W9-CNL-384

The Devil's Tub

BOOKS BY EDWARD HOAGLAND

—Essays—
The Courage of Turtles
Walking the Dead Diamond River
Red Wolves and Black Bears
The Edward Hoagland Reader
The Tugman's Passage
Heart's Desire
Balancing Acts
Tigers and Ice
Hoagland on Nature
Sex and the River Styx

—Travel—
Notes from the Century Before
African Calliope
Early in the Season
Alaskan Travels

—Fiction—
Cat Man
The Circle Home
The Peacock's Tail
Seven Rivers West
Children are Diamonds
The Devil's Tub

—Memoir—
Compass Points

The Devil's Tub

Collected Stories

EDWARD HOAGLAND

Arcade Publishing • New York

For Joe Fox,
Rust Hills,
Ileene Smith,
and Lilly Golden,
editors supreme.

• • •

Copyright © 2014 by Edward Hoagland

All Rights Reserved. No part of this book may be reproduced in any manner without the express written consent of the publisher, except in the case of brief excerpts in critical reviews or articles. All inquiries should be addressed to Arcade Publishing, 307 West 36th Street, 11th Floor, New York, NY 10018.

Arcade Publishing books may be purchased in bulk at special discounts for sales promotion, corporate gifts, fund-raising, or educational purposes. Special editions can also be created to specifications. For details, contact the Special Sales Department, Arcade Publishing, 307 West 36th Street, 11th Floor, New York, NY 10018 or info@skyhorsepublishing.com.

Arcade Publishing® is a registered trademark of Skyhorse Publishing, Inc.®, a Delaware corporation.

Visit our website at www.arcadepub.com.

10 9 8 7 6 5 4 3 2 1

Library of Congress Cataloging-in-Publication Data is available on file.

The following stories first appeared in: "The Devil's Tub," *Yale Review,* Autumn 2005; "The Final Fate of the Alligators," *The New Yorker,* October 18, 1969; "The Colonel's Power," *New American Review,* No. 2, January 1968; "Cowboys," the *Noble Savage,* No. 1, February 1960; "Kwan's Coney Island," *New American Review,* No. 5, January 1969; "The Beaver House," as "Seven Rivers West," *Esquire,* July 1986; "The Last Irish Fighter," *Esquire,* August 1960; "Circus Dawn," excerpt from *Cat Man,* Houghton Mifflin 1955;
"The Witness," *Paris Review,* Summer–Fall 1967.

Cover design by Brian Peterson
Cover photo credit Thinkstock

Print ISBN: 978-1-62872-448-6
Ebook ISBN: 978-1-62872-462-2

Printed in the United States of America

Table of Contents

The Devil's Tub

JAKE THIBODEAU, also known as Grandpa Harley, or Pappy, had been a Wall of Death daredevil for more than thirty years, from the end of the good times—the era of Speedy Babbs and Speedy McNish, Joe Pelequin, Lucky Vinn, Elmo Ballard, the Kemps, the Hagers, Earl Purtle, and their sundry ilk, who still wore leather football helmets then—and was now about a month into working on his sixth marriage, when he booked himself and his motorcycles for a series of pumpkin fairs in northern New England with Smoky Miller's little carnival. Small-time, shit-kicker fairs, and Smoky operated out of his home in central Maine, not Florida, but he was in his own way a pro and knew all of the county officialdom.

It was late August, not a terrible time to be sleeping in your car in Vermont, but a teary disappointment to Vickie, needless to say, who was a Philly girl, twenty-four, and "the oldest old lady" Jake had ever had, as he liked to mention; thrill riders of any age do get a lot of action. But that meant Vickie's six-year-old daughter, Elizabeth Alice, came along with her. The child had been a good traveler so far, so busy adapting to the zany changes in her young life that she was no trouble except in the sense that her mother and Jake sometimes argued about how she would be schooled. She spent much of her waking hours searching the midway for coins, though the concessionaires fed her on fried dough, candied apples, and cotton candy—for free, naturally— and was so small that she could stretch out in a sleeping bag on the floor of the Plymouth pretty comfortably. On warm nights they had the floor of the Motordrome, roomier, slatted wooden quarters, but shared with the four motorcycles and Cliff, the second rider, and his tough-mouthed, bleached-out, short-haired girlfriend, Charlene. (Cliff, whom Jake billed as "Flash Michaels —One of the Top Riders in the World," though he was a beginner, just a dirt-biker, and a stiffie, went in for women of his own age but didn't marry them.) Right now the cool nights had driven Cliff and Charlene to the back of his station wagon, with the Maryland plates and a tawny, ribby dog tied to the fender that would jump and bite you in the chest if you stumbled near, and then again in the ass when you fled.

Money was the problem. They had no talker. He'd left when Jake couldn't pay him enough any longer, so Jake had to do the spiel on the bally platform himself when he wasn't riding on the inside, which was exhausting and also left a terrible silent gap while the show was in progress, when ordinarily you could build another tip from the loads of people wandering the midway who wanted to be told, or assisted to anticipate, what was happening in that big, round, roaring, silo-shaped drome. The banners, adorned with painted skulls and Indian arrows and feathers, read: "The Race for Life. The Dips and Dives of Death. Free-Hand Trick and Fancy Acrobatic Riding Featuring Indian Scout Motorcycles on the Devil's Tub. The Circle of Death." But you needed a strutting loudmouth with a mike on the outside to draw them in and explain the history and the risks and the connoisseurship of using antique Indian Scouts, the most delicately balanced, maneuverable cycles ever made, for this dangerous job, where you doubled your tire pressure but left your tank unfull because too much gas sloshing around might throw you off the wall.

Jake dressed both Vickie and Charlene, brunette and bottle-blonde, in glittery shirts, bare midriffs, leather pants, and high-top boots, so that the tip would think that they were going to see the girls go on and ride, if they paid to get inside. It was like a fish trap. Once each new batch of marks had swum in, they couldn't leave without forfeiting their money and, penned there, listened in frustration to the midway's siren songs till Jake decided that he had captured enough more to strut his stuff. Vickie sold the tickets, Charlene collected them, and a boy named Angel, a gofer Jake had recently taken on, sat on a Harley Davidson that they had on metal rollers on the box outside and raced it as tirelessly as if he were crossing Minnesota. He was sleeping with a harelip girl in one of the grab joints Smoky owned, so he always smelled of onion rings in the morning, and he traveled with her, driving the grease joint to the next town for Smoky, till he could buy a two-bit Honda to ride.

Cliff was thirtyish, a journeyman mechanic, and so stolid he had taken only a month instead of two to conquer his dizziness going round the wall. Not a bad guy, though, true to his word when times were pinched, and energy in the bank for a twelve-hour day. But Jake had served *his* apprenticeship riding on the handlebars of Goldie Restall, one of the legends, from the age of twelve, and then when he could legally drive, jumping a motorcycle over rows of cars on the Joie Chitwood Show. Of course, *these* bikes were stripped down, no headlights, seat springs, and so on, for a different purpose, and he liked to boast on the box that he was "The Doctor of Thrills."

Jake was slim, lightly built, twitchy and boyish in his bad posture, with a boomeranging sort of strength and a thin, browned, pockmarked, croupier's face, alert like a marten's and wrinkled concentrically, though his chin was receding, his undersized mouth lacked several teeth by now, and his nose seemed lengthened, as another effect of aging. He would lose about thirty-five pounds every summer, and when rounding the wall, his thin rigid frame and scraggly long hair flung out behind his balding head made him look like some South Asian holy man on a vision-seeking ordeal. He was cocky in his patter, however, though off-putting and confrontational in his naked yearning for the public's approval, but never a bully or abusive to his women: easy in a divorce. Split the money, didn't fight about custody, signed the papers, "Just leave me my Scouts." It was usually the classic problem of "in-laws versus outlaws," and "I didn't promise you a rose garden," he would say, "I'm the best drome rider left. That's what you wanted and that's what you got," even without the extras the oldtimers had

had, like a lion riding perpendicularly with them in a sidecar, or chasing them across the floor of the drome, and them with a piggy-backed blonde.

He was foxy in manner, and for the best crowds he'd still try a "money run" after a sidesaddle stunt or the crisscrosses he and Cliff had performed, round and round inside the "wine barrel," as carnies called the silo drome. That meant he would simply circle the rim, next to the safety cable that protected the customers, as slowly as centrifugal physics permitted him to, and snatch bills they held out. And if he was between marriages, he'd coast down and straddle his bike on the floor in his epaulettes and Sam Browne belt and admiralty cap and other glitz, looking up at the spectators' faces on the round walkway, and point at the cutest one that was smiling and ready, and say, "Come see The Doctor, Luv," while her boyfriend perhaps turned beet-red. A rider in his prime, at least in the old days, he could stack 'em up in different motels around town until maybe he'd get so tired that one day after the last show, he'd just have his grease monkey—his Angel—boost him over the twelve-foot-high wall when no one was watching and slide down the guy wire in back and sneak away to a hotel where nobody was waiting for him, for a night's sleep.

Vickie had come to his show—although he didn't own it at that point—on the Strates midway in Philadelphia this spring. Elizabeth Alice's father, never married to Vickie, had scrammed, and she was grateful to Jake for tying the knot, as well as excited to split from her irksome kin—hillbilly transplants and binge drunks for a life of bright lights, constant movement, and showbiz folk. It had appeared to be a child-friendly atmosphere too, until Elizabeth Alice mentioned that the other carnival kids "showed me their knives." Jake was always solvent in May because he was a pipe fitter for General Dynamics in the winter, building ships, with a union card—that's how he'd made a down payment on the drome when the owner wanted to close it up, the same week they got married. Vickie was a gentle, rangy girl with fluffy hair and a carny's owl feather tied in it, and bold, malleable, vulnerable features, a low forehead, a clown's personable nose, of the kind carnies want, but was aloof with the towners, and competent with the money box or driving the rattly Plymouth between dates while Jake piloted the tractor trailer that carried the drome. Jake had been a commercial driver for Mayflower Van Lines in the off-season as well, but had drawn a suspension for the sin of having a tail light out when he'd had a drink in him: which suddenly required that their hops be hired out at two hundred-fifty dollars a pop, on top of the second drome payment, and the big Strates organization, a railroad show, dumping their contract because of the ownership change. Jake had been riding this drome, and often driving it, for more than seven years, so he wondered if "management" didn't agree with him.

Vickie was not a quitter, and lacked other options anyhow. She was touched by the twin tattoos he had bought for their right wrists, *I LUB YOU,* and the slight middle-aged waddle he was developing in his fifties (though he claimed he was only limping from shitters), and the way that his eyes often roamed above other people's heads, as if calculating or conceiving stunts they had never dreamed of. He occupied the saddle of a cycle as another man might loaf in an easy chair, or fixing the motor, was patient, even methodical, as if following a set of written directions in his head. Now he was squatting on his heels at the bottom of the firwood drome, twenty-four feet in diameter, passing a cigarette back and forth with Cliff before they *vroomed* their machines and hit the jumpboards for the performance. The intimacy of sharing a bit of spittle was negligible, next to trusting his life to Cliff's timing soon after. Stringy arms, gray ponytail and all, Jake could lift as much as Cliff or Angel when setting up the huge wooden sections and the steel backframe. He'd described to her the thirty-six or fifty-foot outfits with three or four riders, where he'd learned his craft and had had more fun, steering with his feet on the handlebars, and stuff, like riding back-wards, and a lion roaming the floor under you to chase you.

About every April Fools' Day, he said, the light in the sky would change and he wanted to put his lunch bucket down, grab the phone, and call a carny, or check *Billboard* magazine's place-ment ads. Vickie kept Elizabeth Alice out during the show, but sometimes stood underneath the whirlwind herself—by the center pole that held up the canvas that kept out the rain—to watch. It was safest there because "if somebody takes a shitter and falls, you can dodge," Jake said. Angel polished the machines and kicked the crank of Jake's motorcycle before each act. His most tedious task was washing the drome's interior with a sponge on a pole each morning so no shards of debris would cause an accident, and mopping the stairs and walkaround that the spectators used. And he was supposed to gas up. Jake nearly punched him once, when Cliff's tank went empty on the Wall. Cliff was low down at the time, so it wasn't a disaster. Angel was now begging to ride the silo too, but even Cliff had frozen on the midstripe one night—blind and deaf to Jake's shouted advice—too panicky to go up, down, or alter his speed in the slightest, till you wondered when simple giddiness would bring him crashing. Jake was circuiting above, near the red line and the safety cable, trapped in orbit. Not that he couldn't have ducked past by slowing or accelerating, but doing so might have triggered a jerk of Cliff's hands that might have dropped Cliff on top of him. Cliff, having put in the weeks of acclimation necessary to overcome a normal person's sense of vertigo, didn't get dizzy and tumble, but some Hell's Angel Hawgmen in the crowd who had spotted the trouble were hooting at him in the meantime. Jake swerved repeatedly in loops toward where they were standing, jutting his right boot out (he always rotated counter-clockwise) as if to clip their noses off or pulverize their chins.

Hecklers, in their Nazi trinkets, he generally dealt with by inviting them to try the Wall on their Electro Glides or Sportsters. "No, not on my bike, on yours! Be my guest. I got no insurance anyway to lose. You'll puke your guts out and black out and lose a yard of skin."

That's what you lost in shitters—mainly skin—if you were catlike enough when you landed that there were no bones broken. Once his oil pan split, spewing goo all over the wall, which sent him into a skid, and he fell, and the cycle landed on top of him, the wheels still spinning, which cut off the end of his boot and part of his big toe. It looked like a red balloon that had popped, and he lay looking up at the flames licking the wall and catching the canvas on top.

Jake was training Cliff to tense his torso periodically to force a blood supply back near his optic nerves. Jake himself had gone around the barrel as many as five times blind, then slowed to the point where his sight returned, not counting the stunts when he was a young hotshot and wearing a blindfold. The jumpboards took you to seventy-seven degrees; then the slope became ninety, and you had doctored your tires to hug the wall by burning a roughness onto the rubber that edged the wood, because although the wall was at right angles to the floor, you were not quite perpendicular to the wall and parallel to the floor; you were a bit angled.

"If you don't want to whiz, don't do it," he said to Cliff, after that episode, while obligingly scorching a grip on his tires. But Cliff of course did.

Unluckily, there was an individual who didn't, right on the midway: namely Jake's creditor, Phil, the son of the family that had sold him the drome, who had sunk that first payment into a grab joint where he seared sausages for the marks for a living. "Would you like the hot kind, Sir, or the sweet kind, Sir?" How could he bear it? A dozen years ago or more, they had ridden on this self-same Wall together, before Phil's brother got killed on it. But recently Phil didn't think Jake was earning well (Strates hadn't either; that's why they'd canned him), whereas Phil, when the hour got late, left the grill to his wife and was out with a beat-the-dealer craps board fleecing the drunks who'd swilled too much beer, with a cozy trailer to sleep in when he got through.

Two hundred-fifty a pop for transporting this rig? And the re-welding and lumber and paintwork Jake would need to refurbish an oldie—shouldn't that come before paying off his debt? Nobody quibbled with his expertise on the ride, just his crowd-control. And who cared about crowd-handling? Well, Phil the Sourpuss did, and Smoky, the boss, who took a fourth of each ticket, but was quite close-mouthed, like most Maine-iacs. Too much time squandered on the "Come see the Doctor, Luv," tease between shows, or whatever he'd replaced it with since Vickie had joined him? Yet the truth was, you couldn't turn out one crowd and fill up with another, and risk your skin, like a metronome, without winding down in between. Phil knew that. You'd think he'd at least pitch in on the bally box for the show, now that Jake had lost his talker.

He was not a bad talker, or a bad rider either: better than Cliff, though with none of the flash of his parents. His dad had stood up on the saddle, going round the silo, for a deserving crowd, and his mom bottle-raised a series of cubs to be a "King" or a "Queenie" so affectionately that they weren't terrified in the sidecar, like other people's lions, but had laid their throats on the vibrating metal, as if for company, when they roared.

Patty Conklin, up in Canada, had the only other drome still operating. "So let's make this one sing!" Jake wanted to say. Phil, his once-upon-a-time mate, had never possessed Jake's panache, but on the other hand had never married a couple of strippers and been "twice burned," as Jake liked to kid himself. Stick to the amateurs, he'd resolved. Vickie didn't know he was a super-rider, on a scale of one to ten, but did guess that he frittered away time temperamentally, from the behavior of the crowds. Didn't know that a cheap, light, little, brand-new Yamaha might have served the bread-and-butter purposes of the show for these yahoos as well as the purist, antique Indians Jake persisted in using, but recognized that a creditor like Phil must be the enemy, like the fuzz. Her young heart would never be content with a hamburger-flipper; plus, with Jake, there were no black eyes to hide, unlike with Elizabeth Alice's dad, and if any creep had molested Elizabeth Alice on the midway Jake would have "ripped him a new asshole."

Cliff was loyal, too, like an auto-shop mechanic with a nest egg in the bank, out to see the world. His hero was Evel Knievel, or other people from *Ripley's Believe It Or Not,* not knowing about press agents, and yet he reminded Jake of those white horses in the circus that when you stuck them inside a ring loped round and around. Phil was built like a fireplug and was a one-marriage man, while Cliff was dorkier physically and probably too in-drawn to spin the wheel and marry Charlene or anybody else. But he claimed he wanted to go on from here to the Globe of Death, which was a more popular, dangerous reinvention of the Wall of Death, and for which a latticed steel ball hung over the crowd and motorcyclists sped vertically around, or every possible way, in tight tandem inside, with no floor to escape to if the signals went wrong. Split-second timing was required that would be suicidal for Cliff, but it also needed a young man with reflexes quicker than Jake's had become. His eyes were weak from pulling so many G's, his knees shook, and his hands trembled when he got very tired. So Ringling Bros. and Barnum & Bailey would have to wait. Meanwhile, he liked the homey hubbub and fewer moves of these country fairs, and doing what he knew.

Cliff's Charlene was somewhere between Cliff's age and Jake's and had knocked around enough that Jake sometimes felt he had more in common with her. She was sisterly with Vickie but mildly bored by her, and when she found herself sleeping in the back of a station wagon, she offered to work for Smoky, if he had a slot for her, going to his office wagon to ask. She "liked sitting around talking to grownups," as she unguardedly put it. Smoky was a rotund, poker-faced, muscly, cold-weather fellow with burly, hairy fists, though not as hardbitten as the real carnies, who had Florida or Alabama license plates (Alabama being the only state where you could register your car from a P.O. box). He always liked a story, and would hear you out while nursing a mug of coffee, though seldom offering any to a drop-in, or committing himself unless he needed something, until he spat out the window to tell you to move on. He could glance up and down the midway as he did so and estimate how much business every joint, large or small, was doing, and therefore his take, and kept a riot gun in his closet to protect his safe. In friendly territory like this, where the "lucky boys," the gamblers, were permitted to emerge from the woodwork after dark and the girl show got wet, he might tell the sheriff, whether it was true or not, that he had been in Corrections himself.

He turned Charlene away, saying what he owned were the big metal rides—the Octopus, the Scrambler, the Tilt-a-Whirl, the Roll-O-Plane—and needed men for setting them up, tearing them down, and pulling the levers, but to try the concessionaires. Because he recognized her as already with it—Jake's ticket-taker—he laughed and added that even if he didn't pay them off, the cops would love him because he "swept up for them. Every jailbird and loose woman in town wants to join."

"Thank god gas guzzlers are better than a new car to sleep in," she told him, not minding somehow if he knew that she'd lost her apartment, as well as her previous live-in boyfriend, before throwing her lot in with Cliff.

He wasn't rumored to be a chaser, and glanced at Charlene dispassionately. "And then you cut your hair off. Not smart. Not good."

It was true; she had lost her go-go gig in a club immediately. Smoky spat and fluttered a finger to dismiss her.

Without trying the kiddie duck-ponds and bottle-pitches, the balloon-darts and airplane-swings—and disliking the smell of carnival food, she skipped those booths, too—she walked past the Tip Top and Sky Diver rides to the back end again, where the motordrome was sandwiched between the mud wrestlers' tent and the girlie show, and presented herself at Jake's friend, Abe's, who presided over the latter.

He shook his head without even suggesting she peel, however. She wanted to regard this as solidarity with Jake, but in honesty she couldn't and found there were no recriminations from Jake or anyone else who had watched her job search down the midway when she reappeared at his act. Cliff understood that she'd been after income, not deserting him, and Vickie felt affronted on her behalf that their neighbor, Abe, had so summarily decided against her. For a moment she wanted to present herself for rejection, but Jake said no.

"Why not?" Vickie demanded in sisterhood.

"Because it's a wet show. They'd lick your pussy."

He mounted his bally platform, grabbed the microphone, straddled the gaudy chrome Harley that was stage-set on rollers and gunned it, ignoring both Vickie's and Charlene's astonishment. Then, "Why do you think people drive for an hour or two to this fair—to see us?" he asked.

Pissed off because Phil, down the dirt strip selling sauerkraut, still wasn't helping him, and his women were restive, he launched his pitch: "This isn't a pie plate, Ladies and Gentlemen. We climb the Wall! This is the last Thrill Drome in the US. We go round like the planets!" Maybe it stung Phil, he thought, that Phil's parents had always recognized Jake was better on the Wall than him, if not of course as good as them, with a blonde maybe piggybacked, and a lion in the sidecar.

Inside, after the tip had been gathered and coaxed to buy tickets, he had to deliver the ding pitch: "ding" because the coins dinged. Standing humbly with Vickie, Cliff, and Elizabeth Alice in the well of the structure looking up at the circle of strangers (the "sucker net" that was supposed to protect them from falling into the drome had been lost when they left Bridgeport), he intoned in solemn, not gravel-voiced, tones: "Ladies and Gentlemen, before we *go to the Wall,* I must ask for your brief attention. You see us here as a family." He had a hand on Elizabeth Alice's six-year-old shoulder. "That no insurance company will cover. You can imagine their policies do not apply to the dangers we face for your entertainment. And so we have established our own Riders' Accident and Hospital Fund for obvious reasons. We will take nickels, dimes, quarters, pennies, or anything bigger that you can spare to contribute, except for your mother-in-law. Please keep her up there with you!"

A patter of coins rained down, and Elizabeth Alice scurried about, giving her mother what she picked up. Logically the appeal should have been made after the performance, but people wouldn't pause in filing out, and Jake shrugged off the humiliation of being hit by pennies (he'd *said* pennies) like a spatter of flies. The procedure was great fun for Elizabeth Alice, whose natural enthusiasm for such a game was increased by being useful and seeing the change often transformed directly into supper afterwards, whereas the dollar bills and ticket sales went mostly to Smoky or Phil, she had been told. Then she and Vickie left, and Jake hollered out, gravel-voiced again, *"I'm Doctor Harley and this is my living room!"* He roared up the Wall—blackened and resilient, "all rubber and oil," as he liked to say—and soon was steering with his feet in the gritty wind, hands clasped behind his neck, or just by swiveling his hips, but as if he were about to fly right out of the bowl. In fact he'd once done that. His throttle wire broke, he lost control, hit the safety cable, and flew right over the spectators' heads, popping through the canvas rain covering and out of the drome, only being saved by happening to hit one of the swinging chairs of the Octopus, high up, next door.

Other carnies, like the semi-dwarf who had run that particular Octopus, could strut the grounds wearing brass knuckles and swinging their hands like pistons, but Jake didn't have to trifle with playing tough. He knew all kinds of carnies' revenge, including the best, which a smalltime big shot like Smoky, from central Maine, had probably never heard of, but which Jake himself had once wreaked at a state fair in the Middle West when an amusement park owner had gypped him. In the wee, windy hours, when all the patrons had gone and a gale was brewing and the place was deserted, you picked a high ride that was stacked domino-like next to a million dollars' worth of other rides and, wearing gloves, you unscrewed a certain key number of bolts and went home to your hotel. And that was the end of a very short season for that bastard; even the Ferris Wheel fell down. Jake's ponytail was thinner and grayer than Vickie's ("Only one wife at a time," he had promised her at the Registrar's, with Elizabeth Alice holding the bouquet), but his moves anywhere at all near the bike were direct and assured.

With dancers prancing in their skivvies on the bally box only a stone's throw away, Vickie had been watching Jake's wandering eye a bit apprehensively, but it was not drawn to the girlie show. He seemed more interested in the local girls with pretty blouses who had paid three dollars to see him ride from up on his own walkway: which was how she had met him, after climbing those stairs. Nevertheless, she forbade Elizabeth Alice from hanging around the front of Abe's tent, gawking at the feathery costumes and mascara the showgirls came out in. Jake suggested there was no harm in her "learning some of the moves" she was imitating that they did out front with their clothes still on. But Vickie was scandalized: "This is not going to be her life."

Jake didn't argue. He didn't want that fate for her either, but didn't think strippers were created in such a way. He was rehearsing Cliff in memory devices for the crossovers they ought to begin using, if their show was not to go stale. People could watch the merry-go-round if that's all a drome became. He granted him a grin afterwards and patted his shoulder; their lives might depend upon whether he had actually learned. And Angel, whose legal name nobody remembered because he wanted to be called Angel, "because I'm not one" (he claimed the chicks liked that, but so far Jake hadn't seen any who weren't harelipped that did), of course wanted in on the lessons.

It was lonesome, when Jake had off-time, looking down the midway for carnies who were for real, not the man-and-wife thirty-mile-wonders who had remodeled their vans so that they could flip up a flap and sell corn dogs and egg salad at auctions, fairs, ballgames, close by, as a summer hobby and drive home to sleep in their own beds at night, or else put up a pup tent behind the stand. Other locals paid the entrance fee for their vehicles, and then simply camped at the fairgrounds, cooking over a Coleman stove for the cheapest of all change-of-scenes. The horse pulls, oxen pulls, and dairy competitions were old home week, but if a character like Jake approached to chat, it became like a foreign country for them, and as alarming as if some gypsy might steal their pots, pans, and babies.

Then there were itinerant guys working a little pokerino booth, or a high-striker where the marks swung a sledgehammer to ring the bell, or else guessed ages and weights, but who never slid south of New Jersey for the winter, where the heart of the business lay. Smoky had no Fire Eater, or Guillotine, or Headless Woman, or Fiji Mermaid, or Two-Headed Exhibit, or waxen Hitler or Torture Show, or Sword Swallower, or pickled punks. There was a House of Mirrors, from Memphis, with papier-mache ghosts hanging in it, and a taffy booth presided over by the wife of the Hall of Mirrors owner. Also a strolling clown on retainer from Butler, Georgia; and Phil, who knew everything; and the light man, who was from Coney Island and had carried around a Half Boy on the Royal American Freak Revue, and catered to Fat Ladies and Bearded Ladies. He'd sewn dried monkeys onto dead carp to simulate The Seventh Wonder of the World, and replaced the plaster fittings in a curving framework that women lay in to be sawn in half ten times a day. But he was a solitary—unbending if you tried to strike up a conversation. Here today, gone tomorrow, was his motto, which was true but also self-defeating. He'd been a utility man on many carnivals, oiling tattooed individuals and overseeing snake-eating geeks, and now that Thalidomide Babies, pickled in jars, that you bought from a hospital, were a no-no, he was just the light man.

So, Jake walked behind the banner line of the girl show during the 5 PM break—when so many of these farmers went home to have dinner—after prudently asking Vickie whether she'd like to come along, so as not to arouse her suspicions. Abe worked out of Birmingham and, behind that, the Big Easy milieu of New Orleans. He was mellow, vaguely chubby, always in a clean print shirt and khaki pants, smiling readily at anybody, unlike Smoky, and with money in his trailer too, but no more of a weapon than a billy club and an iron tent stake. "Bandits are scared of girls," he liked to say, although he did employ a roughie, not just to help put up the tent and tear it down again, but to protect the girls from rowdies in the crowd, if necessary, with help from the deputy that a sheriff would usually provide, if he was being paid off. "Audience participation" kootch shows were the wildest kind, and only allowed in the same venues that still welcomed a Wall of Death, so Jake and Abe crossed routes at several engagements a year.

"You break your neck," he warned Jake affectionately, again. "An old geezer like you," he said in his Cajun accent, from a boyhood spent in Lafayette, Louisiana, where his father had bought furs from the salt-marsh trappers and managed a rice farm. Otherwise his watchwords of advice were to "Negotiate from strength; the little fish gets eaten up," and "I was a nice Jewish boy who learned one important lesson: beautiful girls need company too." Not in high school, they didn't, but later, in a modeling job, after the photo shoot was over and the gay guys said goodbye, assuming that they already had some other date. If you escorted them to a party, held their purse, shielded them from unseemly propositions but cleared out of their way whenever they wanted you to, you'd become an agent in a year or so. And, further down the road, if you didn't get all huffy at bedtime at the sound of an occasional vibrator in your motel room, you could find yourself sleeping with three or four eye-popping pusses, in all the extra beds the manager could fit in, and topping off one or another, as needed.

"*Compadre,*" Abe repeated, nodding with amusement at the stilted step of Vickie—who to him was just Jake's newest, but was approaching out of curiosity or jealousy, with her arms crossed, rather as though Abe possessed x-ray eyes that saw straight through your clothing. "You, the holder of a Bronze Star for heroism, come to see this old 4-F?"

They laughed. It was their joke that though the army hadn't wanted him, Abe had lived almost ever since surrounded by nookie, except during the winter, when he liked and even insisted upon being alone. Had never married, no children, but enjoyed them, and, noticing Vickie upset that her daughter had followed, he said, "No, no, no, it never hurt a little one to see how the big girls can wind a man around their pinkie. The mystery of women."

He introduced her to Sheba and Carmen, who had emerged from their dressing room for money to go buy softie cones and boats of French fries and sloppy joes, in their high-heeled slippers and fishnet stockings, but sweatshirts and cutoffs, with hair tattily scarved, as a street disguise. Yet, spotting Elizabeth Alice, they ducked back inside, wailing for lace and ruffles to dress her in, and brought Samantha out as well. Ignoring Jake, they soon had Vickie, too, feeling proud and mollified. Abe had a canvas chair for visitors, and signaled to his roughie, a leaden-faced bouncer type, that it was okay for him to eat now. A deputy in a comic uniform loafed nearby.

"You know, I've known this guy for what, probably ten years?" he told Jake, meaning the sheriff, not the carny workhand or the lunk who was the deputy. "And he says"—Abe, sotto-voiced, raised his eyebrows for emphasis—"he gets his money now from letting a certain plane land once a month from Canada at the airstrip. So he doesn't need us anymore, and just gets in trouble from the Christers at election time. So this may be our last gig here. I'm going to do a good blow-off."

The dancers returned with subs, and Vickie left with Elizabeth Alice. Sheba was actually a Sally, but had ebony (or more than ebony) long hair to fit her African name, as Carmen's was fluorescent blonde, and Samantha's flame-red. They were all tall, which made it easier for them not to have to watch their weight: which was a benefit of stripping over modeling. In the flesh, people weren't as particular about a dab of flab, even a love handle, if you remained indoor-white. And unlike some of the Southern girls, Abe said, these Northerners didn't chew and spit tobacco.

When Angel tried to peep around, Jake shooed him away. But Sheriff Leroy showed up, with eye pouches as dark as a raccoon's rings. Though not as weighty in the community as a Southern sheriff could have been, he might still be intent upon soliciting more of a kickback, if this was going to be the last go-round. They felt antsy; Jake had had to pay up too, a hundred smackers, because of "safety concerns." Leroy's livelihood and merriment was measuring degrees of illegality, and the three ladies, despite their legerdemain in appearing quite shapeless in sweatshirts, quickly withdrew after a chorus of Hi's to him.

Leroy had chimpy arms like a dairyman, but Abe's smile merely widened. "Leroy!" he welcomed him hospitably; it was impossible to prevent your own mouth from twitching a little. And Leroy's visit turned out not to be mercenary but sentimental. He hunched comfortably over where they were seated, leaning on the trailer's bumper with the insinuating manner of a highway trooper looking inside a driver's window.

"You know, I was remembering that I saw my first cunt right here. Most any man my age probably did. It was a public service because we didn't get to see it anywhere else. My father took me— it was cheaper than going to Montreal. And you gotta see it before you know what you're gonna do with it, don't you?"

"I'll use that on the box if you want me to," Abe said with a grin. "And if your daddy was a widower when he got bald-headed, I'll bet you he kissed his last pussy right down here too."

That startled the sheriff, but, knowing Abe to be an alien from deep Dixie, and having been acquainted with him for a decade, he had to actually agree. They talked about trailer tires and hitches, and crooked salesmen, and scanner frequencies, until Jake neglected to reopen his own show on time so he could stick around with the sheriff and hear Abe's opening spiel. Abe was quiet-spoken, economical with his energies, relying on the mike instead of shouting, and never strained his memory trying to bring in the name of the particular town he was in. People didn't pay to be flattered at a girl tent. They came for only one reason, and he was in it for the long haul.

"Gentlemen, this is the Fish House. We give you the hole show. You can smell it. We leave nothing out. You'll either go home and enjoy the pleasures of your fist, or else your wife will thank you because we've primed your pump. We have Carmen and Sheba. See whose dimensions you like best. And also our redhead Samantha, who swallows silver dollars, if you know what that means. If you don't happen to have one on your person, we'll sell you one for five bucks."

Laughing, the sheriff left inconspicuously. But when Jake emerged from backstage, he noticed Phil's urgent fireplug figure, beside the grease joint down a ways, wondering why the drome had not been up and running to catch the girl show's marks before Abe had started his pitch, not just the stragglers who were now arriving late. Cliff and Charlene dimly perceived that they had missed a phase, too, and Elizabeth Alice had resumed scouting the midway for coins, brooches, barrettes, medallions, or whatever had been dropped, while drinking a chocolate milk and chewing an onion ring Angel's girlfriend had given her. She was having fun, trying to get ahead of an old guy who was searching for change, waving the wand of a metal detector, so Jake didn't call her back for the "Riders' Accident and Hospital Fund." The screams from the Scrambler no longer frightened her, and the pitchman who ran the water-pistol game, which was her favorite, let her play, gaffing it so that she won.

Jake was surprised, therefore, to find her crying after his blow-off. She said she had wound up, on her way home, at the mud wrestlers' tent, adjoining Jake's drome on the opposite side from Abe's show. Three young women performed—high-school classmates on Long Island a few years ago, and still friends—who knew who Elizabeth Alice was; and after signaling their intentions to Vickie, in the next ticket booth, they had invited her in. They were doing this stuff partly for a hoot, but the experience of seeing women fighting each other in a tub of black muck terrified Elizabeth Alice. She ran bawling out, not realizing of course that they were faking and much less likely to get hurt than Cliff or Jake. Vickie, comforting her, explained that like the Scrambler, it was only pretend, so she wouldn't have nightmares, which she was prone to.

After a while, Vickie carried her back to meet the mud wrestlers: whom she wanted to be friends with anyway, certainly more than with the strippers on the other side. Jake resented the wrestlers a bit, as First-of-May triflers—not carnies at all, but exploiting a fad—whose act would wilt in the autumn rains and maybe never come back on the circuit next year, although he was glad to tap into the extra customers they brought. Vickie didn't share that opinion. In fact, the organizer of it, named Alida, told Elizabeth Alice she had a little girl herself, who was staying with Grandma in Bayside, while Mamma was away. And Alida's husband, who was their manager and also about Vickie's age, was a building contractor, working for his father in his regular life. So he could afford to take orders from his tomboy wife, and the summer off. He'd jury-rigged a shower from the fairgrounds' hose and a portable water heater he had brought along, and they were now kind enough to let Vickie or Charlene use it, even though they weren't covered with mud.

Alida was a ball of fire who knew how to control her money ("very tough on the customers," as bookkeeper for the construction company, her husband said), as well as her diet, and owned a split-level ranch house in the suburbs that she showed Vickie pictures of. Indeed, they wanted a fourth woman for tag-team wrestling or just to spell one of them off—but not to "pick up some unknown girl with a social disease," as Alida confided. She promised no rough stuff, though her nose looked as if it had been broken (she claimed a car accident); and what with this terrible pinch for money, Vickie was tempted, but didn't know how to broach the idea with Jake.

Jake called them one-season wonders, and they told her that his motordrome looked ramshackle—but also that you had to pull each other's T-shirt off in the middle of the tussle, or nobody would come. It wasn't advertised, but word-of-mouth promised the customers that you were going to; and possibly as a result, a snide feud had developed, these last two days, between the girl-show strippers and the mud wrestlers, as to whose stunt was more demeaning, dirtier, more disgusting, the mud fight or the muff-peddling.

"Cunt-lapping," the mud wrestlers called it, when Alida shouted at Abe's Sheba or Samantha, walking by. And if she did, "Eat mud!" Sheba yelled back.

Jake sided with his friend's girls, naturally. No real carnies would waste their energy starting a spat like that unless it had been set up beforehand, building toward a "grudge cat fight" with an extra admission fee, in front of the grandstand. Which was a great idea, come to think of it, except you couldn't trust "the mud people," as he called them—resenting Vickie's needing to shower there—to go easy on Abe's girls. The staging would have to be cautiously done, and he didn't even believe they had the split-level house and their boasts about a construction business back on Long Island. Otherwise, why eat dirt? Their credit rating was probably zilch.

"Like ours?" Vickie asked.

"Yes, like ours!" he'd muttered in anger; and that was before she ever proposed going next door to try working with them for five bucks a minute, while in the ring.

That night it was warm enough to sleep inside the drome on mattresses, with plenty of elbow room and some reefers to cheer everybody up. By the next noon, Vickie found Jake, as he pulled on his stunt pilot's barnstorming costume, in an approachable mood, and once he had absorbed the news, he surprised her by simply saying, "If the suckers want it, and you want that. They'll body-slam you, though. You'll be black and blue." Neither bossy nor pleased, he looked to Charlene to dissuade her. But Charlene didn't oblige, though, being ten years older than Vickie, she didn't seem miffed not to be considered, herself.

"That's all I'd need," she said. Yet she was sometimes so puzzlingly aloof with Elizabeth Alice that Vickie was uncertain about bringing her into a conspiracy to conceal from the child what her mother was planning to do. Who else was there, however, to help while Jake was inside on the Wall? When she asked Jake what he thought was wrong, he suggested Charlene might have given up a kid for adoption. He'd seen that reaction before.

"They don't get over it, but they can wiggle around it." He didn't believe Vickie would be at this foolishness for long. Thus the lying could be over in a day or so. "That butch stuff," he added. "You think they're your friends, but they'll hurt you."

He didn't spell out that he thought his Vickie was rather phys-ically frail, compared to this new well-fed threesome trading on a fad, who no doubt had eaten cereal and milk every morning through their toddlerhoods, while she was being fed potato chips and Pepsi Cola, and who'd never had their daddy's belt buckle permanently scar their breasts at fourteen, or been screamed at as a "shrimp," punishments that didn't make you serviceably tough, just wary and pessimistic. Also he didn't voice his opinion that, whatever the sins of the elegantly milky-clean Carmen, she would be a more feminine influence on a little girl Elizabeth Alice's age than those dykes. He knew Vickie didn't consider them bull dykes, but "liberated."

Hoarse, and feeling nausea on the Wall from doing both the talking and the star turns for his act, Jake wanted to be able to get on the bally platform and simply tell the crowd the truth—then be done with it—saving his poor vocal cords and resting a bit while they filed in. To be able to simply say: "I'm the best there is at doing this, the best left who's still doing the stunt. If you want to watch, pay your three bucks." And in fact he liked having Elizabeth Alice around. More than Cliff's predictable company, going round and around like a circus horse underneath his own looping orbits, she furnished a kind of focus or center of gravity for him, although she was never in sight during the show; she couldn't be allowed in the drome while they rode, of course. But he would fix his mind on her. He wanted to take her out catching frogs in the field afterwards, with some water in a little coffee container.

What happened, however, was that while he, Cliff, Charlene, and Angel were busy at the drome, Elizabeth Alice went peering behind the scenes for her mom, and, from the back of the next tent, she witnessed Vickie, half-naked, calf-deep in muck and spattered all over with black, being toppled again by Alida tugging at her hair, while five dozen men were hollering for the other two young women to show off their boobies and mix it up dirty, too. Elizabeth Alice sank into desperate hysterics that lasted for over an hour.

"This isn't solving anything," Jake protested, during the five o'clock break, after Elizabeth Alice had been extensively hugged to calm her down. Meanwhile, he had already gone to Phil's grab joint and asked for some decent assistance from him, on the bally box, for instance, for old time's sake—but maybe too aggressively, because

Phil's normally mousy wife helped Phil respond by stamping her foot on the idea. "No more motorcycles! Isn't it enough that your brother died on the Wall?" Phil and Jake—who had been gingerly workmates even when they had ridden together—looked at each other quizzically, and Phil told him to cool it and take his time, skip a month in paying his debt, if he wanted to.

It was good being married—not just because at Jake's age, your ulcer might burst on you, or your eyes might red out from pulling so many G's on the Wall, and who else, dude, would ever take care of you then?—but to have people to protect. Yet with such limited options, he ought to search for a bigger carnival for them to join. But when he went to Smoky's trailer to ask for either a financial incentive to stay on, or the loan of a talker from another attraction on the midway, Smoky's small eyes twinkled bluntly. His lips bulged like a boxer's with the mouthpiece in.

"If every single one of your customers doesn't have a ticket stub of mine in his hand when they go in your place, I'm going to boot your butt the hell out of here."

When Jake expressed total surprise, he said that a spotter of his had told him that "that kid"—Angel—had been letting people in if they slipped him two dollars in cash when he manned the door. If it were Vickie or Charlene, Smoky added, he would have assumed Jake knew, but, "Punch him out," he suggested. "That'll solve your money problems."

Of course it didn't at all (although Jake did split Angel's lower lip) but was a diversion, something Smoky, like any carnival owner, was expert at, whether with a town's Fire Inspector or Sanitation Department, or merely a carny like him.

• • •

Vickie was bruised yet not grudging about how the wrestlers had treated her. Alida had given her some motel money for a sound sleep tonight, and she felt like such a conscientious mother, compared to her own, that she needn't fret that too much damage had been done to Elizabeth Alice, assuming her dreams turned out okay. Vickie explained to her that it had been make-believe so they could sleep in regular beds and use an indoor toilet and so on. Jake's pride was injured, then. Needing advice, in any case, he moseyed over to Abe's to lounge in a camp chair behind the banshee banner line, not out of horniness but loneliness. Similarly, the three strippers were too played out to care how macho Jake was. The tranquility Abe could conjure up was more attractive to them.

Abe chuckled at Jake's account of Smoky's imperviousness: not that he himself would really have been less. And he could remember Phil's virtuoso parents in the motorcycle drome, with their lions shitting, spraying urine during the show, sometimes fearfully, sometimes territorially, but smelling worse than the bikes did. They laughed about it together, and living dangerously by the prowess of your body was a bond with the girls, as well. Yet the work did burn them out. Abe would start from Birmingham with three second-string tits-and-asses club dancers, and finish in Florida after Thanksgiving with none of the originals, or the first substitutes for the originals, either. In Memphis, Knoxville, Lynchburg, Pittsburgh, or places in between, he might lose a girl and pick up another one—always pros; he didn't train them. And it was like handling Amazons, he said. Like soldiers, they tended to prefer each other's company to any alternative, and needed their rest and recreation, such as going to a movie collectively, a swim in July, a visit to a pick-your-own apple orchard later, a kitten in a box in the dressing wagon, or enjoying a cry in common when the customers got brutish. He'd give the weeping one her money, and she'd climb onto the Hound, while he phoned the nearest agency, in Boston, St. Louis, Louisville, Buffalo, or wherever, until by and by a new six-foot "bombshell" would arrive, hair-coloring and sexpot pasties and all. If she didn't yet know how raw this hayseed outfit that she'd jumped onto was, Sheba or Samantha—or somebody like Sheba or Samantha—or else Abe himself, would demonstrate to the new girl how to grab a guy who was going down on her by both ears in a manner that let him know he was going to lose them if he so much as hinted at a nipping. And if this discovery revolted her, it was a matter of pride with Abe that she could still leave with a little money tucked in her bra.

"Negotiate from strength" was Abe's advice again, after hearing Jake gripe. He had a beer in his hand but, unlike Jake, had not been a drunk. "You and me are about the same age, but we're pretending the gravy train isn't going to end. We can squeeze it out, but pretty soon every high school kid is going to be looking at what I'm charging for on his computer at home or his girlfriend will be giving it away for free." He motioned toward the stage. "Girlies are girls. You'd think even the bald-headed guys would know that."

Vickie stopped over to check on Jake, then left Elizabeth Alice with him while she went back to the wrestlers' tent to chat with her friends. Abe said he had enough to retire on, but, like a good carny, omitted asking Jake how he stood for the winter; just suggested he ought to put Vickie to work.

"Right?" he asked Carmen—who had the biggest bouffant, black at the roots, iridescent-honey on top, and was now grooming Elizabeth Alice's hair with a comb as long as most of her arm.

"That's how they do it," Carmen agreed. "My poppa used to put his hand in my dress every week to see how mine were developing. He thought he could live off of me, but I've never sent him a dime."

"Hey," Jake interrupted for the child's sake.

Elizabeth Alice had a sort of primary animal energy that put the adults to shame, and maybe was why she lent him that sense of focus when he was on the Wall. He studied his blotched, blurry agglomeration of tattoos for a bare space on his arm where he could have one engraved for her. But she needed more protection than Vickie, and he meant to be faithful to both of them in their separate ways. Having grown up fatherless, but slated to work in the Navy Yard like his mother's in-laws, he was tender on that subject. Although he'd loved his mom, he had taken off when those whirling, flashing wheels and vortexes of light, embellished by sirens, of the World of Mirth show and Goldie Restall its Wall of Death impresario, *vroom-vroomed* into town. His mother's tenement windows looked out on the carny lot, and when he hit twelve he didn't let them leave without him. He was perched on Goldie's handlebars as "The Youngest Rider in the World," until he became immunized to dizziness and, turning sixteen, could legally drive alone. Their team played the Steel Pier in Atlantic City, Palisades Park, the Santa Cruz boardwalk, Soldier's Field in Chicago, The Cow Palace in San Francisco, and Rocky Dell's Great American Shows. Jake learned short-cut auto mechanics too, so you could buy a heap at a junkyard and make it run for a week or a month, with the doors tied shut if you had to. At that one stage in his twenties he'd crewed with the Chitwood Thrill Show, jumping cars over a row of junkers, then rolling them, and stepping out with chesty panache. But that didn't have the intimacy of a Harley Low Rider balling into the wind, not to mention an Indian Scout climbing the Wall "like a bug," as Goldie would say, before he retired to driving a tramcar for gimpy tourists half his age on the boardwalk at Wildwood, New Jersey. As Goldie, his foster father's, longevity showed, it wasn't so much the shitters that were going to wipe you out. Once Jake's drive tire burst, and his knee went right through the floor when he came down. His whole leg was oozing blood and bodily fluids and he had needed a hundred-forty stitches on his face and head. But Jake had had two heart attacks, more recently, since turning fifty (although before he'd met Vickie, so she didn't know), and now carried nitroglycerin tablets buttoned into his shirt pocket, even on the Wall. He'd tried driving a bread truck and working in a loblolly pine sawmill down South afterwards for a spell, but the spinning lights that could still entice a smooth-skinned young lady like Vickie pulled him back. Hugging a perpendicular wall at thirty or forty miles an hour concentrated a grandpa's brain cells wonderfully, and if the pennies raining down on his head shamed him, he pretended they were for Elizabeth Alice.

Yet how could he hustle a gig on a better carnival than this one when he was pinned down to his impossible schedule? Abe shrugged sympathetically. Abe had traveled with a Mermaid presentation, and an Iron Lung exhibit—another grind where you employed a young broad, undressed, to hold still endlessly, while cramped in claustrophobic quarters for many hours—and had toured with Medical Curiosities (your basic Two-Headed engagement) in a trailer. But he preferred a free-standing, live act, and not just a Fat Lady, but the coziness of trouping with a trio of lively showgirls, who for their part often preferred the companionship of a dork like him to all the men they'd known that they had been scared of. Abe was backed by a moneybags in Gibsonton, Florida, who owned his equipment, but otherwise operated independently, hiring his girls, or stable of fill-ins, plus the roughies, and negotiating with every county sheriff as to whether or not "lunch" could be served, which boosted the receipts considerably and thus the lawmen's too. In the winter he retired to his secluded hotel and got a good rest, without needing a crutch such as AA, or anybody else.

"No, I wouldn't trade with you," he murmured to Jake, watching his girls groom Elizabeth Alice's hair and ruffle her dress. In the morning in the motel room, he would hand Samantha the telephone to call her children, if she woke up early, before they set off from her sister's house for school. ("Mommy's working, darling. Mommy will be home soon.") Carmen had apparently stashed one or two in foster care, but didn't or couldn't contact them, which made her jumpy during Samantha's conversations and yet doubly so on her behalf if she didn't call. Those mammary organs that paid the bills did have a bedrock purpose, and Jake, to his dismay, didn't disagree with Abe about a trade, because, after all, after six marriages, he didn't even have Elizabeth Alice in the sense that she would acknowledge him as her brand-new stepdad. She enjoyed chasing the coins rolling across the floor of the drome, or would follow him where she wanted to go anyhow, if he had sided with her against her mom, but wouldn't take his hand as they walked, or emotionally give him an inch.

Observing the changing hydraulics of the crowd, Abe got up and mounted his bally box. "All alive," he said, parting a curtain to show the strawberry-haired Samantha. "The Inner Sanctum of Mystery, Gentlemen. See the Cleft That Shelters and Divides Us. We illuminate the female body for you, Gentlemen. Most of you already know what you are going to see. (And if you don't, you better hurry in!) The Hole Show. I don't need hyperbole. Nature doesn't exaggerate. These ladies display the attributes God gave them. You or I may wear blue jeans or a tuxedo. They wear their birthday suits. Feast your eyes, Gentlemen. It's cheaper than a marriage license. We have it for your pleasure for the price of one blue ticket. We do go back to good old Dixie for the winter, but we leave you warm with memories!"

The tip was so anemic, however, that Abe left Samantha out there as a come-on—Samantha, the surfer and good sport, a California girl in Pan-Cake makeup, who used a special antiseptic to wash herself when she came offstage from the show, and often muttered the doctor's mantra, "Do no harm," to herself, as she worked.

A mark who should have been hospitalized approached Jake and Abe, as they sat together. He talked past them irrationally for a while, until Jake pointed at Cliff's yellow mutt, tied to the station wagon a dozen yards away, and said, "He bites."

Then they had another visitor with a funny grin, this one supporting a duffel bag slung over his shoulder. But it wasn't stiff like a gun, and Jake and Abe, from their decades of sizing people up, recognized that, as odd as he was, he was not a nut.

"No job," Abe told him, as they waited for him to reveal his shtick.

"No, no, no. I'm giving you a present," this character, sandy-faced, an enthusiast, replied. "You couldn't buy this for less than, what, a thousand dollars?"

"How much you gonna pay us to take him off your hands?" Jake asked, who had seen the satchel move as the guy set it down.

"My bad luck is your good luck. It's outgrown my house. I would have had to give it a room of its own." The guy raised his eyebrows to indicate how sincere he was.

Jake glanced toward the motordrome. Vickie was stationed in her bathing suit on a stool on the bally platform, as he had asked, so that people idling by would notice the place for later reference in their mind's eye. Abe's bevy of strippers were re-coating themselves with sunscreen, and showing Elizabeth Alice how. It wasn't uncommon for a boa fancier to try to unload his snake on a carnival passing through, but Abe had told Jake that only Sheba had previous experience of carny life. The other two had been hired out of Boston's Combat Zone.

"Sheba," Jake called, after checking with Abe. "Gentleman has a gift."

She strolled over, handsome and tall, sashaying even though it was not yet quite her working hours, with her Cleopatra-sheeny hair, and her legs promptly assuming a stocking-ad posture, but marred overall by a certain horsey contour to her nose, which she had never found a sugar daddy who was willing to pay to fix. She held out her ring finger kiddingly, while her savvy eyes registered the slowly churning sack.

"A freebie? How heavy is he?" she asked, in that high, phone-sex voice. "You're stuck with him, hey? Can't sell him to save your blessed life? My limit's fifty pounds."

"Fifty's the same as seventy-five," suggested Jake, who hadn't realized she had experience of this kind. Abe, her boss, by his silence suggested agreement, but Sheba was a flamboyant woman. Nobody could give her orders. They both rolled their hands, signifying to her, don't worry about it, but the towner mistook this for a go-ahead and unzipped the golf bag. He lifted out a Burmese python twice as long as he was.

Sheba turned out to actually like snakes, and stepped closer. She didn't touch it, but didn't jerk back when it protruded and flicked its forked tongue to scent her. Jake called to Angel, who always hung around the girl tent if Jake's presence created a pretext.

"Go down to the farmer barns and get me a chicken. Alive." He waved aside Angel's question about how to accomplish this.

"Who would replace me?" Sheba asked. She and the snake were looking at each other. It was so big, as well as so habituated to captivity, that neither fear nor an attempt to escape were its primary reactions. It was a creamy color mottled with reddish brown, and Sheba—making a snake of her black thick whip of hair, holding this across her chest, then flipping it over one shapely shoulder to hang straight down her glorious back—felt no inclination to put more daylight between herself and the snake. The man who had raised it hefted the forward end, while the python kept its tail snugly anchored around his midriff.

Could Vickie, Jake wondered? Not fill in for Sheba with the dirty stuff, but could Vickie handle the python to bally his own show, perhaps? People might think he or she was going to ride with it, and come on in. He wasn't afraid of snakes—he knew them as he knew lions, as a drawing card, and had been acquainted with half a dozen midway snake charmers—but stability was the one thing even the tamest of them required. If thrown around, they automated their tightening mechanism. That was why this individual was receptive to Sheba's stare and her tentatively outreaching hands: because it sensed a confident reliability there.

"Tell you what we're gonna do," Jake suggested, when Angel returned with a chicken that he had borrowed. The sudden flapping and the manure smell had aroused the reptile to center its gaze and prick its tongue, which flickered out like a flame. Jake recognized Sheba's intensity or empathy, too, and Abe smiled at him, because they didn't tell you everything, did they, these kootch girls? And she might be the true type, who would tell a crowd of men that she preferred its hugs to theirs, which was good box office, and weep at the end of the season, when the snake caught pneumonia from the cold and contracted a killing fungus in its mouth.

"Tell you what we're going to do," Jake repeated. "Lay him on the ground, and if he eats the bird we'll take him and only charge you for the wood for a cage."

Everybody watched in mild surprise, as the snake looped into a jumbo coil in the grass, although some of them already knew there was no point in accepting a snake that was going to starve itself to death: which could be the case. Angel gazed toward Vickie, who was sometimes his protector in strange situations, but who was oblivious, and Jake told him to go fetch Smoky, who might have some advice. Elizabeth Alice was drifting toward her mother, but slowly, because she was fascinated.

"It's a girl, don't you think?" Abe remarked to Jake and Sheba, who, unlike Carmen and Samantha, had not crossed her arms self-protectively or stood up on tiptoe as if about to scoot. Her legs were out of range of a strike, but she leaned forward sympathetically. Her brother had kept king snakes, she told them. She tried a kind of Statue of Liberty pose, as if the python's head would be her torch.

In his unhurried manner, Smoky arrived. He had booked several such attractions over the years and they did draw, for a grind, he agreed. You taped a spiel, and some bozo sold the tickets. But he glowered at Angel, with the bandaged lip.

Arms akimbo, provocatively statuesque, Sheba disclosed that at an Atlanta nightclub she had once presented a Venezuelan red-tailed boa constrictor, and had liked him better than the hairy rednecks who reached for her here. Sally being her real name, she wanted to call the snake that. They had given it a generous circle of space in the warm sun, and, when Jake swung the chicken in the air until it beat its wings, then tossed it out, the spear-shaped head reared abruptly a couple of feet and grabbed it in midair—gripped and clenched it to limpness within the moiling coils in about four seconds—and began to sniff and slather it with saliva, and stretch and lengthen it with strategic squeezes in deliberate preparation for swallowing the bird. The people watching dispersed a bit, not in tact so much as in awe of these specifics of swallowing the meal, imagining a larger one. The novices gasped.

"She's a hot one, huh?" Abe told Smoky, who surveyed every problem that arose, or any event, with the same level, skeptical equanimity. Exhibitionists were his wage-earners, but he booked shows, he didn't own them, and so he could afford to be dispassionate.

"Where's that going to sleep?" Vickie asked, in Jake's ear. He was remembering a mark who had tried to give him a lion that the guy had bought as a cub for a hundred dollars, but couldn't keep in his garage any more. He hadn't had it in the car with him, but described the mane, and Jake suggested he give it a chance—just let it go in the woods.

"It's better than a lion," he told Vickie. "And it could sleep in the generator wagon, where it's warm."

Smoky, when consulted about this, nodded neutrally, though they were all going to separate fairly soon: the iron and paraphernalia of his amusement rides, from Abe's Girl-o-rama, and Jake's Motordrome.

"I want her tonight," Sheba insisted, staring persuasively for support at the other dancers, who were exotics too. When they didn't speak in opposition, Abe grinned. "But I always wear a bra, with a snake," she informed him.

"So would I," he agreed, and assisted Jake and her to convince the python that the golf bag was a familiar lair to be zipped back into to digest its meal.

"I love nature," she said.

"Porn is nature," suggested Abe.

"Not so much as the jungle."

"Porn *is* the jungle."

Since they seemed on the verge of arguing, Jake snuggled an arm around Vickie who at least hadn't evinced an active phobia about snakes, and walked away. She'd gradually admitted that she was never going to be able to ride with him, even as a passenger, on the Wall, so he felt in a stronger position.

"We need money, and snakes suck it in. And snakes are deaf. They don't go into a stink from the roar."

"I tried the wrestling," she pointed out. "And I'm worried about Elizabeth Alice's ears."

So, when he had a spare minute, he fixed the child a temporary pair of plugs from candle wax. But she wouldn't wear them unless her mother did also. And Vickie wanted Jake to, but it was hopeless coaxing him because he thought it was bad luck for a drome rider: plus might prevent him from hearing engine subtleties that he ought to know about, or where Cliff was. He'd lost considerable acuity, but would rather get clipped by a car on foot somewhere because he didn't hear it coming up behind him than miss a motor click or a tire sound that earplugs would block out, but might have saved him on the Wall. Your act was your life.

The plugs had the unexpected effect of causing Elizabeth Alice to take a nap, whereupon her mother snuck over and spelled Alida in a match again, "for motel money," as she muttered to Jake. "And she must be sleep-deprived. Why don't you teach Cliff to ride better, instead of trying snakes?"

Again, he was touched rather than angry at her, but answered that the wrestlers were slummers and would beat up on her. He went over during an interlude to talk with Alida's husband, however, and gathered the impression that it was a serious if half-assed venture. Supposedly they were tired of working for this guy's buzz-saw of a father, and a school had been started in West Virginia to exploit the fad and coach women in how to mix it up better in mud, which they wanted to go down to attend.

Angel drove Vickie and Elizabeth Alice to their night's sleep early, while Cliff and Charlene helped Jake milk the crowd for whatever he could. He baited several biker-clubbers in the crowd by sticking his boot out, going round at the safety stripe on top, as if to clip them if they leaned over, and got them howling mad. His right wrist held the reins of death, and his left the reins of life for himself, and thus he constantly twitched these two, as he swerved in breakneck vertical cloverleaf patterns on the rumbling wood.

In the meantime, over on the girl show, whenever a tip collected, Abe would bring out Sheba in a negligee and shorty nightie, with tan-toner lending a gloss to her yummy skin, and the ravishingly docile, Oriental, ruddy-and-heavy-cream-colored python slowly exploring every crack and cranny of her body with its flicking tongue. Jake was hoarse and coughing in exhaustion on his bally platform, but Abe was introducing "Tarzan's Jane." He'd shake his head. "Oh boy, Guys, I truly hate to tell you this, but there's no accounting for taste. She prefers him to you! And so did Eve. We tell it like it is on the inside. We go ballistic at every show. That's why I have to send my girls back to Boston next week to recuperate."

Sheba was wearing stilettos, and Abe squatted to stroke her leg and put one ticket under her heel, stroking the languid python's twitching tail, as well.

"I'll tell you what I'm going to do before we move right on and take it all off on the inside. The first admission is free to the man who's brave enough to come up close and ask the lady nicely to please lift her shoe."

As was usual, a bald-headed gent with gums for teeth, who already knew the drill, volunteered.

"He's saving his three dollars to spend on the inside!" Abe crowed. And Sheba, who liked the toothless part for the cunnilingus, said, "You be right up front now, Sweetheart." She also waved a sweet and silly drunk on through.

"We're not going to hurt him, Ma'am," Abe explained to his wife. "We're only borrowing him, and we'll return him to you a better man."

Jake's place benefited from Abe's charged-up patrons, when they left. He roared the chrome-slutty Harley on its rollers, while Cliff donned a silver helmet, as if they were about to hit the Wall— Cliff was gifted with an imposing frame, at least—and Charlene, perhaps goosed on by Vickie's absence, began to taunt the crowd from her ticket booth, in her spiky, punky haircut and back-street Baltimore accent, about whether she was lookin' at he-men or wimps, in a way that piqued but didn't offend them. "Show me some oomph!" she jeered.

Jake and Cliff completed bolder figure-eights than ordinarily, and afterwards—knowing that she loved the gaunt old tawny dog, and because he saw her watching Sheba flaunt the snake over on the other bally—Jake asked Charlene if she would be afraid to do the same.

"I'm not that good of a stripper." Charlene laughed. "But you mean, would I agree to wear him, if you promised to unwind him when he got too tight? Yes; but I can't bear to watch what he did to that chicken."

"No, we'd feed him roadkills. When you see a rabbit or when you see a possum, you stop. Nothing bloated. And no turtles or armadillos."

He remembered Vickie asking him, the evening when they first had realized they were going to have to sleep in the car, why he wasn't a stunt man in Hollywood. Smart question: Why be a road warrior? He had even been offered (though, like his heart attacks, he hadn't mentioned this to her) a steady income shilling for one of those cheapie Asian motorcycle manufacturers, with a new drome thrown in and a tractor trailer to haul it with, if he would tout their sleazy machines as part of his act, instead of the ancient Indian Scouts.

"You've already got a bald spot, and Evel Knievel can do anything you can do better than you," Vickie had told him. Yet she hadn't threatened to cart Elizabeth Alice back to Philly and let him look for a seventh wife. When she quietly cried, he had apologized that things were hard; and today he recognized that the headlocks and hip throws had shaken her more than she wished to admit, although she remained friendly with Alida, because she had quit snapping at Elizabeth Alice for mimicking Carmen or Sheba's moves. Never having married before, and having lost track of Elizabeth Alice's sperm-dad soon after the little girl's birth halfway through her last year in high school, Vickie harbored modest expectations of him so long as Jake behaved better than her own dad. She watched him look at the Wall not as an occasion for dashing glamour, such as had originally attracted her, or even a cash cow, but as a craftsman's hurdle, with a certain astonishment.

But Jake listened enviously to Abe's patter, as Sheba virtually clothed herself with the opulently tapestried, and undulantly checkered python, which fit its form to hers in order to absorb her body's heat, and inserted its tapered head into interesting locations in order to sample her smells: "Is that ecstasy, Gentlemen? You can kiss her satin shoes and get a red rosebud kiss on your cheek, drawn with her very own lipstick, if you break the ice and push right down in front. She won't bite you unless you want her to. This is her boudoir. The closest gets the mostest. You'll see on the inside what that snake does for her when they're alone!"

Later, still shaking from the vibrations of his machine during those hours in the centrifuge, he indulged in a lengthy shower with Vickie in the motel room, while Elizabeth Alice slept. They made love better than he could have done with any stripper, as he knew from experience, and slept as late as the management permitted, after first waking for Elizabeth Alice's breakfast.

"We live outdoors," he explained to her. "We tune the motors louder than you would be allowed to anywhere else. We wear clothes you'd get stopped for in the street. This is show business. We have fairies and dwarfs. We have women who are sawn in half. We have people who would be wards of the state if they were not with us," he said. And Vickie was placated. She even tried lifting the python that next day, a Saturday, finding it "lighter than Alida," and dry-skinned, not slimy, and patterned like the Persian rug her grandmother, the one relative who had loved her unstintingly, had owned. Tentative but serviceably pretty and twitchy-assed, she stood on the bally platform with it for a while, as Cliff's Charlene did too, boosting their take for the afternoon, when the girl show wasn't open, but kiddies were led by, wanting to see the loud-noise ride.

Yet an old Wall of Death carny had once told Jake that "your mother is your best friend." Naturally he didn't believe it until last year, when his had died, and he'd had to put her best stuff into a storage compartment, along with his own favorite relics, and realized that there was no one now to unfailingly turn to after a heart attack or a terrible shitter. He'd never mentioned the storage compartment to Vickie (this way, you had something left over after a divorce), nor the floaters in his eyes, and the double vision he sometimes experienced when he accelerated too fast. His sixth, or magnetic, sense would thereupon kick in to warn him where the iron cable was. Or perhaps he somehow felt through the fork springs and the wheel base the location of the top paint stripe, until he could distinguish its red again, then the yellow midstripe, and the seventy-seven degree slant that led to the ramp and safely to the floor—although Jake had once performed in a "bottomless" silo act, as a "Death Dodger," in a "Circle of Death," where the body of the structure was lifted off the floor, once the riders got into motion. This was back in his heyday, when carnivals still exhibited "Hitler's Car," next to a Four-Legged Girl, and a Human Pincushion, and "Tortures of the Middle Ages," and monitor lizards as "Living Fossils." You hoisted a reconditioned engine into your banged-up truck and hit the road, with a hand-held air-raid siren for the bally spiel, and a banner proclaiming, "The Devil's Tub." Once you were rotating round the bottomless cask, there was no hope of coming down until it was lowered again.

But late that balmy Saturday afternoon, as the crowds were building for fun and frolic and the entertainment principle was operative that you were going to make ninety percent of your money in ten percent of your time, Sheriff Leroy and the Chairman of the County Fair Association, both of them overfed bullfrogs in this dinky pond, began a portentous stroll down the midway. They stopped at the bingo tent, inevitably, and at the Mouse Game, where people wagered on which hole in a flat board a gray mouse, when released, ran down (the result being gaffed from below according to where the man in charge poked a thread of cheese). Bypassing the American Legion's roulette wheel, they visited the various Lucky Boys at their portable craps or blackjack tables, pausing to josh with them and with Smoky, while palming envelopes or plain greenbacks. They also passed up the rope climb, the radar gun that measured how hard you could pitch, a walk-through trailer togged up as a Crime Caravan, with Al Capone, Bonnie and Clyde, Jesse James, and police-warehouse bric-a-brac, and all of the kiddie games. The ritual was to raise the previously agreed-upon bribes for offences to public morals, and Abe had an envelope ready to give them, which might reduce his pot for the evening from possibly two thousand to fifteen hundred dollars or so. But the mud wrestlers were apoplectic. They didn't know the rigamarole. This was an athletic event! This had been arranged at the beginning with Smoky, they argued.

"All right, keep your shirts on, then," said the sheriff. "We'll see what you earn. If you don't, you go to jail." So they paid him.

Jake, having no sex or gambling encysted in his act, watched these proceedings with only vestigial apprehension. He walked away. Nevertheless, the pair did stop at his bally box, walk around the outside of the drome, examining the system of struts that backed it up, and glanced inside: whereupon they told Charlene to give him the high sign.

"Where's your safety net?" the association chairman asked. His teeny mustache, in the blankness of a very fat face, seemed to be a point of pride with him, and he emphasized this by smiling.

Some bastard must have told him that Jake had lost his sucker net that was supposed to be spread next to the safety cable to catch a fainting customer. Phil couldn't have done it. It would run against his own interests. Was it Angel, out for revenge? Angel was down at his girlfriend's wagon, yelling, "Stinkies! Stinky onions! Get 'em while they're hot!" and ringing a ship's bell.

"It's a matter of public welfare. We may have to shut you down," the sheriff explained pleasantly. But Jake lost his temper.

"Do you guys eat out of the same bucket?" he said.

Sheriff Leroy interrupted him: "It's a free country. Do you want to close up right now and vacate our premises? I'll just have to check your license, if you're driving."

Who else except Angel would know that his license had been suspended? Jake switched strategies quickly and slumped his shoulders in defeat, as you were supposed to do.

"Hard times," he pleaded, indicating the responsibility of Elizabeth Alice's presence with a placating gesture (though a lacey nothing that Samantha had tied around her neck made that seem a bit incongruous), as well as the disparity between his own bally crowd and the sex show's, next door. So they only charged him an extra yard.

Abe was grimacing in sympathy at the spectacle, but when they turned to him, he threw them off-stride for a moment by claiming he had changed his kootch show from the audience-participation of yesterday to just an ordinary snake-charmer's demonstration, with Sheba and the python. "Nothing unsavory. Nobody's stripping."

Then he laughed because bewilderment, and even disappointment, crossed both their greedy faces, and gave them their envelope to split, plus a crotch-thong he said that Samantha had worn. "You can smell it, come Christmastime."

Jake was distracted, however. As a rider, not an owner, he hadn't needed to deal much with this kind of bullshit before. He cut his front tire in weaving by the cable and nearly took a header. If the sucker's net had been in place, he might have grabbed it and saved himself that way, abandoning the bike to fall, but since Cliff wasn't yet in the drome to complicate his descent, he steered jaggedly down, feeling as if he'd gashed a leg, his links with the precious 1928 Indian were so strong. He was glad he hadn't let it fall and get battered more. But that he, the only thrill act on the midway—there were no cats or wire-walkers in front of the grandstand, just trotting races, tractor pulls, country music, and a little demolition derby—should be singled out for a double payoff galled him. Even at only a hundred bucks, it amounted to his entire gross for a very good ride, and he had seen those porky sheriff's deputies with their beer bellies unable to run down a pickpocket, or carry a stretcher with a stroke victim on it to the ambulance without some of the carnies helping. Smoky might be as overweight, but he could practically put up the Ferris wheel, if necessary.

When Jake had checked over the Scout and finished changing the tire, he remembered Angel and went after him. He was not in front of the drome, or at his girlfriend's grease joint. Peering, Jake did eventually catch sight of Angel's pinstriped railroad man's cap among the kiddie rides, up by the Maple Sugar House, at the front end of the carny, but couldn't find him when he finally got there.

Foolishly, he had glared daggers at the boy before beginning his ride, so Angel must have figured he had best disappear.

Jake now wondered whether he shouldn't have looked in the possum belly underneath his drome trailer, where he kept tools and other valuables that might be pawned: even a couple of fifties for "desperate money," as he called it, and photos of people like Goldie and previous wives and his mom, and a ring that somebody had given back to him, in an oilcloth pouch. He should have fired as well as punched Angel, after he stole, but you wouldn't have many roughies working in a carnival if you got all that choosy. Then he did spot him, sprinting distantly from behind the end of the grandstand, across the fields, toward the highway, with a kit bag in one hand and more stuff in the other. What with the heavy traffic, Angel would be able to grab a ride and wave goodbye to here.

The girlfriend selling onion rings was sniffing back her tears, but Jake did not immediately open the trailer's possum belly to learn the worst, although the lock was askew. He growled at Cliff to try and hold the tip while he ate a cheeseburger. (You burned the cheese on the Wall, and the meat was useful for healing your bruises.) Then he hit the circumgyrations like a roulette wheel's metal ball. It was sure a better livelihood than driving a moving van from Bridgeport to Pasadena, and back. From the waist down, he felt part-bike, and relished exercising the fingertip control that enabled him to ride perpendicularly while seated backwards, if he was in the mood for a display of stunts. He followed that with a money run, riding around the top of the barrel as slowly as centrifugal force permitted him to, his right hand outstretched for bills.

He was shaking—he hoped imperceptibly—and his smoker's cough reminded him that, when he was younger, he could have run down Angel in the field, instead of letting him escape. Death he pictured as a great, sudden shitter. Maybe death was another orbit, at right angles to everything we had imagined before.

Standing on the bally platform, Jake handed Vickie the few dollars he'd collected and surveyed the seething crowd. A slow-motion mob; but Elizabeth Alice was dodging families of wandering marks, as she shuttled in and out, searching the packed dirt for coins. Not an ideal childhood, but busier than many. Over yonder, the mud wrestlers were trying to hose the latest load of gunk out of their hair. And Abe was proclaiming that Samantha was "going to swallow a silver dollar in three different ways on the inside." Carmen posed beside her, while Sheba rested in a chair. The feud with the moxie-driven wrestlers had simmered down of its own accord, once Abe had decided he didn't want to risk his girls' good health by promoting a match in front of the grandstand. He really enjoyed his sleepy, leisurely, bathrobe mornings with them in what was generally some lakeside motel room, in the annual cycle of different towns.

Sweating badly and hoarse, Jake began to tout his motordrome again into the microphone. He spoke the truth as a kind of shorthand: "This is the last there is, and I am the best there is, Ladies and Gentlemen. If you want to see a motorcycle ride the Wall, come on in. This is the last go-round."

He had been feeling a familiar nausea, and picturing himself carted off by the sheriff's men as a charity case to the local sawbones or hospital. And now a crushing breastbone pain shortened his breath. So he fished a nitroglycerin pill out of his shirt pocket and put it underneath his tongue. He was visualizing the embalmed body of a young carny workhand of Italian ancestry who had been killed in a fight in Laurinburg, North Carolina, and kept on public display in a loincloth as a local joke called "Spaghetti" in the undertaker's garage for sixty years.

"This is about the last motordrome there'll ever be, and I'm the best there is at it," Jake recited painfully. Although Cliff had stepped away somewhere to eat, quite soon he went inside alone to start the show early and without him, anyhow, after consulting his watch to time the second tablet. He gazed up at the irregular circle of faces rimming the silo, all focusing upon him, and kicked his crank to bring the mini-motor to life—a tenth the size of the biggest Harleys'.

His left shoulder and on down his arm hurt stabbingly, as he straddled the saddle. So he fingered another bitter pill out of his pocket and laid it in his mouth, where the first was still dissolving. The usual headache started. He didn't try to speak any further. Simply gunned himself up the curve of the ramp, onto the circuit of the Wall, and into orbit, round and round and around and around, until, dead, he fell.

The Final Fate of the Alligators

I N SUCH A CROWDED, busy world the service each person performs is necessarily a small one. Arnie Bush's was no exception. He was living in the Chelsea district of Manhattan at this time, although he had lived in central California on several occasions, as well as Chicago, and Crisfield, Maryland, and had put in four years or more in Galveston, Texas, at a point when he was married to a woman who lived there. He'd thought of it as her home rather than his; all of her husbands, as far as he knew, had left Galveston after their marriages to her ended. She owned a laundromat and barbershop, attached, which he had helped her manage. She was a cheerful, practical woman—Ellen—and they'd lived with her two sons in the cottage and patio area behind the business establishments. When he met her, he was a merchant seaman on leave from the sea, rooming in Galveston and hanging around the parks and bars, though he already knew the trade of barbering also. He'd given her a daughter, as a matter of fact—her only daughter—whom he kept in touch with at Christmastime. The girl, whose name was Jo-ann, had grown out of her teens by now, and he was hoping she would visit him if she came north. He hadn't seen her since babyhood, but when he thought of her he imagined that she looked like her mother. Ellen was a smally built, active woman with a bumpy complexion, a pretty figure, black, scalloped hair, and masculine blue eyes. She carped and bitched a bit too much but not so much you couldn't stand it, and since she wasn't as bossy in business hours as she was at home, and since the inescapably boring chores were handled by two employees of long-standing, he had not found that the setup interrupted his independence. Instead, he'd liked being married to a businesswoman; it furnished him with the chance to operate a going concern without the ball-and-chain aspects of owning property. He hadn't married her for money reasons, however (at least, he didn't recognize the motive if he had), but for the special, jumping, bodily impetuosity between them, never equalled for him with another woman, which really never had turned sour. Just the degree of intimacy and understanding they had reached was unforgettable; he hadn't lived four years with anyone else, or given way so much, opened himself. He'd known what she was thinking when she didn't say anything, and known that underneath the peremptory manner she was a homekeeping woman as well, who didn't want to bitch at him if she did bitch, who disliked her own businesses and wanted peace and a simple household.

He had appreciated her youthful bottom, her mother's bosom, and the way she gathered her hair at the nape of her neck. They went to Matamoros together on a week's trip, leaving the kids with the woman who cooked. They dressed in sombreros and paper shirts and saw a cockfight and a festival street dance, and in his memory this trip pretty well represented what a marriage ought to be like. He had delighted in the period when she was pregnant, too, partly because his own gravity had pleased him. And Ellen had slowed down—that ambitious, scrimping fussing—had leaned on him and showed a dreamy side, as he considered, like his. More than at the chance to run the business as he wanted, he'd been happy to see her soften, see her resemble him. And the whole weighty buildup to the baby's arrival—the hydraulics, the clocking of it—had seemed the marvel that it ought to be; and then the hump under the blanket and the red head and skin, the sleeping and the sucking, the rooting, the tunneling, the reaching up, the funny-looking undershirt. He'd called her Joey Milkmouse. He'd hung over the crib: he'd brought home cotton lambs and rubber fish, full of a welling gentleness that mixed with the detachment that was native to him and easily passed for gentleness.

There were certain moments in the routines he detested—at breakfast, for example, which they hurried through. When they were about to get up from the table, she'd mention whatever was on her mind, speaking rapidly and sharply after the silence of the meal. "I want the garbage men to clean up all that stuff they're chucking on the ground; I want you to call them about it. They can't just drive away and leave a mess like that around. And the Bendix people were supposed to be here yesterday. He knows we have two machines out. They were supposed to service us on Monday and they didn't." Sometimes she felt cornered, she said, by the need to hammer at these guys and hold her own, making them do right, though she was thankful to have Bush taking over the worst of it. She wrangled with him at breakfast to get him started strong.

When she was with her kids, she didn't hold out areas of private reserve, but, having been somebody's wife already twice before, with Arnie she was a pensive, smiling chum at best, a speedy co-worker rather than the kind of ultimate companion he'd thought a wife would be. He resented it that what was a climax for him— his marriage—should be her third, and that she didn't flare up angrily, for instance, when a lady called her Mrs. Westrom, which was her previous husband's name. It reminded him of shacking up, or of an ordinary, carnally enlivened partnership, and he was disappointed, if this was marriage, even more than he admitted. He wasn't one to raise a stew about it, however; he was a quiet, self-contained fellow. Instead he paid more attention to the females in pearly slacks who huffed and puffed about the laundromat, eating weight-saver cookies and drinking coffee from the vending machines, and remembered the sea, of course, with intensifying nostalgia. He thought of his teens in Bakersfield and of the many memories of his twenties, when he had gone to sea and knocked around the world—afterward, he'd fought in Italy as an artilleryman. Except for Ellen, the baby, and his two stepsons, he had no ties to anyone, but he discovered that these ties were not indissoluble, either. The boys were runabouts, aged ten and twelve, not lonely or fazed at all, and Jo-ann was mostly Ellen's baby, or the cook's. Ellen's preoccupations were the normalities of mealtimes, meeting the mortgage bills, preserving her neighborly relationships, and seeing the children grow, whoever her husband happened to be; this was his impression anyway. She may have supposed that no husband could be held for long. She kept a bunch of photographs of herself on the coffee table and the chests of drawers to give the kids an atmosphere of family, she said. Bush, who got awfully tired of looking at them, told her she ought to go into show biz.

He was living well but was annoyed a lot. Being a believer in the rule book, a sentimentalist, he didn't like to hear her joke about their having met on the marina, as if it had been just a sort of pickup and as if she were lucky to have gotten married to the man, finally, instead of raped by him. Best were their evenings in bed, lying against the puffed pillows watching television after the kids had gone to sleep, then half an hour's succulence after lights out, and being a person of substance the next day. He was reasonable by nature; he didn't fume and fight as his restlessness increased. But it was really not a man's life there, putting in the bluing, making change. Ellen was defeatist when they quarreled. If she let her confusion show, he was touched; if she was apprehensive, so was he; but she was unrelenting too. In the morning, she would tell him what she wanted done in the same remote, peevish tones, her face assuming the fat expression of someone drawing on inner resources. It was as if he'd as good as left her already and she had her children and friends to fall back on. Apparently, she thought her marriages were a sort of constitutional folly. She said her friends told her she was lucky to get off so lightly every time. Who these friends were Bush didn't know; he only saw a bunch of business friends—the couple at the bakery, the liquor man, the electrician. He didn't think her marriage to him had been foolish, but if that was her attitude what could he do?

He signed on the *Esso Chile* at last, and went off to Bahrein and Maracaibo. He was a wiper in the engine room; on other ships sometimes a steward. Actually, he wasn't on the sea for many years during this second stint before the grittiness and bleakness of the life drove him to land again; yet he did love the ocean and continued to talk about it wherever he was. In his own mind he was a seaman—a seaman ashore. He was nearly as lonely ashore and often thought of Ellen, suspecting, indeed, that leaving had been a mistake. He knew her show of indifference had not been real. She hadn't wanted him to go, but he'd let her pretend she didn't care. They'd been afraid; they'd both pretended it was a matter of small importance—he would go back into the merchant marine, she'd live just as before and maybe marry again. So the proof that he had made a mistake was that he hadn't stayed on the sea long. Every man made his share of mistakes. He missed being part of a household and painted her in pastel colors when he was disheartened, but he decided that it wasn't the mistakes that mattered so crucially as where you were at the end of them all.

Bush was doing fairly well. Stocky and aging, he had crewcut gray hair and a mustache and lived off Ninth Avenue, close to the harbor, keeping up with a few old nautical jokers who patronized the bars he went to. Like them, he hadn't seen much of the ocean from day to day, being hard at work or below decks in his off-hours, but what he remembered was the massive accumulation of what he'd seen. It overshadowed the other job surroundings of his younger years, just as his one marriage dominated the memories he had of other periods spent with women who for awhile had supplied him with housing and sex. He was a sailor, he told the neighbors, and at night or on his lunch hour when he took a stroll he remembered the ocean's agitated sheen, like nobbled tin, and the majestic, chastening pitch of the water when the wind blew, the ship's joints creaking, the heavily lumbering engines, the waves thudding, making a bass hiss against the hull. His apartment, although a walk-up, wasn't too grim. One window faced south, and the sunlight wasn't impeded, because the adjacent block of tenements had been torn down—a process that he knew might pose a problem for him eventually, but in the meantime his rent was low. He had a barbering position in an uptown office building, and managed to live on his salary, saving his tips.

The alligator, like an overgrown brown invalid confined to bed, lived in the big bathtub. If an outsider had been invited in to look at it, he would have gaped, because this was no ten-inch plaything but an animal of barrel-like girth, with a rakish, pitiless mouth as long as a man's forearm and a tail as long as his legs. The cut of the mouth, however, was no clue to the alligator's mood since, like the crocodile mask that a child wears in a school play, it was vivid but never changed. The eyes, eel-gray with vertical pupils, were not as static. They seemed to have a light source within them, and the great body, scummed slightly with algae, was a battlefield shade, the shade of mud. The last time Bush had tried to determine its weight, he borrowed a slaughterhouse scale, fixed a sling, and hung the scale from a ladder, and struggled to heft the animal into place, but he couldn't get its hind end off the ground. Even so, the scale read a hundred and thirty-some pounds. He didn't name the alligator, because it wasn't human; in no way was it human. Like Headley, the fellow who had left it with him years before, he never lit on a name that sounded appropriate—not the Trinkas and Sams that apply easily to dogs. "Alligator" did very well for nomenclature, being a title that loomed in the mind, and "you" served for talking to it.

On arrival, it had still been of a size to permit it to go through the motions of swimming, drawing its arms alongside its trunk and wriggling abruptly downward into the tub until its belly brushed the bottom and its blunt snout bumped the front. It had been four feet long then, and Headley and he had carried it up to the apartment wrapped in a blanket against the cold. The fellow, who was a barfly, a lathe operator, was going south to Gainesville, Georgia, to visit his brother and wanted Bush to take care of the creature until after the holidays. He kept saying that, as big as it had grown since he had bought it—a small water lizard in a pet store—it must be worth lots of money. But he didn't show up again.

Bush laid a plank on the toilet seat and sat in the bathroom watching his new companion porpoise and wallow for exercise as best it could. Once he realized that Headley wasn't coming back, he bought a jumbo junk bathtub from a wrecking company, paying eighty-five dollars, including the delivery charge. He could shower at work, and so the inconvenience of keeping the animal was slight. Furthermore, he soon entered into what he considered an intimacy with it, so that he wouldn't have wanted to give it up. While he knew very well that alligators inhabit fresh water, having it in the apartment, he found a great many of his seaman's memories springing alive with a clarity even surpassing the clarity of life.

The smoldering waves, the sharks and whales, the dull colored, impassive seas on a smoky day—these sailors' sights and many more churned in the roil along with the alligator, who smelled, in fact, quite like the sea. He fed it on chunks of stew meat twice a week, not a demanding chore, and opened the window when the weather was warm to let in the sunlight direct.

At the public library, Bush read that alligators were mild-tempered compared to their crocodile relatives—that a man could swim in a slough populated with alligators without the likelihood of being attacked. He read that they preyed on waterfowl, muskrats, and slow-swimming fish, and he fed it a fryer chicken once in a while, bones included and the feathers left on. He fed it fish, too, always heedful enough of his overtures to its mouth end not to provoke an incident. The furor of feeding time was the main danger, when the alligator, after wringing a slab of meat like a rabbit, threw it up into the air for the pleasure of catching it deep in its throat when it came down, gargling the beef like a strong syrup. Splashing, galloping in place, it chomped and worried the meal, and Bush was touched because, after all, in such scanty quarters there weren't many satisfactions available to it. On less frenzied occasions, it liked to feel its throat rubbed, including the gums of its eighty teeth—just as long as he kept his hands off its muzzle, where the nostrils were, and away from its blistering, satin-gray eyes. The eyes sat on top of its head like two midget riders, and the nostrils collapsed and blew open like a horse's nostrils when it ducked under water.

Though the books gave a vague set of criteria, he couldn't figure out the sex of his animal. He did learn that at only five years an alligator may already be sixty-six inches, which put into perspective Headley's brief role in its life; he would have been jealous to think Headley had had it longer than him.

Except to run water into the tub, Bush often left it to its own devices. It produced a clacking sound by chopping its teeth and at eating times it grunted, too, which he assumed was some kind of adolescent version of the drumming, reverberating boom with which full-grown alligators shook the bayous. The grunt, faintly explosive, contained an animal resonance as well—a *waw*. At the zoo, an attendant told him that alligators rarely bred in captivity, and what he observed of conditions there assured him that he wasn't unkind to keep his at home. Like an eccentric, he didn't even regard the arrangement as strange. He was a dignified man, with a serious nose, his mustache fluffy as a Russian's, and when he got a little bit drunk nobody handled him roughly. Cutting hair every day in the week but Sunday and drinking draught beer in the evening on Twenty-third Street, he had no trouble making ends meet; and he didn't acknowledge his birthdays as landmarks at all, tucking the crimping sensation of being in his sixties into his well-knit walk. He didn't resent the gator's composure, since he himself was self-sufficient.

The alligator slipped imperceptibly toward adulthood, as befitted an animal that was created to live for a century. Its corrugated back was patterned with gray diamonds, although blurred, olive-drab colors overlaid that—not like the bright baby checks Bush saw on the specimens in the pet stores. These little ones were yellow and black and had tiny bills, with a Donald Duck ski-jump effect at the end. Their tails, though, were crenellated already and their eyes, tinted cinnamon-sulphur, were gay, iridescent, and savage.

Like a runner running a treadmill, his big friend surged in the tub, as if a birler were birling. Sometimes it inflated its lungs and then would deliberately try to submerge, swimming against its own buoyancy, until with sensuous relish it released the air and sank down. Another exercise was to seesaw, lifting and lowering its tail, making its hind legs the fulcrum—legs like afterthoughts that were tacked on. Its tail, of course, was the motive force when it swam—a walloping paddle of muscle, which the saurians of the Everglades, three times the size of his monster, swung so powerfully when they hunted at night that they could knock a drinking doe into deep water and seize her. Limber as hide, it whacked up over the edge of the tub and against the wall when the alligator wanted the sting of the blow. The tail seemed to lead a life of its own, twitching quite independently, motorized separately, and when the body moved forward, the tail, which followed after a short delay, was what lent its progress the appearance of irresistibility and crisis.

Bush provided big roasting cuts of meat now, and real mama hens. He found he was trusted more, and he could stroke the nostrils, opening and closing under his hands, or reach behind the ungainly legs to the tender, pigeon-colored armpit skin. He loved the apartment's sea smell, strong as it was, and knew that in possessing such a remarkable prize he was erasing all of that bulk of his life when he'd stayed ashore as a dreamer, working in lumberyards and snipping people's hair.

Reptile leather in the handbag shops began to be labeled "Caiman," the South American relative of the alligator. Then it was gavial skin, and the baby alligators also were unobtainable; he was told they weren't being shipped any more, though his own animal, continuing to grow, seemed prepared to live on forever on behalf of the species, linked back to the dinosaur dynasty. As its girth increased, the grin on its jaws became more theoretical, as if it were pulling the wings off a barfly in its mind's eyes, while in actuality it lived like a very fat fellow, whitening like ash gradually, its eyes a white furnace. The grin wasn't precisely gloating, however, because the two corners sliced back to the very roots of its head—there was more grin, perhaps, than the gator wanted—a grin of chagrin, a grin like that worn by a man whom events have let down and who, grinning to cover the fact, betrays the bad taste at the back of his mouth.

Bush, too, grew grizzled. He read the newspapers and kept up in a less hectored fashion by hearing the headlines read on the radio—the violent malaise of the sixties, the fads and bizarreries. There was a spate of suicides in the neighborhood, and people signaled with mirrors from their bedrooms, or blinked their lights. The streets were tight with pedestrians. He made his home his castle and used binoculars to keep in touch with his neighbors, though he was not himself overswept by the claustrophobia abroad in the world, being accustomed to shipboard conditions. He watched the buildings smoking, and then when the city stopped them from smoking for the sake of the air, that in a way was eerie, too, because so much was going on inside, you knew they ought to be smoking.

The alligator had been ill only twice, when it seemed unable to open its eyes and the eyelids turned blue. It lay with its long maw closed, and a fixed vaudeville smile, propping its head on the side of the tub so that it needn't come up for air. Bush poured bouillon into its mouth through a tube and furnished heaters, and for the time that the illness lasted he didn't attempt to exercise it. Ordinarily, hauling, assisting, he got it out onto the floor every couple of days for a walk and to let it dry thoroughly—let it lie flat, sprawling its arms, while he cleaned the interstices of its skin where fungi might gather. The logistics were not ideal, but the business was very brotherly—the struggle, shoulder to shoulder, to jimmy the heavy body out of the tub—and he didn't get tired of rubbing his hands across the rich hide. On both occasions, the alligator had got well in a week or so. There were some gradual changes, though. Whereas before when he watched the beast's clumsy galumphing he had imagined the alligators in the swamps in their glory, now he began to see his friend just trying to stay alive. The alligator stared at him through its cruel pupils which contained all the harshness of millenniums past—and he wasn't so sure it was going to outlive him. A man downstairs kept fish, and Bush arranged that if he should die this person would telephone the zoo and get them to take the alligator safely. Since he wasn't made to last for a century, he hadn't expected that he might outlive his friend.

Besides the problems of fresh air and space, there was the elaborate question of diet. How could he duplicate the crunchy, glittery nutrients of a jungle river? Of course finally he couldn't—not with powdered Vitamin D and not with steer beef. Sometimes the alligator loped like an otter with constipation, humped awkwardly, and when that happened his own belly ached. These seizures disturbed him dreadfully, especially when he decided they were the result of a deficiency, and one he couldn't correct. Dancing like a bear that had burned its feet, the creature suffered sadly, though its mask was still heavy and comic and rigid. Great gouts of gas came up in bubbles, released from the alligator's digestive tract after much lurching and shuffling. It craned its neck to persuade them to come, after doing an agonized gandy dance, or a dance of death.

During the night one weekend, at last, it died. Bush didn't discover the fact until midmorning, because its position underwater was painless-looking and natural, the head floating just in the attitude of an alligator at peace with itself; he only noticed that it was dead when he saw that it didn't come up to breathe. However, the expression was a terrible one. The expression was like the Angel of Death's, if, as seemed likely, an alligator confronts the Angel of Death with the expression of the Angel of Death. And all of those eons were etched on the mask—all of the meals in the bubbling mud, the procession of species extinguished, the mountain-building, the flooding seas and the baking sun. The framework of daily courtesies was over between them, and the fury and barbarism photographed on the face were alive like a flame.

He might have called the leather-toolers, but didn't. He and his neighbor who kept fish got help and carried the alligator down to the street late Sunday night, leaving it stretched in solitary magnificence across the sidewalk for the city to figure out what to do with.

He had these three memories, then: the sea, the few years in Texas, and the years on Twenty-first Street, with the mumbo-jumbo that filled in between.

The Colonel's Power

GERRY SCHUYLER'S TECHNIQUE with the officers was the soft voice, since the soft voice, of course, was a gentleman's voice, and if they were being loud the roles were reversed. It was the peacetime army and they didn't want that. Except for the barracks end of the life, he seldom had dealings with officious types. His were in the Medical Service Corps, Gerry having the plushy job of running the hospital morgue, which was seldom in official use and most of the time was his private apartment, where he kept his civilian clothes and whiled away hours that he otherwise would have had to spend in more hectic surroundings. Of the four rooms, two were storerooms unconnected with death, so he locked off the rest. He was personable and quick, with a cocked-head approach to the world he was in, expecting to become a lawyer. He enjoyed the lawyer's egalitarian eye, the apprentice cynic's, and was relaxed and responsive with his fellow privates, respectful and friendly enough to the sergeants, and got along with the colonel, a most subtle man with a face like a doge, a pill-taker and amateur sphinx, quite paranoid. After an inadvertent affront to him, there were about three hours before the misunderstanding could not be explained away, but Gerry was just sufficiently quirky himself to be able to spot these emergencies.

The colonel had a master's degree as a chemist-virologist and a sense of humor about doctors, an intimate knowledge of how they were. He came from Florida and was on his way toward thirty years in the army now, uncertain whether he oughtn't to quit, letting the extra pension rights go. His one great mistake had been a disastrous quarrel with his professor at Duke as a young man, after which he had left in a sulk without starting a more rewarding career. He believed in wearing a smile, and he liked to do double takes, show surprise, and appreciated the comforts of life such as soft beds and round slumpy shoulders. His handwriting looked like debris but his clothing was smooth and casual, never exactly khaki. He bought the off-shades available to officers, either a summery-looking tan or a rich business-suit ochre. He had an acute, ironist's face with jug-handle ears and open, unmilitary eyes, which he turned to one side as he spoke, as if slightly shocked at the stories he told—wonderful childhood stories built up with the fancifying talent of a Southerner, about pigs, dogs, and Negroes called Brother Some-thing-or-other. Ordinarily he was all gaiety and games on rainy days or when circumstances were gloomy, as if he were feeling less lonely. Then his fur rose as the weather improved.

Combined with these qualities was a cruel streak, however, which put fallen favorites to work transplanting meningitis. It became a refrain with him—"There's plenty of virus work, Private!"—so that the draftees regarded keeping one jump ahead of friction with the colonel as almost a matter of life and death. That year he happened to chair the Court-martial Board as well, and, while probably no outright miscarriages of justice occurred, when he would come back saying that the prisoner had cried, he was contemptuously pleased. Gerry in a gingerly way argued with him, wondering if, sooner or later, his decisions could help being affected by his attitude. Besides the thefts and AWOLs, another board he sat on considered unsuitability discharges, such as the WAC clerk who gave herself shocks with an electrical gizmo in order to cure her acne, or the corporal who hid in the chaplain's closet.

"I asked him why he didn't take some pills if he felt like that, instead of hiding in the closet. He said he couldn't swallow pills."

"So? If he couldn't swallow them he couldn't swallow them."

"Well, he could take them in water; he could have dissolved them. Or he could chew them," the colonel laughed. "It's a sign of mental trouble not to be able to swallow pills."

"That's what the hearing was all about, wasn't it?"

"Sure. We're letting him out. Don't worry about him. He must be already packing." He imitated giddy packing, although he wasn't nearly as reluctant to grant these releases as were the less intelligent officers. In fact, he was one of the least "chicken" officers around, the liveliest, the cleverest, who cared nothing about salutes, detested swagger, and who, though he was shy in the outside world, was conversant with it—went to recitals and plays and belonged to a club up in New York. He corresponded with German professors he'd met on his duty tours there, and directed the Officers' Quarters with a silken hand. The general got him to host dignitaries, since he knew how, but afterwards he passed blank little weekends alone on the post. His happiest days were the working weekdays, yet the doctors who used his facilities drew distinctions between him and them. He didn't especially take to them either, with their mockery of the army at the same time as they were enjoying status in it. He liked to propose dirty deals for the enlisted men, which he had no intention of carrying out, in order to see them disapprove.

With the sergeants, too, Colonel Wetthall was intricate. For instance, Sgt. Washburn, who loathed blood, was assigned to the vein-sticking room every so often, where she cried and cried. She was enormously fond of him, the main man in her life. The two of them worked cheerfully side by side much of the time. He teased her by calling her Sergeant Wash-born, imitating a mountain girl's speech and then shifting to his manorial smile. He liked functioning on a par with his peppily IQed draftees still more. Digs at the legal profession, or "What now? What's new?" he would say when Gerry appeared, wanting an answer he didn't expect. He'd gather the whole crew to watch him mix media syrup, and then swing around to ask why the floor hadn't been buffed. "Haven't had time?" he said, so that they couldn't tell if he was agreeing or ironic. Because of the colonel's changeableness the under-officers treated everybody with caution, and the sergeants, like humble technicians, weren't formidable unless someone twisted their tails. Sfc. Reynolds, the administrative sergeant, was a self-propelled man from a starved coal town who allowed himself the pleasure of questioning the college boys when they wanted a pass but otherwise, strict and fair, held himself back.

The few privates were tender as mothers from the emotionalisms of stress—a sort of a breakneck golden rule—and knew each other's every heartbeat, lavish like men with high hopes on a raft. Two were displaced druggists, one was a dentistry school dropout from Hawaii, one was a fabrics designer from Newark, and one was a playground director from the tough Bronx. In the barracks Fallon, the playground director, had the bed next to Gerry's. He was a dreamy, competent boy who let his sly jaw down to laugh and got along peacefully with the wildest types, as at home. He was serious rather than kidding, and his ambition was to build a boat patterned after a late-nineteenth century sloop whose owner had sailed around the world.

Gerry's girl situation was probably still for the record as much as for real, but he had a fine girl named Babs Babineau, a Vermont French Canadian. The colonel frowned slightly because her last boyfriend had been a Nisei, but Babs was a practical, nurse-like girl, doing X-rays, with lovely hair and a graceful shrug. Her prim face lighted when she was at ease, or particularly if she was told she was pretty. Though she was ashamed of being in the army, it had been a good move away from her home. She was stiff-upper-lip and misfortune-prone, with a thin-mouthed smile, even, square teeth, a trick knee, a shallow asthmatic's cough. She underdressed for the cold and if she took something hot in her mouth would insist upon sweating with it, not spitting it out. She turned their walks in the country into endurance tests and had a sharp hungry whine like a child set upon. Nevertheless, she was a sweetie, as dependable as she was obstinate. "She? Who's 'she,' the cat's mother?" Babs exclaimed, if Gerry neglected to introduce her around.

Terribly grateful, he lolloped affection on her, and loved the curve she curled into when she read in his rooms, her nylons glinting like two snakeskins, or seeing her come toward him at a distance, with a lean, lonely beauty unaware of itself, and lift her arms quickly to him. Escaping that monotonous city sarcasm was also fun—to be able to say, "Aren't you glad you're with me?" and have Babs's reliable "yes." But such a drab life she'd been brought up to look for says one must make the best of one's lot in the world, that grim brand of puritanism that thinks everything given away is gone.

"If you're trying to remold me, why do you bother? Why don't you grab yourself somebody else?" she said.

Gerry asked the colonel about menstruation, grinning as if he had reasons why he needed to know.

"They used to say it's the uterus weeping for its eggs. The egg that's been waiting gives up hope. It gets flushed out in a rush of tears—if that's not too old-fashioned for you," Wetthall said.

"So it means that it's over?"

"The cycle is over for the moment, yes." He looked at Gerry in a flat, placid mood. Yet the same day the department was racked neurotically by a quarrel between him and Sfc. Reynolds, of all unlikely people—the basis silly, whatever it was—in which Reynolds threatened to let his enlistment lapse at the end of his hitch and the colonel, snickering softly, told him he had enough time left anyway to be shipped off to Germany next week and not see his wife and kids for two years. "Do you want it?"

The sergeant's face swelled. He shook his head.

Gerry was an optimist. Peppiness rather than a lack of grades had veered him into the service before law school, a decision he now regretted, but in the meantime he nourished his hopes on vague chattered pledges of deals someday with other excited young men on the make. And because of his summers spent traveling, he could tell what states the rest of the soldiers came from, often having been to the very town. Since he had crossed on all the big highways, a simple map of America contained marvelous clumps of impressions for him. He was right on the fence in his pleasures, not having lost as yet the sort of immediacies he'd had in his teens. For example, he had a sixth sense, so that visitors never walked in on him unawares and he scarcely troubled to look left and right before crossing a street. He didn't trip in the dark or bump into people when going around a corner. He was full of impulses he trusted. Once he got used to the dirty work, he didn't anticipate that the bodies would play any role in the cozy householder's setup that he had arranged, because they were autopsied quickly, averaging just one a week. But sometimes they'd suddenly descend, like absentee

owners; and couldn't be shunted off. Most patients died at night.
If they survived the sunrise, they usually pulled through until the
next night. Births also occurred then, because of the same corpo-
real relaxation, and he was sent stillborn babies. Oddly enough,
they were easier to handle than the adults, being too small and
too rudimentary to have achieved human dimensions. He was sad
without so much empathy, as if with a cocker spaniel.

A master sergeant in the surgical ward happened to die the
same night as two soldiers who cracked up on the turnpike, and
Gerry's locked-off icebox rebroadcast its claims with a vengeance,
everything baying and hollering. The nurses wheeled down the
lung case, all cleaned up and stoppered, the thumbs tied together
and the penis tied off, but the MPs, an hour later, pounded on
the door with their flashlights as if war had started and hurried
the casualties in with a curse. They were bruiser MPs, rough for
a hospital because of the mental wing whose escapees they had to
run down, and the bodies were ghastly, long, spattered things. An
amazing deadweight spread over the whole instead of being centered, as with a living man. There weren't wounds, only holes, like
a stained diagram. The face of the soldier who hadn't been driving
was peremptory, drawing back—look out!—with a short plain-
tive nose. His friend wore a grimace as if he were hearing a brutal
joke, and still groped for the wheel, which he had lost. Perhaps he
showed some satisfaction too, because this time he had done it up
brown. Despite the need to hose and scrub, despite these coarse,
arrested expressions, and despite the age sympathy that Gerry felt,
the two young privates were a relief to wrestle with, after the old
chest patient who looked so shriveled and mauled, so systemati-
cally readied for death, and now had on an ambiguous smile.

None of the bodies was stiff. They were just heavy, although
they became more stubborn and stone-like as time went on. After
a day or two they appeared to steel themselves, turning a granite
color, in order to bear the hauling which they were being subjected
to. And they were either all there or else not there at all, larger than
life or else insignificant, like a pile of wood shavings under a sheet.
A few stocky men were inexplicably light, but a Fort Dix drillmaster
with a big barrel frame bulked up like a giant compared to a wasted,

frail brigadier general Gerry examined the same day, who sported a harmless look, like a whistler's, like a balloon man's. Though a woman could hold her own, a small fellow lost out, being allowed to display none of his fervor. Even his gore was less grisly—the drill-master's postmortem took hours and filled up two pails. The smiles were the little man's advocate because they wiped away bravery and pain, both together, and leveled off everything else. This cryptic twitch of the lips at the moment of death began to absorb Gerry's interest after the rest had become tedium. Most people did wear a smile. Sometimes it wasn't a bit cryptic, it was benevolent, knowing, or blithe and astonished and rather singing. The marks of gritting the mouth through so many weeks of suffering might remain as well, and once in a while somebody's mouth had turned to an un-mistakable loathing, but never toward an expression of fright.

Gerry worried because he was able to eat heartily after the sights that he was exposed to and the smells that rose up—powdered bone if he used the saw. Did it mean he would adjust to anything? He got very low-key in mentioning his experiences; he avoided mention-ing them. In the barracks at night, the two lines of figures under their blankets unnerved him, with the feet turning up. To lie down himself was like a rehearsal. And the smiles preoccupied him—why in those very last instants? It was a positive action, not merely the mouth going limp as it did in falling asleep. During cancer autop-sies, grape-like, gray, horrible bunches were removed, yet the patient smiled. And Babs saw an old army widow die and, practically cry-ing, told how a smile had quietly preempted her face just in the final seconds, after indescribable paroxysms and pain.

The doors to the icebox grew to be like lids on a Pandora's box that he dreaded opening. Then, in a big comedown, the row of bodies inside might look simpleminded when he pulled them out, might look like a row of public wards. A head on its wooden block seemed about to lift and complain. The doctor, to take out the brain, tipped the scalp over the cadaver's eyes like tipping a hat, as though the fellow were mentally dim, which Gerry later tipped back for him.

• • •

Colonel Wetthall's duties as court-martial chairman, mean-while, produced other nasty stories. He seemed to enjoy telling them to Gerry and arguing with him. A prisoner objected during his trial because a guard had woken him capriciously the night before, and he hadn't managed to go back to sleep. He didn't feel he could defend himself alertly.

"It's probably true."

The colonel grinned. "Well, it may well be true that he got woken up, but that isn't something to bring up in front of all of us. He might tell it to the guardhouse sergeant in the morning if he wanted to."

"No, you should be willing to hear him out. He hasn't anyone else."

"He has the guardhouse sergeant. He has the other guards. He has himself. Let me satisfy you, young man," Wetthall said, still friendly, not ungently. "He wasn't beaten. We asked him that. We were laughing just a little, but we asked him. And we asked him whether soldiers ever have to fight without a good night's sleep the night before, but he just whined. He's a whiner."

"He's a prisoner. I think you ought to take the time to hear complaints. That's not going beyond your function, is it? It certainly shouldn't be," Gerry answered, disturbed because the argument tied in with earlier ones.

"If there is any monkey business, sure. If there are violations. This is whining. We told him if he didn't stand up straight we'd strap a board to his back to straighten it. He didn't like that either. He's a deadbeat, really. He stole a camera from a friend of his and now he doesn't want to be confined. And last Sunday his girlfriend walked out from the railroad station but the man on duty wouldn't let her in to see him, so he protests to us about that too. It's not something in our discretion."

"He's not a deadbeat, he's a prisoner. He sounds as if he needs a little sympathy."

"Yes, his girlfriend does." Wetthall chuckled. "I'm awfully sorry for her. That's a long, hot walk and she does it for this dead-beat. We were tactful, I promise you. We didn't laugh in front of him. We laughed when we went in the other room. I hate to upset you. You have a bleeding heart."

His eyes glittered, sliding away like ball bearings, and the pleasure he appeared to take in teasing Gerry must parallel what he'd felt in the deliberating room. What was he after? How could he relish his power that way and not misuse it? Gerry would be making small talk of the question with the law professors in a few months, but meanwhile the very approach of his independence aggravated his concern.

The barracks commander, Captain Bone, was a shaved-head professional with a brisk, disposable cheeriness, a battlefield, impromptu air. But hard spells succeeded soft no matter who the captain was. They'd sleep on the floor to keep the beds tight for inspection, and polish the floor till it shone like blond hair, rub the brass faucets golden, unscrew the light bulbs to wash them, and seal the gleam on their boots with a lighted match. Like frightened dogs, Fallon and he scrambled under their beds looking for dust, except that they laughed at themselves. Gerry shut himself off in his rooms at the morgue as much as he could. When his time had got whittled down to two months, he was ready to screech from frustration at the previous, squandered twenty-two. The girlfriend illegally brought into the morgue, the diplomacy by which his officers ignored it, bored him, and Babs saw him less anyway, because he didn't use "we" enough, she said, as if his affections weren't permanent.

The occasional weekend in New York City whizzed by. His job had been organized almost to disappearance. The force-fed extravagances of brotherhood that grew up in the barracks were wearying. The sergeants had lost their first novelty. The doctors were knowledgeable only about medicine, although they were so good at dissections that they stirred up his impatience to start on his own career. The colonel remained the best company in spite of the difficulties. A day could pass quickly, working with him, with no hint of their being in the army. But Wetthall withdrew from such familiarity when one of his privates approached discharge, perhaps hurt to see anybody so eager to leave. A new second lieutenant had offended him somehow. During three Draconian days all the property on the books was transferred to him, terrifying the poor man, since it amounted to over a hundred thousand dollars of new responsibility.

Gerry had oiled the tracks for himself, however, until even Captain Bone, whose energy pumped like a piston—who called privates "Duck" from their habit of marching in columns of two—treated him like a short-timer. The bodies departed from his establishment in a wide-stitch, flop-arms fashion, and no one complained. He was popular wherever his errands and other took him. Yet he had begun to pick over an uneasy notion, which was to write a letter about the state of affairs regarding Colonel Wetthall. A report would not itself be a court-martial offense, and his discharge was getting too close for most of the standard reprisals. Fallon was working on meningitis at the moment, but by now they were both so well trained that they didn't care.

One Wednesday afternoon the colonel returned from a hearing with his eyes alive and his lips buttoned up. A case of failure to obey. The two of them argued again, the word in this instance being "scum."

"Scum is scum, my friend, I'm afraid," he said, unbuttoning. "We gave him a good chance to think about it. We gave him about six months, as a matter of fact, so we'll see what that does. We may make a new man."

"Oh, there's only so much thinking to do, isn't there?" Gerry said ruefully.

"Poppycock. Okay, be anti-authority, fine, while you can. Gather your flowers. Just as long as there's somebody else to get the jobs done and take the heat. A few more years and you'll be having to do it yourself, won't you, or it won't be done? You don't really want eightballs running around loose any more than I do. You'll recognize that. You'll have to face the fact that there is a group of unsavory souls who do best out of circulation.—Sergeant Washburn! Ser-geant Wash-born? I want you!" he called, a hog call, his naturally soft voice cracking.

Gerry was surprised at how decided he felt. A complaint, in theory, should be addressed to the Inspector General, but the I.G. here was just a major, without reputation, besides which he had no wish to blemish the colonel's official record. Treachery enough was

involved in any event, because he was still a favorite despite the close
scrapes. Maybe all along he'd been treacherous to one person or another in keeping his mouth shut so much. Mad as the idea was, he
realized that he was going to go ahead with it and that he wouldn't
be thinking it out any further. He could write the Commanding
General, not an enemy of Wetthall's, whose action, if any, would be
unofficial. Although the general was unlikely to act, after two years
here it struck Gerry as appropriate before he left to express, as it were,
one suggestion. He delayed a few days and then sat down and drafted
carefully.

Commanding General
Headquarters
U.S. Grant Army Medical Center
Firegap, Pennsylvania

3623 Med. Detachment
USGAMC, Firegap, Penn.

17 May 1961
Dear Sir:
  I will try to write to you as straightforwardly as I can, not
knowing the exact proper form of address, to tell you of something that disturbs me. I have been stationed here, working in the
Pathology Section, for twenty months, since completion of training at Fort Sam Houston. It may possibly be that the fact that I will
be entering law school in the fall has caused me to take particular
notice of the operation of the court-martial and psycho-medical
unsuitability Boards. At any rate, I have been very interested
and have found I approved of the quality of military justice as I
have glimpsed it. Indeed, I am far less critical of the Army as a
whole than draftees are generally pictured as being, and, without
saying that I am not ready to leave, I have had no meaningful
criticisms to make of it as an institution. It is an idealized institution, which can hardly be faulted except where human error
comes in. The investigation and trial of court-martial offenses is
an example, because, unlike the civilian system by which a man

is tried if there are reasonable grounds for suspecting he may have committed a crime, in the Army he will never be brought to trial to begin with unless a comparatively exhaustive investigation has shown it is practically certain that he did commit the crime charged. Much more conclusive proof is expected in the investigative period; and the hearing, as well as an opportunity for him to challenge and counter the evidence, becomes a time when a group of outside officers go over the evidence once again and the process by which it was gathered in a thorough manner. They are administrators and it is a system set up for administrators. The prisoner is innocent until proven guilty, but he is not put on trial until he has virtually been proven guilty, so there is not nearly the need for professional legal men, whom the Army of course could not provide in its countless outposts, as there is in the civilian court system.

I am sorry to be long-winded, but I want to show that my interest has been sincere. The Chief of my Section, Lt. Col. Wetthall, is Chairman of the Court-martial Board at present and also sits on the other Board. I have been working in close, daily contact with him all this while, often with what should only be called friendship, and have been treated fairly by him. What is bothering me is that he seems to have a cruel streak which sometimes affects him very powerfully, a sadistic streak, if you wish—this is difficult to put. Nothing of this has been applied against me, I have only observed it from the sidelines, and he is not responsible for it, it goes without saying. Nor does it affect his excellent medical work. I am trying to say what I have to say without being impertinent or offensive. Since I know that he enjoys friendly relations with you, and seeking also to avoid harmful red tape, I have written to you about it instead of to somebody else. I believe he takes pleasure in the fright and fear of persons under examination, also in sentencing. From his stories, I am certain of this. I have seen and heard it again and again in the past months, and I cannot see how this can help but eventually affect his decisions in such respects as length of sentence or the actual conduct of the hearing itself. I simply would hope that he would not be placed on these Boards anymore, not that his professional duties would be affected in any way. I hope

you can see in what limited ways I have been disturbed. Thank
you for allowing me to write to you.

Yours sincerely,
Gerald Schuyler,
Pfc.,US51462023

    Showing the letter to no one, he typed it, held onto it over-
night to read again, and delivered it by hand in the course of his
rounds the next morning. He hoped that at least the adjutant
would be the one to open it first and that the two typist privates
at Headquarters Section never saw it at all. He was exhilarated at
breakfast, breathing as if he had just won a race. As lengthy as the
letter needed to be, coming from him to a general, he had side-
stepped saying several things. He had been both clever and honest,
he thought, and if any of the general's own observations corresponded to what he had said, it would bring unobtrusive results.

    Then he began to go sick. He snuck off to his rooms at the
morgue as if he were poisoned, hardly able to breathe, he was so
anxious. Now he was caught in the gears. Now he'd be mashed.
The letter must have already been opened; he couldn't retrieve it.
He stared through the bars on the windows. For his whole life he
had been a lucky fool, trusting his luck, proud of his impulsiveness.
He thought of the letters to friends, written off the top of his head,
which had hurt them. All at once now he would have to pay—in
the army, of all insane places. The Commanding General, a man
he had never seen and knew nothing about except that the colonel
liked him! Brine-green, he leaned on a stretcher and groaned. He
wouldn't be called a crackpot and let off. That was only in civil
life. You were accountable here—you were run up the flagpole.
Oh, good blessed Christ!

    In the late afternoon Sgt. Reynolds phoned. "Where you been,
Schuyler, sleeping? You're supposed to appear every once in a while,
you know. We like your smiles. We like to see you. The colonel wants
you."

    The colonel, when he knocked and went in, looked almost
sicker than he. And Gerry saw instantly that their friendship was

ended. As if he were already discharged and home, he realized how fond of the colonel he had been, how much touched by him, with his lonesome "cultural" weekends, his wide open eyes, and mild, inconclusive, highbrowed expression. Once when the corridors had been stacked with flu patients on litters and the civilian workers went off duty at five as though on an ordinary day, the colonel had turned gray and shaky, but not crumpled like this. He looked like he'd gained fifteen pounds in unhealthy places. He gazed in sagging impersonality at Gerry's middle, not telling him to sit down.

"Perhaps we can discuss this letter you've written. Do you have a copy? You kept no copy? Very well, we'll read mine. You're trembling, do you know that? Your hands are trembling. Someday you may look back from a comfortable distance and think you were quixotic in your twenties—you were a half-baked, nice, idealistic young man with a certain amount of guts, and you'll find it an attractive picture, you'll think it was good to be at that age. But I think you'll be wrong. I think you're what you people call a fink. The old-fashioned way to say it is that there are good men and bad men in the world and both of them pretty well stay the way they start out in regard to that feature, whatever else happens to them. So I don't envy you. You have a long life ahead of you, and you may be able to fool yourself or even respect yourself but you won't be able to trust yourself. You've got a little wild man's hell to live in. It will be like having a robber working for you who you can't get rid of. You'll never know what you're going to do next."

They could hear each other breathing. Wetthall looked at the letter, and Gerry trembled from the immense collapse of his fear. He crossed his arms and squeezed his breath in. In his life he had never been so unspeakably sorry. As soon as he'd found out the colonel would be the one to decide what to do with him, he had stopped being afraid!

"We've been glad to have your ideas on the court-martial system. '. . . have found I approved of the quality of military justice as I have glimpsed it. . . . Indeed, I am far less critical of the Army as a whole . . . can hardly be faulted . . .' When is your release date?"

"June thirtieth."

"We won't ask you to start to say sir after all these months. June thirtieth is a fiscal-year release. When would your release be if we decided to keep you on?"

"July eighteenth, sir."

"That sounds like a long wait, doesn't it? We don't want that. As I say, you don't need to sir me. After two years of not saying sir, we don't want to strain you by expecting it now."

Holding his chin in his hands, he was blowing air into his cheeks and pinching it out, not finding it possible to look above Gerry's neck.

"Tell me something. You write here, 'I believe he takes pleasure in the fright and fear of persons under examination, also in sentencing. From his stories, I am certain of this. I have seen and heard it again and again,' et cetera. 'I simply would hope that he would not be placed on these Boards anymore, not that his professional duties would be affected in any way.' You are scrupulous, aren't you? '. . . Thank you for allowing me to write to you.' Has he allowed you to write him?"

"No sir."

"Am I getting pleasure from your fright at this moment?"

"No sir."

"How do I look?"

"You look unhappy, sir. You look upset."

"I guess I look like you look. You look very unhappy, my friend; you look like a sorry specimen. Do you know that, besides the dirtiest, most sudden thing that anyone has ever done to me, this is a punishable offense?"

"I—not at the time, sir. I guess so, sir."

"*Why* is it? No, I take that back, I don't want to bully you. The answer is that this letter should have been shown to me before it was submitted anywhere and then it should have been submitted to Captain Bone, who, if he could not act on it himself, would have sent it on up to the next man, and so on to the Commander. But tell me—this is not, I think, an unfair question—why did you not give it to Captain Bone, because I think you more or less knew—was it because you didn't want Captain Bone to know that I have been boasting to my private soldiers that I was invited to the general's house and his wife's for tea, and telling my soldiers the outcome of the various cases I try—only the general himself, instead? Or was it so you wouldn't get skinned?"

Gerry had a wild blush.

"Why you people don't think anybody but a captain can skin you I don't know, because they can. You think they're gentlemen like you in the ranks above captain, don't you? You think they wouldn't have attained that high rank if they weren't gentlemen like you."

Humping his chair to face the side wall, he chuckled, clearing his throat. He looked sideways at Gerry. "I lead an innocuous life, I assure you. I talk too much. I'm a snob."

Gerry was trying to answer his accusation, but couldn't get hold of the faintest clue as to what he himself had had in his mind.

"And you wanted to be dramatic—go straight to the top rung, right?"

"Yes."

"Why don't you sit down, since we're old friends?"

Gerry mentioned having considered the I.G.

"The I.G. is a kind of a toy. You frighten them if you go to them." Worn out, he rubbed his eyes. "I think people should see their letters again. They're not to be sent just fluttering off. You're a lawyer, and captains are small fry to you. I'll tell you, if you *were* a lawyer you would be finished after this; you could start somewhere as an accountant if you were lucky—I'm trembling now. You're not and I am."

He stopped and watched curiously, while Gerry, half blacking out in mortification, tried to cut himself off from the crazy man who had written this ignominious letter.

"Tell me again—here I'm forgetting how bad it is—what did you think the general would do? Could you imagine him doing anything other than sending it down to me?"

"No, I can't. I'm afraid I didn't follow it out."

"Of course that's the easiest, to leave it up to the fates. I'll tell you what's been proven, that I've pampered and shielded a smarty sneak. Has anybody ever surprised you so much?" He laughed, better able to look at Gerry. "Anyhow, to get on with this, you say, 'It may

possibly be that the fact that I will be entering law school in the fall . . .'
That's just in case he doesn't realize? ' . . . the Chief of my Section,
Lt. Col. Wetthall. . . . What is bothering me is that he seems to
have a cruel streak, if you wish—this is difficult to put. . . . he is
not responsible for it, it goes without saying. Nor does it affect his
excellent medical work.'

"So that's the meat, is it?" he asked after a silence, with a suddenly gay, strong voice. He straightened and pulled his chair up to
the table in a soldierly fashion, like a scrappy runt of a field officer
with a freckled bald head. "I'm not a man to push to the brink,
you know."

"Sir, I can see that I had nothing to go on except guesswork
and the way it's put is very, very foolish and inexcusable."

"Yes, it's difficult to put. Do you know how you tell a sadist?"

Gerry shook his head.

"A sadist is pretty likely to be the person who talks about sad-
ism a lot and notices it in other people—knows all about who is
a sadist and rings the alarm bell, very excited. Or another type is
quite different. He's someone who is extremely kind and exceed-
ingly gentle, who can almost, you might say, be counted upon to
do the kindest thing when he is in a position of power and when it
actually comes down to the point of doing anything. This might
not remain the case forever, but if you supposed that I was a sadist,
for instance, and from knowing me well, as you say, you knew I
would probably be leaving the army within a couple of years and
that these board duties rotate, besides, and any and all decisions
are passed up to the Commander for confirmation,"—he took a
deep, jerky breath and slapped the letter—"you might get an A,
my friend, if you concluded that the sentences for these couple of
years were going to remain just as lenient as the Commander was
going to allow."

He waited.

"Nothing to say? Young man, I want you to keep out of my
vicinity as much as you can between now and the end of the fiscal
year. I've told you how I don't envy you. I'm going to tell Reynolds to give you more work than you've had, because you've gotten

away with murder in the past year. And I want to hear one thing more, if it's not tormenting you. Why is it that I'm not charging you? Do you think this letter won't be talked about because I'm not? Or am I afraid you'll think you were right and that I'm a sadist if I do?"

"Sir, I'm sorry, I'm very—"

"Get out of here, you're dirt to me," he said, in the grand, army style.

• • •

The purged self-possession the colonel finished with lasted for several days before his muddy qualities caught up with him again, although he didn't single people out as much. Gerry went around with runny bowels and dizzy spells, digesting the scene. At moments he still believed he'd done the decent thing; the alteration in the colonel seemed to prove it. He thought he'd stuck his neck out when most people would not have cared. Besides, it might have been the adjutant who'd read the letter, not the general, which would provide another reason for Wetthall to drop the matter. When reviewed, the incidents that had aroused him continued to, but he realized the colonel hadn't wanted to crush him despite feeling betrayed and that he had oversimplified and been too swift and cavalier about risking someone's career. The memory stung. Sometimes he thought the colonel's predictions were true, because he could relate a bunch of half-cocked blunders of his that went way back and could conjure up a future of ever savager impulses and narrower escapes.

In June he grew almost teary; whole weeks were bathed in nostalgia, a process he had watched as other people's discharges approached. Now it was his turn and, though he hardly spoke with the new transferees, with anybody else who had been around for more than six months, he stopped along the corridors and talked, leaning an elbow on the wall. His days were spent in being congratulated, being asked how he was feeling. As if pregnant, he shared the news. He grinned down gently at his "whites," like an ethnologist, and tolerantly stood reveille, his sleeping limbs slumped into the regulation posture. When he attended Troop Information lectures, he'd known two officers before the present one and his impatience was gangrenous. He was as tender toward himself as a man healing after injuries, unwinding the bandages and wondering that he has survived.

To ceremonialize the two-week mark, he and Fallon and Pvt. Babs held a candlelight party in the morgue. They decided that they couldn't invite newcomers, finally, and sat with wine and pastries as a party of three. The candles were fun, the grinning was fun, although there wasn't a great deal to say. Fallon was a four-square type, domesticating the table with his elbows until it became a comfortable size, with that heaviness Gerry had gotten fond of. Babs, urchin-like and unyielding as ever, had never accepted either his view of her or of himself, so he was glad they were free of each other. But he was worried because she had no prospects, no one to help her. He was afraid that, a month or so after he left, she would panic at the civilian plans she had made and reenlist in the army instead. She peppered out tight little jokes about the world outside, and Fallon told how the baseballs rained down in July in Claremont Park, so that you gripped your head. Gerry didn't say much, conscious of the flashier program which awaited him.

The candles shone through Babs' hands, when she cupped them, with an astonishing pink iridescence. Even Gerry and Fallon could watch their blood move. Fallon said he remembered reading that a candle wouldn't shine through a dead man's hand. He suggested they try out the rule. Gerry didn't like the idea especially, because he'd become still brisker with the bodies since having been told by the colonel that he had a sadistic side too. With the candles glowing before them, however, and not many subjects to talk about, they went in to test if the story were true on a middle-aged corporal from one of the anti-aircraft sites who had been autopsied during the afternoon. He had died in the hospital's mental wing, the cause of his death, a brain tumor, not having been diagnosed properly. It wouldn't have been operable, but the doctors had had a sad time, regretting not letting his family visit him and not having fixed him in quiet surroundings.

Looking down at the man's face again, holding the hot, dripping candle, Gerry immediately recognized the wrongness of what they were up to. Nobody was eager to unfold the hands—his slowness slowed them all down. The aberrant behavior that had confused the doctors hadn't left any tokens behind. In a relaxed way the corporal seemed more soldierly than a middle-aged corporal might usually look, and, if he wasn't too bright, he looked steady. One nostril had widened slightly, as if he were just going to smile a little on that side of his mouth, as if he were with a friend, having finished a hard, marching day, and, pleasurably enough, was just a bit bored. The business was terribly awkward. They were fumbling at it when two starchy MPs, along with the AOD and the MOD and the NCOD, unlocked the door to bring in another body. This interruption seemed to fit in with the silliness of the project so well that for a minute they didn't realize they were in trouble.

The Medical Officer of the Day was an intern who had watched the postmortem, and he glanced at Gerry and at the dead corporal with disapproval, nodding goodbye to his colleague, who would take charge. The Administrative Officer, by mischance, was the provost marshal, a most effective major who lived off-post with his family and who wore an insignia mustache.

"Who are you?"

"Sir, I work here. I'm in the Pathology Department," Gerry said.

"Where are your clothes? You're not in uniform."

"I'm off duty, sir."

The major grimaced at what was in front of him, growing leery and clipped. "What is this nonsense? Why are you here then? What are you trying to burn, for heavens sake?" He walked quickly through the other three rooms and back.

"Sir, it looks strange, but it really was nothing particular," Gerry said, following him at a distance. "We were trying out an old wives' tale."

"You were having a party, I gather. Whose glasses?"

"We'd heard—we were wondering whether it's true—that a candle doesn't shine the same way through a dead man's hand. I'm sorry. It sounds crazy, I know. We were shining it through," explained Gerry numbly.

"Yes, if you work here you know it's off-limits better than anyone else."

Fallon blew out the candle and Gerry helped stow the new arrival onto an icebox tray. The NCOD was the assistant supply sergeant who gave them their clean sheets every week, but he was braced as impersonally as the MPs for the obvious court-martial, as if to witness a ritual ordeal.

"It's pretty cut-and-dried, isn't it?" said the major. He wrote down the time and their names. He sighed, looking around. "See if Captain Bone is still on post, will you, Ashlen? I'm going to get your captain in. We might as well. If you like to burn bodies, you can look at this one. He was a real smart guy. He hasn't a flashlight and he wants to see if his gas tank is empty, so he looks down the hole with a match."

"We weren't trying to burn anything, sir," Fallon told him. Gerry explained again that they were testing an old rule of thumb.

The captain came, with his commission riding lightly on his shoulders, a more adjustable type altogether, but he too screwed up his face at the mess they had gotten themselves into, in their lounging sweaters and all.

"That's sheer absolute idiocy. Who was the bright one? Who had the brainstorm? Can't let anybody off?" He had Babs in mind, but before they could agree, he said, "No, we can't. It's a restricted area. She's not a baby."

Wetthall was called because of his prickly reputation where his own section was involved, and he turned up, although they had hoped that he wouldn't. He listened to the accounts, regarding Gerry with flat dislike and the others assembled with some distaste.

"Don't you realize these people when they're about to get out of the army think that they own the place? It's a wonder they don't run many more tests!" He laughed. After first clasping his hands behind him as if he were hearing an irksome speech, when that wasn't comfortable he stuck them into his pockets instead, and then finally crossed his arms on his chest. He showed none of the ritual air of the NCOs or the duty officer, never mentioned proceedings being taken, and, when the major did, opened his eyes in surprise and averted them as if the notion were news indeed. Gerry, appalled, fighting the sensation off, all at once felt completely saved.

"It doesn't quite have the smell of a court-martial situation, Major, would you say? When you compare it with some of the other things, it seems short of the borderline." He gave a mansion-porch smile, seeing company off.

Captain Bone stood very straight with his eyebrows raised, so that one's heart couldn't help but go out to him; but the provost marshal was a tougher cookie, who also knew how to spread on a smile.

"It seems to be clear as a clam to me. You've got it down like a laundry list. You've got the candle, no less, whatever exactly that means. You've got the wine. You've got the girl in on it. You've got the poor corpse inside there. Whether you add them up upside down or right side up it's still awful funny." He did a palms up. "I'm responsible, Colonel, and it may look sort of like a bad joke to you and to me, but if the relatives knew they wouldn't feel the same way."

"If the relatives knew there had been an autopsy or if the relatives knew the results of the autopsy, they wouldn't be pleased. It's a wretched little piece of history," Wetthall remarked, touching his gaze along the shelves of specimen jars. In subdued ridicule he turned from there to the crease in the major's sleeves and the militant line of his shirt front and fly.

"Well, with all due respect to you, this is my night, sir, I'm afraid. I'm responsible. It seems to be very much cut-and-dried," said Major Kinsey.

"If we had a martinet working in here he'd probably be buggering the corpses," the colonel said softly in his cracked voice. "This is part of my lab. I know the personnel who are concerned. They say they were shining a candle through a dead man's hand, which is an extraordinarily stupid thing to have been doing, almost beyond belief, and you might have to admit that they're missing a screw, but it doesn't impress me as suitable for court-martial action. If Captain Bone chooses to give punishment on the company level, that might be appropriate, but a court-martial action would not be. We can discuss it tomorrow morning with the general if you'd like."

He put on a cordial smile. He excused the enlisted men. The major walked away angry, looking more like a colonel than he. Captain Bone went out to his car, amused, maybe vaguely disgusted. Wetthall left for the officers' billiards room at such a speed Gerry couldn't keep up with him, which was all he was trying to do, just stay behind him.

Cowboys

ZINO'D BEEN THE GATOR WRESTLER since he'd left the Army last spring. Lemkuel's Hollywood was a pretty good carny. Offered lots of attractions but nothing too big for the trucks or expensive to use. Easy to move; played it cool. The hard part for the wrestler was hopping on him and off because if you know about gators you know they can't open their mouth once you're holding it closed—nor the same as the muscles which shut it. That was when the gator's being calm was important. There's a powerful tail also, but this one forgot about his and, as it worked out, only had teeth to eat. Lemkuel told Zino to take some kind of spurs to him to jazzen up the show. Zino told Lemkuel to *hire* a freak.

Zino wrestled with the gator, and Spike, his friend, took care of the hyenas, controlled their jitters and made them laugh at the right times. The third guy who was with them, the paratrooper, took care of the carnival's elephant, gave the towners rides. He did a lot else and so did Spike and so did Zino, but the point is they thought they were tops for handling animals, Frank Buck, Tarzan, and the cat's meow.

Lemkuel's H. was showing Kimberton while the rodeo went on. That's eastern Oregon, cattle country, pretty famous for its rodeos. Lemky's H. was there a week day-and-dating with the rodeo when all the people were in town. Wasn't competition, really, just to get their slough-off, which made a new experience for Spike and Zino and the Trooper, in hick country not to be the grand attraction. May seem silly, but it had to matter, working in a lousy carny, sleeping anywhere, with the numbers stamped indelibly on their shoulders in cattle ink they'd been given by the border cops when the show had zigzagged into Canada to play the suburbs of Vancouver. Beside the rodeo, Lemkuel looked almost the same as the gypsy, nut-game, hotdog stuff that used to creep up near his midway to try for a smidgen of business. And Zino and his friends were on the bum and not true carnies to whom a fleabag three-truck show set up in a vacant lot in Harlem, New York, might be the greatest object of attraction in the city: if the general public didn't know this, so much the worse for it.

Spike was a Marine—had been in the Marines—and he was sure he was the toughest thing God made. No, he let the para-trooper be an equal to him. But Spike didn't cotton to playing second fiddle to that rodeo. Competing cowboys owned the town like Lord and Master. Five-thousand-dollar cars wouldn't draw a glance if one of them was strolling down the street. Cowboys never brag to strangers, excepting ways like flossy chaps or with their hats, but even silent ways irked Spike. He watched the cowboys all the time. He'd squint. He'd reconnoiter vantage spots where he could watch a bunch of bars and several streets, and not ascared of nothing. A Marine.

They're suckers, cowboys, course. Zino had sucker stuff he fiddled with, Chinese charms, and they spent when they won— cowboys don't get salaries, they win or starve so he had no particu-lar complaint. He was peaceable by nature. But usually in a town people would be asking *him* and hanging round and being excited. Here, this town, *he* was s'posed to be the fascinated one and dog *them!* In a bar the cowboys would be leaning on their arms with all their weight, on account of all their hurts and pains, favoring one leg or the other, and everybody'd want to buy them drinks, breathe their burps, listen for the pearls of wisdom—when the cowboy'd gotten drunk enough to condescend to talk. Women would be say-ing those fancy shirts they wore were cute as mink. And, because of the rodeo, ordinary, everyday cowboys who never gave Zino any trouble in the other towns got to thinking they were special. Seemed to take an hour to make a quarter off them.

Spike wore tee shirts covered with the carnival and a mauler-looking leather jacket with LEMKUEL'S HOLLYWOOD

CARNIVAL written out in full on it, the whole shebang, and always threw out hints to people as to where he worked. Here it was like he had had on a Wall Street suit. People thought he was different from them, all right, but they paid no attention to him, didn't give a damn. The cowboys weren't starting trouble, either on the lot or off it. They kept their fights among themselves—stand still trading punches till one guy'd run low, and that would start the tumbling over tables and the throwing crockery and chairs—bartenders were the ones they hurt, because they'd wreck a bar. But Spike lost weight about them, until finally Spike took Zino and the Trooper to the rodeo.

Zino'd served his time like anybody's brother as a draftee, not a Fighting Man. The gator wrestling redeemed him for the other two. And although Zino was proud enough of the carny as carnies went, he knew you had to be a bum to work in one and once he'd started getting some breaks from the world he'd quit—so in the last analysis he wasn't proud; it wasn't like a service outfit to him. But Zino was curious, wanted a laugh. He went along for kicks. Spike was deadly serious. Spike suggested it while they were hosing down the bears. "Let's *go* to the rodeo." He emphasized the "go."

"When we're off they wouldn't be showing either," Zino said.

"That don't matter."

Spike thought about the thing all Sunday, and the next day, soon as they finished the morning chores and before the opening for the matinee, he asked again: "You comin'?"

Zino hardly knew what Spike was talking about—"You comin'?" was all he said—and yet he really couldn't be excused by that because he had a notion. Even if he didn't know Spike's plans he did know Spike. Cowboys were hayseeds, Zino figured. He'd never been worried by hayseeds before, and if a carnie can't handle the hayseeds he'd better go straight.

"We'll see about Airborne," Spike said.

Airborne was sleeping on top of his elephant. He liked height. Spike didn't hesitate to wake him. "Hey, you want to stir some cowboys up?"

Airborne was down—fast as that. Didn't wait to be elevatored on the elephant's trunk. He jumped, and then he scratched his elephant's tongue. She moved it under his hand like diddling a lollipop.

"Do we got to clean?" Airborne asked Spike. Watching them was funny. Paint four dots on a piece of metal and you'd have how their eyes looked. Sergeants' eyes. Zino smiled.

Spike told him yes. It was risky because Lemkuel spotted people with nothing to do; it would be safer simply to clear out—in that the carnival was like the service—but they always made him wash. Being a good soldier. Airborne kept his clothes and face and armpits clean, but anybody taking care of elephants stinks something terrible. Washing doesn't do away with it, but you try. Stinks terrible if you don't like elephants much, which women don't. They argued about the smell and scrubbed and fooled around so long they had to call in witnesses whose noses still could judge if it was there. Finally let him be. No one happened to think cowboys must stink too; they weren't going visiting women. It was habit, washing Airborne any time they left the show.

So now they waited while he got his boots. He'd always fuss. Like putting money in the bank, when you brought Airborne you started off by sacrificing rime, and Spike and him were buddies. The jump boots he had on weren't freshly polished—"These're getting crummy." His second pair was in an airtight plastic sack inside a box inside his trunk, each boot wrapped with felt to prevent scrapes against the other boot, and he was always changing boxes to find one which would "hold up." He blew at the boots to get off lint, then started in with rags and polish. Spike was sympathetic, but Zino told the guy to hang a sign, Museum Exhibitions.

When Airborne was through with the rags, the boots were like you'd see on a colonel, and he was only partly done. He spit and used his finger round and round and round laboriously. Then to cement the shine he lit a match. The shine burned in, he took a razor blade and shaved the white-gut laces newly white. They were permanently put in, a special, raised, jump-boot pattern; zippers on the sides were used for getting in and out. He polished the zippers. Zino made faces and began looking forward to going to the rodeo very much. Spike tapped his foot, whistled softly, and stared at trees. Last, Airborne bloused his pant cuffs to the boots with two steel springs which shaped and made them rigid, and with rubber bands. A sergeant's shine, a sergeant's boots. Zino snorted.

"Are we ready?" Spike asked, trying to keep from being sarcastic. He sympathized with soldiering and didn't want to side with Zino.

"Wait'll I look," Airborne said. "You didn't give me notice." Since he wore no shirt he centered his buckle and the fly of his pants with the line of hair down his stomach, and checked that the huge tattoo on his chest wasn't blurred by hair, was shaven: the head of a screaming eagle, his old outfit's emblem.

Zino kidded: "Did the gooks give you notice?" Spike still watched trees.

"Let's move out," Airborne said, satisfied and grinning. He snapped Spike a salute in fun, which Spike returned. None of this pussyfoot, brush-your-forehead-with-your hand an officer would use; a leaping whiplash, an electric motion, an enlisted man's salute. They stepped off with the thirty-inch step, Spike calling cadence, all regulation. Hup Haupereep Haup. Zino was the slick-sleeve, but they weren't harassing him; he went along with it. Spike's lilt and chat and joyousness made it fun, as good as a band for stirring you up. Kosher sergeants: by the book.

Pretty soon Spike gave them Double Time, letting Airborne do the Airborne Shuffle. Spike was smart, though, and cut it back to Quick Time before Zino thought about the silliness of running; then to Route Step, where they walked as they pleased without cadence. He was a battlefield Marine and he preferred this, quiet and alert, not civilian walking. Put them fifty feet apart on alternate sides of the road with a stride that could last for thirty miles. And as he walked, Spike seemed to clothe himself in solemn battle-green, the aura of war, the time-honored burdens of pack, shovel, and littler gear and crossed, tall weapons—all half-joking; he wasn't a nut. But he started memories of maneuvers crowding upon Zino. The flares and hammering machine-guns; the trim traced mustaches of the officers; the clap of laughter when the top ones joked; the shadow of a marching file in the afternoon, long on the grass like a moving fence; the First Soldier during the hurricane telling them this was the United States Army and to feel some pride and quit their gripes, and late the worst night (not in the hurricane at all but when he chose to make it) standing erect on one foot in a jeep's headlights on a roadside post in his tee shirt and muddy pants and boots, telling the two hundred of them: "Yes, you men are troops now. You done good. I don't swear at men under me, I just run them till their tongues drop out, and the man that falls had better show me blood on him and whites for eyes, because I'll look. But you're men now, you boys, and you're troops. And any of you that were men before are good men now, and troops. You've earned your sleep. Fall out."

Spike said over his shoulder, "Fix your knives." His hand made the start of a motion toward where a bayonet would hang. He smiled, but his lips pressured together; his hands were dandling a weight—in his mind, by God, he was carrying a gun, and a man's-best-friend, not an idiot-stick like Zino's.

The rodeo arena was open-air, surrounded by stands, with a big dirt-floor shed at one end for everything to live in. As anyplace in show business, the way to the performers was through the most inconspicuous door an outsider found. It brought Spike under the stands and next to the chutes, and following the chutes he came to the shed. Airborne got fiercely bubbly, like the average sturdy sergeant about to be tested. Zino recognized the state and despite his own tenseness smiled. Spike was just alert.

"We gotta find where the crum-bums are hiding. What should we do, yell? Maybe we'd scare them. Maybe better if they think we're towners," Airborne said.

The animals looked to be out, the way they kept them. You could be used to the carnival zebras and bears and gators teed off and hyenas snapping and still not feel comfortable, seeing past a couple of grapevine-yard slats those horns which even the steers grew, horns yellow like teeth, high and thick—long so you couldn't see both at the same time unless you stood back. Razor horns mellowed yellow. The steers were packed in the pens so crowded that the horns were like a head-high mass of thicket. Then in another pen, instead of horns there'd be the horses' heads, goggly, watching Zino, all turned in one direction and touching each other, like a school of fish, hanging still or moving as fast as fish in unison with ups and downs and quivers.

The bulls were by themselves and didn't make Zino nervous; they plain made him sweat. Their pen should have burst just from the numbers in it—couldn't have forced in a pitchfork of hay; how were they fed?—not to mention the boards being about as thick as one of their nostrils. Zino'd have circled a field a mile across that one of those bulls was in—and watched awhile to admire it—couldn't have dreamed up a better bull in a nightmare. Not farm bulls: humped Brahmins for spirit, now standing as bulky and still as so many cannon. Twenty bulls in a pen the size of a kitchen. He dried his hands on his pants.

Calves for roping were squeezed in a pen like frogs in a pail and hopping and making the noise for everything else. In narrow spaces between the pens, besides the hay and cowboys' bunks, were dogs, cats, and special, privileged horses with blankets on their hinds and pails of water of their own. The shed held more animals than Zino would have expected to see spread on a whole horizon during a roundup. Right then, as soon as that, he felt sorry he had come. But Spike and the Paratroop were every bit as gutty, straight, and veteran-looking as before. They didn't bluff.

They kept a distance from the animals, not to excite them, and hunted for the cowboys, who were hard to find. Some were hidden in the horse pens, messing with the horses, and some were smoking in the hay asleep. Yes, asleep in the hay, smoking. These weren't the first guys Zino'd seen smoke in their sleep but were the only sober ones who didn't do it for a stunt and had the nerve to lay in hay. Another bunch was in the rafters of the shed with fifths of liquor, playing cards. Turned out to be the ones who at the time could walk without much pain, although their jeans were trussed against their legs for injuries. Zino and the sergeants watched them. Cowboys are really proud of two things, besides their horses and themselves—their boots and hat. And so they're always fooling with their hat, fixing it on their head or playing with it on their knee. And whenever their feet are dangling, straddling a fence or on a rafter, they'll kick them out, kick them back, and admire the spurs and boots from every angle. They wear dainty boots, with personality, pointed slim and form-fit curving—funny to compare beside the Trooper's giant stomper weapons.

Dogs let the cowboys know about the strangers, but nobody was interested. Spike had plenty of chance to look around and map his plan. There wasn't much to see except the animals. Saddles on some sawhorses, a kerosene stove (banked in hay), and pots and dishes. Cots with Indian or khaki blankets; saddlebags, knapsacks, suitcases, little private stuff, a mirror hung on the side of a pen. When Spike had learned the land, he whistled sharply at the cowboys in the rafters and jerked his rifle hand for them to come. They didn't stop to ask a question. Like such a thing was natural, they swung themselves around till they were hanging by their arms and dropped off down among the steers and skeedled out before they could get gored. The steers went wild. The steers thought it was raining men. The fence careened and cracked—but lasted.

"They need some jumping lessons," said the Troop, meaning in technique. A cowboy pounded extra slats onto the pen where it was damaged. Zino noticed earlier repairs the same.

Spike played the situation fine. He took his time. He put his fists against his hips Commanding General-style and let the cowboys wait. Pat Patton's pearl-sided six-guns strapped at his waist would have looked swell, and a cowboy like Earp or Doc Holiday trash.

When the cigarettes burned near their lips, the guys asleep woke up a little. As this happened to each man, Spike jerked his rifle hand at him to come. The ones in fooling with the horses showed up of their own accord, propped on their elbows on an animal's back. Most all the cowboys tried to make it. The guys from the rafters walked, bowlegged and teetery on those high-heel boots. Others got a stick and used the corners of their feet or hobbled on their knees, arms crooked out with pain. A few only were able to crawl on a horse for the view and put braids in its mane while they listened. That's how to tell a rodeo cowboy from a regular one. Oh, the regular, he won't walk like you and me. But the *rodeo,* most likely he won't make it to the can without a horse. It's the falls which do it, not the actual stock. A herd of horses couldn't give a hogtied cowboy half a bump.

Zino was six feet. Spike even bigger, and Airborne, if a finger shorter, was muscled tougher than a shark. They'd murdered the loggers and the apple pickers and the sheepherders and salmon fishermen through Washington—there are no rougher places than a carnival. They'd have given the cowboys a day's work in a fight. But Spike didn't seem to plan to. He just was there to talk.

The animals got restless and stampy. But the cowboys were attentive, scratching their stomachs or tilting their hats around with their fingers, as they were always doing, or tinkling a spur; otherwise still and planted to listen. Spike had been practicing what to say all week, he'd been so mad, and now he had forgotten. He was confident, but he'd forgotten. Pinched his mouth and frowned. Each cowboy looked different from each other cowboy; couldn't treat them as a crowd. That's what bothered Zino. Each hat had its own independently airy-curvy brim, although always leveling sternly with the eyes in front, and its own variety of creases in the crown. And the necessity of hat-room made the cowboys space themselves so that each man was an island to be dealt with separately. And the faces weren't the same. Each had elements of its own.

Spike would do this kind of thing in the Marines, he'd said— on pass go into town and tell the locals what was what—but now the feather-tinkling spurs were all they heard. Spike couldn't start, and Airborne couldn't either, being out-ranked.

Suddenly Spike grinned, squared his chest, pushed his lips against each other and his fists against his hips, pulled himself so straight he was a picture. Loud as ringing metal he began.

"You people! Get this clear! Because your soul may still belong to God but as of now your ass is mine!" (The tone: why sure, he'd talk recruit.)

"The shit has hit the fan. I'm going to take the swagger out of you! I'll bring some order here. I'll straighten you. You'll take the course. I'm going to run you through a grinder! Each word I say is going to be your Bible. *I'm* your law and you'll stand tall! When I say jump you'll jump for me, you people, till you wee and wet your whiskers! Except you won't have whiskers. You'll dry-shave."

Knots and lumps stood in his face. He stopped and looked at Zino and at Airborne like assisting cadre, then beyond them to the pens of stock. The cowboys got the same expression from him as the stock.

"I helped put up the flag on Iwo Jima that the people took the pictures of; I was on the hill. I was in on Okinawa, Bougainville. I was in the Phillippines when the Japs gave in. And I know two things: Japs, they stink and you guys too. When I was going to school I hung from railroad ties when trains crossed the bridge. You couldn't do that now, but I was having fun and goin' to school. And I'm a better man with women." He grinned abrasively. "And I brought in the first Dakota well, my crew that I was in, which meant the state gets rich. And I knew Tony Zale like brothers. Not many guys have done the stuff I did, not you! Cowboys are for kids! Cowboys are for children!"

And Spike looked something fine. He'd dropped the boot-camp patter, but his tightened lips still carried fight, stamped what he was as sure as hash marks up the arm. His voice would fill a company street, and if he'd coughed he would have shouted louder. Those cowboys should at least have been set back. But no, and not insulted. They were enjoying Spike, hunched smiling on their heels like wolves sitting. They held their hats and tippy-tipped their fingers on them as if they had Spike in a jar.

"S'pose I yell Hey Rube like show guys yell. You'd be skinned!" He grinned at Troop and Zino to share how smart it was. Nobody's used Hey Rube in shows for twenty years, but he said that. They weren't near hearing distance of the lot. The Trooper, he was next to Spike's left shoulder, one pace out and one pace back, in shining battle boots, the screaming eagle on his chest.

Zino stood where he could make a run for it. Twenty cowboys to the three of them! But cowboys weren't the athlete he was. They're funny, cowboys. Blind drunk every night; chain-smoke, drink themselves blind. Because they only do the stuff they do for ten or fifteen seconds—stay on a horse—they aren't in good condition. Got no wind: never's a need for wind. And crippled. And always thinking about something. Watching you and sitting on their heels and thinking. These ones did. His back crawled.

Spike faced up to them, had suckled nails. "I'm from the carnival," he said. "Which means in every town the guys who think they're rough come down to make it rough. Everybody. Cops off-duty. And we handle them, *we* make it rough, we chase them through the town. I've always been with outfits like that. Our battalion used to trade the medics in for fightin' troops before we'd hit the sand. Our tankers emptied the tool box throwing wrenches before they'd die. No ammo and a Jap comin' in? *Give him the butt and the steel!"* he roared, so even the cowboys blinked.

He knocked the hat off one. The guy was bald. "Skinheads!" Spike sneered. "That's why you wear them hats!" He kicked the same guy in the foot, which made him howl. "Sorefoots! That's why you wear them boots! 'Cowboys!'" He spat the word. "I think they call you that because you look as dumb as cows. Huh? Answer up! Umbrella heads! Your cattle got your tongues?"

The cowboys grinned. Their mouths and noses got real wide. "Slaps, open up the gate."

Horses poured forth like a dam had burst, in a wall of dancing crazy water—brown as water—out the gate and racing to both sides. Zino bounced as the ground shook and the mass whirled round the shed. Singling out individual broncs was scarier still. They pinwheeled, their hooves topped their heads. Zino fell down in a ball and covered his head. Then he got up to try and survive. Spike was willing to run for it now, but too late. Zino stuck beside him like any raw replacement. The horses were everywhere, plunging and thrashing and kicking each other, fiend-faced, an oncoming merry-go-round brought alive. And now old Slaps got happy-go-lucky and let out a couple of bulls, which were charging but hadn't decided where. Spike couldn't maneuver because of the horses. Soon as the bulls spotted him and his men it seemed that they'd be cooked.

The cowboys didn't bother with the bulls, only to dodge. The cowboys were after the horses. Cowboys are cripples but cowboys can move, just never how anyone else would move and most of the time they aren't balanced steady; every few steps they'll fall. These guys were using their hands to help. Sometimes they almost ran on their hands, skeedling next to the ground like crabs. The slender skin-colored boots seen at a distance made them look barefoot. Several men had a funny run, limping on both legs: each step was a stumble and to keep from falling they went at a run. And as much as they ran they threw their hats, stalwart, sailing hats, so big. They must have thought it wasn't fun enough to rope the horses, because they dove and flopped and skidded, told each other wordless things and yipped and shouted at the horses, sailed and flapped and flung their hats to steer them. The hats were charmed, never crushed or tromped on; kept their gallant complex shapes, as if to wear one was to wear a helmet. Of course Zino and the sergeants didn't care about the hats. They were trying to save their skins. But the way to live was stand right still and watch in all directions. This they did, in the middle of the tumult.

By and by the cowboys got the horses circling. Couldn't stop them, but they got them circling, and relaxed, dusted off their hats with careful swats or with their fingers, and began to eenie-meenie, picking out their broncs. Everybody was inside the horses' circle except the bulls, who charged in and out. The cowboys took it slow, rolled cigarettes, listened to the hooves and breathing. Then they limped along beside the circle—a man might stop, change his mind about a horse, now go again—they stumbled along and one by one grabbed onto a horse's head like hauling in a running catch and shinnied up as effortlessly as rolling into bed—so easy. Course it wasn't. The horses sunfished, seesawed, wrenched around like puppets, and when the bulls got near went off their rockers.

A cowboy scissored with his spurs to liven up a dull one. Another man was having trouble, holding to a horse's neck, his body flat out from it like the greatest jitterbug. Got smashed against a post and really caught a case of the limps. Anybody else's legs would have been mangled. Once a cowboy sat secure, why he'd perch on the rump of the bronc, swing his legs up on its back and ride, with it bucking, like that, hold onto the hide with his fingers.

Mounted, the cowboys had some height. On the ground because of all their walking troubles, as well as legs bowed bad as wishbones, they seemed small. Horses became different too, more individual. Bucked tight jackknifes in a circle; or lunged roomily and straight ahead. Or the mechanical, classic, easy buckers, rhythmic as a circus horse, except the motions bigger. Affectionate horses acted happy. Complainers wagged their heads. The cowboys with horses broken fooled the bulls back into the pen.

Spike was catching his breath. He didn't seem to figure that these new procedures had anything to do with him. Airborne waited for his orders, Zino only wanted to be gotten out of what they'd brought him into. Spike watched everything, partly contemptuously laughing but also interested and entertained. There wasn't a trick he missed, hands on hips, scalp-close haircut, a Marine.

Still, some cowboys hadn't mounted, those banged up the worst. They crawled to the top of a pen, using their elbows for hands and their knees for feet. The rest of the horses were driven past and they got on that way, like straddling the chute. Men who wanted ropes and saddles went for them, and Spike began at last to feel outnumbered, started for the door, although to look at him he was a kid being dragged away. Now suddenly he ran—the three of them—a hard determined dash which would have bowled over anybody on the ground. Riders loped in front to cut him off and squeezed in from the sides and nudged up from behind. They crowded Zino and the Trooper in so close to him that the three hugged each other. From then on Zino never knew what he was doing before it was half done. The cowboys talked a different language, heeey*ah!* and who*oo!* And partly to the horses, and what they said was swallowed in the dust and noise. Their faces didn't seem to move, except the lazy smiles, so he never even knew who'd spoken. And he was running without stopping, the horses with their manes gone wild, and mouths, and hooves about to split his back. The dipsy lassos teased. The cowboys doing it he couldn't even see, just occasionally, smiling lazy at their skill. Spike tried to slam a guy who'd been bucked off and they thought that was marvelous, as with some kind of monkey, though they wouldn't let the cowboy make a fight; it wasn't what they wanted.

The posse had no boss but one guy spoke officially. "Talk is cheap." He grinned at Spike. "You'll live, you fellas. Don't think we're out to kill you. Just havin' a little fun. Dusty up that fella's shoes. Do what you're told until its over." Which was bullcrap because they couldn't hear what they were told and had as much control of what they did as mice.

To start, the cowboys put a horse on either side of Zino and a horse behind him and ran him into the arena. Only place to run was straight ahead, until the horses turned him, and if he tried to stop the horse in back would stomp him. He couldn't fall down in the midst of the hooves, and couldn't climb the cowboys' stirrups because they'd whip him with their ropes. They had a race with Spike and him and Airborne—who could be got to go the fastest—although he didn't see his pals; was lucky seeing the sky. Yes, Spike raced too.

Then they cut it down to one horse and rider; made it like steer wrestling. Ran the man beside the grandstand wall and leapt on him from the horse. The hard thing was to land on target, instead of, when they'd do it with a steer, landing in the right position, heels braced out to plow the sand. One guy who missed Zino wrecked his knee; another struck the wall and was unconscious. And sometimes Zino had a couple of moments to fight them on the ground before the posse broke it up. "Don't spoil him," the posse'd tell the cowboy. Zino couldn't do much, with his breath knocked out; or else the cowboy would have hit the ground and been behind him. He slugged, ran, fell, was hit with those flying tackles off the horses, was bumped by the horses—once got hit with a horse's head; it tossed its head—socked like a club! His eyes were blind with tears of hatred and with sand. He gasped too hard to cry. The grunts of the horses pounding into turns and stops seemed to come from him. Knocked him down; knocked him down again; he gave up fighting, just tried to dodge and let the cowboys bust themselves against the ground. If, as he'd heard, the crucial qualities in battle were the wind and legs to run, he proved as well as Spike and Airborne that he could run.

Finally came a contest at roping and hogtieing. The cowboys who were last won because by then the captives simply waited for the rope exhausted. Even so, the cowboys fascinatedly compared their times for roping calves with these for roping people, and tried to rest them up to make it fair. If a cowboy missed two throws the man might run right out the other end of the arena and be free. Didn't happen, but it gave the roping purpose. And as much as catching the man, the cowboy had to put the loop to bind his arms or else he'd lose out to the stopwatch, busy in a fight before the feet were tied, because no posse would help him now. Spike and Airborne got some good licks in. Zino was too tired. A cowboy hung under a horse's belly while it galloped and roped Airborne from there. Zino didn't see. He reeled in circles. Always a goddam horse pulling taut the rope around his chest until the cowboy had him down and tied. Or else a goddamned horse's nose goosing at his kiester.

The three of them finished up as crippled as the cowboys, without the broken bones. Lay on their backs. The cowboys looked enormous from the ground, and the horses had tremendous chests and necks and wispy little heads; and tall—they reared and stamped—bodies huge and long like walls. The cowboys' hats blocked out the sky. Black sideburns spread down their cheeks and there was hair between their eyes; expressions on their yipping mouths to dream about. The chaps, the spurs, the boots, jean jackets, hats—each item never would need boasting. Zino didn't hope to kill the cowboys. He wanted God to have them die. One made a horse cross over him, kick near his head. He didn't pray. He shut his mind.

Kwan's Coney Island

THERE WAS A SAINT IN THE STREETS, a bland silver man about one-fourth-sized who was rolling along on a rubber-wheeled cart while a priest in lace walked in front reading the blessing. Two lines of men gently pulled the lead ropes and behind the saint's cart a large number of women in black carried candles. A uniformed band of fifteen played a salute to anybody who came up with a dollar bill to be pinned to the saint's vestments. "Wait a minute! Wait a minute. Not so fast," said a butcher coming out of his store after the crowd had gone by. He wore a black band on his arm and, holding his dollar, he kept at a sensible step to catch up with them. The band turned, like everyone else, to wait and, when he'd delivered it, did the salute, all the cheeks puffed, the instruments facing him. He got a saint's card from the priest, which his wife kissed.

Kwan nodded familiarly to the marchers. These parades happened almost every month. He followed until the fireworks stage, when a string of firecrackers were laid down for a block and the head man waved his breast-pocket handkerchief a long time, swearing because his assistants at the opposite end couldn't figure out what he meant. Then a shocking great war cannonade went off, filling the air with its smell and smoke. The kids ran the length of the fuse just ahead of the blasts, and yellow and blue and red stains were left in the street which would last till the next occasion. The saint was rolled into a storefront to stay.

Kwan had been downtown for Saturday night and had come back late on the bus. This morning, delightfully logy, he'd lain in bed past eleven o'clock, although he was never a sound sleeper.

He lived in the back of his laundry, not to save money so much as because he had gotten to be rather crusty and could do without constant company. He liked company only in short doses. After a get-together he took at least a couple of days to digest whatever he'd heard and several more days to finish enjoying it. He had lived in Pittsburgh for many years, so to live here in New York a few dozen blocks from the central neighborhood of his own people was a luxury. In his block were black men and Puerto Ricans and Sons of Adam, as he called the Hasidic Jews, and Italians, as he called the Germans, Poles, Greeks, and Italians, and miscellaneous bums and bearded young scholars. He had a Russian church and a Spanish church alongside his business and, all in all, he could pass in and out with a fine anonymity. Sundays in August now he went to the beach, thinking over the gossip of Saturday night and the fixes his friends had gotten themselves into. Even on a cool day he would go because of the sweltering week he'd put in, as well as the sweltering week to come. He was middle-aged, dressed in his next-to best suit and a clovered sport shirt, with the mild roundish face of a member of the amphibian family, except for his humorous mouth and firm chin.

The hydrants were going but nobody soaked him as he went past; the Puerto Ricans were after their own. It was a day in the eighties with a marvelous high sky the blue of an organdy robe. He took the subway, reading a Chinese newspaper until the tracks emerged above ground. Having chosen his seat especially, he sat back, his hands clasped in his lap, blinking in the sun, and fanned by a dry city breeze. Although his appearance was staid, he was just as pleased at the holiday as the children who chased back and forth in the car. They were more than pleased—they jumped on the seats, they shoved each other against other passengers and partway out of the window. The train made a great many lackadaisical stops, while Kwan mused down at the street below. At Coney Island the pour of humankind off the platform and the festival babble and crush got him energetic. There were mynah birds telling fortunes, merry-go-rounds making music, coin-slotted player pianos. On the hurtling rollercoaster, people screamed and screamed. From the pots at Korn's Korn came a scarifying smell like flesh burning, and the teenagers, running in front of the traffic, plunged for the beach. It was all too much, of course, and reminded him of scenes from his boyhood in China, but he was detached and quick on his feet, inconspicuous, knew what he liked, and liked this contrast with the rest of the week.

He went to his bathhouse establishment. STEAM, the signs said. A lot of the men spent the whole day reading the newspaper in their cubicles. They sunned for a bit on the roof, steamed in the steam room, and never went out on the beach. Kwan sampled the services, getting his money's worth. The fat stomachs on the Italians amused him. Though he was certainly no muscle-man, they were so laughably fat that as soon as they took off their belts they had to hold onto their bellies. Their testicles bulged like bunches of onions. To squeeze in for a shower was like having to push through a herd of beach balls. It was always quarrelsome, because most of them weren't alone through the week like he was but were standing up for their rights in some busy business establishment, and they couldn't lay off on Sunday. And the black-white business was tense. Only a handful of blacks came in to change, but today one of them attached on to Kwan to try to get into the showers. He was in the next cubicle and he offered Kwan part of a sandwich, struck up a conversation until Kwan left with his towel, and then hurried to swallow and stand up too, more and more nervous about it.

"It's pretty packed, huh?"

"Plenty room," Kwan assured him.

The trouble was that his fear was contagious; for a moment Kwan was afraid to go into that bald gleaming mass of bodies himself, forgetting that nobody ever objected to him. The black man hardly looked at *him,* he was so busy being nonchalant and looking ahead to the white men's faces.

"Any space?"

Kwan paused beside the Negro, but there were so many people talking that nobody answered. He pushed through to find a spot, the man tagging after, putting a shoulder in Kwan's stream of water and sloshing his front with one hand. It was a crazy room, with shapes such as you never saw on the street, and much genital-fussing and belly-rubbing.

The exit to the beach went under the boardwalk, where the whites were the jittery ones. The shade was dazzlingly striped with thin lines of sun and a good crowd of people had sprawled in the cool twilit sand. Mothers held kids. The passive families with their spraddled-out postures and scraps of food reminded Kwan of a refugee crowd, and the stripes across everything were doubly weird, but the sea glittered peacefully blue. He had on a new bathing suit and his toes had not grown as old or as crooked as some of these fellows' toes. Adding it up, he cut not a bad figure, he thought. Nobody took exception to him.

A bunch of colored children tore by, throwing handfuls of sand. There were drunks with beer cans, tough policemen, and propped, melancholy souls alone on the part of the beach where everyone else was in transit. They lay on one elbow with their lonely detective novel and their plaid thermos bottle and their brown fleabag blanket from home. It was stop-go. A pair of whites would find themselves on a collision course with three blacks and suddenly stop. By the water the hot sand got cold. Jammed family groups whooped it up; screwballs were yelling. The continual verging on violence was tiresome but didn't directly affect Kwan, who picked his way out beside one of the breakwaters until his body was lapped by the waves. Facing the sun, he braced his back against a large rock and dug his heels in, loving the suctioning. This was his favorite time of the week, right now. He wiggled around for the perfect position, worried that soon the day would be gone, that he wasn't happy enough, but he was. The light, multiplied on the water, was a week's worth of sun. He had seaweed to scrub with and salt on his lips. He smiled so much that he wasn't aware he was smiling, and was all the time closing his eyes to enjoy them closed and then opening them to watch the shimmer and action. Probably five thousand kids were being taught how to swim just in the area in front of him, which made for a steady myriad blare, the yeows and shrieks yiping out of it. Jumping, jumping, jumping, jumping—there was scarcely space for the waves to roll in. When the wind cut the hooting, it blew back again. Old-man-in-the-moon faces bobbed up to blow out the water and suck in some air. Horses chased horses. Mothers were teaching by every method, including the drown-'em-and-laugh-at-'em cry, if only because they themselves were scared. The lifeguards paddled on little rafts which the fishy kids tried to catch up with, and once they had a shark scare, when the police helicopter started to swoop. A guy clambered out covered with black steamship oil, having swum through a slick. He'd been the shark. In the distance the regular sky ride screams were like crying dolls squeezed.

Five children crept past after crabs, although the rocks had been hunted clean. Kwan tried to converse with them with avuncular dignity, pretending to peer round his feet in case a crab might be hiding there. He liked their shouts and the teeming water and teeming beach, the women in bouncing bathing suits. While he regretted not having had children, this was not a gnawing or painful feeling because it had never seemed possible. Marriage had never been much of a hope. He'd paid court to several ladies but always as one of so many suitors that the family and daughter had toyed with him, letting him know how privileged he was. Even so, he had various dear memories of the onanist kind—vigils outdoors, or missing a meal to send flowers he knew that the girl would ignore. Sometimes he'd encountered a colored woman who would come in the back and allow him to tickle her a little instead of charging her for her laundry, and then he had hoped that a permanent amicability might grow up between them. But each time afterwards when he mulled it over, he realized it would only amount to a lot of tickling—no work. If he wanted to share his life with someone, he needed a helper. The flight to Hong Kong to bring back a wife required an enormous sum. To be sure, he had saved toward it, but he was an occasional gambler and he loved his other few pleasures too much.

The mobs were a piece of his childhood, the kids smeared with black sand. He strolled way down to the fishing pier and sat against a green piling. He saw an eel caught and a beer-bottle fight between the men on the pier and the men in the motor boats which were putting about, tangling some of the lines. There was a fight on the beach as well. The white lifeguards in the towers close by had to jump down and help one of their bunch against ten or twelve Puerto Ricans. The police got into it with roaring and clubs and the kids on the sidelines grabbed several girls by the heels and dragged them around, scaring them into hysterics. It was serious for an instant; then it fragmented. The unearthly hordes of people, picnicking, petting, quietly wading, swallowed everything up.

With sharp interest, Kwan watched the ocean-going ships rendezvous with the pilot boat at the mouth of the Narrows. As a boy he had wanted to go to sea and still thought of himself as half seaman, especially because of his one long sea journey. At night in his shop he listened for toots from the harbor, sniffing the salt smells. He liked to walk, so he walked some more, keeping a count of the ships he saw and prolonging the afternoon's activity. When people spat near his feet on the sand he spat back, if not near enough to set off a brawl. The beach was extremely hot. He got up on his toes and trotted under the boardwalk again with the shade-loving crew. The Seashell Bar was there, a whole line of bars, and this was his day for American food. He leaned on the counter as sauerkraut was forked onto his sausage. "Very good stuff. More, man." With big mouthfuls he ate a whole lot. A raving white man kept pulling his trousers off, while the cops attempted to tie them on during the wait for the ambulance. Finally they needed to handcuff him in order to keep them on. He shrieked like a factory whistle and collected a crowd. Kwan scraped with his teeth at a candied apple and winced at the smell of the cooking corn.

The sea was a sizzling, glistening blue. He watched the Parachute Jump, the kids doing stunts. He watched the Diving Bell sink down in its tank where it was nosed by the Porpoise Herd. Couples being jolted out of the funhouse doors at the end of their ride were bloated by mirrors to squeal a last squeal. At the Torture House an elephant was mashing a canvas man underfoot. Santa Claus laughs came up from him. The sign "Chinese Water Torture" intrigued Kwan, since he couldn't guess what that might be. Finally he paid the twenty-five cents. The House was a tent behind a board facade, and the Water Torture was not featured prominently. Both victim and tormentor were yellow as bile, the latter chuckling, apparently. The victim looked up with the face of a calf about to feed, head twisted around to catch hold of the teat. He was papier-maché, and a make-believe faucet dripped on him. Quite accurate characters in a pencilled balloon said, "Let me go." Kwan grinned at all this, but some of the other exhibits made him squint; he had squint lines engraved almost like a sun-squint.

There was a live show. A fat man climbed slowly onto the stage. "Folks can come right down close to me where you can see everything and hear everything. No need to be afraid of me . . ." His face was tattooed as if he'd wished to obliterate it, not simply to become a rarer freak. He had a display case of hatpins and needles and two rows of drinking glasses.

"All you good people want to see everything, want to hear everything. That's what you have here, all the odd people," he said, filling the glasses to different levels, and continued in a mesmerizing, biting voice, "My name is Musical Tons." He laughed to get his body shaking, groaning at the discomfort. "I'm fat, but since I'm not as fat as some I'm also musical." He licked his finger and began to rub the glasses' rims. He did "Dixie" and "I Could Have Danced All Night." But the audience grew sarcastic and whistled along. "Mary, to my right, is one of our features. She's going to talk to you about herself in her own words and will be glad to answer any of your questions. Please listen carefully."

"Now you were told outside on the paper that I would show you underneath my dress, and that's what you are seeing," said Mary, who was unbuttoning her dress in mannish haste. The people giggled with whispers. Faint howls drifted from the roller-coaster. She wore a bathing suit. "I am a Christian woman and I do not show you underneath my bathing suit. It is the same. The ladies may feel of anywhere they wish to be convinced that it is real. The gentlemen may feel of anywhere where they would feel their sisters or their mothers. Now I have cards for ten cents which show myself and I will write on them my name Mary in my own handwriting, which is very good."

She spoke fast and she wrapped the dress around her like a towel.

"Now I am called the Crocodile Woman, which is because my skin is like the thick skin or the hide of a crocodile. It is because of a disease, and which is not infectious, do not worry. I am a Christian woman the same as your wife or your mother. Now I have a message for you, which is that God loves you. Enjoy the life which God has given to you, enjoy your skin, be thankful."

"Thank you, Mary," Musical Tons said into the microphone. "May I direct our friends back to myself? I am going to perform what has been called in the newsprint a remarkable demonstration of hardihood. Pay close attention, if you please."

He took his shirt off. There were hooks through his nipples, and he picked up two five-pound weights from the floor with them. "I'd do the heavier ones if we had a bigger crowd." He smiled around. He had separate smiles for the whites and the blacks but in both cases bitter with scorn. As he swung into doing his stuff, what politeness he'd had before peeled away; he was intense.

"What I do mostly is stick these pins through myself. Want me to?"

"Yeah," called the crowd, caustic and mostly young. He grinned at them and they back at him. The Santa Claus ho's came from the man being mashed by the elephant outside, and Kwan's squint was well-rooted by now, not much more distressed than a standard sun-squint but limiting the amount that the eyes took in.

"You do?" Turning a bit toward the knot of whites, he dawdled, as if such a personal stunt was humiliating to perform in front of a bunch of Negroes, who were quick to sense this, however. Several pressed in, looking at all those blue bruises.

"Which arm?" he asked.

"Left!" they shouted. And plenty of whites were panting as well, until his contempt grew so delicious to him he couldn't bear it and wheeled around to the blacks again.

"How about both arms?"

People broke into smiles and nodded. He leaned from the stage, stroking the longest hatpins. "You may expect I sterilize these things. No, as a matter of fact, just the opposite." He dropped them and rolled them under his shoe. "The trouble is, a platform like this is never awfully dirty; not the real vicious germs. How about it? Put some on for me, would you? Give me some germs."

Ha! They were startled. Those who didn't freeze up were excited. "You want to get poorly, huh? Over here, babe!"

Musical Tons mixed his colors and took from the young and the old, leaning out to give everybody a chance to contribute the smudge off their hands. The women acted as if they were touching a snake, and one fellow had a real brainstorm and licked the pin when it came to him.

"Good. Let's get the worst of it. Give me some more."

He picked a white volunteer to help push the needles through. "You're not much use, are you? Is he, folks?" It was hard going with the first one, particularly on the far side of his arm. The point was dulled so that nothing important inside would be cut. Once the pain started, though, his zest went away; he was deadpan. It seemed like distasteful labor to him rather than pain. Kwan felt twinges penetrating his limbs too.

Anguished figures around the room were painted with blood, but he might have been digging a sewer hole. When he had hatpins sticking through both his arms, "How's this?" he said. "Enough, or do you want 'em through my legs too?"

"Up your old ass, man. Let's see the whole thing!"

He smiled toothily like a dog. "Everywhere? Okay, but your job's the filth. I want all you have. Armpits, that's right, you got the idea."

The racial divisions were gone. It was between those who froze and those who warmed. The pins that were already in obstructed his muscles when he was pushing the new pins through and he looked like a man from Mars equipped for space signals. "How about it?" He pointed to marks on the side of his neck. "Sometimes if I have a big crowd I'll put one through here. Are you people big?"

"Yeah, big. Big as butter," they yelled, with the grins of a gangster movie emptying.

He laughed. "No, you're not. You're too small." He drew out the pins and rubbed the blood drops at each exit point into one of his hands like a powder.

• • •

Kwan loafed in a bingo parlor for an hour—a collection of souls who were more his own age. The sun got low. The whistle-pitched roar from the beach subsided. Instead there were drumming parties and bonfires, shouting, and stone-throwing. A girl belly danced. Gangs of kids with handkerchiefs around their heads were swinging clubs. The beach was like a checkerboard, with whites in certain parts and blacks in other parts. Kwan watched the pitching machines pitch baseballs and watched the Scorpion, the Steeplechase. The lights strung over all of the rides went on, and a boy ran along the boardwalk setting the wastebaskets afire. Kwan steamed in his bathhouse again. He sat in a bar, played bingo another half-hour, then saw the jail pen cleared. As this was underneath the boardwalk, an amphitheater was formed around it by the ramps going up. A large crowd gathered, and, since the prisoners came out singly to the paddy wagon, the process was a long one, each fellow making his moment in the limelight just as dramatic as he could. For some it was the last steps of a death march, for some the last steps to the stake. They stalked like concentration camp victims. They wept dementedly and stumbled, protesting, with glances at the sky. Soon afterward the riot that had been brewing finally broke out. It wasn't anything to see, just cobra-mongoose-jumping and strangled yells, figures running dimly and hammering down with their sticks. First the Italians were outnumbered, and then the blacks. New blacks came, more Italians, and then again new blacks, who were sweeping the bench when the cops sirened in.

Kwan wandered through a side alley to get a last feel of the sand. He took his shoes off for the fifth time that day. He couldn't decide whether to go straight home or stop downtown along the way.

He noticed a colored woman who was sitting against a post in the darkness near him. "Hey you," she said. He was cautious—he had started to leave—but turned and edged toward her, kicking ice cream cups and paper plates.

"I'm Chinese," he said.

"I know you're Chinese. Nobody's mad at you. Nobody's going to beat you up." She laughed. The feet on the boardwalk sounded over them.

Lying down, he put his hands behind his head and clasped the post. She fixed a piece of cardboard in the position of a lean-to. Although she was only a youngster, she had a face with glamorous, rich lines, a nose that flared out when she smiled, and very pretty creases in her forehead with which she could pretend surprise.

"I'm Crystal."

He was impatient now. In his old boardinghouse a Cuban girl had tapped along the rows of single rooms each night, being quick and businesslike.

But she insisted. "Say it."

"Clystal."

"Crystal!" she giggled. "No, Crystal. Say it."

"Clystal." He clutched the pole and watched her tongue.

"Crystal. You trying?"

"I hold on," Kwan said.

"Yes, you hold on as hard as you can. First say it, though."

"Clystal."

"Crystal!" she shrieked in giggles, making him wait.

The Beaver House

THE OMPOMPANOOSUC SKIRLED through a sequence of close-hedged passages with blowdowns everywhere and huge rock heaps in the channel that the water pounded into and next to which the horses had to slide and hop and skid, as Charley's party continued pushing upriver. When the pitch of the ridges permitted it, they stayed above these difficulties, and Cecil lagged behind with the dog pack in case anybody was following. Periodically also the river spread out on its best behavior with a spear-point glitter, a fish-scale glisten, wriggles by the frantic millions glistering in the sunlight—its high-key rattling sibilance louder than a rustle but softer than a roar.

The dogs howled at night, and Cecil's elderly gray shepherd Kaiser got bite marks on his muzzle from unrealistic sexual aspirations. Nevertheless, he'd spring into a pool, spring out, jump in again with a splash, facing the other way around, and playfully chew on underwater sticks, when Coffee was palling with him.

"Are we going all the way to China?" Sutton joked, riding in his tireless fat-man's slouch, and ever more contented to be where he was.

Charley silently knitted up the miles like yarn; old men so often looked like old women anyhow. Though daily they were in the mountains, when they forded tributary rivers or creeks they could catch a glimpse of a grander topography behind these preliminary peaks which had such an extra dimension that Cecil remembered the story of Jack and the beanstalk—mountains which carried the shock of the first grizzly tracks he'd seen, with the indentations of the claws extending out beyond the outline of the toes as a black bear's would never have; mountains large the way a shaggy-throated Western raven was bigger than an Eastern crow.

In the forestland, they'd started encountering black bear tracks, but whenever the country opened into grassy parks and rockslide areas where the sun hit hard again, the bear marks had been left by grizzlies. "Wherever you can't climb a tree," as Charley explained it, because if they could catch them the grizzlies ate the blacks, but a grizzly couldn't climb trees like a black.

Though Sally hadn't the best nose in the pack, more than any of the rest of them she now understood that bears were what most interested Cecil, and focused upon puzzling out bear signs for him. One fine day she turned up a set of prints with each hind paw as big as both of Cecil's boots, each forepaw the size of his two hands, and claw tips that registered like five dimples in the dirt a finger's length in front of the toes as a kind of last word and a shock even to look at. The bear had strolled about, scuffing its sandy feet across bare rocks but then walking in wet places as if for the pleasure of feeling soft mud on its toes.

They'd camped early because Charley wished once more to get rid of his nagging premonition that somebody—white outlaws or a Sikink raiding band—was trailing him. With Sutton he rode back a few miles to lie in wait beside the path while Margaret worked at housekeeping repairs and Cecil lingered over the bear's progress, wondering if he couldn't insert himself into its mentality—whether besides following its tracks he wasn't able to pause at the same places and peer in the same directions toward which the bear had pointed its ingenious nose.

At first the creature's meanderings seemed rather muzzy as he painstakingly followed it around. Then the chronology of where she'd gone and what she'd munched on seemed not muzzy at all, but personal. He almost forgot she was a grizzly; she was a fellow citizen of the valley of the Ompompanoosuc, enjoying its complexities like him, and he tasted several of the plants that she had sampled or feasted upon and smelled the traces of herself she'd left. He was startled when, after a mile or two, her tracks abruptly swung across a short red beach, straight into a deep stream just where it entered the river, and vanished into a purling current which was only ankle deep before it shelved into the thicker water. The current was still chipping away at her last print as if she were right beyond there, under the black surface.

Cecil explored this tributary, with its tea-dark water and red beaches, for another mile, until her tracks reemerged in a marshy patch—she'd probably traveled on the other side—where the dogs sent up an explosion of birds, and frogs plopped desperately for cover. Two beavers which had been dragging a birch bough out of the woods rocked back on their heels, clattering their teeth, as the dogs raced at them. Then they tumbled into the nearest of their stick-hauling canals, which was so full of water the dogs didn't dare to try to grab them.

All the trees at the spot were beaver-bit. White chips lay all over, and unfinished business—stumps with topknot twirls of sappy wood, tree trunks that had split in falling, and loose branches—everywhere. Beavers, deer, and bear that were nocturnal back east were out and busy in broad daylight in this new country. A marten, too, hung spellbound in plain sight, watching Cecil from a spruce. There was lots of beaver feed, aspens and birches so dense that he was wiping spider webs off his face. He stumbled, the dogs tangling his feet—how silly it was to have so many of them with him, scrapping and tussling with each other.

The bear had nipped off fireweed shoots and nibbled biscuit-root, parsley, and cow parsnip; had consumed several frogs, to judge from the prints and scraps left in the mud, and parts of half a dozen rotting fish and clusters of salamanders that had been eating the fish. But when he noticed that these tracks appeared smaller than the earlier ones, it occurred to Cecil that this might be a second bear. He was suddenly glad all the dogs were along, and if they were nonplussed a bit by the bear's activities, they were bolstered by him, their magic man, as he liked to describe his position among them when he felt smug.

Red-rock side hills rose prettily three hundred feet in the sunshine to ledges that supported junipers and pines. The little canyon had no end as yet. Modest waterfalls twined down and you could see a game trail descending from higher terrain. The floor widened into slough-grass meadows, as Cecil dawdled past beaver dams and ponds at a deliberate pace, the water gradually dwindling till he could observe the opposite beach so clearly he saw tracks emerge from, reenter and reappear at the edge of black water there.

He sat down awhile to soak his feet, rest his butt, and check his rifle. The gray shepherd had not been enjoying himself even at this easy pace, and Cecil was reminded of a dog in Maine whose master had brought it into a bar one night, intending to get drunk and pick a fight with some of the other loggers, and you could see that the dog knew very well that in about half an hour its master would be on the floor, that it would have to jump into the fight and try to save him, and would feel the spiked boots in the room, the fists and axe handles on its ribs. He realized that Kaiser, who a hundred miles out of Horse Swim had already regretted leaving his German master, was gearing up regardless to face the charge of a bear in order to save Cecil if he had to.

Smoky was also fearful, but Smoky was afraid of his own inner deterioration even when there were no bears nearby. Roy's hound Yallerbitch, like Sally, was hardly bothering to trail the scent, it was so strong—perhaps was trying to ignore it—and the two huskies, as tall on their feet as Cecil's hips, clung close to him, as did the goat. The goat had grown a veritable mane up to the top of its head from all of its adventures and, devil-may-care, was scratching its hip with the tip of one horn. But why had he brought the goat?

Tracks had materialized from another direction. Again he was puzzled, because although he wasn't seeing two sets together, his impression was that they weren't the tracks of a single bear. He knew that adults didn't travel together, yet the difference in size wasn't so disparate that it could be a sow with her yearling cub. The tracks were alarmingly large—but with his gun and his dogs, what had he come for except to trail bears?

He was sneaking slowly along like a deer hunter, but pulled up short at a ring of sparkling drops of water fifteen feet wide on the bank, where the bear must have climbed out after a swim and shaken herself. Thereupon—realizing he'd just been staring at other tracks—he remembered that since this was June it was the courtship season, a brief, uncharacteristically sociable period for bears. Twice in Maine he'd crept up close to mating black bears to watch them play and paw and nuzzle one another, and belatedly he recognized that the wayward footprints crisscrossing the creek had not been made by a lone animal foraging but by two creatures courting. That was why it had been so simple to see what they had been eating: they hadn't finished anything.

Of course he wanted to drop back for at least a mile. There were never cubs near mating bears, and cubs were what he was after. What was he doing? What foolishness, to track this bear of bears so carelessly; and with the dogs, a surreptitious withdrawal was now impossible. He was in a brushy stretch, no trees to climb. The hound and the duck dog were ahead, Coffee, Smoky, and the huskies behind them, and the goat and shepherd next to him. The creek had been dammed into a two-acre pond in front of him on his left side, and he could see the impressive dome of a beaver house across a diffuse swirl of currents; also a smaller one. On his right side, he had a few dozen yards of meadow grass to operate in, then dense alder bushes that would provide better cover for a bear than for him, and finally the steep side hill with occasional trees spaced about on ledges above that he could never reach if he was being chased. A game trail descending from unknown territory seemed only to add to the sinister possibilities of whatever awaited him.

He heard his dogs already breaking sticks, scrimmaging with a mystery beast around a bend in the path, and hoped that maybe it was just another beaver. Moving sideways, he held his rifle against his chest, but stopped dead when he caught a reflection in a clear puddle ahead of him which seemed to be that of a grizzly sitting dog fashion in the brush with a head like a stump, plain brown and stationary as though neutral, head-on to him, not facing the yelps of the pack. In contrast, the commotion in the alders grew to an uproar as a second grizzly, as purple-colored as a plum, plunged around a boulder in pursuit of Sally and the huskies. Bits of flowers were stuck to her lips from the vegetation she'd been feeding on, but the enormousness of her front legs at such close range astounded Cecil. Under the bulk of her hump, they were undiminished from her shoulders all the way down to her paws—paws that promptly veered toward him, as lithe as a cat's. But she paused and waved the right one as if a dog had bitten it, half upright on her haunches and fulminating as if her privacy had been outraged, as well as the sanctity of her foot.

He didn't fire, because he thought he'd be killed for sure if he did; and despite all of her violent manifestations, her elbows as thick as a ship's timbers, she had a prissy and fastidious air that delayed her slightly. Sniffing for information, she was uncertain where to rush or who to charge. He couldn't guess whether she had met a human being before, but in spite of her air of fussing, there was a pell-mell daring about her, a freedom such as he'd not seen in many animals. The dogs had run straight to him for protection, had then scattered when they sensed how frail a reed he was, but now were circling tightly—Moose on three legs—in order not to abandon him, while the shepherd, his hackles up, his muzzle high, although his hind legs were cringing, backed into Cecil's knees, preparing to die defending him, just as he would have died for the German grocer in Horse Swim in front of a holdup man, or if a drunk had owned him, under the hobnailed boots of bullies in a bar.

The male bear broke from a standstill into a lope, bigger, calmer, bluffer than the female but scarcely looking at Cecil—looking at the goat instead, which was still hanging next to him. Cecil fired a shot into the sky, not because his friends would ever hear him, but to try doing something to save himself, and yet afraid of wounding either bear.

That loud report decided the female. She bounded at Cecil like a round-backed cat going for a mouse. He was so scared he dropped his rifle and snatched at it wrong-side-to. He would have been a goner if she hadn't been blocked for a moment because the male, intent upon the goat, collided with her. Cecil sprinted out of the way, but the billy did the one thing he had learned to do when chased by the dogs. Instead of running as quick as he could, he stopped so as not to be mistaken for an antelope or deer and swung his little horns around. The bear didn't even pause to swat him, simply lifted him in his mouth, puncturing the ribs on both sides of his backbone, and carried him horizontally and alive like that toward the same thicket of brush, till with a last twist he died.

Cecil ran for some poplars by the pond, though they were not substantial enough to climb. He had no other place to run, and had been so close to the goat he'd heard the bear's teeth in its back. He heard the female start after him again and noticed the shepherd dog still braced to die for him at the old spot—knew therefore that the dog would be spared. Though he was running for his life, he could barely subdue the impulse, formed when he was a child being chased by older kids, of falling to the ground, rolling into a ball, and surrendering, to be let off with a few slaps. The dogs couldn't save him, at best could give him a few extra instants of life, but as she closed the gap, he glimpsed Coffee and Smoky darting with the utmost agility from either side to bite her thighs—noticed, too, with preternatural clarity, Smoky's lips beginning to twitch and drool as if a fit was overtaking him. Cecil had dropped his rifle once and for all in wriggling through a brushy tangle, and found that he was unexpectedly next to the male, which was already chewing at the goat like a lion on a hunk of meat and rose bristling and roaring. Shedding his hat and jacket for the grizzlies to examine, Cecil turned into the water, hearing Smoky grunt as if more than just his breath had been smashed out of him. He was splashing knee high in the pond when he remembered a cruel series of rotogravures in the Pittsfield *Register* of a grizzly wading after salmon and biting them in two. Either of the bears could chase him like a groundhog on the land and like a fish in the water.

He had nowhere to swim except away, and could see the dogs arrayed about the meadow in positions of collapse or stupefaction. Smoky was writhing in a fit while the she-bear rocked over him, waiting until she understood what ailed him before she finished him off. That gave Cecil another delay. He was belt deep by the time she came after him. Spotting the big beaver house, he resurrected from his trapping days the memory of the nesting chamber that would be above the water level inside, if he could somehow reach that. He floundered forward into the deepest water he could find and ducked under, pulling himself down by grabbing lily and bullrush stems. Making up for his clumsiness with the gun, which had nearly cost him his life, he swam and crawled along the bottom among a welter of branches the beavers had stored for food, grasping them to keep below the surface except when he had to gulp a breath. He could hear the dogs barking from the shoreline and the bear searching for him, thrashing across the pond with what sounded like explosive noises underwater, snuffing and sneezing as she tried to nose him out.

He knew beavers and beaver houses from Maine, and pawed through the murk from snag to snag, past cached piles of succulents, to locate the main igloo of sticks without revealing himself. It was conical and four to five times the length of his body across its base. After he had groped for much of the way around the structure, he felt the lip of the underwater porch and finally the precious gap that was the entrance hole. A beaver swam out past him hastily like an underwater muff brushing against his arm when he began wriggling inside. He punched and ripped his way up through the claustrophobic L-bend of the passage, terrified that he would become jammed and drown before he reached the air. Would there *be* air? Or would he feel the grizzly grip his legs and be wedged inside that stick tomb with only his head safe in the nesting chamber while she gnawed on the rest of him? One of his arms did get pinned at his side, but he kicked and pulled himself up to where he could finally breathe, his free hand seizing the grown-up flabbergasted beaver that was cornered there, while he wrenched his other hand loose to strangle it, although he suffered a serious and bloody bite. Feeling badly scraped along his hips, he lay exhausted with just his head and chest in the chamber for a considerable while before he thought to congratulate himself.

It was too low for him to sit up, but by jackknifing his knees he could lie wholly dry inside. The flooring was of shredded wood and moss and grass, lighted faintly from the area of the smoke hole, where in the winter the beavers' body heat would show outside as steam. Though he was shivering and rubbing the wounds in his hand, he found the supply of air sufficient. He moved the four whining kits from where they had huddled to the edge of the exit, and sure enough, the live parent's wet and chattering head appeared after an interval and removed each, and also the dead beaver afterwards.

He was lucky. *Well, you poor sap, you're all right for now,* he told himself, fingering the ceiling a foot or two above. His impulse was to push, *push* and try to make more room, but he resisted doing that lest he turn frantic, resisted thinking about the fearfully narrow passageway from which he would have to swim out of this cell—he wouldn't have been strong enough to break through the roof, even if the grizzlies hadn't been waiting for him.

Exploring the weave of sticks, his fingers found a blunt-headed arrow of the type that Indians shot at ducks. The beavers must have pulled it from the bottom and treated it like any other useful piece of wood. He was so awed and so scared and wrung out that he soon fell asleep, waking horribly as the house shook. Something had stepped on it; and he heard a snuffle. Were his dogs looking for him? The whole intricate basket-weave of the edifice shook like a bird's nest in the wind but resiliently absorbed the weight of whatever was walking on it. Figuring out whether the beasty voice he heard was bearish or only doggish ought to have been a simple matter, but he was not in good shape to decide. The creature felt like an elephant, the way his mind was running, and yet the lodge was springy under its tread as though ready to give and give if necessary but never be clawed open. Ultimately the animal did depart. He heard marsh birds flying over, which he thought a peaceful omen. Later two small birds hopped about picking at seeds or bugs over his head, perhaps a pair of wrens: *tsuk-tsuk.*

Still jackknifed in this inner sanctum, he calmed down enough to nap some more, and fitfully imagined what was happening outside—the forlorn, bewildered dogs waiting about, the purplish, pussy-bodied grizzly wading after him, venting her spleen on bushes and trees in the meantime, before she climbed with her mate out of the canyon on the game trail to higher country. His mind drifted high and wide above the little creek and the Ompompanoosuc's main valley, wondering if he had ever had three better friends than Sutton and the others. Yet he could have died so painfully and quickly. And once he'd shot his mamma bear and trained and harnessed her cubs and built his raft to float with them to the coast, he'd never see his friends again, except perhaps for Sutton, who on the other hand might never go back East.

Margaret would latch on somewhere with another white trader or trapper, not with Sutton permanently, he thought—at least his jealousy made him hope not. Charley would die snugly of heart failure while hilling potatoes on his homestead. And *he* would return with many stories for his children, with maybe a Thloadenni wife, and a sensational bear act, for which he'd sport a green frock coat and red silk hat and wow the crowds. But the gypsy in Sutton was more powerful than the gypsy in Cecil, and Sutton's grin as he stared at the mountains they were entering wasn't that of a settler like Charley; it was a traveler's pleasure at moving along, whether he ever found any gold or not. Cecil would wind up in Massachusetts, but Sutton might end up in China.

A sow bear bred once every couple of years, and once every couple of years she wanted her privacy, thought Cecil, managing a smile at what had happened. With the return of his common sense came claustrophobia, however. He dreaded reentering the passage and becoming wedged underwater. He remembered his father's death of cancer, scrunched up in the maple-sugar tub on the wood stove. Sucking his beaver bites, fighting his panic, he debated for a long time whether to go out head first or feet first—which would be the worst way to drown? Or if he panicked lying here, he would never get out; could rave till doomsday in this tomb, securely enchambered by the same basketry that had stymied the bear.

He lowered his legs into the tunnel, kicking carefully to learn how far he could maneuver like that and keep his head out of the water. A bend or bottleneck stopped him, and he hoisted himself laboriously up again and turned around, under the two-foot ceiling, remembering a stillbirth he had witnessed when the child—a nephew, his sister's son—had died in the birth canal. Putting his head and shoulders into the icy water, he thrust his body halfway down head first, but was unable to reach the sticking point and quite quickly pulled back for breath. He was so much bigger than a beaver. But the more he hesitated, the grimmer the outlook for him seemed, so without thinking any further he committed himself, remembering that the tunnel was only ten or twelve feet long and if he went into it deep enough he'd soon be out.

The worst moment of his life occurred after he had pushed past where his legs, crooked at the knee at the top of the passage, might still have extricated him backwards. He was completely underwater and inside, his legs immobilized, his arms struggling, but was stalled belly down at the L angle that led outward, whereas he should have been positioned belly up in order to bend and maneuver. He had to rotate himself in the corridor, inching slowly, unhooking his clothing as it caught on spiky sticks, with no chance at a breath of air if he failed. Then his right calf cramped on the last stretch when he thought he'd already twisted free. He wriggled his whole body, desperate as a hooked fish.

Once he was breathing again, his head well out of the water, underneath an azure sky, the pond without a ripple in it, and no bears rampaging on the bank, he was sure he'd live to be ninety—he would make sure that he did. He heard a dog yelp, and another one, from where they had been waiting for his body to float up. His legs and back cramped as severely as if they would stay cramped for at least a week, the way they had one time when he had fallen into the Androscoggin River during a log drive and nearly drowned. As then, he scrabbled sideways like a crab to shore.

Poor Smoky wasn't dead, but his spine was broken. Nevertheless, he dragged his hind end towards Cecil, his foreparts moving as stiff as crutches, apparently in full faith that some magic touch would be able to heal him. Cecil, after retrieving his rifle, simply sank down next to the dog under a tree that he could climb if the grizzlies returned. He cleaned the gun and stroked Smoky, while preventing the others from bumping against him as they competed apologetically for recognition, and watched the hope die in his eyes.

Moose's left hind leg would need to be dressed and splinted. And Sally, who he hadn't known was pregnant, was lying in a daze with a bloody litter of puppy fetuses that she had miscarried strewn around her tail. Cecil himself was dizzy and sick, and vomited. In much pain from his back, he lost his temper when White Eye started licking the stuff up, but quit shouting at him when Smoky woke up whimpering from his slide into a coma and flinched. He had to shoot him, finally, as the rest of them slunk about and crouched. Glancing at Smoky's body afterwards, he saw that the colors of his coat were not really as much like smoke as like the marvelous salt-and-peppering of intersecting light and shadow that disguised a wolf or coyote in the brush. A beautiful dog; and of course it hadn't been the coloring of his fur or even his epilepsy that had betrayed him to the grizzly but Cecil's foolishness. He hated leaving him unburied for the bears to come back to.

"No goat and no Smoke, huh? Yes, we figured we might have to slit open somebody's gut to find ya!" said Charley, when Cecil and his sorry canines straggled into camp after nightfall.

Margaret hugged him. Moose was injured the worst, and Sally was bleary, but Sutton pointed out that the old shepherd's face appeared to have whitened clear back to his ears and throat. "He got two years older all of a sudden."

Shivering, coughing, Cecil lurched around to find a bearable attitude in which to prop his bones while telling his story of hiding in the beaver house. His hearing was sharper than usual, and when he listened to the horses munching grass, it didn't sound peaceful; it was a violent sort of crunching, like the noise a bear would have produced if it were munching on him. When he wasn't giddy with the tale he had to tell, he fell silent and glum, though he ate hungrily.

"You figured you were safe, huh? A skunk bear could have dug you out—that's how they eat all winter, tearing beaver lodges up. So if a skunk bear could have got to you, what makes you think a grizzly couldn't have?" said Charley.

A "skunk bear" was a wolverine, a beast Cecil hadn't yet encountered. He wondered whether or not the skunk bear's proficiency meant he might at last have extricated himself from inside if his life had depended upon it.

Charley, who softened in response to his silence, remarked a bit sympathetically that when he recalled anything he wished he hadn't done, "It ain't what you did to a person—because there was always reasons there. Maybe the reason wasn't good enough, maybe I'd do it differently now, but there was *some* good reason. No, it's generally what you did to a dog. Do you know?"

He was obviously reluctant to go ahead and tell them what may have troubled him. "How about you?" he asked Sutton, who laughed.

"Oh, I guess I've done some dirtier things to people in my time than to doggies. I guess if you rub shoulders with thousands of people you've got more opportunity to do somebody in, and most of us are different when we're young—that's when you bash somebody."

Charley said his friend Ben with the hot springs, who had been murdered, had come up here from Nevada along the coast on the freight boat, starting from San Francisco, and had walked in on the Hainaino River trail, like him. He was a prospector; he didn't mind a two-month walk, looking at all those pretty creeks and meeting Haidas, Tsimshians, Hainainos, Tlickitats and what all else. In Nevada he'd had a wonderful big dog that had been with him everywhere and understood English and Spanish and Injun or whatever was on the menu and still had a lot of life in him. He loved that dog, but all he'd heard about was how cold it was going to be up in British America.

"He was making preparations, fussing like you do when you're planning the best trip of your life, worrying about things you don't need to worry about. He got so concerned about this dog not being a 'winter dog' or a 'snow dog' because its fur only went as deep as his first knuckle that he had a man take him out and shoot him. Couldn't do it himself, and the bloke that did it for him came back and said, 'You shouldn't have shot that dog; I've never seen a dog as intelligent as that, that knew what was going to happen to him and why.' And when he got up here, of course he had plenty of dogs, he trained a dog team, because he liked tinkering with dogs, and he learned they could either grow a coat or else get by without a coat, if they had the heart for it. He never did find a dog so bright and loyal as that dog that he'd destroyed."

Cecil, who'd expected from the beginning to lose most of his dogs in fracases and pursuits, asked what Charley regretted doing himself, but Charley had said all he would.

Sutton responded with his story of letting his circus's hippo go into the Mississippi. "He was swimming upside down, he was having such fun, eatin' duckweed. You could argue that he froze in the winter; probably he did. But if he got far enough downriver I don't think so. If he swam to Baton Rouge he could have got into the Atchafalaya swamp and lived forever. He was letting that current catch him and take him down and he was about the fattest fish you could imagine."

The Last Irish Fighter

WEST OF TIMES SQUARE was a place sometimes to see show-girls in their daytime purple glasses and long pants. But all Kelly saw were two clean-cut nuns with boy faces, and a girl he'd never have known was a girl without looking twice, and a woman kissing her baby, and another one kissing her kid, and another, not kissing, but holding pressed lips to the neck of her child. A pigeon tossed a piece of bread like a dog with a rat, and a cat or a baby was crying, you couldn't tell which. A lady and a street cleaner swept side by side, until they got past the front of her house. Kelly lounged by the windows of stores. He watched a cop in a phone booth clicking the switch on a tiny fan and smiling so gaily he must have been calling his girl. And in the street he saw the white and smoky flitter-whirl of pigeons: the pigeons felt so good their wings were going as fast in spurts as ducks'.

On Eighth Avenue a card said GUARANTEED under every object in the pawnshop windows. The bars had their guaranteed drunks. The windows of the barbershops and greasy spoons began to show pictures of fighters, autographed and with the manager's address, and in a doorway sat a shoeshine-boy ex-boxer, his hands now agile and awhirl with brushes. That was what happened to your colored boys. But over a block, on Broadway, Dempsey had a big restaurant, and Kelly knew of plenty of other prosperous businesses that fighters owned. This was Boxing's Street, just like it was Pawnshop Street and Whoring Street and Get Drunk Street, although a wise man never messed with those last two. Madison Square Garden was here and *Ring* magazine and Stillman's Gym and the famous tavern hangouts and the managers' offices and the Boxing Clubs and Guilds and Associations, Commissions, Corporations, Organizations. Kelly started feeling businesslike, like somebody going to work. He sauntered, though; he sauntered down to Forty-Second Street where Better Champions was.

The door to Better Champions Gym was marked by the guys outside it—not guys you would see anywhere. Some of them seldom went inside; just seemed to mark the entrance. Old posters lined the stairs, but since there wasn't any light nobody more than glimpsed them. At the top, by a window, was a huge white chart of ink on pasteboard which listed all the fighters whose fees were paid as of today and warned that no other fighter should attempt to enter without his money ready. Other signs were stuck at angles on the window, where you couldn't miss them, saying, "Pay!" and signed "J. D." Nothing had started yet and the managers and people standing around were watching who came in, and gossiping. It was like a judgment being passed, and Kelly didn't go too well; got blank indifference. He hated it and worried that the owner of the gym wouldn't recognize him as somebody who'd paid and would shout at him for heading for the locker room.

Among the quiet fighters changing, his uneasiness seemed silly. But even the other white men's faces were different from his, from speaking Italian or German or whatever they spoke, were shaped different. A Negro face—American Negro, not Spanish or British West African—looked like a countryman's. Nobody was much like Kelly. He was plain old native-born cop-Irish, without much Irish and without the cop.

He snorted at the locker room. Dirt was thick. Paint had given up peeling; flap a towel, it flittered down like snow. Jogging in place, he swung his arms up over his head and down and rocked his elbows casually. He shared a locker with another fighter who hadn't come in yet, so Kelly had to find Peapod, the guy who kept the keys, a small colored man with a round wild face made wilder still by a wall eye. He was on a window ledge reading comics, but climbed in for Kelly quickly without grumbling, once he had been found. Hurriedly he walked, with short arthritic steps, unlocked the door and said, "Awright?" with such an upward, sidewise glance it might have been a word of treason. His eyes were full of water and shifted constantly, just as he himself did. After each time he spoke, he'd move away, as if he'd laid a bomb. He moved off now.

The wonder was that the door didn't fall when it was unlocked, with its broken hinges. Kelly sat on the bench, taking his time. He rubbed his leg hair. It was blond compared to the hair on his head, and seemed so thin or seemed so thick, depending on the way he thought of it. Creaselessly as gloves he smoothed his workout socks on, tied the high-top shoes—perfect fit for secondhand. His trunks too had been a bargain, but now the locker looked awfully bare with only the other man's equipment in it. Kelly had started to train again last week after a lapse of a year since he'd quit boxing the last time. He had no money and no manager supplying equipment.

"Peapod, I'm supposed to use that same stuff, ain't I?" he shouted.

"I didn't hear," the key man answered from behind some lockers.

"Huh?"

"I didn't hear about it," the voice repeated, sure enough, farther over. He must think, once his position has been given away, you'd lob grenades at him. Kelly's buddy had come, the one he shared the locker with, and Kelly looked disgustedly at him.

"Guess you got to go and talk," said the guy with friendly softness, thumbing at the gym. "And if you don't get any place you could try me, because I'm boxing today and I could probably let you use my bag stuff. You try first."

Kelly stepped over the benches cluttered with clothes and gear. The main room was full of gabbing groups. He looked for the manager whose stuff he'd used for several sessions by promising he'd spar with one of the manager's boys some time. The conversation in the group stopped for Kelly—for a stranger in civilian clothes it wouldn't have—but began again once they were sure they didn't know him. The manager Kelly wanted did a double-take and turned exasperatedly. "No, I can't help you. My kid isn't working out for a week. It isn't worth it."

"Just your gloves?" Kelly said.

"No!" He was sharp. "It'd be enough you use my gloves if you were working with my boy. I shouldn't have let you before this. Those gloves cost money. That's why you don't have none of your own." His mouth was as small as one of his eyes. Kelly tried to wheel away from him insultingly, but couldn't finish doing it before the manager had turned his back.

So what now? Sheepish though it made him feel, he'd have to borrow from the fighter. It was embarrassing. He passed a guy who motioned at him. "No manager?"

"Not right now," said Kelly. "I had Timmy Hannahan in Boston till he quit."

"How many fights you had pro?"

"Thirty-three. Won twenty-three," he added to stop the guy's sarcastic eying.

"Must have laid off a long time. You look old enough for fifty, sixty fights to me." The manager smiled. His large shadowy glasses sat on a large red face. His body was square and soft and his hair looked handled. His smile went through a lot of changes. "I'll let you use a pair; I heard the disagreement. I'd like to watch you work. I've seen you, but I didn't happen to watch. You seem like you could throw a heavy punch. From Boston, huh? Hey, Peapod!" he called into the locker room. "Give this boy a pair of my speed gloves." He turned and smiled and pinched his nose and blew it out the window into Forty-Second Street.

China was the name of the colored fighter who shared Kelly's locker—he'd been to China, maybe fought there. "I know how it is," he nodded, seeing Kelly chipper. "You feel like you own yourself again when somebody takes an interest. Then when they start paying your bills you know you do." China was comforting for Kelly to be with because he was older, one of the few who didn't make him feel far past his prime. China was over thirty and getting flabby, but, turtling into the shell he made of his arms and his shoulders, he did okay, even got some TV. Sharing a locker meant he could stash money for the future. He was wise.

• • •

The first people started hitting the bags—thunderous, playful bursts in passing just to announce their arrival. When the sound came into the locker room everybody moved more slowly, since they'd have to wait their turn. Kelly liked to listen and be lulled, like a connoisseur.

"All right, you got 'em! Don't ask me again!" crazy Peapod hollered in his small voice, glaring murder at the wall when he brought the gloves. China grinned with Kelly, scrubbing street sweat off his thighs before he put on his trunks. China's mask-like fighter's face was puffed up as from poison ivy or a month of crying. It looked sympathetic naturally.

A fly buzzed too long near Kelly and he brought his left hand from the bench and grabbed it in the air. Hand-speed was a talent. He slapped his mitten gloves together happily.

Better Champions was divided, half for the rings and half for the bags and tables and skip-rope space. In the middle was a huge, old desk with a big sign, "James DeJesus," and a littler sign, "Pay Me." A cushioned swivel chair went with the desk and a square was roped around them with the red-velvet-brass-post paraphernalia of a movie house. Kelly put his things on a radiator near a back window, where he would be out of the way, and began to fix his hands. He liked the job, did it carefully. The first of the strip of bandaging he put between his last two fingers and, holding it there, made four folds across the top of his knuckles. Then he began to wrap the strip around and around the punch of his hand, smooth and tight and supporting, and made an occasional excursion around the heel or around the wrist. He could have done the pattern in his sleep. It always ended the same. Each fold lay perfectly flat on the ones it overlapped, even when it went diagonally, and when the last of the strip was reached he tucked it under the front wind. From the second joint of his fingers to the wrist his hand was firmly sheathed. Tape he didn't bother with for working on the bags.

The wad of bandage for the other hand took a lot of shaking. It was twisted and getting grey with dirt, but would fit his hand ideally. Everybody used handwraps over and over, like old shoes. Along each wall boxers were doing the same as Kelly wherever they could find a space to sit their stuff, a bench or a candy-soda pop machine. Most had hotel towels, easily recognized from the next guy's, and were wearing shirts and robes; Kelly only had the towel. And exuberant ones were blasting a speed bag just for the roar, naked-fisted, till some Old Mother Trainer fussbudgeted over and put on their gloves.

With the bandaging done, Kelly felt like a fighter, hands like disciplined weapons. He flexed them, testing the play, and limbered his shoulders. He slipped on his gloves and gently tried them out against the wall. Rising up on his toes he started to shuffle. His muscles heated and blocked together so that he felt their power. They bunched easily, nor too gracefully, with the catch that carried extra power. He felt tough, as tough as any middleweight he saw.

There was a guy over there who could sledge in a *punch*. He was steadily smashing a heavy bag with punches that would bring on internal bleeding. At the next bag was a straight-out high-puncher, two equal fists and nothing in his inventory aimed below the neck. Straight rights, straight lefts—all his moves were the same and carried higher than his own head if they missed. Kelly wouldn't want to be that specialized, but he could match the type, he reassured himself. In one of his best fights his opponent had lost his mouthpiece and Kelly had slaughtered the mouth so badly for the rest of the round that nothing could be done to patch it up. Next bell, it still was dribbling. The ref had stopped the fight. Spot-target hitting and plenty high.

The workout started with warm-ups, went to the big bag and the speed bag, and finished with rope-skipping, shadow-boxing, table calisthenics. Kelly was going to be third on one of the heavy bags and in the meantime occupied himself toe-touching and with setups and trying all his punches, both as he threw them and in the classic style. He figured little situations, punched accordingly. He feinted, sliding into his crouch and out and poising himself. He stretched from the waist in a circle, touching the floor, and in a shuffle pushed his fists up beside his head like horns. He galloped high knee-action spurts; back-pedaled, poking the tips of his hands down at the places where his feet had

been; and limply stomped from side to side as in a comedy routine to use the muscles on his ribs; and bounced and bounced,
scissoring his legs, twisting on them with deliberate wrenches;
and simply stood idly and snapped his head in each direction to
build resilient muscles in his neck. Then when the bell rang he
walked around and loosened like everybody else. Three minutes
and a minute rest. No matter what he did, how easy or how hard,
it was organized like that.

"Where you been keeping yourself? Do you expect everybody to spot you?" he heard at his ear. It was the manager whose
gloves he wore. "Yeah, I found a fellow who heard of you, but he
wouldn't have known just seeing you. What do you think, you're
famous? Maybe if they've heard of you in Boston still I could fight
you some up there. No manager, you're sure?"

Kelly shook his head, formed his lips for "no." He crossed his
feet with nervousness and rubbed his head. He wished he had his
towel with him; he ought to use it between rounds.

"I don't know, I seem to have a skill, I don't let nothing by me,
opportunities, I mean. The other fellow doesn't see it and I grab it up.
Like you, I spoke to you. Nobody else even noticed you. I'm smart,
I don't go sleeping, I'm watching all the time. And here you might
be worth some money and I'm the only one who saw it. How old
are you?"

"Twenty-eight—twenty-nine," Kelly said without pleasure.

"What'sat mean?" The manager leered. "Don't you know?"

"No, I know, I got to be twenty-nine a week ago."

The manager looked at the floor in sudden seriousness. "Well
that might not be too old. Let's see you."

So he watched. Kelly wasn't doing anything; the new round
hadn't started. But he watched. It was silly. Kelly was confused and
didn't like him. His glasses had black frames which hid his eyes
almost as much as dark lenses would. He handled them continually
as if with pride, so that it seemed he thought the glasses made him
better than somebody who didn't wear them. And his mouth was
always moving, and he handled it and pulled the lip to show inside.
When he breathed out loudly his face would redden. The bell set
Kelly going again, but in the middle of the round the manager

interrupted, "I'll let you have my card." It read, "Howard Straws, Manager of Fighters," and gave his phone number. "If I'm away the fellow next door answers, and I answer his, and we don't steal nobody's fighters. I can trust him."

The rhythm of the round was spoiled. Kelly fumbled through the last two minutes. Ordinarily he was confident. He had a solid, balanced crouch and moved without committing himself foolishly. He knew his shadow-boxing showed experience.

Ten guys bobbed and weaved near Kelly and each took up the same amount of space. Except for their styles only the names on their robes told the ranked contenders from the kids. The trainers treated them all the same. They spent more time with the people they were paid for by the managers, naturally, and more time went to big names, but they were nice to everybody and never deferential. The fighter they scolded might be anyone and would deserve it, but they didn't do it often. Little sad sacks the trainers looked like: they didn't change their faces or their posture, couldn't be excited. They'd trained the old-time greats and no one seemed as good to them as fighters of twenty years ago. Another reason was they'd fought themselves and had their faces bashed lopsidedly expressionless. Grave and pitying a badly beaten boy, they looked almost the same as when posing for an arm-up victory picture. They stood around and watched, a towel across the shoulder and a leather skip rope looped around the waist. As much as the managers talked, the trainers watched. It was their job.

Kelly started swatting a speed bag; the owner didn't mind. Stared up at, it was like a black bull's eye in a slicked circle worn by its contact with the wooden frame. He played with it expertly: tapped it into motion and its swing into the proper line, then pasted it smartly with the various surfaces of his fist and bashed it with a straight, life lopping punch or an action like shotput-throwing. It was as tempting as a hanging pear. He tippy-tapped ,and got it swinging crazily, and then tick-tocked it. And all the time he pranced his feet, high-kneeling to the rhythm of his hands like a baton twirler. These were the bags that let the whole gym know what was being done with them. The groups of managers moved away, not liking the competition, but the trainers listened and chewed out loafers if they were concerns of theirs, or, if they weren't, told them to give the bag to somebody who'd use it.

The owner—one of those godawful wild men a manager had dug up from some ferocious slum—wanted the bag. He had a head like a pineapple—spiky hair and a brain that narrow. In the ring he set himself flat-footed and shoved stuff out. So he swung wild? So he had plenty left. An opening was blocked? There'd be another. He pawed as if he were swimming, as primitive as that, and even on the speed bag shouted "Bam" and "Boom" and puckered his lips in concentration till they sweated. Speed bags were supposed to help develop speed and aim and certain sorts of stamina. The big bag built up power and taught you stance and how to set the feet and get off the punch. It was thicker than a man and larger than the target on him you could hit and, like the speed bag, working it was fun. Kelly's turn came and he nuzzled the bag between his head and shoulder, then rocked it away with a punch from the hand on that side and followed up with one from the other. On its return swing he caught the bag on his opposite shoulder and repeated the game. He hit the bag a couple of punches as fast as he could, and raised the number to three, six, always using just one hand, until both arms were weak. He hit it freely then, however way he felt, so that it swung in high lurches, and *whop!* he'd snap down, fists pressed ready on his chest, and let it swing over him, be up and lacing it when it had passed. He ran combinations—strings of lefts and rights in a certain order—or dug rapid-fire with one hand until he couldn't hold it up, it got so tired.

The last minute he lazed: nuzzled the bag with his shoulder and pushed it around like that, or openhanded it to get it swinging, and took his time, punching irregularly so it dipsy-doodled. He practiced twisting aside and guarding himself and crouching. He put his head in its path and dodged and ducked. After the bell he walked around to keep from stiffening and toweled himself all over roughly for the pleasure. Everybody did, except celebrity fighters who had a trainer dry them. But in spite of the crowdedness of the floor and the number of other fighters he had to change direction for, everybody was absorbed in their own training and trying to be as serious as if they were alone. Rope-skippers had a corner of their

own where endlessly they flicked their hands—it would be training for a poker dealer—and skipped the strip of leather frontwards,
backwards, right-foot, left-foot, slow- and triple-time. "You don't
train for him, he take your head off," said a trainer, sprinkling water
on the floor to make a circle for his boy to shuffle in. "He punch
outside; you punch inside." And where are the hands when the feet
go here? And learn the trick of falling forward to grab the crooks
of an opponent's arms.

A heavy stepped under a frame and with a continuous roar
blurred the speed bag to invisibility, an ideal-build heavy just
growing out of the lighter weight, each pound put on to fill real
needs. The noise got so great the trainers relied on signs. The
bag didn't burst because the speed he hit it with distributed pressure evenly. Fighters usually killed the speed bag's rhythm with a
Sunday punch once in a while to rest their arms until they started
it going again, but this bozo batted it steadily for the three minutes, varying only the ratio of his hards to his softs—the pulse,
the beat of his hands crissing and crossing stayed always the same.
He controlled how hard he hit without the help of taking longer
for a stronger blow, and his arms, at a peak of condition, needed
no rest. Because of the varying force, he hit the bag at all points
in its arch—it didn't go at the same speed, but was chopped into
spurts which only a dead-eye could follow. Yet the noise he made
was one noise without parts, a swelling and sinking thunder. His
head led a charmed, miraculous life in the midst of his flying fists,
and during the biggest racket Kelly was scared. This kind of a
guy could send a hundred at you as fast as they could follow one
another, all rocks heavy as your body was; sure, stoppable, one or
five, but not a hundred!

• • •

"Hey." Howard Straws turned Kelly to face him, taking his
chin. "You haven't done much yet, so I want you to quit and box
two rounds instead. This fellow needs a sixty-pounder for his boy.
I can look you over, and be better for you. How much you weigh?"

"One-sixty-three."

"Good. Feel okay? Won't be for a while. You got plenty of chance to change." He put his hand on Kelly's neck and steered him to the locker room. It was a queer sensation, having one's neck and face handled. Kelly had forgotten since he'd quit boxing, had to accustom himself again.

"Crackers will handle you—you know which he is? Well it don't matter; he'll know you." Straws slapped Kelly's shoulder. "He's a bum. I'll tell you confidentially they're all bums, every fighter here not counting mine. You look okay. Nice to see an Irish boy still fighting. The fans'll like that. There're not many like you—just Irish fans, no Irish fighters. We could bill you as the last one: might go fine. We'll see, we'll watch and see. Pea, give this boy my fighting stuff," he yelled at Peapod, and he took his hand off Kelly's neck and began making dirty-finger signals at a buddy, flipped a greeting at another. Then he sobered and straightened his sleeves and French shirt cuffs which had gone awry.

The last Irish fighter! Kelly's spirits sank. It was true: the Irish had gone on to better things; he was a freak. But right now coming to the gym fitted his life so perfectly—he was drawing unemployment and living snugly with a woman. It took so little time, half an afternoon, and a fighter got two thousand clear for network TV, after all the cuts, and being white and Irish would bring breaks because of the fans. He put a cup on underneath his trunks and removed his bridgework, and settled down behind the rings to wait, might be an hour. He sat beside China, who was talking with a friend, a studious-type sax player who came often. China went to his rehearsals. One ring was for boxing. The other was for shadow-boxers and was full. The flashiest show was being provided by a former welter champ, now just another tanker. No ordinary duck walk: a bouncing spring-legged exhibition, hands on hips; he went like a frog. Did standing-up gyrations like a top. But throw a punch and he couldn't see it, and his legs and lungs went zombie-spongy in the first five rounds. Kelly was older than him, which was why China was encouraging. China still earned a living fighting and didn't worry about injury and didn't hate the sport and didn't always have to fight upstate—New York City fans would watch him. He simply trained gently and then went out and fought his fights to the promoter's satisfaction. Kelly's hopes were modest like that. Kelly loafed and wondered who among the twenty guys sitting on the bench he was going to box. Crackers, the trainer, was pointed out to him, a small bowed bug of a man.

The walls of the gym were painted black, but light reflecting off the neighboring buildings through the windows glowed benignly off the floor. Somebody's speed bag went like an outboard motor. The brown guy in the boxing ring put zing in every punch, dug them in like nails to last a century. All the power from his knees up and neck down wadded to his fist. No matter how far it had traveled he was adding steam to it when it hit. The sparring partner was jarred a good five feet by every punch; whatever he threw in an exchange he had to get off first. He was driven to the ropes and partly through and James DeJesus, owner of the gym, was standing underneath and jumped away like he'd been pinched. A manager next to him though, didn't, even put a hand up to support the fighter. Jim grabbed his coat and yanked him back.

"Always get away when they're knocked through like that, let 'em fall! Let 'em hit the floor instead of you, 'cause that's what they're liable to do, hit you. God protects 'em." Jim swung around to tell a larger group. He chuckled with soft sarcasm and grinned obscenely. "God protects 'em just like he protects the drunks."

"Easy, Luis," said a trainer. With each punch Luis's feet scraped the canvas with a vicious noise and a sharp snatch of air came out of his nose. Accompanying his punching, the two sounds echoed louder than the speed bags' roar. Now the pair touch-boxed; Luis in order not to hurt, his sparring partner not to make him mad.

Then Luis made gargantuan gargles with the water: mouth as big as the trainer's hand; his thighs thicker than his buttocks; his calves like shillelaghs shaped of muscle—so much noise and size and vigor that the water seemed still clean when Luis spit it out.

This manager of Kelly's couldn't seem to rest. Again he called him, into the middle of a group. Kelly crossed his arms and fixed his face to be polite and calm.

"Where you fought?"

"Where have I fought?" Kelly repeated, looking around at the jury of managers as Straws adjusted his glasses on his nose and squeezed his lips. "Boston more than any place. I fought in Boston Garden and Revere and Chelsea, Worcester. I fought in St. Nick's here as main event and I fought in your Garden once as last prelim."

"Who'd you beat?" said Straws. They all watched Kelly when a question was being asked, then looked away as his mouth opened for the answer. He did too, looked down at the backs of his arms.

"Who? Oh, I fought some guys that would sound good. But I didn't beat them." He laughed. He didn't make up stories. It was easiest to tell the truth.

"When was this?" Straws acted like a D. A. when he had a crowd.

"Oh." Kelly paused to think. "Not so long. Off and on. I'd start and I'd fight and I'd quit. Two years ago was the last."

"Well, you behave yourself." Straws tapped Kelly's cup to make sure it was on. "So what do you think of him, huh?" He put his hand on Kelly's neck. "You were all asleep, huh? And I got him."

The other managers shrugged noncommittally.

"Yeah, get in," DeJesus told two featherweights. He dropped a rock of rosin in a box and crushed it under his shoe and dumped the powder in a corner of the ring, banging the box on the canvas. He strode back to his desk, pausing to bang a window shut he didn't happen to want open. "I'll open the windows," he said grimly, picking his nose. The featherweights toed the rosin while they waited for the timer clock to work around to where they'd start. A trainer climbed onto the apron and gave them their mouthpieces, slicked grease on their cheeks. They went to opposite corners then. One took hold of the ropes and did knee bends, jouncing hard. The other hit his gloves together, readying them, and danced and tapped his head guard up so that it didn't block his eyes. At the bell they circled to each other so their backs faced away from the corners they'd chosen and their ties to them were cut.

Two styles: One guy hung his left way out loosely at his side and rocked it with anticipation. His right was cocked more normally. He was a lunger. The other put his fists beside his cheeks and close enough to thread a needle and darted forward, back, and forward a few steps with continuous excitement. Of course in the midst of throwing combinations his fists didn't always return there, but it was how he began and ended. The complication of fighting him came from his nerves. He would choose his spot and brush his nose with his thumb and bump the head guard up from his eyes and start his little frenzied bobbings and the frantic seamstress motions. But when the open-fisted guy waded in to make the fight, the seamstress broke it off, sidled to the side and chose another spot. He wasn't afraid. He'd slug it out as hotly as the open-fister, but only when his jumpiness was stilled. Or else, another possibility, he'd work to such a climax of nervous and preparatory motions that he'd have to let fly.

Any number of fighters could use the shadow-boxing ring at once, and fast, because the real professionals moved fast. They'd done their rigamaroles a million times and went by rote. They pedaled backwards, caroming off the ropes and zigging in and out between each other; or slowly charged, launched heavy pulverizer uppercuts. Kneeing knees, kicking feet, shoulders shoving, foreheads butting— the ring rocked with a collective rhythm that the spectators could tap to. And there were no collisions. The kids went slow, attempted little, watched where they were going, but more credit went to the professionals. They missed a guy as skillfully as they'd hit him.

"Stay in. Chuck, 'nother round'll do it," a trainer told a fighter who was climbing out. The fighter grunted disagreement. The trainer made a face. "Chuck, you need it." No success. The trainer flopped his head disgustedly and threw the towel at the bench for the boxer to pick up himself.

"Whoa, Bessie!" came a yell. "What do we think we're doing!" A bulky man in a pin-stripe suit with his tie flying, watch fob hopping, rushed the fighter. "Gettin' the goddam hell out of the ring before our time is up?" He slapped the fighter twice across the ear and pushed against him, shoulder against chest, forcing him back to the steps to the ring.

"Okay! Yeah, okay," the fighter said and got back in.

"Hey! Hey!" roared Jim DeJesus. "I don't want no shoutin in this gym!" He spat and his voice hit the wall in echoes. "If there was a woman and a child up here, what would they think of that shoutin' you did? Ya bum! Hit him again if you want instead of

the shoutin', but *don't shout,* ya sonofabitch! It's *written right in the rules on the wall!*" He spat and strode around his desk out of control. "Sonofabitch!" He unzipped his fly and straightened himself and zipped it up again. He muttered comments to surrounding managers and spat again. His eyes swept round the gym and fixed on that one shouting guy as if he had killed women and children wholesale. Jim was scary, yes, but fighters had nothing to fear from him as long as they kept their mouths shut and obeyed the rules. He sometimes even seemed to look on them with favor, when they had been exceptionally quiet. Same thing with trainers, as long as they did what he told them. It was the managers he had his hands full with, unless he joined in with his wolfish grin when they were kidding. Kelly, buried among twenty fighters on the bench, could listen safely. He cushioned his towel behind his head and stretched his legs and laid his arms across his lap. Close his eyes or watch what rounds he wanted to; that was Kelly's "job." Not only got him out of the house, it couldn't be better.

Little half-pint chose himself a spot, brushed his nose with his thumb, went into his hovery knit-needle bit, elbows stuck out almost farther than his gloves, and waited for his man to come. But the other guy was slow; by the time he'd come the place had gotten hot or something for the seamstress and he'd strode away with stretching steps on ballet toes and taken his intent and bobbing pose elsewhere. Twice this happened, and the lunger, the loose-fisted guy who didn't bother with a guard, was feeling miffed. When he got there this time they mixed it up like so much scrambled cat. The lunger hooked his left up hard to bust the seamstress' chest. Again he did; again he tried. And down from up beside his cheeks the seamstress brought his gloves and stabbed lefts to the nose.

Kelly paced in order not to stiffen. Couldn't sit all day. Two tough middleweights squeezed past him with polite excuse-me's. Both were veterans—one's face was smashed level like a welder's hood except for his eyes, which had receded. They were through with the bags and carried their jump ropes, tapping the wooden handles briskly. And then they'd vault and shuffle in the shadow ring. The makeup of that ring would change from people who were starting the training session to people who were finishing. Kelly knew at least he wasn't boxing either of them. He wondered who, looking around the benches; several middleweights were waiting. He seated himself again and let his eyes half close. Straws was tweaking the chest hair of the trainers he could reach where it stuck out above their undershirts. When they moved away Straws yawned and turned as if to talk and was disappointed: nobody was near. His regular crowd was pushing around and about among them a small Italian-looking guy, also a manager, his face a meager version of DiMaggio's. They squashed his hat on his head for a joke and pushed him from behind whichever way he went. Kelly wondered how the manager's fighters felt. Finally they stopped to check their suits for wrinkles. Straws went to one of the groups which had just formed to tell the story. The members fixed their belts and smoothed themselves, their eyes shining from their laughter. They combed their solid-looking, molded hair and tried to coax the pushed one over. Straws opened his belt and tightened his shirt, spat on the wall and took out his nail clippers.

Crackers, Kelly's trainer, signaled.

"Ready?" Kelly said. Instead of answering Crackers snuggled the head guard over Kelly's ears and strapped it under his chin. He checked his hand wraps and slid on the gloves and tied them with hard swift tugs; his lips bulged a bit from the exertion but otherwise his face stayed blank. Flashing a finger once down the lacing of each glove and once across the head guard's strap, he finished with a slight okay sign, and quickly turned away.

"How's this guy I'm fighting?" Kelly asked.

Crackers half turned and mildly spread his hands to indicate a shrug. He wasn't far enough around to look at Kelly, but he made the effort of partly turning. Likewise, his mouth opened: didn't say a word but opened partly.

"Which is he?"

Crackers angled with a thumb. The fighter was being laced: Kelly's weight, all right, little taller, but a good physique, light coffee skin. He wasn't a name. Looked tough, but who didn't? His trainer was drilling him some: small gestures and murmured words, working him like a machine. In the ring now was a fight of reelings and thumps; you wouldn't hear too many of them before a man went down. One man was fishing for the other's head and trying to keep from getting cut in half. He landed painfully on the other's eye and suddenly had no worries for his middle. A thicket of defensive whistling stuff was put in front of that eye. He should have changed his target then, but didn't.

Two cutiepants had the ring for a round. Always popping their hands against each other and making adjustments of target before they'd trouble to throw a punch; and little downward conversational sorts of glove movements like a couple of deaf-and-dumbs. And any time a punch missed, the other guy, instead of counterpunching, was sure to stop and catch the arm and make it continue its course until the thrower had been spun around, just for the fun. As Kelly watched, one cutie sent the other head-first into the ropes with a glove on his elbow and a motion like helping a lady board a bus. Kelly was experienced enough to know the tricks, but it was just hard on the legs and a nuisance, always being fuddled and spun and adjusted and having to cover yourself from punches from the rear. Revenge or maddening a guy was the best you could do with them. He walked beside the benches unkinking his arms. His opponent had started shadow-boxing, one hand fronting for the other like a bag. Kelly and he exchanged nods when they passed. Kelly remembered seeing him on previous days, but not how he'd fought, which was frustrating. Santos was his name.

They were side by side now in the ring, toeing rosin, holding to the rope. They walked again, with longer lunging steps and stamping as if crushing bugs. "Lemme see," Crackers called. He rubbed the grease on Kelly and handed up a mouthpiece. Kelly crossed himself because it would be foolish not to. The bell rang and they shuffled to each other, shoved their gloves out wary and wide to touch in courtesy, and cook up their stances. Each kept his punches under wraps at first. Kelly was a stand-up fighter who cocked his hands for slugging, not to guard. Santos was a picture fighter, doing everything correctly, and he crouched. He looked impressive. He looked good.

Santos fought by the numbers: left jab and so forth. Kelly'd hook to the ribs to counter his lead—block it with the right hand,

which he'd have to bring up, and instantly hook with the left.
When the guy started catching those on his elbow Kelly countered
instead with a looping right slammed over Santos' left hand as it
came—didn't pause to try to slip it, took the punch to give one.
The looping right was ticklish, positioned like that, but even if it
hit his shoulder its power gave the guy a scare. He'd want a defense
and was unprotected on that side. So Santos began throwing flurries, which meant Kelly had a chance to turn straight on and slug:
Santos would stay there. And Kelly got to Santos, kept his flurries
short. The guy had one of the best physiques in the gym, but his
punch somehow didn't come up to what was promised. Kelly, as
Straws had thought, threw heavy leather, but in a rudimentary,
stand-up-fight-me, stoic style, and he was slowed down by being
out of shape and old. To match Santos' flash, Kelly tried to punish,
using single punches; this was his defense. His savvy partly equal-
ized the difference, but he couldn't string together combinations
the way Santos could—a lead with a cross with a hook with a hook
with a cross with an uppercut to the face. However, Santos had
no bite, and didn't look like he was going to grow it either, being
already grown. Kelly: let *him* whang you to the gut a time or two
with both his hands and he would bleed you, or at least that's how
he'd been. Santos moused from lower ones, bending down, and
brought his elbows to his belly. He headhunted, Santos did. Kelly
roundhoused rights like swinging a bucket at the head, to please
the guy, but Santos would move back. Hadn't tagged him yet, and
Kelly felt the patter of his fists against his face—Santos must get
mad, to land so many punches without hurting, although he was
scoring points. Kelly did the coming in. Santos flaunted foot speed:
let him flaunt it backwards.

At the bell they tapped each other friendly on the head and
Kelly went to Crackers for regreasing and to have his mouthpiece
washed. "Doin" pretty well," said Crackers. Kelly paced as soon
as Crackers let him, too stirred up to stop for long. Felt like old
times—and he remembered he'd been good—everything came
naturally. He didn't sucker for this joker and he punched regardless. Many of the managers were watching—oh, not with worship
on their faces; he could imagine the usual "Bum" being passed

around; but watching, still. The paying fans who were here might clap a little at the end. They sometimes did. Kelly was looking fine, even against a hit-and-run like this. Well, he was better than a hit-and-hold; Kelly wasn't yet so old that he'd prefer a lover. And, to give Santos credit, he winged his left in well.

He likes to run: we'll run him in the ropes, Kelly thought when they began again. Santos was hard to trap. Once he dodged so it was Kelly went against the ropes, and Santos figured that he had him then and rushed till Kelly frightened him by lolling there, arms spread. Kelly grinned insultingly, but couldn't draw poor Santos close enough to slug. Yes, next time he did, and Kelly nailed him on the bottom rib and got a groan. He was the opposite of frail, but surely hated to be hit. He jumped up on his bicycle again and pedaled back, Kelly after him.

Such a clean-looking guy to chase. Tee shirt sparkling white, white stripes on his trunks, white laces, white shoes, white sock tops, purple gloves and new black trunks—so clean it made you feel like you were trying to mess up something nice. Kelly did a little better defensively, picking off some jabs like baseballs caught, and slipping others past his cheek and out of sight. His face was flushed from what got through.

The best bit happened at the finish of that second round, where it was placed most happily. Santos must have gotten careless. As he tried to duck as usual past Kelly near the ropes, Kelly reached him with an elbow and shoved him back. He tried again and Kelly grabbed him like a crate, both hands, and shoved him into place and uppercut to his heart. He fell against the ropes and bounced. And Kelly timed the bounce and uppercut to his heart. And left-hooked to his cheek, to show the world he could head-punch, and left hooked to his heart. And uppercut to his heart. And smashed him on the heart. The guy pitched up and down and dove for Kelly's arms. He pinned the left till Kelly punished him so bad he had to let it go. Kelly battered at the upper belly and the heart. Santos covered up, but that was no defense. Kelly whammed and whammed, shoved him with an elbow to set him right and punched him on the bottom rib and left-hooked to his heart. And Santos pitched around and quit his covering up and dove again to catch the arms—pinned them momentarily, but Kelly worked one loose and hit the heart. And then the bell.

They tapped each other on the head and shoulder, tickled each other on the neck, as awkward as it was with gloves, and walked together to the stairs. Crackers gave them each a hand to lean on climbing down. Kelly's legs and arms were quivery. He couldn't seem to stop dead still. Aimlessly he strolled till Crackers grabbed him by his gloves and made him stand just where he was. He was like a child being stripped of stuff; he stared off absently, letting Crackers do the work, twisting his lips as a child might when Crackers took the mouthpiece out. Kelly was allowed to lick the sponge, but not to put it in his mouth. Crackers watered him and dried the middle of his body; when he began to need to reach to dry the arms and legs he handed Kelly the towel.

"Was okay. Course the man didn't hit. Hope you wouldn't fight with your face like that against some ones."

Kelly grinned. He scrubbed his sweat and walked, driven by his muscles to keep moving. He proudly glanced around at everybody to see how much they liked his stuff. He couldn't tell. Nobody even looked at him. Peapod from the locker room was searching the floor for cigar butts—not cleaning up: he smoked them in his pipe. The managers were chatting. China was boxing now, but complimented Kelly, clinching deliberately to have a chance to nod approval. There was a friend. Kelly was happy. The feeling of those final punches had been etched right on his arms. He was going to knock off twenty pushups on the rubdown table. He leaned against it for the shake and shake of the contortions of the fighters on it and flexed his hands and felt real good, real rough, real big. He'd plant one and he'd lobo anybody.

Straws was coming with a crony who wore a suit so shiny that you couldn't tell the color, whether blue or black or green. "Don't tire yourself," Straws told Kelly. "Listen!"

The crony started in: "I have a boy who's got a fight in two weeks, and if you wanna get yourself in shape too you can fight with him this week and then next week if you've done okay, I'll let you have five bucks a day for fighting him. Of course, he's

better than the chicken-charlie you just fought. You wanna try?"
He talked as rapid-fire as a sightseeing guide.

"Who is it?"

"Rudd. You know him?"

"Yeah, I'll try him," Kelly said. Rudd was a comer burning
up the field, the kind that Kelly'd have to fight soon anyway.

"Damn right you will," Straws told him. "This afternoon. He's
not fighting till the end, so you'll have a rest. Plenty of time. You
relax."

"Good opportunity for you," said the crony.

When he left, Straws confided: "These crumbs drop tips. I never
miss a word. That's how I picked you up and that's how I heard he
wanted a boy to work his boy with. I don't miss nothing. Don't nothing these bastards do get by me. And another thing I was thinking
was about this previous manager of yours. Are you positive I'm not
going to have to buy you from him?"

"No, he died."

"He didn't sell you to somebody before? I don't want no law-
suits and the last thing in the world I'm gonna do right now is buy
a fighter. Maybe he sold you on his deathbed."

"No."

· · ·

Paid, no less! In one in ten of these bouts the sparring partner got paid. The money wasn't much—three-and-a-quarter a
day, or less after Straws took his cut—but being paid alone would
feel good. Kelly clapped for China and was partly clapping for
himself. With China every defense move was utilized, and every
kind of punch, very complex fighting. In the early rounds he'd rest
along, and later when his opponent's defense became shoddy from
exhaustion there'd be murder. China wasn't one of those old men
so out of shape they tried for first-round knock-outs, although he'd
pick one up that begged him to. Kelly looked out at Forty-Second
Street, the traffic, sunlight, sky. The sky was wonderful and big;
the sun was fun, not hot. High up, seagulls sailed, so sharp they
looked the shape of bats.

The Spanish-speakers' hair grew neatly long down the backs of their necks, while American coloreds as often as not had a wild scrap of hair back there like a pirate might tie with a string. Italian fighters were normal enough about the back, but grew their hair so high in front it doubled the height of their foreheads—which was to scare you with. What did the Irish do? Goodness knows; Kelly was the only one. The Irish punched. He wished he were acquainted with more guys. The Ecuadorians he couldn't talk to, and the coloreds had Harlem to gossip about. Besides, he was older—like the man over in the corner who'd fought Joe Louis. Louis fought a bum a month, the saying went, and this guy had been one of those bums—still scraping up an occasional fight because of the one Louis bout.

Two beginners were boxing now, kneading with their fists, safe distances apart. Their styles were full of fragmentary little poses they were trying out. When they did get close, they footballed with their shoulders and covered face and body with crossed arms until they couldn't throw a punch. They ducked too much and took each other's guard too seriously. From nervousness they let their hands, rigged tightly for defense, go out so far that they were useless both for punching and for stopping punches. If the youngsters did move fast it was from agitation. They'd flinch back even as they hit, in fear of counters, which destroyed their power. Kelly laughed; most anyone got hit; a winner absorbed better. One kid was still learning not to shut his eyes. And when the pair worked into clinches, without a referee to help, they couldn't come apart.

"Yeah, this is it," a manager at the door informed a Negro kid, and indicated James DeJesus. Jim had walled himself away behind his rope; he was studying snapshots, probably of relatives. The kid had trouble getting his attention, but then Jim listened, nodding in impatience at every sentence as if he'd heard it many times before, although not otherwise being rude.

"Yes, you're from Birmingham," Jim said, "and you came here and you want to fight. But where are you going to eat, where are you going to sleep, boy, huh? How?" With a motion of exasperation, "Pick him up!" he snorted at the managers who'd grouped around. They were the cheapest (including, Kelly noticed, Howard

Straws), who didn't have their stables full. The first to examine the kid, a bald and bag-eyed man, made a fart noise through his mouth and lifted his leg like a doggie weeing. It was his favorite sneer. DeJesus had turned back to his photos and didn't seem upset immediately—he'd seen the act before—when all of a sudden he shook with rage and, stuffing the pictures into an envelope, went over the rope with his lead pipe after the manager, cussing his filth. The guy ran down the stairs ahead of him, and two minutes later was peeking around the door again like a child chased out of a playhouse.

In the shadow-boxers' ring a bunch was shuffling blank and timeless as a marathon except one lively kid who leaped and scissored like a dervish. The bookies' representative was there. The bookies pooled their information and only sent one man to sessions. He was easy to spot because he didn't dress to be conspicuous, the way the managers did, in bowler hats and velvet collars, and always kept a hand around his pockets checking on his multitude of slips and on his rolls of money. The hand that wasn't guarding pockets was used for feeling fighters. He'd wave them over, ask about their families and if they'd win their scheduled fights and what was new and what they knew and what was funny, laugh with them, and then rest his hand on them and slap them to congratulate them that their health was fine. Meanwhile he'd be feeling muscles in their arms and shoulders and the special muscles in their necks which might absorb the K.O. from a knockout punch. Legs he'd judge by eye as often as he'd squeeze them. When he was through he'd stop and make a mental note of his appraisal, pick his teeth.

Standing in the door was a young light-heavyweight with face not yet in the final fighter's mask. He was in his best suit, preened, and leaving to box on the coast, Kelly'd heard. He carried his suitcases too easily to notice right away. He seemed afraid to enter his own gym without being welcomed, the bashful, gawky stance trying to be so suave. He was afraid because of his suitcases and best hat, best suit, best shoes, so vulnerable to being poked fun at, his very, very best, stripped of all excuse. For another reason, his wife was lingering in the shadows with their baby son. She was timid-looking, black like her husband, and had come to see him off. When the fighter did move into the gym he shambled. His legs couldn't keep up with his body and his head bobbed, his arms waggled ludicrously out of rhythm, not because the suitcases were heavy, but because he was scared. Kelly was impatient. When Kelly slicked himself up in his traveling clothes he didn't fall to pieces and go bashful; he was cool.

The light-heavy's manager greeted him and shook hands with the wife, told her how swell her husband was and praised the son. The light-heavy edged to the side, smiling with embarrassed pride. He set his suitcases down and clasped his hands to keep them out of trouble, planting his feet stiffly. The bookie wished him luck and he tried to stay alert and bright for whatever might be wanted of him. On top of the shyness, though, an excitement sang in his expression. This type of guy didn't leave his neighborhood except to box; and now there'd be the taxis, the airports, cross-country flights, hotels, the big shots patting him, swank restaurants, and TV cameras and newsmen and the arena mob. In the newspapers you read sob stories about Negro ex-champs—how sad it was that Beau Jack, the gallant lightweight of the Forties, should be a shoe-shine boy. Should Beau Jack have been a shoeshine boy straight through instead, and never been Beau Jack at all? And was it bet-ter that Joe Louis owed the government a million after being the greatest modern champion for thirteen years, or for Joe Louis to have spent his life in Detroit's Browntown heaving coal?

One event the fighter insisted upon. Again and again he looked at James DeJesus until his nerve was up, then touched his wife so she would follow. Jim acknowledged the trio by jerking his head for the guy to speak, not rudely, but to the point. It was his way with fighters. He didn't make them speak up loud, like he would managers, and for shy ones he would lean his ear much closer than he'd lean it to a manager's mouth.

"Mister DeJesus, I'd like if you would shake hands with my wife so she would know you," the light-heavy said. "This is Mister DeJesus. He runs everything."

Jim courteously responded, even to admiring the child, and would have slugged a man who cursed, but finished soon enough to show he took it as his job. He spat on the floor during the interview, but that was nothing—he'd have done that talking to George Washington. Children of white fighters he would often kiss with that same spitting mouth.

He was concentrating on his photographs again when, hearing one of the managers say hello on a pay phone more than once, he felt obliged to give some lessons.

"You can do it however way you want," he started gently. "It don't kill me. I'm only telling what I think is wisest." Pacing up and down beside the booths, he waited for a call to demonstrate. There was one, and he whirled and sprang for it. "Better Champions!" he snapped. . . . "What?" Instantly he slammed down the receiver.

"Now there was a case," he lectured, "where the party did say something, but I couldn't hear what it was. If you can't hear him you can't talk to him, can you? So hang it up." Jim grew enraged. "If he can't make you understand him, he don't know what in the hell he's saying! If he don't speak up with his business quick, hang him up! He don't have no business! Maybe might be the wrong number! Hang him up!" He raced into another booth which rang. "Better Champions!" he shouted furiously and slapped the receiver back again. "That was a different case," he told the crowd of managers. "I couldn't hear the woodhead; I couldn't hear a thing. It wasn't that I couldn't understand him, I couldn't even hear him!" The idea flabbergasted Jim and he turned logical: "And who would want to call you bums but bums anyway? And what do you want to talk to a bum for when you got so many here? Who else is going to call you? Only a bum would call a bum. Hang up quick."

In the ring a beginner sprawled against the ropes, taking a thousand and never trying to clinch or get away. Feverish, holding his breath, he pawed and pummeled back. Every kind of fighting style came off the street. The other guy was sinking 'em in with long snake arms and myriad spidery feints. But the more he hit the beginner, the more the beginner tried to hit back. That was guts; now give him a trainer.

Rudd, whom Kelly was to fight, was listening to another fighter. "I told him right in front of the ref, 'You keep on running on me and I'm going to stand on your feet to hold you still till I can slug you.'"

Rudd listened with a real respect. His answers were too soft for Kelly to hear, except for the Negro-backsticks accent, but he understood when Rudd shrugged with his hands to get out of talking. His weight didn't spread into height like Kelly's, and his arms were short, but all of him was muscled as machinely as a fish. Kelly nodded and Rudd nodded back from politeness, obviously not knowing who he was. A modest face, but awfully flattened, and his career had only begun. His nose seemed to cover the front of it, dwarfed his mustache. Kelly felt his own nose. The thickening couldn't be ignored, but he laughed because a manager had kicked another in the seat and started a slapping bee. He fidgeted his hands to keep them off his nose. That didn't help enough, and finally he had to walk. Walking started him thinking how his muscles felt and balling them and stretching. He wanted to do well.

"Well, we'll see if this is glass." Straws, switching on a smile, tapped Kelly's chin, although his eyes were searching him. "But he don't let his legs do nothin', he don't learn. Fights almost pier-six."

"You hit him, he goes down, he hits you, you go down?" Kelly asked.

"No. He don't go down." Straws squeezed Kelly's chin. "You can jab him silly—not what his manager wants you to do, but there is sure to be somebody in in the next two weeks who puts on shows and I can give the sign to jab and we might have ourselves a bout. If you're good against Rudd, they'll give you one. We'd lose the little money and we'd make the big." He made a face and shoved his fist at Kelly full of threat. "Get him!" Kelly walked away. They tried to put across to you how much tougher they were—tougher—how superior in every way; wouldn't even leave the fighter that.

The Number Four Contender of the Welterweights, and Kelly's favorite fighter, hopped into the ring: favorite fighter to watch; he'd never spoken to him. Usually the guy used bags, and so to see him was a treat. He'd whip his body up and down and pump out punches fast as Kelly'd tap a finger. He both started and finished exchanges and always knew what he was after. He'd paste your facial openings shut and leave you sorting out your parts. From the country of Colombia, he chuckled Spanish to his sparring partner, and through the mouthpiece it emerged monkey yunks. Number Four's equipment was in nifty piercing reds and greens. He himself was chocolate-brown, a well-formed five-foot nine. And what a face he had—eager, mild, unmarked, an unhurt nose. The man in with him was a little younger, maybe twenty-one, and jounced his warm-up footwork with a consciousness of being outclassed. His crushed face was merry as he returned the jokes. Their grins were each distorted by the mouthpiece, but Number Four's was less so. He let his upper lip slip up until he looked as though his mouth were full of gum.

They blocked their arms out in a box for touching gloves, touched elbows too. The partner's style was raggedly gutty and wasteful, composed of constant straight-out pushes trying to wear his adversary down. So Number Four gave him the same—rifled level breastbone shots with longer arms. Then Four softened— didn't want to discourage the guy with his own stuff—switched into more natural ways, and pushed the partner gently back when he got in too close for Four to bomb him. If the guy insisted upon pressing close, why Four'd collapse and lean on him with all his weight until in a bout the ref would have had to break them. Or, if the partner hunched low to escape the stoning. Number Four would simply lean down hard across his back, trapping his neck in an armpit, until, again, a referee'd have broken them. In between these sapping clinches he romped out punches in assorted styles, hooks, jabs and upward-movers—uppercuts and golfed-in bolos—and crossed his arms to stop the counters, grinning when the other guy threw stuff because it opened him up the more for attack. Of course Four didn't need an opening to punch. He whacked 'em in, openings or not, hit the biceps if that's all there was, but hit and hit, hit and hit; befuddle the guy and fox the judges' eyes. Down he bent and up, chop-stepped, and shook the golden talisman that hung around his neck into a fling. His body almost rubber-shimmied in exigencies of golfing blows and of defense. But it looked easy. As part of readying his own, it seemed, he picked off punches, as breezily as that. Real horse-hoofs: tucked 'em in his palms. And when he slipped a punch you'd think he'd glanced across the street, so simple and so neat. Just casual. Or as if in a rhythm. And all the time he pumped in punches quick as sharks.

The partner naturally had got depressed. Number Four dropped his arms, quit offense and when the guy let loose his all, just wriggled with delight at the massage. And rocked against the ropes to hear them creak, rocked and rocked, began avoiding punches with his body, curling kitten-wise this way or that, sucking in his tummy; arms stayed at his sides. Around the ring like rubber he rocked, limp and lax and scarcely getting hit. One rope's spring propelled him to the next. Eluded and evaded everything as if it were rehearsed.

He stopped that business, took a few and let the guy get to him and raised his arms and fought in close. He fought like you would see him on TV against class fighters at their best, who'd have their way to some extent, Four unavoidably being hit and thus sharp-punching at tight targets like the nose and eyes and solar plexus to cut and pain the man and jar his aim; of course he'd hit the jaw whenever he could. This guy wasn't quite the same, though, this poor kid with features bull's-eyed in a wad. Number Four drained everything to quarter-strength for him. And on Four's face that mild, eager, searching look like always when he fought.

He frauded for the fun of it now, Four, pretended to be hurt and woozy—buckled knees, drooped head. He 'possumed helpless in the middle of the ring, fumbling for a clinch, woodenly walking into what was thrown, exposing his heart and tummy. But as the partner got engrossed, Four sharp-shot a bunch of aces to eyes and nose—kept quarter-force—and by mistake, it must have been, he clonked the partner's chin. This put the sags and staggers in the partner's legs; he braced them wide-apart and quivering. Number Four put out his arms as stiff as railings for the guy to rest on and, when he could stand up by himself, just nuzzled languidly head to head with him and slowly shadow-boxed, leaving his own stomach open-target for encouragement.

When the guy felt better Number Four spoke Spaniard to him, apparently telling him he'd let his face alone, to cover up his trunk. The partner crossed his arms. Number Four whipped golfing bolo rocket punches down from shoulder height which smashed in on the navel, real divine whirlo bolo punches arching like a scythe which made the paying fans shout. Showoff, yes, but full of zazz. Little Peapod paused in hunting cigar butts to watch. His eyes, instead of being muffled with subservience, were lighted fiercely.

They wrapped their arms around each other's shoulders and went to get rubbed down. Both faces gabbled Spanish happily—Four Contender's mild and eager, the partner's like a penny put under a train.

Shuffling, Kelly wrung his wrists and rolled his head around on his neck like a juggled ball. He fiddled with his trunks to sit them higher on his midriff so the legal target would be lessened, and wiggled his feet—the socks were smooth, the laces tight—and closed his eyes, rested vacantly. For a while he was just conscious of his body, how comfortable it felt, not springy like a kid's, but plenty big and tricky. No, he wouldn't be hurt, he felt too fine; he was in his prime. Good old boy that never gave him any trouble. He found a private corner behind the rubdown tables and looked across the straightening bending bodies to the whole of the gym. It was a madhouse. In the ring a skinny fighter was taking a beating. Every time he got off something the sound would show he'd hit an arm. Every time the other man chopped in his right there'd be the soft thud of hitting home. The ring shook and squeaked. Spectators clapped. Shadow-boxers stomped the floor. Skip ropes slapped and whispered (when you couldn't hear them, watching them you thought you could). The skippers thumped their feet. Big bags jerked and shivered up at crazy angles, to the thunder of the little ones. Fighters shuffled in a maze of warm-ups. Several languages were used. The managers goosed and sparred hilariously, pulling ties. "Who?" DeJesus yelled above the uproar; a name was wanted on the phone. *"Who? Cufflinks Prince?"* He gaped with disbelief and leapt up, spitting like a hot frying pan. He would have thrown his arm except it was attached. *"You know that bum's not allowed in here!"* His two poor legs hardly could support his fury. He hawked a real whopper up and let it fly. From the fighting ring, sharp anguished gasps and snorts of heavy labor; the blinks were in the skinny fighter's eyes, his head was being knocked back and forth with faint flesh-squashing noises as fast as if it were a bag. It shivered like a melon, unattached to him, and flung off hair sweat, tiny tears and spittle drops which could be seen. His head guard looked about to split—it looked as though the lacing of the head guard was lacing on his very head and couldn't help but split. And still the punches came in succinct thuds. Speed bags reverberated savagely through the gym and underneath their roar were sounds of shaking rings, DeJesus' fury, managers' catcalls, whizzing skip ropes, shadow-box gyrations, heavy bags being plastered, plunging calisthenics, until the gym seemed about to fly apart.

Rudd paced as though his rounds were soon. Kelly asked him, "When do we go in?"

"Are we boxing? I don't know, when they tell us." Rudd pointed at a doe-eyed Negro. "I've got him too. He might be first." He paced alongside Kelly companionably but silently, looking at the floor. Their strides weren't matched. Rudd seemed to churn along with tremendous energy, slow and channeled. Even walking, his legs hardly stayed under him; they were geared to driving ahead so powerfully. Fighting, if he didn't come on at you, he'd fall flat. Kelly'd watched him on TV against a classy boxer-puncher tiger who assumed a fancy stance and moved in like the dreadnaught that he thought he was. Rudd, also moving in, had ragged him twice; and all the offense and the class went sick, the tiger dropped them like a stone to cover up and bob down in his lowest crouch. Rudd chased him till he'd knocked him out. His face was scary to anyone who cared about his own: it had a dozen widgets from sewn-up cuts and over parts of it a slick scar-skin had grown in place of welts, a skin so shiny that if he'd been white it would have looked like bone. Under the skin-thick reinforcement buttressing were eyes swollen into Oriental slits, cheeks Indian and huge, brows, nose, chin, each immense—that was what you punched at, features. When Rudd had first puffed up he'd probably looked like China, permanently crying, which made a funny contrast with a smile. But now he'd gone beyond that. He just looked puffed, as with weary sleeplessness, no emotion, only puffed. And his nose, although gigantic as three noses, had been leveled down until it was becoming just another buttress pad across his face. Twenty-two, Rudd was.

This was no way. Kelly went off by himself again to get into a better frame of mind. He was still in his twenties and younger than plenty of active champs had been. What did he have to worry about? He'd sparred with Tony DeMarco when both of them were kids in Boston, and Tony had ranked Number One behind Basilio for years. Kelly slipped into his fighting stance, arms set loose, hands quite wide. It was a good reliable stance for any general purpose and boosted his spirits because he was proud of it. He really began to feel like fighting. It was a mood to be worked into by walking, by getting grim, thinking what Rudd hoped to do to him and what the rounds could mean if he did well and what specific punches he was going to throw. Soon he was ready to knock the stuffing out of anyone.

Five minutes later he munched the mouthpiece out of Cracker's hand and slid his shoes around, looking solemnly down on the people. "To the meat," Rudd's trainer was telling Rudd. Kelly smiled and bit his mouthpiece sternly. More than the gloves, the mouthpiece in his teeth made him know that he was going to fight. He crossed himself and circled the ring, dancing and thrusting out his arms. A grave and blank expression settled over his face to cover up the rising heat he felt. He went to a corner and faced away as if Rudd's name were being announced, ground his feet like crushing bugs, plotted how his arms would go. Twice he glanced at the clock, and ticked the time off in his mind, turned as the bell was about to strike and scrabbled a cross in case he hadn't done it right before.

Most anybody would exchange hands at first, a lead for a lead, a cross for a cross, in a study period, but not Rudd. He probably couldn't lead, he was so crude. Plod and halt, plod and halt was his pattern—halt if he could drag his legs underneath him fast enough. His gloves pointed at each other by his stomach, making no defense attempt. Kelly jabbed him as Straws had suggested and the reaction was an uppercut one-two, the right hand's path a mirror of the left's. Neither got to Kelly; he stepped back. Rudd, ungainly guy, hadn't any follow-up or plan—jabbing him you might as well have pressed a button which turned out uppercuts and roundhouses and looping overhands; the last two he threw only in excitement. And the side of the glove seemed the same as the punch of the glove to him. He didn't care. Everything went all out. Everything was spadework for a K.O. He had no subtleties or medium attack.

Kelly put his hands further from his body than usual and hit Rudd with straight things to keep him off—not that it bothered Rudd so much, but his arms were shorter than Kelly's. He was the opposite of a counterpuncher, being entirely aggressive, but he acted like one with those automatic uppercut answers to each of Kelly's jabs. He had a horseshoe in his glove—Kelly's forearms caught the uppercuts and even there they hurt. Kelly warmed more to the round and stung Rudd with a combination to the head which at least made him lift his arms. The next one he sloughed aside like a snowplow, as elementarily as that. Kelly grinned across his mouthpiece at Rudd's crudeness. Pretty soon he'd quit this caution and slug naturally, working from the body up. He winged a straight long left to Rudd's mustache and curved a right which ended on his eye and dug a left hook to his heart. All went through.

It seemed like he could score at will, because Rudd's arms were down. What doing? Kelly's belly almost left him, that's what! The second uppercut—no aim adjustment made for Kelly's doubling up—hit Kelly's chest. The third, immediately after it, from the left hand again, would have rubbered Kelly flat except he stumbled to the side. Instead of his chin it hit his shoulder. He was way down, face gargoyled in pain, clutching his arm across his middle and trying to pry his head in underneath them. He couldn't have stuck his arms out for a clinch, his belly was too caved; it hurt like a vicious cramp. He quavered backwards as though on ice, groping with his feet. Rudd kept throwing, misses because Kelly had moved, sometimes roundhouses instead of uppercuts, although the arc made was the same. Ponderous, Rudd pushed after Kelly, but Kelly could go faster and gradually recovered, his cockiness not wholly scared away.

What a funny fighter! Western-movie-type: no punching volume, only force in what he threw. The trainers had accomplished nothing except stretch him out to go ten rounds. All that remained for them to do was give him his feet and a guard and teach him to lead and to hook and to jab and to cross! Kelly would stick him with jabs, and there was a sneak straight right he'd called on in the old days, and his rainbow right brought down from the sky. Power-crazy Rudd with his windmills from ten feet out should be no permanent problem—he didn't even seem to keep track of where his own hands were, but would sort of discover them before he punched. Ugly, octopussy style. Kelly hung out of Rudd's range and sent him stuff which had gone soft by the time it landed. But he reached his eyes. After all the receding they'd done and the cartilage surrounding them, still they could be reached, and got their corners cut each feature bout. Kelly'd frame a mouse around both eyes.

When Kelly came to closer quarters, Rudd began to shove. Strange shoves, the purpose not to set up Kelly for a punch, but to set himself! Kelly was a sack of something to be lifted, and all Rudd thought he needed was the leverage. He'd try to tip him in the right direction with a shoulder jostle and put his head against his neck and place his feet, and then let blast; of course Kelly wouldn't have it go that far, and Rudd was anything but hard to fool because the fact of Kelly's being a human, not a sack, came as a surprise. Blocking those uppercuts was murder on the wrists and elbows, though, and once when Kelly grabbed Rudd to tie him up he found he couldn't hold him—he couldn't clinch! So what to do, stand and trade blockbusters with the guy, or spar and run and guard his health? He had no choice. *That* missed Kelly, and *that* did too, thank God, and Kelly landed one, he thought. But Rudd was happy to take five in order to throw two. Rudd lurched, ape-footed, heaving up his paws. On TV when his man was macaroni on the ropes he'd go into a wild and stamping dance with punches flung exultantly as whoops. Study him, study him, Kelly told himself. He was giving up the possibility of looking very good. Cautiously he held him off. Rudd was familiar with delaying games, but he didn't make allowances for them, didn't even get mad. Mad, he couldn't have swung any harder. "Work, Charlie! Mix, Charlie!" yelled a fan. Kelly backed away, thankful Rudd was slow. He tried again to tie him up. The arms that clung onto Rudd were no stronger than two noodles; into his stomach big bombs burst. He got away sick with pain. To fight a guy he couldn't neutralize by clinching was terrifying. Hit him and run, hit him and run was the only way to last, and Rudd had learned Kelly's rhythms now, such as they were, and went after him quicker. Kelly was trapped and hurt twice in the corners right in the belly. He couldn't punch free. He pulled himself out by a rope one time, wobbling in pain; the next he caught hold of Rudd's head and tried to bang it on a ring post. Rudd's trainer shouted angrily.

They tapped each other on the head and on the fanny at the bell and circled the ring in opposite directions until they came around to where Rudd's trainer stood. Kelly leaned on the rope, exhaustedly resting. The trainer would have lagged with Rudd, but Rudd wouldn't let him, made him give Kelly attention. Kelly's nose, cheeks and forehead were regreased, also his gloves, to protect Rudd (whose hadn't been). His mouthpiece was rinsed and crammed back in his mouth. His chin strap was yanked insultingly. "Fight him!"

He hated to leave the ropes, his middle was so tender. The bell alone was a stimulus to Rudd, who started lifting uppercuts immediately. But Kelly flared: the "Fight him" and his trapped imminence of being clobbered. The very ropes were wrapped in cloth a funeral black. He closed with Rudd and slugged, which was his natural fight and not the sharp-shooting boxing. He used long rights and overhands and long left hooks that packed their power at a distance where Rudd's shorter stuff would not. It was a pleasure to his arms, and sweat flew off Rudd laughably wherever he got hit. He smacked him in the throat and made him gag, then had to move away in front of Rudd's slow, dragging charge. Moving meant he couldn't hold his range; either he missed or else Rudd grazed him. Rudd was a machine, with unvarying swings. All of a sudden Kelly shook him with a looping right which flattened the glove and, while the moment lasted, frenziedly swarmed him with close-quarter chops and hooks downstairs to disembowel him.

What Rudd returned to Kelly drove his stomach to his backbone. It collapsed him. He got more. He didn't count the punches. His legs would still work, compared to the rest of his body. Palsied, they carried him back, Rudd following and landing. Nothing hit belt-line like the first, but gloves blitzed into his face and chest. At each one Kelly's whole body shivered uncontrollably. He groped backward, trembly-legged. Rudd followed with the dragging gait. Kelly pushed out his arms to hold him off and fought the shakes and fought to clear his mind. *Jab! Jab him!* he started to remember, when he felt the ropes against his spine. He jabbed with both hands desperately, but Rudd plunged through and hit him on the lowest rib, hit him on the lungs and hit him on the liver. Kelly couldn't breathe. He was smothering with pain. His legs went trembling stiff; his head dropped forward. Rudd hit and knocked the mouth-piece out and nearly tore the hinging off the jaw. Kelly put his face into his palms and, half-unconscious, bent between Rudd's gloves. He couldn't move or hide or breathe. . . .

Rudd supported him against the ropes. Kelly clung around his shoulders, clumsy, coming to. With the action of actually help-ing and raising him, Rudd began slow-motion uppercuts, so as not to stall the round. A little while and Kelly crossed his arms and let Rudd use more force on them and fifteen seconds later was answering with tappings of his own. The middle minute passed in light and dream barragings of each other, perfect punches hard as pats. When Kelly put some bite in his, so did Rudd, and, Kelly having cleared his head, the fight resumed except Rudd remained outside of Kelly's jabs.

Kelly's mind and reflexes were functioning okay, recover-ing. The pain had numbed and wasn't hampering him. But, like a pro, Rudd watched the clock, and like a twenty-two-year-old, he couldn't bear to goof around the last few seconds. He plowed through Kelly's jabs and socked. Kelly was a bag of sand for him to lift. Lift him he did with belly punches and, like a sack being slit and emptied, Kelly sank away to shapelessness. The strength slid out of him like so much sand and he clung limply, slobbering on Rudd's shoulder. Rudd spanked his ass. The people clapped.

Crackers stripped off Kelly's stuff and Kelly fixed his eyes on him as if he were a doctor; he wanted to sit down but Crack-ers wouldn't let him. Crackers' face was screwed into the lines he wore when tending battered boys. "We yelled at him when he was lickin' you so bad, but you know how they never hear. He's worse, he's dumb." Kelly didn't try to speak. He wanted to lie down. Crackers kept examining him for cuts; he must be red. Finally Crackers shrugged and slipped from under him, so that he couldn't lean, and patted him and left him with a towel.

A towel. He focused on the fact of holding it, and touched his midriff gingerly and flinched. His eyes were fuzzed. In arena fights he'd taken maybe two or three beatings like this, when he was much younger. He groaned and was ashamed of groaning. He'd better not sit down; his body troubles would just harden on him. Actually his jaw was the sorest, but nobody minded a sore jaw as much. He walked a little bit. Two rounds in a gym—was it Rudd or was it him? Didn't matter, this was quits—he'd started coming again mostly to kill time; never again. A trainer and a fighter were arguing. What was there to argue about, how bad your organs were being rearranged? Kelly walked gently, not to let the pains harden.

A woman was in the gym, on spike heels, and stacked, and colored with an orange stripe up her hair. Kelly wondered if she belonged to Rudd, because he ought to have a good one. With any sort of a manager to move him he would move and Kelly might be telling grandkids of the day when he'd been walloped by a champ. Rudd's new partner was faring better. He was skinny, with ingratiating eyes, and was simply blocking punches, nothing else, and so he wasn't getting tagged. Oh, he'd feel for a chance to use his hook, which was his treasure obviously, but never more than started it. A trainer watched, placid and motionless, and next to him a peppy youngster bobbed and bounced, exercising, pumping his arms and simultaneously chattering gaily to the trainer, although the trainer gave no evidence of listening. The youngster's sweated hair poked wildly in all directions, while the trainer's stayed correctly combed. Kelly's middle grew more tender as the numbness lessened. Kelly would be like the trainer, not the youngster, from now on.

"Pretty tough boy, hey? Yeah, I wish I had him. Who doesn't?" Straws glanced over Kelly's frame for bruises. "Good experience for you to box him and you're lucky—anybody else'll seem easy.

His manager says he will still let you box him and a little later he'll start paying you. You remember how he said he'd pay you?"

Kelly stared at Straws, unbelieving.

"You remember, don't you?" Straws chuckled nervously, patted Kelly. "Yesterday he said the last week he would pay you, son."

"You'll make me cry!" Kelly burst out. "You don't want to lose your lousy cheap three bucks you paid DeJesus! You're afraid to lose three bucks! You'd drop me afterwards and when you finished taking out expenses I couldn't buy a candy bar with what you left—and I'd be in the hospital!"

"You're a catcher, you're a bum!" Straws snarled and backed away as though from something vile and went to Crackers, thumbing at Kelly with a bitter-twisted mouth. Crackers gave no sign of a reaction, didn't even shrug. Straws went around to managers and thumbed. Some laughed at him for having gotten stung; some said so Kelly heard: "He don't like it, he don't work," and looked at Kelly bleakly. They had you if you still wanted to box, but Kelly didn't. He showered slowly, trying to sponge the pain away, slowly pulled on his civilian clothes, put his store teeth in his mouth—the crusher in his present mood—and sat caved in. He tried to talk to Peapod and his voice squeaked from the belting of the voicebox; his nose, swollen, hindered too. You had to go on living your whole life after you quit boxing. You couldn't be all busted up inside and sick and crippled because you'd taken extra punches when you'd got too old. A kid paraded to the mirror naked, a little jiggling nod of pride accompanying each step. It wasn't only stuck up kids who jiggle-headed when they walked, but punchdrunks too; except a punchdrunk couldn't help it, and his face was molded grisly as a burlesque queen campaigner's, instead of, like the kid's, being snottily untouched.

Circus Dawn

THE HIGHWAY TEEMED with people and cars. More and more the town was waking up to the terrific fact it had a circus in its lap. Cars were stopping. Cars were pulling off the highway. Hardly any went by, unless to turn around at the gate of the amusement park. The convoys of circus trucks had to thread their wagon trains through a bottleneck of cars, something they were expert at. But every once in a while a big interstate diesel truck hove in sight cruising along on a schedule. The old electric horn would blaaaat, blaaaat and the air brakes f'ch-sssssssssss-f'ch! The driver'd be cursing, knowing if it wasn't a million-dollar fire it must be a circus to jam up things at this hour of the morning.

The cars were from both directions, the fathers bending to the windshields as they drove and the rest of the family almost out the windows watching for the lot. The cookhouse they sighted first, since nothing else was up. Arms pointed. "There it is! There it is!" The cars eased cautiously onto the grass. The families piled out and clustered with neighbors from home to chat about how exciting it was, all the funny-shaped, colorful wagons, and how much land it took, and was that tent there (the cookhouse) the big top? Was this the whole circus? The parents joking about how long it had been since they were up so early and agreeing they should have brought rubbers and this was an experience children mustn't miss. The kids tugged. "We'll be late! They're *doing* it all!" The parents lagged stodgily, still overcome with their virtue and accomplishment in getting even this far, and worrying about wet feet. . . .

Chief and Fiddler luckily were out of earshot. Just looking at a mass of townies, Fiddler could hear the chatter in his ears, from so many, many towns, always the same chat. It was better when the sun wasn't up and they were mere silhouettes—a whole horizon dark sometimes with townies—or on a foggy morning when you'd have to figure out where voices came from, if you wanted to. These were precious minutes while the townies lingered near the highway. Soon they'd be everywhere, like gnats.

The Seat men and their buddies appeared on the edge of the lot by the highway. They must have walked from the diner. A single figure separated from them and strode to a parked jeep, jumped in, and barreled toward Chief and Fiddler. Chief chuckled, "Boss! It's the Boss, boy!" which meant it was the Boss Chief, the Head Canvasman. The jeep was equipped with stake driving apparatus. The Boss Chief would put in the little clumps of stakes that anchored the big top's center poles. White people called him "Chief" like any other Indian, but the Indians had named him "Boss" because he was the only one of them to reach a boss status and get paid like a boss. The Boss Chief was minus an ear. As a kid he'd bet somebody his ear against theirs, the story went, and lost. Then he'd turned more serious—become a boss.

"They must have been telling him their troubles," Fiddler said.

Candle flames flickered in the depths of Chief's eyes. He didn't reply. He hurried to meet his friend, Fiddler after him, kicking through the grass. The grass grew shin high. The cats and elephants and ponderous seat wagons hadn't stomped over it yet. It wasn't as lush or as Irish green in the sun as grass on the eastern lots, but brown and nice still. The show would take the ginger out of it. The grass would grow after the show left, but not like before.

The Boss Chief skidded his jeep to a halt. The pair of bright-eyed Indians punched each other mockingly.

"I see you got it all laid out, Mr. Menagerie Chief."

"Yeah, I got it fixed. Where's your tent? Where's your poles? Where's your blasted tent?"

"We're waiting on you! You ain't spotted all your wagons yet. You ain't even got your train unloaded." Then the Boss Chief quit fooling. "Was your boy with you?"

"Him? He was sleeping, weren't you, Fiddle? He was in bed." The tone of voice was not so much scornful as matter of fact.—Is he of age?—Not yet. Fiddler flushed.

"Maybe it'ud been better if you'd both been in bed," said the Boss. He was speaking as a Boss. In spite of his grave expression, his eyes glittered in sympathy with Chief.

"But he did pretty good this morning."

"Yeah?"

The circus water trucks hauled a whole slew of wagons onto the lot—the runner raced in front, beckoning directions—then cut them loose and powered away, just as quick as that. "There are the cages!" shouted Fiddler. The big lay-out Cat clacked and clanked toward the wagons as fast as it could, the little pinman hanging on behind like a monkey. The cat seemed certain to bulldoze right into the wagons but at the last instant spun in its tracks, hooked on to a string. It was cages, but the wrong ones, the act cages and the dog wagon. Fiddler had to be patient. The lay-out cat maneuvered, snorting and starting and stopping, and the pinman bobbed on and off, unhooking the wagons one by one. Then the cat returned to the lot entrance and pulled Fiddler's entire line of cages into the deep grass behind the cookhouse, where he wanted them. They rolled prim and well-kept-looking behind the big cat. He was proud of them.

"He's got to see his babies," Chief laughed as Fiddler rushed off.

The cages were behind Number 4 Wagon, the Ice Box, in two-foot grass where the manure could be raked out and left as it fell. The pinman scarcely had a chance to chock the wheels before the townies were on the spot to find out what was up. The lay-out cat steamed at them as it went and scattered them momentarily. Fiddler opened his tiger cage just to look at "his girl," say good morning. The townies scurried and swirled in his wake. She came to the bars with a flat, blank, murderous sheen in her eyes for the townies. He stood within easy range of her paws; his face nearly brushed against hers at the bars. Past his ear she roared her tiger's roar—more abrupt than a lion's, bristling with the actual sound of breath, like a gasp, titanic. Fiddler could hear the townies trip over themselves as they fled back.

But then they were coming again. "What in the world have you got there?"

"Yes, ma'am," he said, and shut the cage. The lady had folds in her neck like a chicken's wattles.

The lay-out cat returned with more cages and put them behind the first string. Frank, the rhino, had pried the boards off the bars of his cage; the fastenings weren't right. He was exposed to the public when he shouldn't have been, bumping his horn on the bars, boisterously swinging his head as if he was aiming a home run.

Like a conscientious soul, the pinman suggested, "You better tell the guy who takes care of him, that batty guy that talks to himself."

"I can do it," Fiddler replied. He petted Frank, reached between the bars and took hold of Frank's head, laid his arms along both sides of Frank's face. The head remained still. The eyes closed blissfully.

"He'll break your arms to bits, kid!" the pinman warned. "I've seen you do the stupidest—" The cat lurched and carried him off clasped on for dear life, the nosy son of a bitch. What business was it of his? What a sucker's job he had.

Frank's head was formed like a turtle's, even to the hooked lip and dull turtle eyes; but his ears flared out like the bells of trumpets and his horn was wedge-shaped, high. His body was big as a bus, long, made for ramming. Frank closed his eyes, let out a deep breath and propped himself on his elbows to be petted. Fiddler scratched behind the huge ears, over the eyes and in the itchy areas at the base of the horn.

"What's his name, mister?" a kid asked.

"Frank."

"Can I touch him?"

The people were crowded around. They'd blow cigarette smoke in Frank's eyes and get their fingers crushed—more than their fingers if you gave them time. Fiddler started boarding up the cage. He was trying to make the fastenings stick when—"Number 12, hey, Fiddler!" Red sang out in the distance. Fiddler glanced between the cages. Yes, the wagon was there. He had to leave Frank's cage no better than he'd found it. Kids were climbing on all the wagons, peeking in the air vents.

"Get off there! They'll scratch out your eyes!" Fiddler yelled. He didn't wait to see the results because they were always discouraging. The day's work had begun.

The lay-out cat driver set Number 12 Wagon precisely where Brownie wanted it, next to his truck, and Brownie gave him a salute. The Animal Department in full, impressive muster moved forward to help unload the wagon. There was Taylor the madman, Brownie, the boss, and Coca Cola—the wagon ladder almost came down on Coca Cola's head when they opened the door; he didn't have the co-ordination to get out of the way; Chief caught it and saved him—there was Coca Cola who'd graduated to Coca Cola and aspirin from wine, and Chief, Fiddler, Red.

After the ladder, the next thing out of the wagon was Nigas, the Department's dog. His real master was serving a life sentence for murder, so he belonged to everybody. He was fox-red, small, spunky, with eyes black and hard as two beads. He was in ecstasy to be free in the sun and grass with Chief, Fiddler, and Brownie, his favorites. After Nigas, the wheelbarrow came out and the stakes, hammers, the water barrels for humans and animals, the top, the poles from the wall racks, the butchering board and sawhorses, the axe, shovel, cage tools—brushes and scrapers—the crum boxes, and the stray tiger cub in its cage. Everything was painted red except the tiger cub and the top. The Animal Department's color was red.

Fiddler went up on the wagon and caught the ropes that were thrown to him and lashed one end of the top to the wagon. Meanwhile Chief drove five stakes, shocking them into the earth a foot at a blow with his big sixteen-pound sledge. The canvas went up, the poles were set, the lines were noosed to the stakes and guyed out, and the flaps of the top tied out for ventilation. Next door the horse tops were going up, although the horses hadn't come up from the crossing yet, and Murphy, the Ringstock dog, was running and barking like Nigas. The Animal men were lucky in not having to put up much canvas. Their cages were exhibited in the big top, so they only needed a shelter large enough for themselves. The crum boxes were placed in a square inside the top. Coca Cola had to open his right up and burrow after aspirin and Coke amongst his crummy stuff to send him into Happyland. "Crum" box was the word for his.

Chief grabbed a scraper, stakes, and his hammer. Fiddler took the broom and a coil of rope. The scraper and broom were each iron rods about ten feet long, the scraper having a small iron bar at one end instead of a brush. They were toted on the shoulder. They see-sawed when you walked, and all the townies wondered what they were for and followed to find out.

The lot was still bare and open. The four ticket wagons and the silver office wagon were spotted at the front of what would be the big top—the sideshow would be catty-corner to them—and the commissary wagon marked the middle of the backyard, with the cookhouse on one side and the Wardrobe and Band wagons in the process of being spotted beside the half-raised horse tops at the other. The cookhouse was up; the sideshow poles were up; the horse top canvas was stretched out on the ground, billowing a little wherever a breeze could get under it. But in the center of it all the grass grew undisturbed. There wasn't a pole or a bundle of canvas. The stake drivers had hardly gotten a fourth of the way around.

Passing the cookhouse, Fiddler and Chief could smell the ham cooking, the biscuits, the Cream of Wheat. Fiddler was hungry as hell. When they reached the cages, there were the same kids climbing to peer in the upper vents. "Get off there; they'll claw your eyes out!" Fiddler ordered.

"*Get down off there!*" said Chief.

They did.

Chief drove the row of stakes faster than Fiddler could tie the rope between them. The people ranked themselves along the rope, holding on to it. You had to give them something to hold on to or they'd simply press closer and closer to the cage until they were pushed up against the bars and you were pushed against the bars and they could hold on to the bars. Mothers would lift up babies to kiss the lion's nose. It was unbelievable. Even using the rope, when the first wagon was opened, the leopards' wagon, some kid got carried away and ran under the rope and nearly escaped Chief's arm. The leopards were crazy to get him, lunging with their paws—he was almost close enough. Chief chased the kid back. The mother wagged her finger at the naughty child to play such a prank when the man didn't want him in there.

Chief worked fast. There was never a chance to fool with the animals when Chief was there because he worked fast. He put the pressure on Fiddler and deliberately kept him from playing with the cats. Earlier, Fiddler's petting the animals had been a point of argument with them, but now Chief just stopped him whenever he could. "Get your hands outa there!" he'd say. Chief would give each cage a rough once-over with the scraper, pulling out the dung. Then he'd go back and cut the meat, fill the wheelbarrow and come with it—and Fiddler had better be through. It was Fiddler's job to brush the residue of straw out of the cages so the floors would be clean for the cats to eat off of. "Clean as your plate," Chief said.

"Are they tame?" a voice asked, presumably referring to the leopards.

"Nope," said Fiddler. Chief didn't answer questions, which was the best policy if you could block your ears and not hear them repeated and repeated and repeated. Of course, the questions were repeated and repeated and repeated even when you answered them, because new people came.

"Across the wide Missouri!" Chief boomed out tunelessly for no reason and turned to Fiddler with a toothy grin—a missing-toothy grin.

"Missouri?"

"Sure!"

"Missouri? Oh, yeah, that's where we are, isn't it? That's the river, the guy in the diner said."

"Sure, Missouri River! Big River! You had schooling, boy. You should know that stuff!"

The only other sign of drink in Chief besides this sudden out-burst was the headache wrinkles over his eyes, and he'd had those all morning.

"You should keep track where you are! I didn't have much school, but I know," Chief concluded.

There were five leopards: Rajah, Sweetheart, Taboo, who was black, and Minny, the fat one, and Rita, who was wilder than the day she'd been caught. They lived together harmoniously except when one of the females would get in heat and go stir-crazy. Rajah, being the only male, enjoyed himself. He had a large, square build and was supercilious when you petted him, demanding to inspect your hands, then stalking back and forth indifferently. Sweetheart was the gentle one. You could put your arms between her paws or stroke her lips or *kiss* her lips—Fiddler had done that once, as an experiment. Taboo was glossy black and slender, pretty, quite trustworthy. Minny was the old one, a fat, quiet, well-adjusted cat. Minny had a policy—not to try particularly to hurt someone she knew would not hurt her—an easy, lazy policy. You could pet her back and flanks and neck. She'd curl her upper lip but not really mind. Rita was the nuisance, lightning Rita always flattened in a corner, watching her chance. Her eyes were deep gray-blue and her spots were navy blue, not black. What should be white on a leopard was gray on Rita, so that sometimes she looked dingy. But now and then the blue would mingle with the gray and make her very beautiful, misty blue, loose-muscled, small and slim and gray. Fiddler would ache to touch her.

Chief worked like an automaton, it seemed to Fiddler. He was patient. He didn't hit the leopards. He let them get out of the way of the scraper. But he didn't pet them or treat them like friends. He just raked out their cage and went to the next; and Fiddler took over with the broom.

Fiddler avoided hitting the cats almost as well as Chief. Rajah, Sweetheart, and the panther, Taboo, were on their feet, prowling and sniffing. Minny was lying down but she'd get up when the broom nudged her and lie down somewhere else. Rita dashed at the bars if she felt threatened, and when she saw she couldn't reach

Fiddler she'd get out of the way. Sweetheart and Taboo stayed beside the bars, pacing fast in flowing, perpetual motions, one black, the other golden-yellow spotted black. They moved in opposite directions and never looked at each other, slipping by effortlessly. Rajah was master of the cage, so he wouldn't exercise in any one line. He marched obliquely from front to back and along the walls and across his females' paths. Rajah was unpredictable. Fiddler had to go slow to keep from hitting him with the broom.

How'd you like to have one 'uv them for a fur coat, Gin? —I'm sure I'd love it, dear, if you could ever buy it for me. I wonder if that bud ever gets in the cage with them damn'd things. When do they feed 'em? How dangerous are they in captivity? Those are what, panthers?—Leopards, silly.—One of them's a panther. He's black—. They've just painted him black—you can see his spots; look—you have to look carefully. Mister, when do they have the big tent up? Mister? I'd like to see him stick his hand in there.—Benny, you've seen more than enough. There are other things, Benny; come.

"They're beauties, aren't they?" a kid said to his girl, and he put his hand on her shoulder, twined his fingers in her hair and tickled her so she giggled and wriggled. "But not like *you*. You're prettier. You're much better." The lucky bastard!

From the highway drifted a funnel of dust and in the middle, in the clear space, pranced the horses, ready to perform, proud and prancing, white and palomino, brown, black and calico.

"The horses! The horses! Here comes the horses!" Fiddler shrieked sarcastically to watch the townies scuttle. He pointed and some of them did go, particularly the girls. They skipped away.

"Mommy, the horses! The horses!"

The leopards gyrated. The horse scent threaded in to them and they could catch a crack of a glimpse at the corner of the cage. They lay aquiver on their bellies, gorging on the sight. Their gulping eyes were brilliant. They shifted their feet to center the weight over the muscles—sprang! on-off the ledge above the door and caromed round and around and around the *top* of the cage eternally, never coming down. The leopards loop-the-looped, did edgewise figure eights across the cage from floor to ceiling. Fiddler snuck the broom in and out so cleverly it didn't interfere. But when he grasped the handle tight his hands hurt him; the scars were stiff and painful, turning reddish.

Some of the men on the horses were old, battered winos, who clung on through the kindness of the horses and who would have been much healthier not wearing clothes, their clothes were so filthy. Some were cowboys, who sat lackadaisically like burrs. And some were the ordinary stalwart, rough little half-pints who are always found around horses. The horses weren't bothered. The horses didn't care who or what was on them. They spraddled their legs or pussyfooted, clicked hooves, did tricks. They didn't wear saddles. They ignored their riders and came preened and prancing, nodding, nipping each other in a drove like spangled gypsy horses, like low-slow-frisky-flying flashy-painted tropic birds, like no horses Iowa ever could have seen before.

The crowd grew behind Fiddler. Newcomers more than replaced the horse enthusiasts and it would have required a staff of twenty expert sightseeing guides to answer all the questions. Fortunately one question drowned out another; all Fiddler heard was a babble. Most people seemed to get the idea that the big top was put up early in the morning. They would arrive far too soon for that great event. Others, intending to beat the first wagon to the lot and watch the first stake driven, would arrive much too late. In any case, flocks of townies appeared just when Fiddler was working and, whatever they had planned to see, they all hurried over to watch dirty straw being raked out of cages so dark the animals were sometimes mere shadows in them unless you were as close as Fiddler. The townies gathered and they yapped. *Which is the most fierce? Are these animals used in the ring? I wish he'd show us his claws; I wish he'd make him show us his claws. Could you explain. . . keeper, oh keeper, could you explain. . .*

The wagon next to the leopards' contained three separate cages. Three lion cubs were cramped into one, a cheetah was in another, and a barrel of a jaguar in the third.

Round as a lapdog and nearly the weight of a tiger, the jaguar was strange. Nobody understood him. He'd been with the show, in that same cage narrower than the length of his body, for many years. But his face looked young, unformed, like the face of an overgrown, lowering boy—a school bully's. Piggy eyes, eyebrows contracted. He was a riddle. He dreamed and dreamed all the time. He'd wake, whack the scraper, roar and chew the ornamentation on the bars, snap at somebody's hand. Then he'd doze off again and be safe as a rug for a day, sprawled out with his eyes rolling in dreams, rising only to drink water prodigiously whenever it was offered. The jaguar rubbed his chin on the bars. The musty, pleasant, early sunlight made him blink. His head was square, his coat as short as the fur of a lion and a deeper yellow than a leopard's coat, the bulls-eye spotted pattern more pronounced and striking. The most versatile of cats, with burly, wrestler lines, the bowed legs of a climber, the dense hair of a swimmer, and grizzly bear-sized teeth to fight an anaconda or a crocodile. The jaguar didn't give any trouble while Fiddler worked. He kept out of the way.

Beside the jaguar lived the cheetah. She was like a woman, nervous, light and slim. When she came in heat they would try to make love through the partition screening. It was ridiculous. She was shaped just the opposite from him. Her bones were long, quick, and the graceful muscles on her legs were for running, not clawing. She was dainty and cooperative, with nails and fur and flat flanks like a dog's, and only the small cat face to remind you what she was.

The cheetah's cage was as easy as the jaguar's and Fiddler was well started on it when there was a commotion between the wagons. A family straggled through. The mother had trouble getting over the wagon pole because of her skirts. "What's this, the animals?" she wondered.

"Do you see the rope, ma'am?"

"Where?" piped up the little girl, peering into the jaguar cage for a rope.

"Geez, he's big, I'll say, ain't he?" said the son, shoving close to the bars beside his sister. The collars of their sailor suits were at the level of the cage floor.

"Don't get hurt!" the mother warned.

"You see, ma'am, if you'd just stand behind the rope they wouldn't get killed," Fiddler explained with superhuman self-control. "The rest of the people are behind the rope and their children are safe." The jaguar's pudgy paws flexed unbelievingly. He edged forward. Fiddler decided not to let the lady "learn a lesson." He yanked the two kids back and sleepily the jaguar half struck at him instead.

"Oh! Help! Thank you very much!" the lady said.

"See, if you'd stand behind the rope—"

"Yes, we will, thank you; we were exploring. Come here, Joanie."

Fiddler's anger was a sodden lump in his chest. It didn't come out. He thrust his hand in the cheetah's cage and up to her face. She hissed like steam with pink, wide-open mouth. Her eyes stared away until they forgot, and she forgot, still staring away at nothing. Fiddler petted her slowly, gently tugging her ears. The townies *ooh*ed as if he were a hero. He pushed the cheetah aside and continued working. Fiddler used the broom methodically and well. Chief and he were proud of their cages.

Wasn't that lucky! Doesn't that man know his stuff, though, honey? What would happen if one of them things got loose! Huh? What would it do? —I can tell you what I'd do!

The lion cubs were seven months old and the general size of springer spaniels, with forelegs thick as Fiddler's arm and hard as blocks of wood. Their paws were swollen, immensely muscle-packed. The cubs had seen the horses briefly when the wagon was first opened. They'd bulled into each other scrambling for ways to get out and they'd kept it up because of the fresh air, the sudden flood of sunlight and moving, talking figures. Probably also the horse scent trailed across the lot from the Ringstock tops and kept them excited. But the moment the broom was in the cage they forgot everything else. The cubs were murder on the broom, piled on—40, 80, 120 pounds—took fat, chopping bites, clawed, and hung on. Fiddler sweated, even in the morning chill, and he was hungry and the cuts on his hands hurt from dragging the goddam broom out, jamming it in with them fighting it, pulling it out.

"Look out how you're doing, fool!" Something laid hold of the broom violently behind him. Trouble with the townies came in bunches.

Fiddler exploded. "Leggo of that!" A man had clamped on to the end of the broom with both hands. "Leggo, you stupid sonofabitch! What in hell do you think you're trying to do?"

"Can you see the child? You almost hit the child!" There was a kid inside the rope, a girl around six.

"Hit her! Can't you keep your goddam kids out of our way? We've got to clean these cages. We've got to watch these cats. We can't be watching what's behind us all the time!"

Chief was at the last cage in the line. He walked down, carrying his scraper high like a spear. "Listen, you mister, you keep your kids outa there! We ain't got eyes in the back of our heads! You keep your kids outa there!" Chief was drunk and grim. He was as tall as the townie and about three times as broad. His hair bushed up wild and black. The eyes were wedged in his iron-red face like two stones.

Ostentatiously the townie examined the kid's head for injuries. "All right," he said. Fiddler turned back to his work, making sure to be no more careful about what was getting in the way behind him than he'd been before.

"I didn't *misbehave* in a long time, Fiddle! When was the last time? Not for a long time till last night."

Always play along with a drunken Indian.

"In Chicago you went to every cathouse on Eighteenth Street and scared the wits out of all the nigger girls, and then in Milwaukee you went and told the giant his mother was a giraffe. He was a 'sonofagiraffe.'"

"Hah, hah, hah, hah, hah, hah, hah, hah! Yep! *He* wouldn't get down off that stage. I told him, 'Get down off there, you'—hah, hah, hah, hah— 'sonofagiraffe! We'll see who's bigger!' *He* wouldn't do it. 'Sober up, Chief! Sober up, Chief!' he said— he *squeaked!* That guy, he wouldn't get down. But that was in Wisconsin. Long time ago. I didn't do anything wrong since Wisconsin, boy. That's a long time."

"Yep."

Chief went back to the wagon he'd been working on, closed it, and left to fix the meat.

The best method of cleaning the cubs' cage seemed to be to pinch their tails and get them next to the bars and keep them frantic after one hand, pinching and snatching, while with the other you swept all the straw as near as possible, then really latch on to the broom and *pull*. Fiddler did. He finished with the cubs.

It's like a grab-bag! What's next? I remember from the first man! This is better than the circus. I'm glad we didn't sleep. Oh! Beautiful, tigers!

Ajax was so tall that, sitting down, the whole top half of his body was out of sight in the upper recesses of the cage. Even Fiddler at the bars had to stoop to look at him. *Let's see you touch him, mister! Naah, he don't dare.*

The lay-out cat spotted the elephant wagon, Number 31, just beyond the cages.

"You're late! Goddam to hell, you're late!" Bull men popped out of the grass and went to work like crazy because the bulls would be along any minute now.

"I'm late!" the driver gave it back. "The sonofabitchin' truck was late! You bastards'd —" The cat spun so sharp it hurled dirt clods in the bull men's faces and took off.

Snippy, Ajax's mate, watched, tentatively crouched down on her paws, her head cocked quizzically. She paced a quick circle in the cage and resumed her crouch.

"You, Snippy. What did you do?" said Fiddler, feeling warm with affection. She looked at him. Her eyes had just a glint of pink in the usual tiger gray. She didn't look at him for long. Her gaze streamed into the crowd and at the rhino, whose cage faced hers, and beyond. Her big body drew compact and then, instead of doing anything, she relaxed and looked at Fiddler idly. The gaze blurred; she looked past him. *Ooooh, it's scary! Lift me up! They could sure tear through a place, couldn't they? Now is that a male and her a female? They must know him. He certainly isn't afraid of them, is he? Henry, we need something like that to catch our mouse.*

Snippy got up and hurried in a tight circle and crouched lightly down again with the pink glint in her eyes that was not a color but a trick of light. But she was in the path of the broom. Fiddler tapped his fingers on her paw. Absent-mindedly she rose, circled the cage, came back, looked at him. The pupils of her eyes adjusted to the light. The black shrank and the gray replaced it, perfectly concentrically, as it transformed from black. Snippy looked over

Fiddler's shoulder, scanning the crowd. Her ears twitched back. Somehow, somewhere she'd developed such a hatred for certain people in the show—the sideshow impresarios with their tuxedos and sharpie, grease-slicked hair, for instance—that she'd pick them out of multitudes of people and keep a bead on them, roar and rage if they got near. "It's too early, Snippy," Fiddler told her. "They're not here." She padded in a circle, crouched softly and stared past him, not searching for anybody now, just staring.

"Johnny! Say, Johnny! Johnny . . . Johnny!"

From experience Fiddler had learned "Johnny" or "Jimmy-Mike-Bob-Harry" meant him, and that if he didn't want to be shouted at for the rest of the morning he'd better answer this particular type of guy.

"Yep?"

"How do they catch a thing like that?"

"I don't know," Fiddler said to cut the conversation off.

"They dig a hole in the jungle, don't they? And cover it with stuff so's something'll fall in?"

"If you know, why do you ask?"

"'Cause that's how I caught my wife!"

"George!" squawked a woman. People snickered.

Ajax sat peacefully while the cage was being cleaned. When Fiddler told him to change sides he did, pausing only to bend and look out at a dog which was barking. The dog yipped and ran. Ajax was so enormous the bars were actually no bigger than some of his stripes. When he sat down, again the upper half of his body was hidden from sight. *Whew! Jesus Christ, I'd give a year's pay to shoot something like that! Would he eat me? Poke him so he'll get down so we can look at him. How much would that big feller weigh? How much do you feed him in a week?*

Frank, the rhino across the way, raised a rumpus when he saw Ajax. He aimed his horn and plunged at the bars. Some of the people were afraid he'd bust loose; they pushed back. Taylor was raking out the cage and he kept right on. When Frank calmed down the people began to throng in toward the cage again but then they stopped as if they'd come up against a brick wall. Taylor didn't use bricks to make room to work in. He didn't even need a rope.

Taylor talked. "My penitentiary name, yaah, Taylor. I'm ex-con." Fiddler could hear a smattering of words and he could read the lips; he knew the words from hours of listening to them. Naturally, today Taylor was discussing The Downfall of Heavy, the Porter: "He's here some place, the guy wha' killed 'um. He killed by beatin'—two did. They beat 'um —Heavy—he tol' me to make him a suit, he used to tell me that. 'I ain't no tailor! Screw ya! That's my penitentiary name! I ain't no tailor! Lissen!' I told 'um. He was askin' for it. I coulda told 'um in Des Moines. He was a boob! He was booby! He oughta huv' been in the hatch! They oughta huv' got 'um with the striped suits! 'I'll make ya a *striped* suit,' I told 'um once time, '*Striped!*'—hah, hah, hah, hah, hah, hah, hah, yaah! 'Ya're a boob!' I told 'um."

People couldn't stand to have that kind of thing spewed in their ear. The townies wavered back, gawking at Taylor as much as at the rhino. But every once in a while some new person would barge into the vacant space, dragging and lecturing children and not paying any attention. He'd get a load of Taylor in his ear, a real blast from behind, from ambush, and jump like a shot deer—"The guy wha' killed 'um. He's here some place."—and peep around for Heavy's murderers, for penitentiary guards, and wilt out of hearing. When one young man made the error of laughing! "Tee-hee, tee-hee all ya want!" Taylor gabbled, foaming. "Tee-hee, yaah, tee-hee! Tee-hee! Tee-hee! But they beat 'um. An' oh they took 'um and beat 'um so the blood came out 'uv his sides and in his ears. I saw it. They had 'um down. They took him and beat 'um. You c'n tee-hee!" Taylor threw himself on the ground, shielded his head with his arms, thrashed and struggled, made gushing motions in front of his mouth and ears. The people cleared out. They came to watch Fiddler. Taylor got up, continued working and talking to "'umself," and Fiddler had double the crowd to cope with.

The second tiger wagon was harder to clean. The male was almost as large as Ajax and he wasn't sitting quietly. He pawed the female and she laced him with her pretty orange paws. He was panting. Saliva bubbles showed on his chin and the ruff of fur on the back of his neck was mussed. He couldn't stay away—traipsing back and forth, every which way, all heated up, much too big for the cage, as big as four men in a bathroom. Beautifully she snarled with ivory teeth white as the fur on her face and lips as black as the blackest stripe. Her face was round like a prize pussycat's— the fur stuck out in a collar. She was gorgeous. When the broom blundered too near she sprang, grabbed it seemed like a yard out of the cage at Fiddler, dropped a roar like a pile driver on him. She jumped back then and bounded across the broom, turned, snapped it up but let go instantly before Fiddler could even brace for a fight. And the male kept beside her step by step, sometimes with his tongue out to lick and sometimes with that hot mouth yawned and the four tusks like thumbs ready to catch her head and hold her still. The head bobbed and the jaws that could have enclosed it glided over, flexing. She boxed his ears. She stung his nose. With her starched, prim frills of creamy fur, her orange paws and black paint-stroked, yolk-yellow body, she boxed his ears.

The trucks towed the first series of floats, each neatly draped with canvas, onto the lot. The flags went up the cookhouse poles, Old Glory and the "Hotel" flag which meant it was time to eat. A hundred bums and winos began pulling themselves out of hibernation in the grass. Fiddler could see at least a hundred. It was amazing how huge a personnel the circus had at mealtimes. Chief appeared down at the leopard cage with the meat. The winos were making cracks about "breakfast" as they passed the wheelbarrow on their way to eat. Fiddler finished with the tigers in a hurry. He did very well, considering what was going on in the wagon. *What's the scoop? Is the big tiger trying to eat the little one? Do these animals become tame for you when you take care of them? Is it true that a lion is the king of beasts? We've made a bet.*

The coarse sand-and-turpentine lion smell gave the last wagon away. It smelled as good as any perfume to Fiddler. He loved it. Big Joe was lying right by the bars and Fiddler sunk his hands in the handsome red mane, hiding even his wrists in it. "You Joe!" he said. Joe grimaced and bit the air irritably but couldn't turn for Fiddler without some effort because Fiddler had caught him sideways to the bars. Before Joe decided to make the effort Fiddler had him enjoying it, squinting, rubbing his ear on Fiddler's arm and groaning with the pleasure of being scratched deep under his mane.

Far across the lot the elephants came gallumphing, bugling split-off noises. The bull men rode, some on the necks and some on the heads, holding on to a corner of an ear and letting their boots dangle down between the eyes—in the circus, all the "bulls" were females. The best bulls briskly wore their men like hats and gallumphed so rhythmically the men went up and down like sailors and could sit with no hands and their eyes closed. Bingo, in fact, rode with no hands. He only had one and he probably had fleas; his hand was busy. The lead bull, Ruth, the queen bull, carried Bingo. She pretended she was going to toss him off. She trumpeted and flapped her ears in preparation. Bingo wasn't a bit disturbed. He called her bluff.

The elephant boss rode a gray horse which kept the bulls in line by butting and bullying them—a real swashbuckling horse. On the highway that horse not only bullied the bulls but also the townspeople's cars, cleared them out of the way, and on the lot its job was forcing paths through the mobs of people. It was the toughest, cockiest horse in the world.

The bulls had been traveling fast from the crossing—the horse had made them—but now they eased up and shouldered through the clustered wagons. Their trunks swept above the grass and wrenched out clumps as people flick a finger. They held their heads steady so the bull men wouldn't be thrown off but let their snake trunks play and curve and snuffle up Black-eyed Susans in the grass, empty Crackerjack boxes. Today the bulls were brown. Elephants were supposed to be gray—everyone knew that; zoo elephants were gray. Even the bull boss's horse was a pachydermous gray. But the bulls themselves only looked gray when the town they happened to be in had gray dust. They were covered with dust. They blew it on themselves, they collected it, they prided themselves on it, grew bristles on their backs especially to catch it. Like chameleons, they changed color as they moved from place to place. If a freak town had red dust or white dust the bulls were red or white that day. Iowa's dust made them brown and they chugged along, swaying from foot to foot. The horse lined them up in the high grass where they would be out of the way of the rest of the circus and the bull boss dismounted, uncoiled his black whip, laid the lash on the ground. The men grabbed hold of an ear and slid off or clung to a trunk and were lifted down.

There was an Indian on bulls. Daisy, his elephant, was the tallest of the herd and he took advantage of her height by standing on the crest of her head and shouting, "Chief! Hey Wampus!" Daisy cradled him with her trunk and set him down.

The bull boss cracked and slithered his whip, holding the bulls in a row and not minding at all if an occasional backlash kept the townies out of his hair. More than half Fiddler's audience had left to see the elephants. From every part of the lot the townies were running—kids and fathers and older sisters and mothers, strung out in that order. The poor bull men, trundling bales of hay, were having a hell of a time in the traffic.

"Rope them off!" Fiddler laughed, secure behind his stakes, when three kids tumbled under the lion wagon screeching "El'-phants" and just about rollblocked his legs from under him. People dashed for the elephants as if for the end of a rainbow. Hallelujah! But the bull boss kept an incompressible zone of fifty-one feet between the bulls and the townies. He was in the center. His whip was twenty-five feet long.

The bulls rocked backward and forward like pitchers winding up, tossed their trunks up and down. Finally the hay was brought. The bulls broke the wire binding of the bales for themselves. They stepped on the bales and let their weight crush down, all the time solemnly waving their trunks like massive wands. Then the trunks plunked down, furled mouthfuls of hay. The elephants ate.

In the lion wagon Bessie growled, sounding like gears stripping. Joe would get up for the broom but not Bessie. She made a terrible, crinkled-up face and glared like a child in the quiet stage of a temper tantrum. Fiddler aimed the broom to hit her in the soft spot behind the elbow on the side. Bessie blocked it, jerking her elbow back with a grinding, crotchety growl. The tigers would have been hopping and roaring, they were so nervous, but Bessie chewed the broom lazily, lying down. Something on it must have tasted very bad, because her lips drew up; she let go and acted as if she were going to sneeze. Her lips scrunched up so high Fiddler could see every one of her teeth, even the molars. She got up, gave up, and stood out of the way. She scraped her tongue between her teeth and growled to herself a scratchy, feathery growl.

Chief-on-Bulls came under the rope to escape the crowd. He was going to see Chief. "How's your Chief, kid?"

"He'll be fine if we can get him sober."

"Where was you last night, Bullfrog?" Chief demanded loud as a bull from where he was feeding the jaguar. The three of them, Little Chief, Chief-on-Bulls, and Fiddler's own Chief, had traveled together in 127 car and been buddies since Chicago; but Chief-on-Bulls hadn't been there last night.

"Nooky! Nooky, you cat-taming sonofabitch! We had a girl on the flats! We took a girl out'uv Sioux City. They must'uv had the alarms ringin' last night. We had her in the Columbus Discovers America float, with the canvas over—cozy, dark, plenty of space."

"What is this story?" blurted a shocked matron.

"You got a daughter, lady? You keep her home tonight, unless you want her Discovering America!"

Chief made the animals work to get their meat. He made them pull it through the bars. The jaguar's arm was far out of the cage, fastened on to a piece. "Git it! Git it!" shouted Chief-on-Bulls, punching one hand into the other and strolling down toward Chief. He was tall and raw-boned, with a Roman nose. He was Alaskan. He'd sailed south on a fishing boat to Seattle and started bumming east to see "the States." But by the time he'd reached Chicago he was ready to turn right around, join the show, and head west again to go back home.

"You brave?" Chief challenged, loud so everyone could hear.

"I can tar the daylights out of *you!*"

"You see them cubs? You feed them baby cubs, let's see you. Fiddle'll teach you how. Come here, Fiddler!"

Fiddler came.

The bull man took a couple of chunks of meat and the lion cubs struck at them so fast reflexes saved him from a scratching, nothing else. He jumped. "Wow, Devils!"

Chief grinned and bent next to the cheetah's cage with a tongue-shaped, bloody piece of liver. "Whatcha gonna do, Cheet?"

Cheetah crept to the bars with mouth stretched full-open, dribbling, hissing, eyes insane. Chief, delighted, hissed back, dangled the meat close to the bars, where Cheetah jabbed at it with helpless dog-feet. She stamped on his hands as they snuck in the cage and teased her feet. Chief laughed and hissed. Cheetah dripped saliva on the floor and hunched in desperation, mewed. Chief mimicked the mew and finally let her snatch away the meat.

Fiddler didn't know whether he thought that kind of thing was right to do. He went back to the big lions' wagon.

Chief fed the cubs and moved to the tigers. Chief held the meat on the end of a prong and the orange paws swiped at it, making a wind that ruffled his hair.

The lion, Joe, nosed the bars. He was hungry. Dots seethed in the brown of his eyes and the colorless drool from his mouth wet his paws. He stared at the ground, the people, Fiddler, through everything as through air. He grunted once with gruff impatience and then once at Bessie, turning his head, to keep her back. In his eyes the pupils were perfectly round and fixed, like celluloid disks, but the brown seethed with floating lines and dots.

"Here's this fella's!" said Chief, bringing Joe a dripping hunk of meat and bone. It wouldn't go under the bars. It got stuck. Joe tugged with his claws dug like fingers into the bone and his teeth grappling, growls rumbling out of him like breakers. Chief drove the prongs at the meat again and again. It took both Joe and Chief to get the meat into the cage, there was so much of it. Joe's mouth was smeared with blood and he was excited, swishing his tail.

"You ain't got none of them fellas in Alaska!"

"No," the bull man admitted, "but we've got bears that 'ud make them circus bears piss in their britches!"

Chief told Fiddler, "You eat. I'll take the crap back."

"That's all right. I'll help you."

"Eat! You eat, boy!"

"Okay."

Fiddler felt just as hungry as Joe or the cheetah. At three-thirty the previous afternoon the circus had given him supper. If anybody had tried to stop him now as he walked to the cookhouse, there would have been blood on the Iowa grass.

The Witness

I HAD BEEN TRAINED as a hospital technician in the army, and instead of the gleaming lab job uptown by which I had hoped to pay for graduate school, I was working in a defunct office building on the edge of the Lower East Side. It was a lab job, but what a lab! My cornflakes-and-cream face began to thin. I lived in a hair-raising rooming house, wondering what my BA was going to be worth and what would become of me. At the same time, however, life down there seemed bracingly rich. The pigeons of Venice wheeled over the roofs and the fountains of Rome spouted up from the hydrants. Churches in eight languages. You could buy diamondback terrapins and whole sheepskins, octopuses and sackfuls of beans. I still think somebody who lived near me could have traveled all over the world without seeing a face which really surprised him. The streets had the spicing of danger a young man likes—"Count Draculer" ruled in the block. Next door to my room was a death's-head guy who wept more than most people laugh. "My wife, my poor wife." I used to smile when we met on the stairs, being polite and supposing that he was laughing, until finally I distinguished the words. The family across the backyard kept roosters which woke me up in the morning.

Where I worked was a bleaker, Chicago-like district of factories, empty at night. It had been bustly about 1900 and was full of April-fool structures with gargoyles that goggled down. A fop stood on the edge of the roof of a perfume warehouse looking into an oval mirror. A large Christ close to him held a cross, and our wild-faced, collapsing building had MARY along its front in archaic lettering between wreaths of stone. My boss was a man named Darwin Hanes, forty-five. He wore a Purple Heart pin, and ties that announced that he was probably a fruit. He was earnest, kind-natured, a flurrier at work, and rather the pure scientist in his intentions, except that he'd flunked out of medical school and dieted on nothing but personal bloody noses in the twenty years since. Anyway, he kept a room for projects of his own, with tubes of Tb and guinea pigs sneezing—we mopped down the floor with iodine. He was round-faced, pouch-eyed, and he made his acquaintances uncomfortable by staring at them for long, long stretches when he talked to them. Alone in the world, he was in that state seen commonly in New York where you give the person about five more years before he goes into a mental ward.

His cronies were Puerto Ricans, flattered to have an American friend. Darwin had learned Spanish during one of his self-improvement spates, and blew hot and cold on them, both sexually and just as chums. Hot and cold otherwise, he was touching answering the phone, full of belief and civilization, and had a scientist's pride; then the choked pain in his voice (the doctors thought him a nut) when the man on the other end said he was sending a couple of patients over for tests and expected a kickback. He'd start shivering slightly, almost as though exhilarated. The world was all black, and, bastard of bastards, he'd make his way! If the girl in question came in with starched sleeves she preferred not to roll up for her blood test but took off the blouse instead, Darwin insisted on coughing until, despite my embarrassment, I pushed in to watch. He had a blackboard on which he did gene transposition equations, patterning himself on J. Robert Oppenheimer, perhaps. He'd put on a mystical stare and brush at the chalk on his hands absently, living the life of a genius as far as he could. He would come in in the morning having "seen the whole thing in front of me" just before falling to sleep, and would sit half the day at his desk muttering over the records he made of experiments, without much result—he'd "lost it."

A great man's life was variety, so he never stinted on phone calls or shopping around for equipment. He was interested in immense centrifuges, in the newest of sterilizers, and barrels of culture media. He believed busy men picked up the phone on the first ring—"Yes, yes, this is he"—taking notes on the margins of whatever was close. He had a soft voice that strung the salesmen along.

There wasn't much work, although enough not to pass the day reading, and I looked out on Lafayette Street a good deal, which was a large brutal one-way thoroughfare, always a drama in progress. At my window I got to be sort of a fixture. The drivers sped by, keeping up with the lights, and under the traffic's roar it was hard to distinguish other sounds, only the most frantic yells. More than once, happening to glance outside, I noticed everybody on the street had stopped and faced in our direction because of some appalling thing which had been going on underneath us for several minutes. A cross-section of business people came into the area, along with the garment workers, but the neighborhood acquired its peculiar tone from the bums wandering in from the Bowery a few blocks away. Though they were only a handful at a time, because of them nobody could ask for a drink of water at the soda fountain, get a car pushed, or ask any favor whatsoever. When the traffic light went kerflooey, we must have had six or eight accidents before it was fixed, since everybody assumed someone else had called up about it. They were shoeless and bloodied bums, heaving, gasping, and threshing bums. One never knew what might be wrong with them and never investigated. Once during the summer I remember a woman sat on the sidewalk from lunchtime on, apparently making different sounds. Several men stopped and peeked up her skirts but didn't do anything for her. A telephone company driver talked with her awhile from his truck; and a lady and a friend did busy themselves, except that they hurried on all the more hastily for their distress when three cabs refused to carry the woman anywhere.

It wasn't possible to watch, just as it wasn't possible for me to be very effective in helping without that becoming a full-time job. No one else did any more, not the priests or the nuns walking through, not the cops, though the cops did whatever eventually was done. The station house soon knew my voice as a crank's. It seemed I was running downstairs all the time—feeling pulses, dragging bums who passed out out of the road. I considered myself a kind of a last resort. The group at the gas station across from us would boot a man in the seat of the pants and bait him into "insulting" them so that they could grab their billy clubs, wrenches, and tire tools and give him the run of his life. I shouted as loud as I could; I'd point from my window, establishing that I was witnessing it. Darwin never looked out, even when nothing was happening, and if he saw me hunch up from what I was watching, he left the room in a blaze of exasperation with the street and with savagery and with his own tender heart. He was sometimes hysterically harsh when he found a derelict trying to get warm in the hall but then was unhappy the rest of the day.

I was the laughing, skinny young man full of "minority" sympathy. I'd laughed at fraternity life, laughed at the army, and now in uncertainty I laughed at the city here, although it was the thinnest defense. In the bazaar-like streets around where I lived I began to flinch at the richness, not that it didn't delight me but because I was living amidst it too; nobody was going to come get me out. I had a girlfriend in the building named Ida with a preschool son and a husband long gone. We shopped from exotic market stalls or ate in great Chinese restaurants or went to the Statue of Liberty. She had nice black hair when she looked after it but malnourished skin—an eager, vulnerable girl scalded as tough as a cat. Her eyes were marvelously brown and big, a very light, shining brown. We used to joke that she polished them, and, without contradicting the skepticism which had got knocked into them, they fluttered with accessibility. The lids constantly closed as if holding them in when I turned on my little charm, such as it was. Since she was the first person who'd ever been specially taken with it, I turned it on as hard as I could.

How she needed a man. She'd trot at my heels as close as a colt when we went down the stairs. She was a Japanese whorehouse in bed, and scornfully mocked me for being a mere boy, years younger than her, when her lopsided liking for me stuck out. She ate on eighty-five cents a day Welfare money with Tony, her son—powdered milk, pork hearts in government cans, and peanut butter. She fried powdered eggs and baked surplus flour. Forkfuls of butter and peas were a pleasure to her, and herring on crackers or a lamb chop was food for a queen. Her boy needed galoshes and toys and everything else and already worried about his mother. "Somebody" would give her a new pair of shoes, "somebody" would give her a sweater, he said, much too young to be hinting. He'd ask me to carry their garbage can down, and if I had change from an errand I'd done for Ida, he ran to her with it as if it were some kind of medicine.

She got colitis, bladder infections, aches in her ears, and every few days appeared to be out of her mind—she yelled in a hollow monotone. Her ovaries formed knots from nervous tension, and it was at one of these times that she thought she had gotten pregnant, which pulled us apart even as we pretended to join together. Fiendishly helpless, she was dependent on clinic interns and procedures whenever she or Tony got sick, and since the furnace broke down about once a week, this was often. At midnight Tony would suddenly wake up laboring to breathe, his temperature a hundred and two. A doctor or ambulance wouldn't be sent unless it went higher than that; and without my handouts she hadn't a cent for a taxi. One autumn night when I wasn't home she went into the street with Tony in convulsions in her arms, and found and convinced a patrolman that help should be called, afterwards standing beside him for twenty minutes. He was a young man and kept wanting to stop the police cars which passed. He went up on his toes, looking to see if the policemen were friends, but knew he would only be reprimanded for not having waited for the ambulance. In all these problems, the money I gave her was scarcely a starter because if her sanity really had cracked for as long as a couple of days, wheels would have been set into motion by the Welfare Department for taking her son away.

With each of us frightened, we sometimes had quite ecstatic excursions, as gay as one gets when the roof may fall in. We rolled the stroller along the East River at Delancey Street. The freighters that came sliding by seemed to fill it completely. We'd race them, while Tony hollered. I was fascinated by him. Week by week he was developing, and very much looking around for an older male.

He watched me shave in the morning—"Is that how we do it?" He peered in when I took a shower and came up for regular "battles" with me. I grew very tender, toting him upstairs when Ida stayed late in my room and we put him to sleep on my couch. Then they spent the night, both in the bed. Such cooking, and dashing with tidbits for me—if she didn't claw me she gave me the moon. Once I had become a passion, she used every tool. She encouraged my fondness for Tony and told me he loved me, prompting trips up by him too to say that he did. The next time we were alone, he would say carefully, "I don't love you. Gene. I don't, you know." She thought me elegant, gentle, and fine, and the security she needed so desperately came into it.

We went out at five in the afternoon, when the pigeon-fanciers were up on their roofs. White swoops and black shadow patterns. And every Friday a farmer sold tomatoes, comb honey, and cider and cheese in the storefront he rented—yellow cream, to make the sick well, and even cornflowers in the summer. He talked Ukrainian with his old neighbors, having left Ninth Street twenty-five years before. It was a link for him, and he was the man who'd made good on their block, and their tie to the woods and fields. He had flat farmer's arms, blue eyes, and a reprobate's face, the slack cheeks and lax mouth. "Just the pure stuff, nothing put in it," he said, like an article of faith, when we asked if the cider was sweet. His pear crates and his heavy old shirt and work boots were as good as a trip out of town.

Often we whooped out to Tompkins Park where there were the modern, sinuous slides. Dusk was the ideal time. Tony crawled through the whale-shaped pipes, giving out screams, and went up to the other children. He always seemed infinitely dearer than them. I followed as if he were mine. He'd negotiate some over a toy, then turn to me and throw his ball, or hike onto a higher slide, wheeing down with the tentative relish of someone enjoying what he knows is likely to be his chief recreation for the day. He always was interested to hear what we thought he'd particularly like to do next year, and he enjoyed these dusk go-rounds in much the same way that we did, for the magical sinking light and the teeming park emptied except for a few muted kids at the swings.

He climbed the big slide with boosts from me—it was too high for him—and slid cautiously down. One afternoon they all had got hold of a pup tent and we helped put it up on the baseball field.

Tony had a luminousness, a resonance to him that was pitched very clear, a sing to his affections and words, perhaps just from growing up in a kind of state of emergency. After each bout with flu he seemed changed, a little bit older. He had awful dreams and toilet troubles and slept with his mother, but otherwise wasn't more nervous than plenty of children, so that whatever effect all of this would have was left in the air. Though he cried during Ida's lengthiest rages and spent many consecutive hours at the TV with that deadweight stare of a child, he remained promising. Of course Ida's hope was Tony in school, that there he would get the support he needed; some bright, cultivated teacher might take him in hand. He'd begun at a pilot-program nursery school and the teachers excited her with their comments. She and I had our ups and downs. My helping hand would be abruptly withdrawn, if only because she'd refuse it. In a day the world of dried Navy beans would return, the hard-as-nails mother. There was a middle-aged lesbian woman who paid Ida's phone bill and gave other aid in emergencies in exchange for the loan of the place certain mornings, and these visits increased. The plastering fell more frequently, provoking wilder reactions. The laundry piled up when the hot water failed and fifty cents wasn't forthcoming from me to take it around the corner. I wouldn't know what was happening downstairs, except that I'd hear a groan or two when I went past and resolved all the more to keep my distance, tired of catching sore throats from them, but worrying about the boy.

That Christmas: what a Christmas that was. No money, his mother bewailing into the phone. She'd determined to find some means of buying him a decent spread of presents but she had failed, and the failure knocked all her palisades down, the wolves howled—she was terrified about everything. We had had no contact for a couple of weeks, but the day before Christmas I overheard part of it and went down with a ten dollar bill for a tree and so forth.

"For who?"

"For Tony and us," I said, in the door.

"More games. More games and games and games," she told me in the most utterly exhausted tone, although already letting me rub her forehead. She rocked with it. "The dog act," she called it.

"You won't leave me alone. You won't stop knocking, will you? I must fill a function for you. I'm a pool you can splash in and see some results. You can see what a kick you have. You won't stop dropping in." Her skin shone with sweat and her eyes with exhaustion and her pale face looked flattened out. Soon she ran out of words and stood there, the uncleanable apartment in a shambles around her—a two-dollar strip of linoleum that was colored to look like a rug. "It's so painful when you just come and go. You don't stay, you don't say anything, you watch us and after a while you go again." But she gave up resisting and we rushed out and bought a bristly green tree and a bundle of presents, threw snowballs, and put on the radio for the carols, got benevolently drunk, and poor Tony had the kind of a day that he had much too often, a hectic heaped one which he was supposed to appreciate to the hilt, after the climax of weeping and tensions in which all the bones of the holiday had shown through—all the bones of the grownups' needs, of which his enjoyment was intended to be the relief.

She showed me she made up his bed like an adult's, since he was in school, and showed me a plant he'd been given and a drawing he'd drawn. She talked about getting a job once he was old enough, when she'd get off Welfare and burn all her rags. Rags they were too, a pitiful closet. I was brought up to date on everything, except hints were thrown out about new boyfriends in order to keep it all interesting. We talked through the weekend, Ida rooting for me wholeheartedly—my absurd boasts. Her mouth was like her accessible eyes, vulnerably wide, with a deep-set survivor's smile, a beautiful smile that probably owed part of its permanence simply to being such a large one. I loved looking at it while lying beside her, force-feeding her eyes. She was very acute but always the all or nothing type, and I was experimental. I had never been loved before and was somewhat the tyrant, or anyway fascinated by how variable women were, passion was so different from friendship. Her hair, if it wasn't limp, was lovely and springy. She had heavy, long, slick-skinned buttocks on rather short legs, and sharp breasts. I hung a bathtowel on myself to show how potent I'd gotten. She said she was glad we had met while she still had some of her youth left to give me. Her cheeks, as wide as a cat's, could be middle aged sullen or wonderfully girlish. She had toil-ridden hands and a workhorse neck because she'd supported her family from the age of fifteen. She believed in the soothsaying stars as well as her dreams, the latter of which sometimes awed me. On the street, if I spotted her half a block down, she looked intimately linked to me like a relative, but all out of whack, preoccupied, miserable. She lived such a hair-trigger life that she'd wait half the night by her door for me to come home when we'd fought, yet be far from amenable. And I played her the dirty trick of connecting her in my mind with the maids my family had had in my early teens whom I'd never got up the nerve to try and lay but had wanted to. It was especially dirty since she was so conscious of caste. She'd had to leave school to scrub people's floors, and she would have hated me.

Darwin, meanwhile, was fizzing along. He concocted electrical devices as well as his medical stuff. He was the kind whom one feels the sorriest for, where the energy's there but amounts to nothing. He set a room aside for Ohm's Law, with shelves that almost met in the middle and equipment that hummed from the floor to the top. He began buying equipment in earnest, having inherited a few thousand dollars from an uncle who had died in Columbus, Ohio, and at once became secretive. This was the break that would bring the bonanza. Nights and Sundays he gave to the Law (Sundays his favorite day now), alone in the building except for the painters who had studios; and no love was lost among that bunch. Whenever you stayed in the building late you discovered new mysteries about the people. The fad was to buy camouflage cloth from the war surplus stores, so that, seen from the outside, the windows looked kooky and jungly.

The crazier a person was, the less tolerance he seemed to have for his neighbors, the less mercy or pity, and the harder he was to deal with. We had a woman we used to give leftovers to after lunch, but she wouldn't open the door no matter how loudly you called out her name. You had to put the food down, knock, and then leave, making plenty of noise so she'd know you were gone. Garbagecan Maisie. Darwin was called Quasimodo by the painters and, in turn, was raucous about their dead ends. He called me Lad, which, feeling as green as I did, I didn't mind. In his wilder states I was Androcles, never suspected of plots against him. He *was* quite like Quasimodo, in fact; once I had heard the name I couldn't forget it. He was cheerful and singing much of the time, blinking and deaf to the outer world. I could see him up in a belltower kicking and pushing away at the bells. His own plots were hair-raising, involving his tubes of Tb as they did. Of course he never carried them out but I had my first taste of powerlessness listening to him, because if I'd phoned the Health Department it was I, not he, who would have been judged to be nuts. With his animals, while he was humane in the short-term ways like water and food, his experiments grew very probing.

At my window, being left to myself, I went through a knightly period. If I saw a colored lady unsuccessfully trying to persuade a taxi to stop for her, I would go down and signal one and hold the door open, so that the driver wouldn't realize that I wasn't the passenger until it was too late. And a muscular, rebel Negro in a wheelchair lived around the corner. He would need to go out for food or a bottle of liquor, hating to ask a favor, and yet there was no other way to get over the curbs. When he was sober you'd see him swallow his pride and do it, but if he was drunk he would spin in his chair in circles for fifteen minutes on the edge of the traffic, yowling and sobbing, as the people avoided him all the more. So I used to go down for that.

Darwin took to working far into the night and bought a cot to sleep on at the office at midday. Either he slept scarcely at all or he slept like a dead man, wildly irregular. He cooked for himself and cooked for his mice, and the smells combined with the hammering from the locked room (he was putting up still other shelves) was crazy. As always when he was most withdrawn, he looked his most clean-cut and pleasant. He quit joshing with patients, worked in silence, and contaminated some of the culture plates in his haste. He had laughed at the neighborhood's burglar alarms, which were always going off, ringing all night, but now he installed one himself. The work we were given fell off. I spent long lunches watching the *bocce* on Houston Street, more Italian than Italy, really, or walked to the library or to one of the kosher sandwich emporiums or, in the summer, to the public pool near Avenue C where upwards of a thousand children would be swimming and the shrillness was universal like sunlight. Long lines waited behind the diving board: two lifeguards stood ready. Each kid climbed on and walked to the end, every step broadcasting that he hadn't the faintest idea about how to swim. In he'd plop. The guards took turns going in. Sometimes, leaving the lab at night, I passed by the local high school and found the whole street spread with trumpeters blowing away, the very bleakness everywhere else accentuating the gaiety. Postponing going home, I'd look through the paper for anything uptown to do. In the winter, if worse came to worst, I just sat in the subway where it was warm, reading the news with the men who dreaded going home to their wives. It was a year of intense wretchedness and happiness mixed, each deepening and giving the other color. On the subway, I amused myself by imagining that everyone sitting there was in armor of various sorts.

Ida's laugh became nearly as throaty when I kissed Tony as when I kissed her, since it was plain that I loved him a bit and that her hopes of marrying again weren't going to suffer because of her son. Her dependence made her even more of a hothead and made me take her for granted, besides. We avoided each other for days, despite his pathetic attempts to bring me back, when he'd knock at my door on his own initiative and tell me his mother wanted to see me, "needed" to (this after I'd heard her drunken yelling). But if we suddenly met, we'd get into each other's arms again, the sarcasms crackling, and her soft buttocks filling my hands. She'd lean her head back for a kiss. She compared her husband and me, both bastards, and laughed. "Has the dance palled?"—meaning her rivals. I'd never made so much love before, and found it was habit-forming. Success brought success. I chased, phoned, and dashed about, pushing, pushing defenses down, wet in the pants and wet in the mouth, this brimstone to her, naturally. The poor woman could hear the high heels through the ceiling if I brought someone in—I soon didn't. She'd upend her apartment and clean and explode, and the next day, hearing her yell at her son, I'd show up scared at her door for his sake, wondering who I should call. She asked who I was; had she met me before?

"You thump in here as if you're some king. Well you're not, you're just Johnny Average to me, and you better believe it. You're disgusting. You walk up and down those stairs—you're as arrogant as a turkey—I don't listen for you any more, you know. I'm not your biddy. You think he loves you. He doesn't love you. And I don't love you. I'm just curious to see what you'll come up with next. I learn, you know. I don't give a damn if a man like you drops dead in the street. You're just a fucker—yes, you're flattered, aren't you, you're such a boy. You think that's a good thing to be. You love me to kiss your chest. You think it's such a magnificent chest, don't you? You think it gives me a charge."

When she didn't drive me out, she clutched at me like a life ring, and didn't hear a word she said, because if I left she hadn't a clue as to why but would stand with the tears slowly penetrating the glaze in her eyes. Holding each other, we watched Captain Kangaroo, who was such a slob that he was a comfort. Tony, letting his oatmeal congeal, stared funnel-faced too. My notion was that, regardless of what happened between me and his mother, someday I would help to put him through college, or get him out to the country for summers. I hoisted him over my head, gulping down my delight in being a father; and the two of them lined up next to the door when I left for work to kiss me off.

Once she thought she was pregnant, everything was intensified. She talked about Tony for hours, as though lonelier now, bored with romancing, only the mother. The round-robin trading of sore-throat germs went on, like her crescendo-type suffering, standing past midnight behind the door. I felt horribly trapped. Why in god's name was I living down here? Half my attraction from her standpoint was because I came from another world. And why had I gotten myself in the fix—I'd forgotten how new the experience of winning love was. I'd made use of her and now it was nothing but castor-oil pains and a sanity stretched to its limits. I was scared to death. She with her neat, small ears, French nose,

and her scrub-woman's lumpy arms—at my dreariest, I could imagine us going through the clinic mill and the intern's glances
directed at me wondering why. The battered old tenement faucets rang like sleigh bells, and we were as merry as mourners,
she sitting beside my knees. She hated men, worshipped men, and
I rubbed her forehead, where the slamming she'd taken had registered most, the deprived and underdog bones. But she bloomed in
exultancy, maneuvering her figure. She looked like a movie star.
It was my baby. We were knitted together now. I was chilled to
the bone! I'd never imagined such passion existed, much less that I
might be the object of it.

When this aghast reaction of mine was clear, Ida got into
more of a rage than anything else could have put her in. The luster
went out of her skin. She turned into a fiery sick cat, bedraggled
and humped. "Why didn't you let me alone? All right, we played
house nicely and you found out you couldn't care less for the likes
of me, I was beneath contempt; so why didn't you leave me alone?
Why did you leave it up to me? It was so peaceful without you, I
was getting along perfectly. But no, you wanted me on the string
for the times when you hadn't anyone better. You revolt me, my
friend. I don't want your baby. You figure out how to get rid of it.
I haven't the energy to spare for you—I need what I have for my
son." And, indeed, her efforts were all to shield him and keep up
his routines.

• • •

Darwin puttered or pounded throughout the day in either his
guinea pig room or his "juice" room, while Lafayette Street grew
still grislier. Bums are straight out of a comic strip anyway, with
their charcoal-smeared faces, their staccato-gapped teeth and gal-
lows bird postures that look like they've already been hung. When
I watched a man chased down the street by a man with a knife, it
was slapstick, like the comics, not TV realism. In the first place,
the knife was outsized, and the man in front completely the wrong
shape for running, and the man following him, though less bloated,

ran like his feet were in boxes, plus the outlandish pursuers who were trying their best not to catch up. Real street fights were broken up into whirring fragments with baby-like *waaahs,* and bums fought with wood slats like Punch and Judy—the outcries, the shadow-show fury—till, after a long inaudible speech, the winner would take a few theater bows. My troubles at home didn't help remove me. On the contrary, I lost my perspective, I could see only the suffering. When I was pipetting something, I'd distinguish a child's shrieks under the rush of the cars and look out the window and see one being whipped on the legs for minutes on end by her father. What could you do? To step in directly would make it worse for the child—the mother already was doing her best to distract him—and to call the police would be more drastic yet, once the guy talked his way out of it and got the girl home. The only weapon was simply to watch—to *watch,* so that the fellow knew. Long after the family had left, I would be jumping up from my desk to lean out with cramps in my chest as if it were still going on.

In the army I'd worried about being "dehumanized," although in fact the army had softened me, but here was a vastly more brutal environment. The truck drivers shouted Giddyap at the bums pulling pushcarts. Even the street was caving in because some foundations had been misdug, and it threatened to block up the subway. I was just high enough to be out of throwing range if I shouted at people. When I was outside, myself, though, I quickly got expert at looking away. Either you watched pointedly or, for safety's sake, you looked away. One time a troop of housewives and I followed four or five friends who were beating the wife of one of them, stopping and pulling her into doorways, until our staring, our numbers, dislodged them.

Ida was shifting furniture to cause a miscarriage and doing hot baths. Going by on the stairs, I heard the brass ring to her voice, on the phone calling friends. After a minute she'd tap at my room to tell me the latest, since it was me in her body budding. Steaming with fear, she went up to Central Park and leapt off the boulders. My hair stood stiff to hear about it. I hugged her, begged, and yet finally had nothing to say, realizing how little the difference was between jumping off boulders and going to the doctors that Darwin knew. She was petrified; she said that her life was a wreckage; she felt hot to the hand as if she were running a temperature and could hardly put two words together, afraid that they might take Tony away, and frightening the daylights out of me. All of a sudden, however, worried that it was some cruel piece of egotism, I would look at her and be tremendously pleased at the pregnancy, sexually excited, and go over her with my hands. She felt the same way immediately. We made the most tender, delicious love, with her stomach the center of it, never so sexy.

Darwin considered me some sort of link to the rest of the world, and joked about "raping girls" and other misconstrued normalcies, though disarmingly gentle about it. He told World War II stories, sitting across from me at his aluminum table and wiping his ribs with a towel if he wore no shirt. He liked to keep to a schedule, to overwork, which wasn't easy in a lab such as ours, and occasionally to take time off for an indulgent talk with me.

"I'll tell you, lead your own life. Nobody has any business with you. They won't understand what you want to do. They'll laugh at you out of ignorance. So you don't ask permission from anybody when you pick out something you want to do, you just go ahead, and then you won't have any problems," he said, the brief phrases to add pithiness. But this successful man's manner was rendered incongruous by the misfit's tone, the schoolboy solemnity he gave everything. It was in his mouse room that he could seem to be bluff the most briskly. The hundreds of rustling creatures did seem like employees, another twill factory in operation. He inspected them with overseeing interest, or picking them up, injected their stomachs, their poor little pots, with that undeniable affection which experimenters, seeing them always as plural, have for their animals as a group.

Our peppiest moments came when a bold bum would wander in wanting his heart listened to. Darwin got shouty, but if the guy didn't run out of the office or wasn't insulted he usually would change around. He wrapped his stethoscope affably into his hand like the doctor he'd wanted to be. He'd sit on the edge of the desk and chat like a boy with a younger boy, wreathed in smiles, not so puffy-faced now. These were his cheeriest periods of all, as if he realized that he could still be a part of the world. The bum inevitably blossomed out too, thought he was awfully skillful to get so much free attention—blood pressure taken—and even forgot his worries about his health. The loudest voices are the voices of bums. The final survival energies, drawn if necessary from everywhere else, seem to go to their throats. We had several memorable specimens, stuffed into their clothes like badly made puppets, the clothes brown and gray and all torn—stains, a scrap of a beard. They were bodiless heads. They were so badly off the only reason they still could walk was that they had wasted away to nothing. But the voice mushroomed, as strange as the lush, unnatural plants which grow out of dead things. Or sometimes the only piece left of a bum was his laugh.

"Wherever I happen to be I'll come in for a checkup every few months, just to be on the safe side. I'll look-see if I can't see a fairly intelligent-looking doctor some place pretty close around. I don't like to walk too far away for it. That way you don't have to worry, you know nothing is sneaking up on you, and if you do what the fellow tells you to do you're gonna be okay until the next time—little heart murmur or something, it's gonna be all right. Oh I can take the cold, I'm very good on that. I know the techniques. They trained us with that. I was up on the DEW Line three years you know. I was up in the Arctic. A lot of these bums wouldn't last a day. Three years of that and you'll take the cold fine; you can take anything. Yeah, you'll see some snow up there, you'll see some dandy cold."

He was like a boy who was shining shoes, this one, with his pert line of gab and the patronizing smiles we gave him. He had hands like a turtle's skin, and strips of newspaper inside his socks, a red toucan nose, a white and red face like a ham bone, and he shook like a soaked sourdough from his illnesses. His ragged coat flapped in the wind like a flag when we watched him leave. Right away he begged from a car at the light, not to lose the boost to his confidence: he put his hands carefully behind him and stooped like a bon vivant to speak to the driver.

We also watched the fences at the garage. I laughed but Darwin was bitter like any respectable citizen under siege. It was hard to tell what was going on because they also worked at regular mechanical jobs. They filled up the station with cars and sweated all day, with a reputation for piddling cheating. But then these cryptic vans would pull in, *Pong's Produce, Old Reliable Pipe and Joint*—ten-year-old trucks which had been painted over a dozen times. They'd move the whole garageful in order to stick the truck in the back, getting very excited and busy.

There is nothing likeable about criminals. They're sneering creatures, ready to turn vicious in an instant, and it was an exacerbation to have them placed opposite us. Of course it made little difference to them when I waggled my finger. They'd grab up tire irons and chase a man. If a Negro drove in for gas, they gave him a Queen Isabella bow and had him wait, pretending to be just about to come, in order to see how long they could keep him. "You goddam bow-and-arrow, get outa here!" They worked, they threatened, in absolute incoherence—a shrug, a lunge at the breastbone. They couldn't talk without jabbing their hands at the person, the mark of respect being not quite to touch him. My stomach got turgid and hot as I'd watch an incident develop. For some reason I went back to the screw-you signal of my boyhood and pointed with that, trying to make myself heard. I shook in confusion for the next half hour whether I'd stayed to watch the scene out or whether I'd ducked away like Darwin. They robbed their own pay phone when they needed change, and the Puerto Ricans hated them too and used to write "warps," "gunnies," on the wall at night after the place closed. One Sunday Darwin watched a car which they hadn't been able to fit inside completely stripped, down to the axles, by three Negroes. He was delighted. It yawned there Monday, while the men fumed.

The four were related, I got the impression, except for a muscle-bound fellow who seemed the most decent. The dominant guy was a blast of straight vigor. He worked a twelve-hour day in his shirt sleeves into December, never ceasing to bluster and shout. He ate with his left hand and worked with his right, talking over his shoulder to the hired, muscle-bound one and yelling ahead to his fat husky brother. The brother, with an unpleasant face, kept up with his share of the jobs but sourly. He had the children who played nearby, attractive twins. The fourth man, who was maybe a cousin, was nervous natured and thin and tall. He had lithe, precise hips that pumped when he walked. He was the most unpredictable and independent and had an oddly chic wife who came and sat in their car every few days while he worked. She looked nice; she was a softening influence, very much gentling him. A snide scowl snuck over him when he got the snow shovel and ran for a bum (they'd let the guy go in a corner and start to pee first). The two children did not have a dampening effect, but when his wife was around none of this happened. He resented me—he was the one who stared back. If I passed on the street he usually quit working sarcastically, though we never spoke.

Virgil Grissom and Hubert Humphrey were driven through on their way up from City Hall. We had a vegetable wagon clatter by daily that serviced the luncheonette downstairs. I looked down at the part in the horse's mane. The Hoodoos fought with the Roman Emperors in the next block. And we had Light and Gas men. They were trying to pump out a manhole before doing some job, except that it filled up again every night. In the morning they strung tapes around the hole, hung warning flags, and set the pump going, and smoked and Coked the day away until the last hour, when they took everything down again. And a mailman made constant pickups—it has to be seen to be believed how many are made.

By the garage was a liquor store owned by a man with a villainous voice and a face shaped like smoke, gray as smoke, who flapped one hand smartly behind when he zipped along on a delivery. He parked in the station and was friends with the bunch, although he considered himself a cut above them. Ours was the civilized side of the street. Right below me was a classical tailor, who suffered like a sunfish in a pail; and, next door to him, a womanly printer whose window display had not been changed for fifteen years and whose mouth was as large as his stomach, the better to laugh with, presumably. He cut the ads for his son-in-law's business out of the paper and carried them around like snapshots. Then his cobbler friend, as skeptical and as seamed as a jockey. He hammered so neatly it was like a stage set: stroke, stroke, the sole was fast; and the nails in his mouth for comic relief. He had a comedian's mouth anyway, and he'd go out and pet the vegetable horse. Two Puerto Ricans ran the luncheonette in eager immigrant fashion. The best thing about them was how they walked off at six o'clock, rolling like seamen, relaxing so hard. They were agreeable and got along fine until the slap-dash cooking cut into their business. They responded by cooking more hastily still and by stinginess with the portions and reducing the menu, so that it was another sad story.

We had plenty of people around and yet we had nobody. When something happened and I would go down I would be on an empty street. In my way, I was expert at preserving my own skin. I never "closed" with anyone, just put myself close at hand. When a car jerked out of the traffic one time with screams from inside, I opened the door on the girlfriend's side to help her get out, not the man's, and retreated as he came after me. "Oh you better run—he'll kill you!" she shrieked. I could see Darwin's pale face above me, and the jockey squinted behind his window as if he were watching a dangerous jump. Darwin believed he had a sixth sense, which made him especially fearful. By now he was sure I'd get clobbered. He told oodles of war stories, remembering more as he went along, and displayed the scars of a beating he had received from some young homosexuals in an earlier phase. They'd tattooed the star on his hand, which alone would have made it impossible for him to return to a more normal life, he claimed. Breakdowns and other new chapters were revealed. An old anxiety about robberies returned. He stopped inviting his Spanish friends up because they might see the equipment and be tempted. He checked the door to the roof twice a day. "That's where they come, off the roof." While he was scared to sleep in the lab, he was even more afraid to leave it unguarded. He used army phrases, shaking his head and gritting his teeth. He even quit leaving our leftovers outside the old lady's door down the hall in case she broke in some night after more.

But he was for *me*, telling me twenty times that he would be my character witness. It was often the police I was battling. In civilian clothes a guy would march off a vagrant, refusing to show him his badge, just whacks. Or when they stormed in in response to a call, arrowing down Lafayette the wrong way, these were the large, lengthy scenes, spreading across the wide street, repetitious but excruciating after you had seen a few. The gold-badges slapped with open hands, as a detective would. The silver-badges poked their clubs like bayonets until a pretext came for swinging down. I bought a camera and drafted letters to the *New York Times*. I fretted on the outskirts, trying to copy cap numbers, and more than once I only saved myself from being arrested by backing off. The standard ending became to find myself being forced to lay my ID cards across the roof of a police car while all the stuff was written down, to stand there, hands on top of the car, in front of the open door—it functions as a sort of station house—until the decision was made as to whether to arrest me, too, or not.

I got nutty, no question about it—more compelled and susceptible, quick to tear and quick to tremble. My eyes had been rubbed raw. The fire escapes on the garment factories filled up with people if a Negro was involved, and some of them would rush downstairs and fuss alongside me on the edge of the action. My ragged nerves were like theirs. I had seen so much violence by now, so many atrocious injustices, that any beginning carried its whole plain progression for me—I understood Darwin's sixth sense. The police were the same, for that matter, and so were the gas station toughs. Everybody picked up from the last time. Anger from then, or anguish, whatever it was, piled onto the new occasion. In a flash the despair poured back, and I would be leaning over the patrol car hood again, my teeth practically chattering.

"No, no sir, buddy, you take out your fucking license yourself! I don't handle nobody's wallet!"

It was December, that awful Christmas, and we had the procession of Santa Clauses coming out of the subway all day with their locked boxes and Santa Claus bells. Their terminus was a mission nearby on Houston, so we had the entire city's street Santas, who were really just ordinary bums dressed up in red and white, limping along much as usual—they didn't bother with stomachs for them. We also had Fire Department exercises going on within a couple of blocks. I needed a vacation badly, needed to get to the country; I was irritated simply by humans and human activity by this time. If a bus driver reached the end of his route and wanted to turn around, I argued with him. The signs on a church or a synagogue that said that it closed at 8 p.m. stuck me as pharisaism. At my cheerfulest I typed myself with the bearded, anachronist Jews in shiny black coats, only a very few left, who still hauled their pushcarts through all this madness in the old style, purple with sweat, having no relation whatever to it.

Though the frog tests I did on Ida continued to run negative, she wouldn't menstruate and the doctor thought that he felt a pregnancy rather than cancer—he said it was *something*. I would drop in on the way to work, if possible, because of my own shakiness, instead of at night when I would have to stay longer. I gave her money and horrified hugs and pained, gingerly looks which tried to convey affection. It's hard to reconstruct exactly what she was feeling since I was trying to avoid being aware of it. She "suspected" I didn't love her, though of course I believed I had never pretended to; and she really thought a good deal of the time that she was going to die or at least be made sterile. She dreamt of water, of babies, of me, of death, and raged against being a woman, while at the same time she was trying to shield me from what she was going through, that is, except for the nights when she heaped her sufferings on me in blinding half-hour explosions, her voice like a flatted cornet. She ate and threw up as if she were pregnant, and looked taut and scrawny with that violin-string attenuation of a cat which drags itself. Then, next morning, what a Liz Taylor opened the door, bellying gay as the clouds! I'd bite her. I had a permanent cold from exhaustion.

Her room and a half had her marriage furniture in it, appropriately mismatched and in faded bright mummy-like colors. When there wasn't another reason, my heart went out to her for the apartment alone, so unspeakably dismal and small, and she without even the subway fare to get out. The layers of paint and linoleum extruded dirt from tenancies fifty years past. The two beds took most of the space. The books were her husband's Genet, the decorations her own sporadic attempts which she couldn't get rid of when the mood left until she saved enough money to buy something else. I regarded the place as mine for loafing ("your doll house," she said), and we still had rather happy, whimsical evenings sometimes, with billing and cooing, no barbarities. We lived on three different planes, mine being the mundane. Ida was in a shadow world, smelling life, smelling death, the surface realities scarcely a glimmer part of the time. She drew upon every ounce of her concentration to manage the details of Tony's existence, yet he chirped out the window obliviously. He had the most marvelous shrieks and chirps, like nothing I'd ever heard before. I almost wanted the baby born. He shot with his gun out the window too much and chased the cat hard, had very pitiful moments, but mostly one wondered whether he wasn't living on borrowed time, whether such glee in defiance of logic and of his surroundings wasn't going to have to be paid for. Certainly in other respects he could go either way. He was slummy-faced, coarse, and tough for a while, as if growing up to be somebody I wouldn't be able to care about. Then in the afternoon, maybe, his eyes would spread open, his face would go soft, as he listened to one of his mother's tales of Aesop. He was precociously gentle whenever she reached her rope's end, just as Ida after an incendiary couple of hours always stopped short and knelt down in order to make it up to him with an effusion of playful intuitive love.

Twice the social worker dropped by unannounced for what was called a Complete Drawer Count. And the tenement pipes rang like railroad bells. "Just hold onto me," she'd whisper, as crazy as eels. It was *"Please* don't stare!" or else "You're not looking at me!" when I was too anxious and pitying. The truth, as we waited for word from the doctor to act on, was that the danger that she'd have a breakdown was worse than the risk of any abortion. She was Catholic, and I rubbed her resisting back by the hour while she talked. I was a futile substitute, but she was afraid she'd lose Tony if she went to a priest, and she made me afraid to go to one too. Listening, I couldn't fix on a plan for any of the eventualities. There were other shouts in the building but not pitched like hers, and she lay with her head in my lap, so that I saw the tears in her nose and the swollen blood vessels. Tony writhed on the floor.

"I've taken so much and what have I got to show for it? I have you here, younger than me, almost a child really, because you were hard up, and now you like to think of yourself as wonderfully kind and honorable. I don't care who's with me. I don't even know where I am. Have you ever felt neuter? Well that's how I feel. I don't feel like a man and I don't feel like a woman. I'm dead, I'm an idiot, I don't feel. I wish I were a tree, or have I read that somewhere? I must have. Nothing is original with me, is it? I don't believe in God but I'm afraid of Him. I don't particularly like you, but I loved you—that's not original either. I don't want to sleep with any more men or have any more babies but I don't want to be sterile. I see horrible figures in dreams, but they're the best company I have except for my son. I'd do anything not to die, but I want to die."

Just as dreaming of having a breakdown is said to tap off the pressure building towards one, when the janitor in our building cracked up Ida appeared to revive, to catch a kind of a second wind. It was a hectic long night. The guy was afraid his relatives were going to kill him and begged for help in heart-rending yells, but he was the one who was armed and they were only afraid for their lives. He ran into the tenants' rooms for protection, and when we ran out, he followed, afraid to be left by himself. With his knives in his hands, he went down on his knees and begged us to spare him.

Soon we were to find out she wasn't pregnant at all, but I'd sunk into a state where my laughing and joking were of no use. I couldn't eat. I was worn out, bewildered and worthless as far as assisting her was concerned, and unable to pick myself up or take a sensible trip or take some good pills. There had been no chance to collect my wits and hunt uptown for a job. I thought I'd never get out of this, and the winter shut most people indoors, so that the suffering seemed that much worse. If you dodged past a barefoot beggar, the blood on his face had froze. The old Jews took temporary respites, but the bum pushcart pullers continued wretchedly. Many drivers hardly acknowledged their right to the street anymore, so long after the heyday of pushcarts.

It may have been an impatient attempt to scare the man or a misjudgment because of the novelty. Maybe the cart didn't register on the truck driver's eyes, being neither a pedestrian nor a motor vehicle. Barreling along and simply not seeing it, he clipped the cart from the rear, spinning the man in front of him. He didn't begin to brake or swerve until it was done.

We called the police from upstairs. Darwin had bought some goldfish and was tinkering with the aeration. By now it was established he never was going to go down on the street if something was happening; and I didn't object; I didn't want to go either. But I'd seen the accident. The man was lying there with nobody touching him, and I still had a sense of being "medical": in fact, appeals on those grounds were occasionally made to our window from down on the street.

He looked dead from close up. I asked in the liquor store if we oughtn't to phone for an ambulance. The fellow was doing paperwork.

"Nobody can call an ambulance except the cops. You know that. What's the matter with him?"

"He was hit by a car," I said. I'd disliked his preposterously sinister face for so long; he turned round and grinned.

"Yeah? Well, probably you ought to call the cops, don't you think?"

I was unable to answer that. Outside, I looked up and saw Darwin worrying in the window, as were the printer and the two Puerto Ricans on our side of the street, although they had no apparent reason for worrying about me. A nervous tick in my cheek asserted itself; I realized I was bone-tired.

"Phone for an ambulance," I yelled to Darwin. The victim appeared quite decidedly dead, however. For all the illness I'd seen, he was my first dead man, and yet since he looked like hundreds of magazine pictures—the ragged refugee dead by the road—the sight could not have been more familiar. Every night going home I went by at least one drunk passed out, usually in danger of freezing. Dead as they looked, I went by assuming, like everyone, that somebody else was going to stop, because to see to them would have tacked on an hour or more to my day. This was absolutely routine, but I felt for a pulse with a sadness that had a momentum behind it—he *was* dead, I knew. Sick, shaky, I wanted to laugh. The pity I had withheld so many times had caught up with me.

The traffic streamed by. A couple of the gas station men came out to wave it on so that their entrance wouldn't be blocked, and the truck driver passed cigarillos around. He was very upset, an outspoken, balding person in a checked wool jacket. It was after four, nearly dusk.

"They shouldn't be let on a street like this. I mean it's for stuff that's going through, you're supposed to go around twenty-five, thirty-five miles an hour. Poor baby. That never happened to me before. Right out of the blue, they step in front of you and you've killed somebody. Poor bastard. Jesus." He walked around between us. I didn't nod to agree but, on the other hand, didn't find him objectionable. The difficulty was that I had an exact image of what I had seen. As crisp as a diagram, the truck had traveled in a straight line. The cart had been in the path of that line and at no time had the truck hesitated. The impact with the man was too searing to bring to the front of my mind but it was indelibly there. The daylight, dim to begin with, was rapidly vanishing.

I went up to the lab, since I could feel myself get incoherent. The man was dead; no sense in gawking about. "Oh, all bashed to hell, that's all," I told Darwin. "Hit him from behind." The truck had *McMartin's Scotch Whiskey* on it and a pasteboard bottle, and the driver, we saw, walked into the liquor store and provoked enough interest that the proprietor at least poked his head out the door. The Texaco bunch toed the cart frame. "Vamose," they said to a carload of Spanish, keeping the driveway clear.

From the gestures, a consensus was forming by which the push-cart man was to blame. Nobody checked him again, and I wondered if I hadn't been too quick in presuming him dead. Though this was nonsense, I came down. They were by the truck, looking for damage. Without much basis, I got the idea the guy might have handed out a few bottles as I was coming downstairs. The cart man, in Raggedy-Ann clothing, was partly thrown on his side, with his head bloodied and his seat all cut up from a bottle of wine that had been in his back pocket. Amazed, I recognized him as the one who had sat and chattered to us about the DEW Line in such an incongruously lively way. All of that spunk and spark smashed up like a broken doll—it revolted me.

"They shouldn't let them out on the street, or you'll even see them up on the sidewalk. No light on him, no way to see him," the driver complained. The others wanted to drag the cart over a bit to let the traffic pass by faster. "Leave it. It's way the hell out there," he said. But with a scared, guilty face like mine might have been, he swung back to me as if I was the one he wanted to convince because I was next to the body.

"Nevertheless he *was* on the street," I said.

"Nevertheless?" He sounded the word, mixing respect and sarcasm. "What are you, a doctor?"

"No, he's not a doctor, he's just a Nosy," chuckled the thin mechanic. I'd always been glad it wasn't one of his huskier partners who had taken the special dislike to me, but I saw he could beat me up easily.

"I knew him a little," I said.

"You knew him?" Bolder, the driver asked with his eyebrows *why* I knew him. I hunched by the body, feeling righteous and safe. After walking off, he came back and stared down at the man in sad disapproval. He leaned with a nervous snort, touched the man's rear, and smelled the alcohol on his finger. "Maybe the noise frightened him." His hands did the noise, then the cart veering into the traffic suddenly. Charades over drunks were so commonplace, one had to remind oneself that this fellow was dead; and although I was glancing for suspicious bulges on them—the way the garage crew was looking at me, I might have been the man who had run the bum down.

"I knew him. Yeah," the store owner said, leaving his doorway. "All the bums around here." He puckered his mouth, looking down, as if to convict any customer of his. The driver asked who delivered his liquor to him.

Why was I being so punctilious, I wondered? I'd sympathized with the driver at first—why get him in serious trouble when nothing constructive would come of it? The man would be just as dead. In the same way as the gas station bunch had taken his side partly to spite me, wasn't my attitude the reverse? With their long-flanked red faces and their choo-choo-choo vigor, I'd never seen them so close before. It was like bars being removed. Here they were next to me, no barriers. And they all had the camaraderie of living in Queens and shaking their heads at the neighborhood. The dynamic, blocky, all vigor guy kept leaving to heave himself onto the fender of the *Pong's Produce* truck and practically disappear inside its motor. "You live in that place?" he asked me, pointing.

"I work there."

"You work there?" He laughed at the building facade with its blotchy camouflage curtains and the wreaths around MARY.

"I'm a medical laboratory technician," I said, trying to invoke the immunity more than the prestige.

"Where do you live?"

They listened, these people I had been pointing at, judging and needling for months. It was too late to leave and I saw that by staying here to argue this issue I had lost whatever effectiveness I had been having up in my window. It was like the police interrogation would be. When they heard where I lived they guffawed.

The cart had carried junk cardboard, ground almost to powder by the traffic by now, and pedestrians pumped past as thick as the cars. By standing still I got the sensation of managing some kind of a show. The most touching detail was a handful of wooden letters the size of a child's blocks, O's and H's, which were strewn alongside the gutter. In warm weather the cart must have been used as a hot dog wagon.

"Tell me something. Why are you all the time sticking your hand out the window? Are you trying to make a U-turn?"

We all laughed. The all-vigor fellow pushed up on his arms from the *Pong's Produce* motor to hear it repeated. A postman in a truck made a pickup, dragging his sack past the body. Infuriated that I was trembling, I searched for the top of the bottle, thinking that if the seal was still on I might prove the man had been sober. The early darkness was very confusing.

Once the cops came it was the trial in advance, acquittal quickly a certainty. They copied the license number on the tail of the cart. They shared with the gas station people that extraordinary beefiness found in the city. The owner of the liquor store emerged to touch the victim's rear end and convey the idea that he had been drinking, and the expression on the dead bum was no help. Besides being so very surprised-looking, he looked haughty and quarrelsome compared to when he had chattered to us about Hudson's Bay. It was the face of a man with freezing wet

feet, with scarlet, goose-pimpled hands and neck, who was trying
to ignore the shouts from the traffic and ignore his misery. When
I drew my mind back to those moments before he'd been hit, I
remembered no drunken appearance. He'd pulled like a dutiful,
suffering horse that knows that its work is the lesser of evils. Now
he looked like a crunched gutter mouse made up for the role of a
bum, with the stubble and stock ruby nose.

"Old bums like thàt, they don't carry a light, can't hardly control what they're pulling, and they turn their ankle or they slip
where it's wet—had a little too much—and out he goes in the lane.
It's a crime when they're out like that," said the thinner garage man.

"Actually, the light was pretty good then," I argued in a de-
spairing tone to the police. "I work right across the street, and he
was coming down very fast, right by the curb. The poor guy was
right in front of him. I don't think he ever did see him. It was
much lighter than this, plenty of light. He didn't have his headlights on, himself, as a matter of fact, so it doesn't make any difference if the cart had a light of its own because it wasn't dark enough
yet to need one."

Hoots from the witnesses. The scorch-faced owner of the liquor store said, "No, he had a load on."

The driver glanced over to where he was parked. "Well I
turned 'em off, naturally, but I had 'em on, they were on."

"Sure, his lights were on."

I was chilled by the gas station group, for whom until now
I had been pretty much of an abstraction, up in an upper story.
They were giving me total attention. The stream of Santas
climbed out of the subway, limping by us, and the ambulance
came; another mail pickup was made. When the body was gone
it required an effort to remember there even had been a body.
As in the rehearsal, when they talked to me the police turned to
look at my building. With their faces trained neutral, they asked
how I'd seen through the camouflage cloth.

"I'm a medical laboratory assistant. We don't have that.
We have the sign about blood tests in the window."

My home address registered badly again, as it would have in
court, and perhaps I hammered too hard at the light being so good.

Also, their first impression of me was marked by my searching look as to whether we'd crossed swords before, a look which must often betray petty criminals—that and the way I dropped my head like an exhausted bull in the ring, very small, windedly quivering. The uniform looked different to me. That charcoal blue—business blue. It had become almost impossible for me to talk to police without being hostile or supercilious, and so it was like a job interview, where my name was being written down but I knew I would never be hired.

I left work right afterwards, in a tumultuous funk. The killing, the codger gabbing away happily in our office only the week before, and everybody's closing over the facts of the accident—I felt as if I had flu. Darwin seemed queer as a coot with his star on his hand and his goldfish and mice and heavyweight name, and I wanted out.

As I crossed the Lower East Side, the record stores blared, the peddlers' trucks jingled, mocking me with a storm of sounds. A priest in an overcoat walked up and down on Elizabeth Street, since he hadn't a cloister, holding a flashlight over his breviary and whispering the words. Kids were clouting a ball. They towered it up seven floors, then tried to spot it before it fell. A cat was making love to a dog. The light was so mutedly rich in night colors that my eyes led a life of their own. The vivid neons had a handmade gleam more stimulating than neons uptown, and the squint I'd developed, the squint of a person who couldn't walk five or six blocks without seeing a man slugged, an arrest, or a beggar, widened out in spite of itself. My eyes crowed. I heard Hindi, Rumanian, Cantonese, Polish, each lilty. A guy was thocking an oud with a spoon. Two beatniks had hung a piece of cardboard on their fire escape to communicate with the girl opposite "Hey, Sweet!" Children spilled whooping across the sidewalk, and the off-Broadway theaters seemed like opera houses up in the Yukon, dowdy, primitive structures, newly white-washed, in the midst of a wilderness boom.

In my block the bookie's bird store had become bona fide. His life's enthusiasm was these evenings, when he really sold birds and sunflower seeds. He sat on a bin in his pigeon coop engulfed in wings, while he talked through the wire to a couple of pals.

The whole block was dream-like and misty, the light Parisian, with every building a different color and height and shape, the fire escapes zigzags of rusted orange, and the rooftops running along in a dum-de-dum-dum. Now I was squinting against the beauty—I must not be strong enough to live here. I caught a glimpse of two fencers upstairs in a loft, and a man inside a locked girdle store was playing his fiddle to a macaw. I looked at the lemons in the street stalls, at the mounded-up oysters and booties and Preen, feeling utterly flattened. That Ida's future should depend upon what I might choose to do was the worst circumstance of all.

She was plenty crazy at first that night: acute concentration on me. Her squeeze when we hugged was too strong to have any meaning as such and had none of the sexiness that was best at arousing concern.

"Something happened?" she asked. She was stroking my back to loosen it. With her harrowed face, which was so much more anxious on my behalf than anyone else's would have been, she looked at me with an open love that overwhelmed me in shame, that she should be sorry for me, tenderly reading my muscles for tension, after the way I had dodged in and out the last weeks. A large face, like a boy's from medium range, like a woman's if you were close or away several yards. Brown eyes, black sweaty hair, and that great wide survivor's smile of hers, as serene as a smile in death. I got a fresh sight of this gritty girl who thought she was carrying a child by me and who was living on powdered eggs and charity clothes and plain lonely terrified misery. I realized how little I'd done, how execrable it would look to me in a few years if I hadn't shut out the memory altogether. My god, how little I'd given her! Beer to help her relax at night? Not usually, unless we were necking. Blueberries, avocado, if I was having them? No, not unless we were eating together. A forkful of buttered string beans would have given her pleasure sometimes. I must have been mad—her son standing between my knees looked at least twice his age because of the life they were leading—I'd lost perspective completely!

I ran out and got mushrooms, steak, and oregano and so on, and spoiled the meal only by hardly talking. Tony wanted the fathering element of it in equal proportion with the food, so he sat on my lap to eat, which he did with politeness and dignity. It was a funny meal. My affection for him gushed up until I could scarcely swallow, watching his every move, and with Ida I was the penitent husband. I'd forgot how at home we could be, although she assumed my silence was because of her pregnancy. But her glance lost its glaze; she got peaceful and sweet. She drew the big circles under my eyes with her finger.

"You've had a worse time, haven't you? You've worried more. You're very generous. Yes, you are," she said when I shook my head. "And I'm not after you, you know, that's not what I want, you mustn't feel any pressure like that." At her simplest and most attractive, she went on about how nice I'd been. She meant it, but at the same time I was thinking that we were half married already, and how fine it was to have supper this way, that to go through the further formalities might be right for me too. Once she was given a little stability, there would be just her warmth, no jaggedness. I couldn't bear picturing the boy dragged off to an orphanage, and felt protectively head-of-the-house. I began reaching under the table, and told her the accident story, more detached about it than I would have imagined an hour before. We hurried the dishes, mouth to the sweater already, and got Tony to sleep. She was a bit gaspier than I liked but very giving. Small breasts with large nipples, and an overall skinny toughness I loved—geisha-small feet with high arches, a mouth like a plum. It was another night when the loops bound around us made us relish each other all the more.

The next day we found out the loops didn't exist. I stayed home from work to get over the pushcart episode and she came in at noon from the doctor's and said he had made up his mind it was a false pregnancy. The explanation was skimpy because we had paid out so much already she didn't pay to have a long conference; but we scarcely hugged once after that. I left the house in blank angry relief and didn't go near her apartment for almost two weeks. I sought out a Negro girl I'd been flirting with, to enter that brittle, tight little set, the dark half of which wanted to go up in the world and the white half of which wanted to go down. Since I, of course, wanted to go up like the Negroes, I didn't quite fit at the parties. She was the life and direction at them. She was impatient, tense, prickly, a virtuoso with people. We had one banner day, plus three club-foot attempts to repeat.

The district absorbed me all over again. I wandered as I hadn't since first arriving. Moist, late December weather with wind and sun, when winter hovered just overhead, giving one more day's grace, now another. I got the exuberant sense that here in one spot was my whole fellow family of man. The racial mix on the streets brought a racial peace which was affecting if you went into other parts of the city. For both colors the process was rather like learning to fly—so many thousands of hours of looking to be put in—and down here we'd gotten farther along. Avenue C had a small-town flavor. Because of the cobblestones and the loose babies, traffic crept; the pedestrians virtually ignored it, so that there was a vacation atmosphere. I used to go into the Siberia branch of the Chemical Bank for the fun of looking at who was assigned there. This was in a grotesquely ancient building across from a live poultry market and a garment ends warehouse, and the tellers were dazed from their banishment from Madison Avenue. Italian ices had been sold out of baby carriages by Puerto Ricans during the fall, and practically every block had its *shul*. A *shul* was a hole-in-the-wall synagogue with four or five Stars of David built into the front, looking defiant and jubilant, from some ghetto in Europe and bursting with hope. In the zany designs of a lot of the blocks you could see the failed architects who at last had been left a free hand; they sometimes went Moorish to celebrate. The neighborhood was as rich historically as the western range of the same period, but was being bulldozed away. I strolled and gazed through the misty weekends—at the patchworks of relic wallpaper on the sites half-demolished, at the wash lines, the three downtown bridges—snacking on Old Country foods, and talking such talk as one enjoys slightly wistfully with a cab driver in more affluent years.

At the lab I tinked tunes on the urine bottles, lining them up. I treated the test frogs to beef liver for having been right about Ida from the start. Darwin was chiseling holes for a new wiring system. Five months instead of five years seemed the prognostication for him. He was eating graham crackers globbed with butter

("I can't stop") and got bigger and bigger, more like an overblown boy of fourteen. The woman whose door we left food at was also taking a turn for the worse. Twice she let her sink run until it overflowed. When we picked the lock we discovered her sitting in bed with her feet drawn up under her, watching the water. She creamed her skin and dyed her hair yellow, so it was hard to tell if she was senile or out of her mind.

I understood Darwin's fondness for mice. If you look at them they're graceful and comely. You can see them as panthers, you can see them as pandas. They cluck like a muffled henhouse, whereas guinea pigs sound like puppies down in the cellar. Light as a leaf and taut-legged, they skittered about their cages and sneezed from the bits of sawdust stirred up. They scratched their ears and cleaned their tails nattily and basked upon piles of each other as on piles of cushions, holding a nibble of food in their paws. Given food, they'd hurriedly wash their faces before feeling ready to eat, and when they were hunched on their hams, their shoulders bulged out like extra pouch cheeks. Their tails were their pride and spiritual spine; they always were handling them, bending them around to clean and inspect. Stiff, up-curved tails signaled a fight; or a nervous mouse, with kissing noises, vibrated his tail out stiff and straight. After endearing, midget yawns, they often slept in a row like suckling pigs, and pressed their paws against their cheeks. Or they burrowed head first in a pile so that just their fat rears and pink, bird legs and rubber-hose tails stuck out. As they sickened, their white tails zoned into gray; they sagged and wizened like little sand bags. Sometimes they fled death in leaps, so that it clenched them in mid-air and they thudded down. Sometimes they lay on their sides, scrubbing their noses in spasms and coughing and sneezing, and went rigid like that, rolled up in the pose in which they'd been born and scrubbing their pulsating nostrils. But it was generally a homey, humming room; Darwin and I often went in there.

My problems were solving themselves. If I was too scared to quit my job, the job was foundering under me. Obviously there would soon be no job. Although I was still at my window and my preoccupation with the violence got worse, I didn't dash down to the street so much. I avoided knots of the Harlem Negroes who worked near us, and I would break into sweats of fear at odd moments, walking through a dark block on the way home—I developed a whiz-along walk. The subway was more than ever like an armed camp and, when I came out, I would see everybody facing in one direction and a man there trying to box with a bus. One day a cement truck stopped revolving. Rather than funny it was frenetic. The driver cried. I'd gotten infallible at sensing a fight, sensing its start and exactly its course. Seeing people clumping in front of me, I'd usually turn off but sometimes I kept numbly on through the thick of it as if mesmerized.

The garage crowd amused itself by setting off leftover firecrackers from the horde they'd blackmarketed during the summer. They were having a lazy spell and would hire a passing bum to do some of their chores for a quarter or so. Ida was jumpy with me once our Christmas reunion was over, and Tony, taking his cue, was also cool. Yet we remained a threesome. He'd run away from me but when I caught him and lifted him up he hugged me even as he was struggling. Ida was furious at my treating her like a taboo object. She moved away as if not to let me touch her any time I came close. Although I couldn't conceive of sleeping with her after the suffering that we had gone through, her person still seemed as much mine as a wife's. I refused to stay out of her room when she dressed. I pinched her elbows to see what she weighed and if she was eating enough. I touched my tongue to her forehead if she looked pale to feel what her temperature was. I used to rub her whenever we talked—rubbed and rubbed. I'd spank or order her around, give gifts as usual, fondle and advise her son—everything except sleep with her. Now that her life wasn't a shambles, wasn't about to break apart, she was left with it, which was not very pleasant either. It was a precarious, temporary sort of friendship we had, both of us riding along until I would go my way.

January was uneventfully dreary. The boiler next door blew up and ours went on the blink for a week out of sympathy. One afternoon, at work, late again about six, I heard the electric horn blast, "You goddam spear-carrier!" A bum hadn't washed a car well enough but wanted his money. I winced at the window, it was all so familiar. The four mechanics were cutting across the lot in diagonal paths, toward the man or away after their monkey wrenches. The wife of the thin one was in the station, so he was trying to subdue his cousins a little, walking slower than them, waving his hand. The fellow was standing his ground on the theory that perseverance would carry him through. Standing quietly, he wasn't easy to see because his color just matched the shade of the darkness. His clothes showed up better. He was dead still. You had to look twice. He was only about in his forties, and everything happened very fast. When he saw the crowbars, he used language too. I was violently agitated. My face had lurched into a flinch; I'd stopped breathing. I was so clocked into the gears of this kind of stuff that every part of my body went sick as if as part of an allergy attack—I knew, I knew, I moved like one of the gears myself.

I was tearing downstairs. Outside, the whites were already in a half moon around the guy (the wife in the office door). "It was a shit, nigger job. You don't get nothing for that," said the blast-vigor brother with the voice like a highway horn. He had really too much energy to focus it on the one guy. The fat brother slouched in a posture of venom, but the muscle-bound hired man was less interested in hurting someone than in being strong. My lean opponent was between, holding them off as he cursed in an undertone for the Negro to run. In harassment he pointed at me as if "look what was coming."

"I done a good enough job. You weren't paying nothing but chicken feed anyhow. What do you want? You want to gyp me," said the man. He muttered that slavery wasn't going on any more. Not young, not quite humbled down into middle age, he was in the galled period of life when he had no impulsiveness left to save him. They encircled him, seeing how he took it, poking at his calves with a tire iron, and they called him one or two names. The auto trunks where they kept their weapons gaped open sinisterly. I'd drifted to the edge of the sidewalk on my side of the street with my tentative gait, my quick-backtrack gait, which had saved a great many necks by this time, including my own.

"I done a good job for you and you're going to keep my money?" He hadn't determined upon defiance, it was just happening. "What

a poor sack of fish you are. You're cheapskates. Go on back to your
tiddle-prick then. Go play with yourselves."

A moment went by before they could believe their ears. As
one man, they turned and rushed for the woman, roaring, to drive
her inside. The circle opened for that, but he still wasn't running;
it was written into the lines of his body that he wasn't running.
I'd never been faced with a situation where there was no running,
so all my gingerly jumpiness was no help to me. I was picking
my legs up and putting them down, twitching them almost like
some sort of tail, but nevertheless remained frozen right where I
was. I was nothing, unable to cross the street, unable to function.
When they came back their feet shook the pavement, and a visible
panic pushed up through his knees. The lean mechanic pointed at
me to hold me where I was, and it was as though I were pressing
against a thick pane of glass. The fellow did try to escape but had
waited a second too long. They ran him into the wall and held him
there tight, waving their shovels and irons. "Call the cops! Call the
cops!" they were yelling to Musclebound, in order to establish that
they had phoned first and that an attack on them by the Negro
had followed Musclebound's call. He shoved a dime in the phone,
beating on it. I could see the white faces like flowers behind me
in our building's windows. It was closing time; most of the lights
were off; the cobbler was getting into his coat. I think I was yelling—at least my mouth was open. The Negro had covered his face
with his hands. Since he didn't try to dodge loose, they didn't hit
him more than a couple of times. I was weeping with the collapse
of my nerves and because I'd done nothing; I'd been unable even
to move.

The police dispersed all of us, finally. I was shaking and finished with this. After spending a few days at home sleeping, drinking milkshakes, I called up an uncle of mine in the Midwest and
borrowed enough to move uptown and devote myself to making a
different start in the city.

I Have a Bid

O N A FARM ON THE LAKE ROAD IN ATHOL, among the chickens that fed on the hay seeds on the floor of the barn, were a blue-tailed rooster and a frazzled red hen. The hen, though she had once been a regular layer, had gotten so nervous lately that she'd almost stopped because several others picked on her, pecking hard at her neck and tail feathers, making her run from the rest of the flock. The rooster, nearly as unhappy, was an extra. He hadn't been eaten at the broiler stage because he had looked so energetic and promising but, not being number one or even number two, had been much bitten by the older roosters, who still outweighed him. Like her, he had lost some of his feathers and was scabbed on his comb and rear end, so, one spring evening when Mr. and Mrs. Clark were going to the Tuesday-night livestock auction to sell a couple of newborn bull calves that they didn't want to bother raising as vealers, they caught the hen and rooster as an afterthought, grabbing them off their perches with the aid of a flashlight, stuffing them into a gunnysack, and tying the neck shut. Clarence and Helen Clark were a bulldog couple. They'd been able to burn their mortgage papers ceremoniously years ago and had sent two of their three kids through Lyndon State College's full program to become white-collar folk in the cities downcountry. Close-knit, they spoke the same language, active in the Elks, the Masons, and the Athol Grange. He'd had heart surgery once, but was fit nowadays, still milking twice a day, with Helen's help, fifty-one Holsteins and two Jerseys for cream.

The sale was held in a low, sagging, peeling building, the former livery stable behind Athol's hundred-year-old, three-story hotel. Inside were pens containing half a dozen sheep somebody wanted to get rid of, a few pigs and piglets, goats, and twenty or thirty grown cows, but mostly a great many calves of both sexes and many sizes, a few days or several weeks old, each with a number scrawled on a disc of paper that was glued to its hip. The cows were elderly ladies whose milk production had fallen off, or maybe prime milkers who'd ruined themselves simply by treading on a teat when they'd stood up, or young ones that had caught an infection they couldn't shake off, or good producers the farmer was selling to pay his tax bill, or buy his kid a second-hand car. This fellow would stay to watch the proceedings, or pick up a new animal for himself. But Rog Boyle, the auctioneer, had a poker game afterward where you could lose that money for the tax bill or the new cow or the graduation-present car before you even got home.

A couple of bidders for the slaughterhouses down Boston way were sitting in the small set of bleachers by the auction ring. Each of them had a slat-sided tractor trailer parked outside, as well as the dealer who owned a local killing-house nearby, to keep them honest. One of the packing-house bidders, too, operating his own semi-rig, was from town—Al Boyle, Rog's younger brother. When the auction finally closed, about 1 a.m., he'd highball down to Massachusetts and bring back a check by noon that might clear him more money than the dry-cleaning establishment he also operated had earned during the rest of the week.

No particular love was lost between the brothers, after they'd been trying to shave dollars off of each other every Tuesday for all these years, and that caused some fun and fireworks. "Keep it honest, keep it honest," Al would mutter kiddingly, in the bidding at the bullpen, if Roger seemed to be pulling imaginary bids out of the empty air to boost the price. But he was never heard to tell Roger the same thing during the card game after the sale, if Rog had inveigled one of the farmers who had some cash in his back pocket into his office, where the Seagrams was. He'd play, himself, for a little while before hitting the highway. And Al had a reputation as a lady's man (as a dry-cleaner had more opportunity to be), like their father before him. Rupert, though seventyish, was still going strong on his Sugarbush Farm, horse-trading and all, with a penniless widow tucked into a trailer behind the barn to service him, as well as his wife in the house. Rupert had been the auctioneer before Rog, wilder in style, but less crooked by repute.

Besides the sellers and buyers, a considerable sprinkling of people sat in the bleachers just for something to do—people who didn't have cars and lived downtown in an apartment that Welfare paid for. One of them might bring a box of kittens or a litter of puppies to give away. You'd see neighbors you might never encounter at church, and perhaps in genuine distress—selling a yoke of oxen for meat that had been the man's hobby for the last dozen years, and now he was either too old to work them or too poor to feed them anymore. Or he was selling a big bull that had come damn near injuring somebody and everyone was visibly afraid of, but too valuable as steaks to just shoot. What also made it interesting for the Clarks was observing how the cattle were graded: as top commercial beef paying fifty cents a pound live-weight, or as cutters and canners, ten cents lower. A three-teated cow might sell not just for hamburger, whereas a veteran prime milker wasn't going to be so tender. There might be a handful of pretty good producers mixed in with the culled cows that if you could write a check for about six hundred dollars without fretting and had a spare stanchion at home would give you fifty pounds of milk a day or better for the next couple of years, and then resell for meat. The trick was to figure out which was which, during that brisk minute each cow, scared, mooing, was goaded around the ring—udder swinging, knees knocking, head lunging—and how much you could afford to risk on a lady that might be a loser, or a real pleasure to have in the barn.

The Clarks had a summer person living next door, named Press, who had a pasture he wanted to keep open; his family liked to see cows out the window. Or, rather (with summer people it was always complicated), he was going blind, so he couldn't see them, and was getting divorced, so his family wasn't coming up. But he had loaned the field to Clarence and Helen for heifers, and Clarence might buy four or five at Rog's sale before Memorial

Day and see what price they brought in October, when the grass gave out and the first snow flew. Every acre of his own farm was at work for them, meanwhile, as hayfield, night pasture, or for growing firewood, maple sugar, or else feed corn. Helen had gone to the Athol school with Rog—a stocky, short man with sweat on his upper lip and a harsh voice and jeering eyes, as he'd always had, in fact, even in junior high, though she fancied she could have snagged him instead of Clarence if she'd wanted to. He had made more money, for sure, but it was scarcely a choice she regretted. With the poker, you could never have felt secure financially, and a betting man liked other risks, plus the brutality of the work (selling horses for dog food, on the side, and dragging downed cows half-dead out of people's pastures with a tractor to hack up for the mink farm) must slop over into his domestic life. She knew she and Clarence erred sometimes on the stingy side, which contradicted their Christian doctrine, but they were respectable citizens, unlike Al and Rog—with that horse-trader father, Rupert, who had the wide-hipped widow living free of charge under his wife's nose in that trailer, even if he was a good farmer. Rupert had once even brought in a freight car load of Western cayuses (courtesy of widow, Melba, who had lived there) to auction here at what had been Rupert's dad's livery business; and Al had been known to return from Massachusetts with a strange young woman in the cab of his truck, who either joined the Hippie commune down the road or ended up waitressing at the Busy Bee. Till she left him, nobody had ever asked Al's wife if she knew.

• • •

It was exasperating to Rog that he wasn't a better salesman, that his voice wasn't melodious and he hadn't a glibber gift for gab. He stared straight at people, without the softening technique of looking to one side and introducing a joke at the tippy-tippy moment when they wanted a gentler encouragement to buy. One on one, he was quite a trader, remembering the figures, doing quick math in his head, and a judge of men as well as of flesh. And the old-time summer families had liked him because he was as good as his word. If they asked him to check on their places in the winter, he would, or at least send a guy, especially during deer season, when summer cottages got broken into by idle hunters. He understood, too, their special sense of urgency about "quality time," as most of Athol didn't. These were busy, successful, professional people from the city with only a few weeks' vacation every year, and they weren't worried over spending a few bucks; their priority was wanting to crowd in as much country experience for their children as they possibly could. So he would procure a lamb or a goat for them on short notice, or a lively puppy, or even a Shetland pony with hair hanging over in its eyes, or a tame old saddle horse, promising to try to find a considerate berth for it somewhere after Labor Day, or else board it, if he hadn't simply rented it or borrowed it from somebody his customer didn't know about. As an auctioneer, he valued time, as well, and as a guy who had grown up hard-scrabble and looked down on by the snobbier folks in town, he rather liked chatting with summer people, if only to spite the locals, who looked down on them also. But he was certain he lost thousands of dollars a year in auction commissions and side-sale fees because he couldn't spiel to a crowd with soft soap and sweet blarney like his father had. Rupert, a slipperier fellow, a drinker, was honest enough, but had caromed about, was absent a lot. Rog had done a creditable job with his own offspring by comparison to how he had been raised—had educated them to find better work than helping him, and so was forced to employ two fatherless nephews of his, who were not as bright as his own boys and made him lose his temper.

Rog had had a hernia for a number of years—was afraid to go under the knife—so even with the truss he couldn't lift much, or jump into the stock trucks that backed up to his ramp and heft the calves or shoulder the cows out when they arrived, the way he'd always used to do, and get up and in there again when they left. He depended on the nephews for that, which was frustrating, just as he did on his wife Juliette for the computer and written work, and upon that eldest kid, a slick-haired boy in fluorescent shirts and black jeans who played the electric guitar in a roadhouse group, to do some of the microphone patter because Rog's voice broadcast so bluntly and harshly. Besides, he liked to be handling the goods and animals: oddities like a wheelchair, a rocking chair, a hand-whittled cane, after somebody died, or a freak llama or whatever. And he knew cows like his father knew horses.

"Awful nice place to gradually build a herd, here, boys, because you get some disposal sales. People build up a real careful quality succession and then have to sell it," Rog told the crowd. But Helen Clark whispered to Clarence with a laugh that because of all the bloated bellies and blown-out faces in the stands, there were a lot of "disposed" individuals also, who'd never been off of the dole. Except for bingo on Friday nights at the Catholic church, it was the only live entertainment left in Athol. Not that the Town Hall hadn't doubled as an opera house, where concert pianists, barbershop quartets, Chautauqua lecturers, and mezzo sopranos performed till probably the 1920s. After that they had had theater groups and talent nights, "until the satellite dish became the state flower," as Clarence said, and poker was an alternative to being born again.

• • •

Karl and Dorothy Swinnerton were sitting in the front, along with the killing-house buyers and gambling-minded farmers, although, like the Clarks, they were not what Rog would call "closers," and would need some tickling to bid at all, and anyhow owed some small debts to him. They had Press, that blind summer person with them—which was kind—and liked to bring home a wholesale carton of garden seeds, or a packet of flashlight batteries, or a trio of mallards, mysteriously squirming in a feed sack tied at the neck, or a fat Belgian rabbit, ready to be either somebody's meal or a child's pet, or a wheelbarrow, or a black pig. A collie with silky hair and tricolor markings was fastened to the leg of the grandstand nearby, too awestruck to yowl, in need of new owners, and Dorothy did miss the presence of a dog. They'd lost a litter to distemper and the grieving mother had wandered onto the road and got killed. This bitch was too old to tempt people with children, but might suit them if Karl could be persuaded that it wasn't too mild to chase after their thieving fox. Dogs had been part of his livelihood. He'd meat-hunted and fur-hunted with them, trained and sold puppies, guided a little with coon and bear hounds, and to have none at all underfoot was depressing, although his cough was so bad that they'd sold off their livestock and he couldn't work regularly as a housepainter. He was the son of a farmer, but glad to have given up that confining labor for inter- mittent painting, where you could move into contact with other people but also had time for hunting and fishing. Nevertheless, he and Dorothy lived back in the woods on a patch of the old fam- ily property—forty acres and the hired man's house that they had bought from the other heirs when his parents had died. They ran a few cows on it occasionally, and still had three Herefords trip- ping over tree roots, which they would butcher when the price of beef went up. But in the meantime Dorothy was worried about Karl's emphysema, and that the money to pay for it might take their house, if the V.A. doctors couldn't help. She was cooking for a price for this summer person who had bought the rest of the land and the main house—at least had bought it from the people who had originally bought it, and was loaning the Clarks the big pasture—but was now unfortunately going blind and talking of staying past the summer, a puzzling sort of decent, lonely fellow of fifty, younger than Karl and herself, but divorcing. He had some money, but who knew what would happen to him?

This weekly gabble and ruckus at Rog's was an outing, and served to let Karl and Dorothy see how many of the people they had known for years were now living in trailers or else apart- ments in town, eating starch with their feet propped up in front of the Box, and not seeming to mind too much. Both of them had spells of dreading that they were going to end up in a dab of space rented by the month, eating government peanut butter and government rice and waiting in line to have their tickets punched whenever they needed something. Karl's only town activity was the American Legion—meetings every month on the second floor of Memorial Hall and marching in the parade on the Fourth of July and a roulette booth at the county fair in August to raise money for the Legion's annual college scholarship for a high school graduate.

But more importantly, he judged a man's character by what he had done in the war—meaning mostly his own war, the Second one— or might have done if he had been in it. The World War I vets, grumpy and reticent and dying off now, were also favorites of his, or Darryl Curley, for example, who owned the construction company and was a Korean vet who hadn't even joined the Legion when he came home. Yet when the National Guard unit over in Chelsea had auctioned off its Sherman tank, after acquiring a newer model, he was the local who had bid for it, against gun collectors from as far downcountry as Georgia, and hauled it to park it in front of the Quonset hut where he garaged his equipment. That told you something more than whether he drank six-packs in the Legion hall. And he wasn't a stick-in-the-mud like his father, who had got out of serving in the Second War on a farmer's deferment; or a goof-off like his brother, Randy, who sometimes helped the Hippies run drugs. Thousands of bucks had gone into that tank, and Karl stopped once to look at it. Although a lot of the Korean War had not been fought on tank terrain, Darryl, an impatient man who made money hand over fist and seldom gave Karl the time of day, strolled out of his office with a certain chesty pride. "Just a glorified steamroller, isn't it?" he said companionably, silent otherwise, as was Karl.

Now, Helen Clark and Dorothy Swinnerton were friends from playing pinochle together and cooking church suppers, when they'd gone regularly, whereas Clarence and Karl were more gingerly when they nodded, although they had also known each other for forty years, from school and then playing football on the Athol Loggers town team in their twenties, both being linemen and dependable. But Clarence, who paid his bills by return mail, and was now a Fundamentalist deacon—read the recitations, looked over the budget, and carried the collection plate—took apostasy as seriously as Karl took not serving your country in wartime, "right or wrong." Yet you had to look at a man's kids, beyond his churchgoing, Karl thought. The two families had been on the phone chattily like neighbors on Grange matters at one stage, when the Clarks' son and Karl and Dorothy's dear daughter, Margie, started going out together, riding Bill's motorcycle around. And one night Bill rode it right off an embankment, on the Border Road, with Margie holding onto him from behind. He had a helmet; she didn't—can you believe it?—and they each seemed at first to have got off okay. But then when her seizures started, he lost interest fast. Made no bones about it. Told her he wanted to have kids, which entirely unnecessarily hurt her. Now he had two kids and a snow-fencing business, two franchises, selling Vermont cedar to Springfield, Massachusetts and Hartford, Connecticut. And where does their churchgoing fit there? Karl had said to Dorothy—until they stopped mentioning it—who was more forgiving, and suggested that that might be part of why they went—although bumping into Helen a lot less, herself.

But with Rog, somehow you had good kids. Educated; good cars, when you saw them; white-collar, out of the town and part of the larger economy, so to speak; and with well-spoken grandchildren for Rog, when you met them, petting a billy goat on a visit to his auction barn—though Rog was a subspecies of crook, actually, if you thought about it. Not so much the poker games, which were between adults, and not so sleazy as you might think, because he'd let you owe him money without a fuss. He liked cash, not bookkeeping. He wanted you to pay him in hundred dollar bills when you could. But he had fallen in with the Hippies, too—like Darryl's off-base son, Randy Curley, who was said to be shuttling marijuana to Boston or New York City in his pickup sometimes, packed underneath a load of maple syrup or Christmas trees—but worse. The Hippies showed up at auction night occasionally, to pick up some cheap chickens, if they'd built a coop, or a pregnant ewe that they might want to milk for some health craze of theirs, or maybe motor oil in bulk, or car parts that Rog had got from a supply store going bankrupt. Rog had learned to call, if his foraging at clearance sales turned up items that he guessed might fit their habits, which he saw included endless tinkering on their junker cars. They didn't do card games, as a rule (that must have seemed tame compared to tripping out on acid), but in due course he met a bearded kid from Brooklyn, who, after slapping together a two-story, peaked-roof board house on four acres in a weed-tree woods—the whole lay-out had probably cost him a thousand bucks—for his wife and kids, and, not buying into the peace-and-love claptrap completely, was looking for some action. Rog—who, once again, had raised his own kids to be more trustworthy than him—took on this twenty-something-year-old hustler whose father drove a subway train and put him to work on a rough commission, going around to families whose head-of-household had just died, looking for stuff that might look antique if you trucked it to a place called Hudson Street in Greenwich Village in New York. Not that Rog had ever been to New York, or this kid knew antiques, but between them, and Rog's connection as a fellow Woodchuck to the bereaved families, they got a pretty good thing up and running. And Rog was not above pulling a gun on the kid—it being perfectly legal to carry a concealed weapon in Vermont—to show him the danger of not coming clean on the money he was being paid for this old stuff by the dealers in the big city. But this kid had grown up in a tougher neighborhood than Athol ever was, and the next day he came back to Rog with the proposal that he, the kid, fork over a hundred dollars apiece for any functional handgun Rog produced, and then he'd sell it for what he could get for it in Brooklyn's gangland, with no questions asked at this end. So Rog practically vacuumed northeastern Vermont for loose, second-hand, shootable pistols of blurry provenance (not only that practically any man who died had had one), and paid his youngest son's college tuition thus. And the Brooklyn police would call the Vermont state police when a murder weapon was found to have been shipped new by the manufacturer to Vermont: where the trail swiftly petered out.

Rog had told the story to Karl in deer camp one November night, after the kid and his family had left Hippiedom in Athol for somewhere else, but couldn't be persuaded to feel guilty, drunk or sober, about anything that might have resulted from those business transactions, once the guns were whisked down to New York. His children were a priority, and he'd also invested in a few farms bought lately from old people who wanted to go to Florida in a hurry, afraid they might die first, but were intimidated by the notion of turning either to a bank or to a real estate broker—signing the papers for Rog by kerosene lamp right there on the kitchen table. And he did mail them their payments regularly, although he usually had shed the farms at a profit in a matter of months. If you owed him money from some ill-considered poker game, he might show up at your place quite pleasantly around dinnertime, eat with you and your wife, and, without haggling, suggest either the hay tedder or the dishwasher would do, or that more-white-than-black, broad-withered cow. He would put any of the three in his stake-side and maybe deliver it to a farm that he was in the process of buying, and come back for mashed potatoes and pie the next night, if your wife wasn't too mad at you and him. His brother, Al, the livestock trucker, might have tried to get a blow job thrown in—but that was dangerous fun, like running cocaine, as that Brooklyn tiger had also done on his return trips from peddling guns, and as Al was sometimes rumored to do. Rog believed in what he called "the logic of moderation," such as his father, Rupert, the horse trader—like Al—had eschewed.

Karl Swinnerton had hunted with Al and Rog for a season or two because they had a good tidy camp up near Goon Mountain's ridgeline, where some big bucks bedded down for the night or else retreated from the next morning's gunfire down in the valley. On Opening Day, these might scramble right past the porch, having grown used to its presence near their deer trail during the year since last fall. Al, Rog, and Karl, who were not friends now, had regarded themselves as a raffish tribe, not just Logger teammates, but all high-school grads: Rog, a horse trader's son making a more steady go of cattle dealing; Al, a budding rolling stone who had lucked into the dry-cleaning business; and Karl, born a farmer, who was trying to support himself as a trapper, selling pelts, and guiding tourists to good fishing holes in the summer. Al was a fly-off-the-handle, seven o'clock drunk, however, who would snap off a shot up a deer's flag end, ruin half the best meat, and make it drag itself, suffering, instead of waiting another second for a side shot, or maybe frontal, to kill it; then for supper forget a pot and burn the bottom through; and, as they used to kid him, needed a woman to pick up after him.

Al was a demon fireman on Athol's trusty pumper, though, putting out blazes with the "Cellar Savers," as they called their crew. He had more public spirit than Rog or Karl in that sense, volunteering for longer than the customary stint of three to five years, and was less tardy or crabby in showing up when he'd grabbed no sleep after a trip. He wasn't fire captain material, but was often the first man in. As a trucker—even only a short-run man who seldom ventured south of Massachusetts or west of Syracuse with his trailer loads of cows—he affected a sort of a man-of-the-world air, as if he was just back from Louisiana or L.A., and full of truck-stop hokum. Like Randy Curley—who delivered furniture manufactured at the mill in Chelsea on longer runs to department-store warehouses in the Midwest or South, as a substitute for the company's regular drivers, but didn't own his own truck—Al had been falling in with the Hippies on Ten Mile Road. He smoked pot more than he used liquor, which was a departure for Athol men of his age, although he hadn't tried LSD, he claimed, or transported the stuff, as Randy was rumored to do.

Stillwater Swamp, which edged his and Dorothy's land on the east side, and stretched about ten or twelve miles, north to south, and five to seven or eight across in its width, was what Karl had known his whole lifetime, in fact. The full-furred otters, foxes, and bobcats, the cedar trees limbed and dragged out for post-and-rail fencing and patio furniture, the cat spruce and balsam fir pulpwood cut for the paper mill, the black ash that he split into splints that Dorothy made baskets out of, the cherry wood, and sawlog yellow birch, and bird's-eye maple in the high spots, and tamaracle, and pickerel, perch, and stewing-turtles in the sloughs. Plenty of deer bounding about, plus a dozen or two dozen moose, so you'd never starve. And now the Japs—some Japs—had bought the whole swamp as an investment from the Wall Streeters, who themselves had bought it only a year or two ago from the original lumbering company that had been working it from when Karl was a boy. And the bulk of Goon Mountain, overhanging the swamp from his western side, he didn't even know who owned. Just its ledges, springs and dimples, going up two thousand feet, where the hawks nested.

Sitting with Dorothy on the bottom rung of the auction house grandstand, he couldn't help wondering why he was down on his uppers, while Rog, Clarence, and Al—to take three obvious examples—were not. Al didn't own things except for his dry cleaning business and his blessed truck; no land, therefore less property tax. And Clarence was a hoarder, so well organized that you'd see him look at his handkerchief to see if it was clean before he blew his nose into it, and already drawing social security checks. Clarence was as comfortable with being faithful to Helen as Al was in tomcatting, though Karl figured that neither pose meant much. Clarence never had the nerve to flout any of the other norms either, and Al hadn't beat his wife or brought home some doxy, just cheated on the sly. Clarence had surely saved enough money for Helen and him to go to Florida and visit friends of hers who had invited them for a month in the winter, leaving Bill with the farm, but, like a coward, he didn't. Though he wouldn't admit it, he seemed to be afraid of beaches, islands, the sea, or whatnot, never having crossed the Atlantic for two weeks on a troop ship, like Karl. He was a jittery man, like most solid citizens, if you scratched at all beneath their surfaces, Karl thought. The lawyer in town had been arrested for speeding, and pot found in his car; a doctor in Chelsea had lost his license temporarily for selling prescriptions to a drug peddler; and the richest local family, who owned the hardware and grocery stores, were skinflints. They drove Caddies and had cottages on the lake ten miles away that they moved to in the summer, and had Karl paint their houses instead of doing it themselves, like everybody else, but had never helped the poorhouse poor or the farmers being foreclosed on. Rog made more generous distinctions, as a matter of fact. He seemed still bitter, remembering his father and mother squeezed from pillar to post, and people avoiding him, snubbing him, as a schoolboy from a family pushed off their farm, until his mother's uncle passed away with no living children and left them another, down the road. So when someone died and Rog went over and bought stuff to sell, he tended to treat them according to how their people had treated his people when he was a boy.

Rog auctioned off some cowbells, monkey wrenches, a gooseneck lamp, a horse harness, and a job lot of plastic razors and ball point pens that he distributed practically free. Then boxes of china—"*Chinese* china, made in China"—and glassware, bags of lawn seed and of lime, a dozen banties cackling in a bag, a pair of snow tires, and some cans of barn paint. "We could use it on the walls but we can't afford to, boys. Got to sell them in order to pay the bills."

About the tires, he said, "They're not hot, boys, but they may have stood out in the sun long enough to feel a little bit warm," because he had a reputation he liked to foster of maybe buying items that had been stolen at some distant point. With garage sales on every roadside killing you all summer long, you needed a gimmick besides trading in vealers and the "Antique Barn" that he maintained out on the highway. "A deal or a steal!" he proclaimed, although he'd never been convicted of anything. "Open those wallets, boys. Awful cheap. I just don't want to get lonely in here. That's why I do it, boys—charge you so little—to give you some fun and festivities."

Dorothy went over to a row of sacks that were squirming, set against the wall. Having gently palpated the occupants, she decided she wanted a pair of ducks, for those big, gamey eggs that they laid for pies or a breakfast to stick to your ribs. And Karl had suggested she ought to write a book on how to find duck nests in the grass, or institute a contest in hen-robbing at the county fair, she was so good at it. That was their vacation every year, parking their camper next to the carnival people's at the fairgrounds, living amidst that hullabaloo for the week.

"What you want, Dot?" Rog asked. His dead older brother had had a crush on her in high school. He sold a chainsaw, a used TV, a dirt bike, a car battery, a radio scanner, a trayful of tomato plants ready to go in the ground, a bedroom mirror, bush clippers, a tool box, three milking machines—yelling the prices bid, until somebody raised and closed the matter.

"I'm overextended! You've got me over a barrel," he told the cozy crowd, maybe sixty people watching. "That's why I'm takin' almost any offer." When everybody knew he had two cars, one of which was a new Toronado, a cow truck, a camper top to clip onto his pickup, a couple of snowmobiles, a three-wheeler, and a four-wheeler, and a boat with an inboard motor sitting on a trailer in front of his house, not to mention the couple of farms he was currently speculating on. Sawdust was strewn across the dirt floor and the railings were painted white, but otherwise the big room was fly-specked and dingy, the air very bad. Leaking bags of insulation bulged downward between cracked beams, from which light bulbs and insect-zappers dangled.

The sows in the pens were squealing, and the aging cows waiting to be auctioned and butchered groaned, flinched, and hooked at one another nervously because they were from different herds, where by seniority they might each have become prima donnas, but now were crammed with strangers into a claustrophobic enclosure and in some pain because they hadn't been milked for at least one cycle, if they hadn't missed more. The fifty or sixty calves, penned at the other side of the auction ring, meanwhile were bleating in fear and hunger—none had known their mothers for more than a day or two—the little Jerseys as slim and tan as fawns, but wobbling tremendously, and the Holsteins still more ungainly and misconstructed because they had been overbred lately with artificial insemination for maximum milking: at least so the Swinnertons thought. Money problems had made Karl and Dorothy edgy, but they were similar enough that they managed to blame themselves more than one another. They knew that being interested in money generated money, at least over a lifetime, and that if you weren't, then you would have to scrimp in the last few years of your fifties and sixties, before the government began giving you health insurance and sending you monthly checks. It was almost a bargain you made with God, Dorothy thought. Hard times for good intentions. But many people who made money weren't greedy as much as full of nervous energy, like Rog, who didn't know what else to do. Always looking for something to buy that he could sell—dry goods, a backhoe, an emu, a consignment of canned pears. In a little black doctor's bag—joking about "good medicine"—he carried wrapped cash, in instances where that was appropriate, and liked land in particular, now that so many dairy businesses were folding, drowned in debt.

Rog's wife, Juliette, was French in origin—that is, her parents had emigrated from Quebec during the Depression—and possessed the French virtues of frugality with money and classy middle-age looks: hair brushed and tucked, clean clothes that fit. She sat on a bookkeeper's stool at the auctions and never lost track of the math or who bid what, even when Rog and his ringmen—the nephews—were momentarily confused. She had black hair and white skin that she didn't let tan, and had kept a Catholic rein on her kids so they all got through school without police trouble or pregnancies, ready to go away to college. Juliette was proving canny now, too, Rog said when he dropped by the Swinnerton's house once every month or two in order to chat, because when you're nosing around for defunct farms with old people clinging on under a load of debt ready to throw in the sponge—and who might rather be somewheres else anyway, whether back in Canada or retired down South—they were as likely to be French as Yankees. They spoke some English, of course, but for a real heart-to-heart over coffee and White Roses at the kitchen table, with Rog's doctor's bag full of greenbacks lying open on the floor close by, Juliette's emoting sympathetically with them in French was better—was invaluable.

One of the gunnysacks jerked like a jumping bean. "Wonder what's in there! Wanna bid for it sight unseen?" suggested Rog, turning from a set of truck tires that his nephews had rolled out for the auction. Dorothy and Karl had only seven chickens left at home, having lost two slow hens and their fine brave tall rooster with the cream-colored cape. Dorothy happened to see him ride off, lying heavily across a fox's red back, with his head right next to the fox's black face, although upside down. His neck had been gripped in the fox's teeth, the feathers wet and disarranged. Still alive, he gazed desolately at the sky. Though Karl would spot the fox eventually and be able to shoot

him, to have only seven layers seemed a dreary, scant, precarious number, on the verge of having none. It was plenty for their
present needs, even allowing for the baking she sometimes did,
but since her earliest memories Dorothy had never known a yard
with so few chickens in it. Suppose she was asked to bake cakes
for a birthday, a funeral, a church supper? All the fuss and to-do
of thirty fowlish, feathery personalities was part of the home life
of everybody she had grown up with—maybe as poor as church
mice, but always eating three or four eggs for breakfast. And for
the social cooking she'd done—the potlucks with deviled eggs,
custards, angelfood, eggy salads, tarts—it had been essential she
have numberless chickens scratching in the dirt, under the leaves,
for bugs and sprigs that turned their yolks orange with good
woods vitamins for children or sick older people. She'd peddled
fryers too, and cottage cheese and home-baked pies to the summer people, when her children lived at home and none of her
aches and pains had counted for anything, and she would gad
about in the car, bringing the kids along if she needed to or she
thought they would benefit from meeting somebody who struck
her as interesting—or if Karl was painting there—often on the
lookout at that time also for possible articles for the weekly paper, whose editor was encouraging Dorothy to try topics like
"How to Dig a Stock Pond," or "What Marriage Means," or
"Athol's Earliest Settlers," or "The Marsh Mallow: Where the
Candy Came From." She dreamed up two for every one that she
actually wrote, and wrote two for every one he ever published.
Darryl Curley had dug them a stock pond with his earth mover,
and Mae, his wife and Dorothy's best friend in those days, had
shocked her by telling her how she, Mae, once had to jump out
of Darryl's car while it was moving and scraped herself pretty
badly on the pavement. But you couldn't write that.

The pond still steamed beautifully in the chill of the morning, but hadn't had ducks on it recently because of a snapper living
in the depths that had been big enough to grab them from below.
Last summer, however, Dorothy spotted her climbing out to lay
her eggs in a sandbank. Karl grabbed her, they cooked her, and not

two days later a wild mallard landed and began eating duckweed; then a blue heron. Later a white egret appeared (she looked it up in her bird book) and, like the heron, stalked around eating pollywogs, salamanders, crayfish, or whatever for half an hour before flapping off. This was unusual, but also signaled that the coast was clear for Dorothy to buy Muscovys for the pond. Starting from when she was barely of school age, she'd been in charge of finding eggs for her family, not just hidden in the water grass, but up in the hayloft, where the banties burrowed holes to brood a clutch. She told Press, the blind summer person, about that and about her articles. He was a nice guy, and good for five dollars a day, at lunch.

Karl was behind on cutting next winter's firewood because of his emphysema, and hadn't dug a new garbage pit, although the one they were using was full, and the garden fence that the deer got through wasn't fixed, and squirrels ran up and down in the attic because neither of them quite felt like climbing the ladder to lay out poison or nail up the holes. So although twenty-three Plymouth Rock chickens were offered for twenty-five bucks, she didn't bid; the commitment would be too much. They knew an old bachelor who had no other company except his chickens and, lonely in the winter, brought them into the house. Rog would think she was getting soft in the head if she bought too many. His brother, Boyle, three years older, who had made major before retiring to play golf in San Antonio, had delivered fuel oil around here before enlisting in the army, after she and he broke up. But he'd thrown snowballs at her, pulled her pigtails, or thrown mud on her as early as primary school to flirt. It was funny how distant you grew from certain people—a person who looked just like he had in tenth grade except for the pudge in his neck and gray in his hair—in spite of probably forgiving him more nowadays for the dumbbell he'd been than you ever did then. What happened was that as you grew more patient you also got less interested, more understanding but less sympathetic. Karl's estranged brother, Marty—now a produce manager in a supermarket downstate—and this Boyle brother had cracked up cars together to impress each other and the girls, while Rog and Karl himself had scarcely registered on Dorothy, being too young. Now, when Karl would go to the veteran's hospital for his cough, Rog—balding but vain about his good teeth—might actually wink at her, and she would wish Juliette were there to take the heat. Juliette, impassively keeping the records straight at her auction desk, with pricey earrings on and her raven hair highly coiffed, would not be rattled by a wink. Although their marriage was a long one, she had changed her tastes in cars, clothes, and adornments lately. They ate out quite a lot, and Rog claimed she wanted him to buy her a condo on Cocoa Beach in Florida, where she thought she knew somebody. Though a fine mother, she stayed out of community activities unless her own fractious French family got into a dispute. The two of them sometimes did engage in noisy fights, when the word divorce was heard, but you wouldn't believe it, looking at how unflappable she was on the dais. Pretty women married Don Juans, and Don Juans married pretty women.

The nephews held up four grain sacks, each with a goose's orange-billed head protruding out, elegant, wriggly, but angry. "Just like a watchdog for your dooryard, they'll be," hollered Rog. When Karl was tempted to bid, Dorothy reminded him of how independent-minded geese are, and liable to bite anybody. Karl had served in North Africa and whispered with a smile that they reminded him of camels, who could be bad-tempered too. But they lost the geese to a woman, whose mother and daughter Dorothy knew, for $8.80 apiece. With farmers, you couldn't tell from their clothes how well off they were—who was here to truck home nine thousand dollars' worth of milking cows and who to acquire a magnetic key ring for a jalopy's dashboard. But these people were well off.

For a minute the loudest sounds were the steady bleating of the week-old, frightened calves—sixty, seventy of them now—and the old cows' anxious lowing, wild in timbre like a zoo animal's.

Rog's "Yes! Yes!" sharply interrupted their distress, as the bidding on a wicker sofa rose to fifty-five dollars and he scrutinized his customers to judge how interested they were. "You lunk, you! You stay with him!" he shouted, when one of his nephews quit staring at a man who'd bid just as Rog rapped the gavel and gave the sofa to another.

He also sold a second-hand living-room organ, five bags of 5-10-10 fertilizer, a roll of linoleum, and then pulled a clutch of New Hampshire Reds out of a bran sack which, being more barnyardy than the Plymouth Rocks, flapped their wings frantically when he swung them high. Dorothy could picture them inhabiting the dirt flat behind her back porch and had Karl bid a dollar-and-a-quarter, dollar-fifty, two dollars apiece, at which point—just bidding against the soup pot—they did get them, and Karl cut more air holes for them to breathe in the bag. He never tried to buy anything else immediately after winning a round for fear the whole thing would get going too fast and he might lose his head. And whereas most people leaned forward, Karl leaned back when he bid, turning sideways so Rog and the nephews wouldn't think he was eager to bid again. Besides, he already had three house cats at home, and a pig to eat, a wheezy ram named Samson, two ewes, each with a grown lamb, a leftover tom turkey named Emcee, and a woods turtle they'd picked up on the road a year ago, with the numerals 1939 carved on its bottom shell, though they had argued about whether to believe such a date. Dorothy claimed no.

Clarence and Helen Clark bought twelve turkey pullets, and for thirty-four bucks, a naked-looking ten-pound pig as pink as flesh, held up by Rog by its trotters, shrieking in terror and blinking after the darkness of being tied inside its bag, though its ears stuck forward like a cap's bill, shading its eyes from the spotlight. They stopped beside the Swinnertons in collecting it, and Helen, in her churchy manner, asked, "How's it going?" of Press, and whether he wanted to go to the midweek service at Solid Rock Gospel with them tomorrow. He wasn't stone-blind, and smiled at her; said, probably next time. He'd been a stockbroker, had some money. Dorothy's parents had sometimes entertained summer boarders from the city, fattening the undernourished ones on butter, cream and syrup, and quieting the jittery ones with hay-wagon rides, taffy pulls, horseback trails, and outdoor barbeques with cocoa and marshmallows roasted on a stick at the end in the firelight. Through this sideline, she had met interesting people as a child, who were briefly friends during July and August, and a few of the kinder ones had tweaked her, as she got older, with the idea of going to college, like the girls of her own age in their cashmere sweaters and riding boots and helmets that they brought from home, until she'd tease them into riding the old farm Dobbins bareback ("and don't you dare whip him"). The boys were easy to fend off, compared with the locals, and she rarely envied the girls when they went home to different lives. But several of the sympathetic grownups had instilled some carbonation in her (as she thought of it, watching bubbles rise in soda pop) that may have led to her newspaper columns later on, and her attempt to start a mail-order candle-making business at another point, and probably, she thought, her tolerance for the endearing but irregular means of breadwinning her husband would put together. The kind of people who came up from the city to spend a spell on an ordinary family farm like theirs—spinsters of both sexes, or sickly people after an operation, or clerical help with two weeks off, or vaguely impoverished artists who might write songs or draw Christmas cards for a living, or professionals "taking a break"—were eccentrically assorted. You would witness the visible recovery of people who had been "flattened," as they said, by a death in the family, of neurotics who used the scary term "nervous breakdown" to describe how they felt. They rocked on the porch, blinked in the sun, took short "constitutionals" with that comical, arm-swinging gait that city folk used, until they'd go breathless, and then might help feed the animals in order to relax. One even brought her own cats. Anyhow, collectively they'd proven easier to manage than her parents had expected, mostly because they were so "eager to learn," as they might put it if they thought they'd been living wrong. They wanted to be shown how to relax, and pitched hay, stacked wood, kneaded bread, kindled the kitchen stove, to get the hang of it.

Helen and Clarence Clark were too tidy a couple to want to look after sick New Yorkers, even if there was money involved. Yet they would make this little pullet project pay. It was never much, nothing grand, but they never had to explain themselves to the lady at the bank; just walked up to the teller's window like anybody else, no appointments with somebody at a desk. And their boy, Bill, who'd smashed up Margie so bad on the motorcycle, had that same close-to-the-vest solvency—a rental-truck franchise run from right in the yard, and his planing mill nearby and picket-fence sales downcountry; plus his plans to refurbish the defunct railroad station for tourism purposes. He was small potatoes, next to Darryl Curley's construction business, but because he was reaching out-of-state toward where the money was, people like Rog said he would grow bigger. A clean-faced boy, not a drinker like some, and yet he'd chopped Margie off right where she lived—telling her the medications for her seizures might deform a baby. It made Karl want to shoot him. Although a girl like Margie you couldn't keep down. She *was* married, and with a baby in the oven that in the pictures they took at the medical center was already sucking its thumb, comfy as you please—her husband a nice decent man who worked for Darryl off and on at a gas station he had bought, or drove a school bus, as Margie had—a mechanic who enjoyed draining oil pans and changing mufflers in the garage, but was trying to get his act together. He seemed half a beat too fast, it seemed to Karl and Dorothy, as if agitated by anticipating Margie's seizures that no longer came. So when they could find humor in it, they joked about the pair as being a match-up like Jack Spratt's, who could eat no fat, and his wife no lean.

A hay rake, a tangle of tire chains, and a case of root beer were sold. Then a brown goat Dorothy decided she wanted was lifted onto the block. Whenever she felt a sad swing in her mood she'd find herself looking for an animal to bring home. It was a buck, standing stock still, not trembling with fear but so insouciant that it tipped its head backwards and scratched its white-speckled rump with the tips of its horns. She and Karl were still arguing the merits of buying it ("Reminds me of a camel"), when she lost the animal to a Greek with bushy gray eyebrows, who owned a shoe store over in Chelsea and bought goats "for cultural reasons," as he had once explained. Indeed, at the State Beach on the Fourth of July you'd notice the entire clan, with Greek music blaring from a stereo and charcoal reddening to coals under a flayed kid. People "kidded" them about whether the skin would end up later in shoes.

Irritated, she bought the next sack a nephew held up: which contained two white Leghorns and a banty that "laid green eggs," the farmer that had owned them yelled—giving a thumbs-up to Karl because they'd used to drink White Russians together at the Osborne Bar twenty years ago. He still drank and Karl didn't, but Karl was the person with a killing cough. "In Heaven they've got no beer! That's why we drink it here!" he sang.

Dorothy bought a green-headed, red-legged duck for a couple of bucks as another addition, although they would eat him when the pond froze, if he didn't turn out as personable as Emcee, the huge, bronze-plumaged tom gobbler that ought to have gone for Thanksgiving dinner years ago, when they'd still had enough cows for Karl to hum along with the radio when he milked. Emcee survived as a relic from when they had had practically as many cats as cows in the barn, but none more personable than Emcee, who swayed his head like a master of ceremonies to the talk shows, too.

Tangled-up piglets muttered and squirmed in other bags, and jittery rabbits stamped their soft, forceful hind feet. Geese protested being pinioned, amidst the din of cows mooing, pigs of butcherable age squealing as if in foreboding, a dog outside barking. Whenever birds or animals were sold, a slight wave of excitement swept the room, partly sympathetic, partly cruel, because anything living could be fun. Both fun and problematical, although a bachelor could buy a box of cockerels for hardly more than a buck apiece and feed them scraps and have his suppers for two or three weeks on almost no outlay.

"Once poor, always prepared," Rog reminded the crowd. "I'd have to stay home from school some days so Al could wear the shoes!" Al, who sat there sporting a stockman's cane and five-gallon hat, waiting for the serious meat-cow bidding to start, grinned, not betraying whether it was true. Rumor had it that Rog had engineered his start by setting a few insurance fires, then sending a retarded brother to jail to take the fall. Even now it was said to be hard for him to get his buildings insured. But Al's story was more curious. In the 1930s and 1940s the dry-cleaning store had belonged to an immigrant who gradually outlived his family and had no relatives to turn to when he grew old and sick. Most boys in town would probably not have worked for him as a presser after school and doing deliveries, or been allowed to by their parents because he was a Jew. But Al, with an adventurous, exotic streak even in adolescence, did, and when the man had a stroke, it was Al who drove him to his doctor's appointments and to the hospital and saw to his needs. This developed into a friendship between opposites—youngster, old man; "Woodchuck" and European exile. He didn't have a lot of last words, Al said, and most were in another language, but what he did come out with that Al, at the bedside, could decipher was not about being lonesome in a foreign land, but *Don't put it off, do what you want!*

The will was complicated but left Al the business, though the house went to somebody else, who sold it for nothing like a shot. And Al had husbanded what he'd got for half a dozen years before he started wheeling and dealing with beef on the hoof—Karl meanwhile out in the winter woods, running a six-hour trap line in Stillwater Swamp and another in a swamp adjoining Stillwater that he snuck into across the border in Canadian territory. It was certainly better fun than dry-cleaning would have been, or staying twenty years in the army, as the other Boyle brother had done. But you paid the piper eventually. He looked over at his drinking buddy from the Osborne Bar whose banty's green eggs would now be theirs, but who was whittling a duck decoy from a chunk of basswood to pass the time. After he painted it up, he might get half a hundred for it from the tourists, as folk art, and Karl was wondering whether every other clown was finding some kind of a racket to exploit, except for him. He went and bummed a cigarette and got away with two drags on it before he began coughing. Then he simply held the thing until it burned to the end, while he and the whittler talked about the run of spawning rainbows at Skinflint Falls.

During this lull, as three late balky cattle were being unloaded—underfed, underbred, dazed and dumb—Dorothy examined the collie that was tied under the grandstand, looking for the cloudiness of cataracts in her eyes, or abscessed teeth, and snapped her fingers softly to see if the dog turned at the sound, and if her response expressed more curiosity than fear.

"Hey, hey, whoa." Karl bustled over. "This isn't adopt-orama."
But she said again, "Reminds me of a camel."

Rog, returning from the cattle pen, said that some pretend-
farmers he had rented a place to over on May Mountain had aban-
doned her when they pulled up stakes, owing him money, and he
hadn't wanted to shoot her. Karl, instead of drawing Dorothy's
hands away, then repeated her check of the dog's vital signs, and
felt her throat and undercarriage for a tumor or a hernia, tested
her side vision, looked at her gums for anemia, her ears for mites,
and at her rear for the bloated appearance that worms produce. He
decided she had some husky in her, a cross he approved of because
the wider head would usually bring a calmer temperament and a
better sense of smell. Carrying over the box of give-away kittens,
he was pleased to see that she sniffed each one with separate interest, and offered her two pinches of sawdust with separate scents
(goat pee and cow piss) to watch her react. He thumped her ribs
to see whether her lungs were sore, felt her joints for the twinges
of arthritis, and her individual toes, and succeeded in holding her
attention for a full minute by conversation alone, which was one
of his tests of a promising dog.

Back at the cow chute, Rog was in a snit because one of the
cows being unloaded couldn't walk properly. Mad anyhow at the
rough job his lamebrained half-brother Kiddo was doing with an
electric prod, which caused the other animals, well or not, to bang
themselves sideways hysterically on the ramp. He chewed out the
farmer for bringing him a mink-farm specimen. "You know she
can't pass inspection, for Christ's sake, for human consumption.
You can't park her here, dead at the door!"

"She's not sick! She stuck her fucking foot through the slats
on the truck!" the other guy argued—his overalls smeared with
fresh shit, his expression pained—hundreds of dollars he'd hoped
for lost.

"Meat for the mink. Won't make Massachusetts," Rog insisted,
cold-shouldering him.

"Dottie," he said, turning and using his older brother's pet
name for Dorothy. "Do take the dog." He also turned to Kiddo,
softening his tone and touching him. "Put her back in his truck,

but go easy on her." Kiddo was illegitimate and had caught meningitis as a boy, which damaged his brain, but he had taken the fall for
the family when the insurance investigators caught up with Rog's
last fire, and spent several years in jail. Rog—watching the cow
collapse again, more patiently now—was said to have given Kiddo
a collection of arrowheads when the boy's prison term ended.

He sold a welder's helmet, a kitchen sink, and a second-hand
possum-fur cape, as the row of regulars sipping beer waited for the
meat bids to begin.

"More chickens. Mutt chickens," said Rog, pulling the Clarks'
blue-tailed red rooster and hen-pecked brown hen out of another
live-looking bag—both of them gasping for a breath of air and
blindly blinking in the light—and revolved them to make them
flap and squawk and get the lumps out. "Here's your alarm clock,
boys. A young fella. This one ain't got the staggers yet. He'll wake
you up no matter what kind of rotgut you drank last night or how
late you got back from catching the clap in Montreal. And here's
his wife to go with him and lay you an egg every morning."

Karl, going after that rooster, bid a dollar for the pair, telling
Dorothy he was sorry now they hadn't bought that billy, because
you could stake him down at the end of the field to draw in the
deer. "Keep your goat meat and shoot venison."

"Yes!" yelled Kiddo, a lug with a short mustache, staring
straight at Karl as if they were partners, when a widow woman
made him go to two dollars.

"Yes!" yelled Rog, when the widow, who managed a meager
operation on sixty acres with her deaf daughter, went a quarter
higher. She pursed her lips, knowing she was being made fun of.

"Awful cheap at that price. You only live once. Going to be a
butter-and-egg man?" Rog asked Karl. But Karl could take a joke
and soon had the sacked birds huddled trembling between his legs.
His father had liked birds; had had a swan at one time, orphaned
or broken-winged, and even a peacock once, picked up at a flea
market. Karl himself had raised pheasants a dozen years ago as an
attempt at a business proposition, for training bird dogs or selling to a sporting club for field trials. And geese, with their white

hind ends, gray wings flapping vigorously, and peremptory heads, appealed to him—like the wild ones clearing out in October and returning in April. As a young man at the time of World War II, he had yearned to learn to fly for the Army Air Force, but not been accepted, and settled for the infantry. And in the swamp, cutting cedars or tending his trapline, or playing softball on the town team on the diamond behind the drugstore, he would later cock a wistful ear when the regularly scheduled airliners or some private plane flew over.

As Dorothy collected the collie dog, just tied with a string around her neck, Rog—sly and fiery but dumpy-tummied—got rid of the last of the pigs, plus a night stand, a bed frame, some shovels, and a crateful of toys from a bankruptcy sale, before the kids who were lying across their parents' laps fell completely asleep. A black, confident-horned, fed-up-sounding cow, which in her home herd had no doubt led the others out to pasture and back again, began to bellow, as if protesting for all the rest of the animals that her udder ached and her legs were exhausted from having no place to lie down, and that they all were hungry and scared.

"*Live* cows," Rog exclaimed, rubbing his hands, scratching an itch, as people laughed because last year the local meat-locker man had suffered a suspension for selling steaks from a dead one after somebody, probably Al, his competition, turned him in.

"Buy you a ladylove that will earn her grain," Rog said, as the first Holstein was prodded into the ring. The big spenders pulled out their clipboards, and the Welfare parents who had come for the entertainment hoisted their children and began to leave.

• • •

After dropping the blind man off at his house—he joked that darkness was the same as daylight to him—Dorothy and Karl examined each creature by flashlight before they went to bed. Already the blue-tailed rooster, hardly out of the stifling bag, had started to interrogate the silent barn to learn if he would need to fight another rooster for supremacy at dawn. The nameless collie was ravenous and, after feeding her leftovers and bread, they put her in an empty horse stall, deciding not to collar, leash, license, name, or tie her up until she had proven that she wanted to stay. But during some pillow talk, they settled on Sheila, after a gentle spotted setter that Dorothy's family had once owned. By daylight Sheila looked like a winner, however, a stately, quite trusting dog, her muzzle whitening, in the last third of her life. She didn't bark to be let out of the stall but, when she was, toured the property in the balmy morning air quite independently, and at the house's four corners found where the previous house dogs had buried their bones; also, in the gully beside the stream, the spot where Karl's trailing hounds and bird dogs used to be chained. Nothing displeased her, and she remained around, lying in the sun, and later in the shade, in the same places that previous dogs had chosen, and peaceably introduced herself to Dorothy's sheep, cats, and fowl with an air of already understanding whatever she saw.

WITHDRAWN